A VEILED AND DISTANT SKY

Sherry D. Ramsey

The Nearspace Series:

One's Aspect to the Sun
Dark Beneath the Moon
Beyond the Sentinel Stars
A Veiled and Distant Sky

A VEILED AND DISTANT SKY

Sherry D. Ramsey

TYCHE BOOKS LTD.

Published by Tyche Books Ltd.
Calgary, Alberta, Canada
www.TycheBooks.com

Cover Art by Ashley Walters
Cover Layout by Indigo Chick Designs
Interior Layout by Ryah Deines
Editorial by M. L. D. Curelas

First Tyche Books Ltd Edition 2022
Print ISBN: 978-1-989407-37-0
Ebook ISBN: 978-1-989407-38-7

Author photograph: John Ratchford

This book was funded in part by a grant from the Alberta Media Fund.

For Terry, Emily, and Brooke, for everything, always.

Away, away, through the wide, wide sky,
The fair blue fields that before us lie,
Each sun, with the worlds that round him roll,
Each planet, poised on her turning pole . . .
   –from "Song of the Stars" by William Cullen Bryant

"I've spent my whole life focused on that next veiled, distant sky. Maybe it's time I start paying attention to the one I'm beneath, and what's here with me."
   –from the personal journals of
   Amber Malka, Ryphen, 2216

CHAPTER ONE
A Rude Awakening

"Captain? Mom, are you awake?"

Maja's voice buzzed tinnily through my comm, but I woke at the sound as quickly as I had when she'd been a child, looking for solace or comfort in the quiet dimness of a far trader at night. Now she sat night duty on the bridge of the *Tane Ikai*, but my mothering instincts held their keen edge. I rolled away from Hirin and pressed my ID chip implant to answer, pitching my voice low so I wouldn't wake him.

"I'm here, Maja. What is it?"

"Sorry to wake you, but I'm picking up a distress call. Thought you'd want to take a look."

"Be right there."

I sat up and pushed the coverlet away, blinking and shaking my head to clear the fog of sleep. The ship lay peaceful but never silent, as the soothing hum and tick of drives and systems filled the darkness. I felt around for jeans and t-shirt to slip on.

"Luta? What's up?"

Apparently Hirin's instincts weren't too shabby, either.

"Just going to the bridge to check in with Maja. She caught a distress call."

"Want me to come along?"

I shook my head and ran a hand through my hair to smooth it. "Go back to sleep. I'll call you if I need you."

"*Okej.*" He rolled over as the door to our quarters closed gently behind me. The guidelights in the galley and near the bridge entrance limned the corridor with pale yellow light, and I stepped softly along the metal decking so I wouldn't wake anyone else. When I emerged into the brighter lights of the bridge, Eta Cassiopeia A shone brighter and nearer than it had on the main viewscreen yesterday. The main star in the binary system was partially shrouded by the whorls and swirls of a cobalt-tinged dust cloud. We were still too distant to get a visual on our destination, the planet Xaqual. With only two wormholes connecting this system to Nearspace, and only one inhabited planet in the star's Goldilocks zone, in-system travel was light. A ship in need of help might not get a lot of offers.

The bridge was quiet and only dimly illuminated for the ship's night cycle, the starry void outside the viewports swaddling it like an inky blanket. From the puddle of light at the pilot's console where Rei would usually be stationed, Maja swung her blonde head to smile at me. A tight and worried smile, but a smile, nonetheless. Now more than a year aboard the *Tane Ikai*, Maja had developed a taste for space travel that she'd never had growing up. No doubt her relationship with my communications officer, Baden, helped in that regard. Still, she'd qualified in both basic navigation and piloting during that time, so I believed in her commitment to staying aboard the *Tane Ikai* and being a contributing member of the crew.

"Just picked it up," she said, turning back to the board. I slid into the secondary pilot's seat beside her and called up the comm screen. It showed a standard automated call for assistance from a ship called *Amber's Ranger*.

"Any information on the ship?"

Maja frowned. "Well, I ran the name and ship's signature through Pika's database—"

Never one to stand on ceremony, the *Tane Ikai*'s AI inserted herself into the conversation. "What we found didn't make sense, Captain."

I sighed inwardly. I'd agreed to test a copy of Jahelia Sord's AI, Pita, with whom I'd admittedly had a useful relationship when we'd all been trapped on a Chron station months ago. The AI program code had been a secretive PrimeCorp beta project, but now, with PrimeCorp dismantled, the Protectorate was interested in the program's potential. The AI was designed to make internal adjustments based on its user's personality—and Pita displayed a very similar personality to Jahelia's after spending time installed on Jahelia's ship. I knew Jahelia had named her version of the software PITA as an acronym for *pain-in-the-ass*, and I'd been known to tease Jahelia that it took one to know one.

Now my brother Lanar, the Protectorate Admiral, had persuaded me to test this version of the code based on Pita, to see if and how a new iteration of the software would change in a different ship environment. While Jahelia was unwilling to make exact duplicates of her program, the copy installed on the *Tane Ikai* still displayed a personality very similar to Jahelia's. I'd named her Pika, explaining that the change of just one letter was an homage to the original program. Secretly, though, it was more of a comment on that personality, because in Esper the word meant *sharp* or *stinging*. And Pika did have a bit of bite. I felt I was continuing tradition.

"Let's see what you have, Pika."

The screen changed to display data for *Amber's Ranger*, and I ran my eyes down the particulars. A single-pilot, skip-capable runner class, planet of registry listed as Mars, expeditionary classification. Registered to a Mars citizen, Amber Malka, last filed flight plan—

"Huh."

Maja nodded. "Last flight plan filed included this system, but that date—"

I looked at her. "2205—over eighty years ago? That can't be right."

"My data is correct, Captain," Pika said in a voice that dared me to argue with her.

Maja mused, "Expeditionary means a wormhole spelunker, right? Could they have gone through an unknown wormhole and . . . I don't know, only come back through now?"

I blew out a sigh and sat back from the screen, drumming my fingers on the edge of the console. The sound echoed louder than I expected on the shadowy, nearly-empty bridge. "Possible, I guess, but where have they been for eighty years? And why isn't there another wormhole recorded for this system? If they went through and didn't return, it should be listed and marked as unsafe in the database."

"Unless they found one and didn't report it?" Maja shot me a meaningful look.

We'd discovered last year that PrimeCorp had sponsored unauthorized wormhole exploration in the early days of the expeditionaries. No-one fully understood, even now, the extent of their unofficial sorties outside Nearspace.

"What about it, Pika? You have access to some of the data your original program copied from the PrimeCorp main database. Any mention of Amber Malka or her ship?"

"Interesting," the AI said after a brief pause. "Amber Malka was indeed employed as a freelance wormhole explorer by PrimeCorp periodically, according to these records. But they make no mention of a foray into this system. That information could have been expunged prior to Pita's accessing the data, however, so its absence is inconclusive."

I shook my head. "Possible, but there's probably a more reasonable explanation—maybe the original *Amber's Ranger* was scrapped and stripped for parts, and this is another ship with the old drive and signature. Or the ownership was transferred, and the ship's only been making in-system runs since then . . . oh."

Pika was quick to voice what I'd realized as I spoke. "With only one inhabited planet in Eta Cassiopeia, that would be a lot of . . . joyriding?" There was a smug edge to her voice that made me question for the umpteenth time why I'd agreed to her installation on the ship. I'd hoped her prickly personality would mellow through interaction with my crew and our diverse personas, but that didn't seem to have happened.

"Well, in any case, we should investigate, right?" Maja held her fingers poised over the board, ready to alter our course. "Whatever the explanation, someone's in trouble."

"Absolutely. How long to intercept?"

Her hands skimmed deftly over the board, entering the parameters. "I make it about three hours if we use the burst drive."

"Three point two-six hours," Pika clarified.

I stood up and nodded. "Let's go, then. You know not to run the burst drive at full the entire time, right?"

Maja glanced up at me, a familiar *oh, Mom* look in her blue eyes. Years ago, my words and her look would have started yet another fight, but fortunately our relationship had evolved since then.

I patted her shoulder and smiled. "Of course, you do. I'm going to catch a couple more hours of sleep, and you call me when we're half an hour out from that ship, all right? I'll wake the others then, so we'll be ready for whatever we find."

She returned my smile and turned back to the screen. "Aye, Captain. See you in a few."

Back in my bunk beside Hirin, though, I lay on my back and stared up at the stars through the viewport above the bed, specks of white fire dotting the charcoal black of space. The *Tane Ikai* had been peaceful of late—busy and profitable, with scattered moments of excitement, but blessedly ordinary compared to the events of a year ago. A distress call from an eighty-year-old exploratory vessel seemed like it might threaten that peace, and I wasn't at all sure I liked the notion. But if someone was in trouble . . .

I rolled against Hirin's back and shut my eyes resolutely. If far trading had taught me anything, it was that you couldn't control everything. Whatever answering the distress call might bring, we had no choice. And I might as well be well-rested when we arrived.

"THERE SHE IS."

We were close enough now to *Amber's Ranger* to make out the shape of the hull. Runner-class ships had evolved over the decades into sleek, speedy machines, but the contours of this one ran clunky and outdated by comparison.

"Drives appear to be offline," Yuskeya reported from the navigator's console. The tall, dark-haired Protectorate Commander was now an official liaison aboard the *Tane Ikai*, which meant, in effect, that she sometimes went places and did things in pursuit of a peaceful Nearspace that she might not have managed if posted to an official Protectorate vessel.

"Distress call still cycling," Baden said. "No other communications, and no-one's answering my hails. Checking all channels." My communications officer didn't need to assure me that he was being thorough. If anyone out there was making a sound, I could trust Baden Methyr to pick up on it.

I tapped my fingers on the arm of my command chair. It didn't look like we'd be solving any mysteries from a distance.

"It would fit inside Cargo Pod One," Baden suggested. "We could use the remote arms to bring it in."

I pursed my lips, considering, then shook my head. "Not without knowing more about what's wrong. I'm not in the mood to have a derelict ship explode inside one of our cargo pods today, thanks."

"Well, someone's going to have to go over there, then. Looks like a single airlock at the rear. There's another door, but it's not an airlock, so no good to us out here."

"Unfortunately, we can't extend the docking tunnel because it's not compatible with that ship—it's too old," noted my pilot, Rei dam-Rowan. Her deft use of the manoeuvring thrusters brought us in close to the drifting vessel, whose hull showed the usual scars of extended space travel but no serious damage. "Whoever goes will have to cross on a tether."

"All right. Yuskeya, you and Viss and I will head over to investigate," I said. "Bring your med kit."

She nodded and rose, crossing gracefully to the nearby medical bay with long strides. When Hirin and I had first acquired the *Tane Ikai*, the bay had been merely a First Aid station. Over the years, as Hirin aged and I didn't, we'd added more diagnostic and treatment equipment, but we still called it First Aid. Maja slipped into Yuskeya's vacant seat to take over the nav board.

"Viss, bring whatever you might need to run diagnostics on the derelict's drives and systems, in case the problem isn't obvious."

Viss Feron was a deck below us, in engineering, but the comm between him and the bridge was always open to keep him in the loop. His deep, gravelly voice came back. "They're almost a century old, Captain. Not making any promises about what I can do with them."

"I have the utmost faith in your abilities," I told him, and his laughter echoed over the comm.

"I may be able to assist, Captain," Pika said. "I do have specs in my database for over three hundred types of Nearspace vessels, both contemporary and historic."

"Great, Pika. Work with Viss when the time comes."

I thought I heard Viss groan faintly.

Hirin caught at my hand as I rose from the big chair to let him take over, his grip gentle but firm. "I have the utmost faith in your abilities as well," he said in a low voice, "but be careful, all right?"

I kissed him quickly on the cheek. "Careful is my middle name."

"Stop it, whoever's in that ship will hear me laughing from here," he said with a grin, and let me go.

"Rei, we'll go out the aft airlock," I said. "Get us as close as you can and keep an eye on things through the exterior cameras. If anything looks sketchy, get clear immediately."

"Ahem," Hirin said in a mild voice. "I'm in the big chair as of fifteen seconds ago, Captain Paixon, so I'll be making decisions affecting the ship at least until you get back. We'll leave if and when I say we leave. Correct?"

Sometimes I still have these momentary lapses, where I forget that Hirin and I co-captain the *Tane Ikai* now. Years of flying on my own while Hirin was sick have left me with what he calls an "incurable compunction to be in charge." I deny it, but secretly I think he's more than half-right.

"Aye, Captain." I threw him a mock salute. "Sorry about that."

Luckily for me, he seems to find it amusing most of the time. He nodded. "Apology accepted. Now get into an EVA suit yourself. And I think you should go out the bridge airlock. It will be easier for Rei to manoeuvre close to the other ship."

Rei muttered something about it not making any difference to her, and I scuttled to the side of the bridge to comply and get into my EVA. Viss appeared then, clunking across the bridge already encased in one of the suits from engineering, helmet in one hand and diagnostics box under his arm. Yuskeya reappeared from First Aid with her med kit in hand.

"Captain, hold up."

I turned back to see Baden holding out his techrig to me. "What's this?"

"The outer airlock door will open for you, but the inner one will probably be coded. If whoever's inside can't let you in, you'll need to hack the code." He pressed the techrig into my hand. "This will do it."

I sighed. "Illegal tech again, Baden? I thought we'd been over this."

He grinned and backed away, holding his hands up, his sea-green eyes unrepentant. "I got it from your brother."

I put my hands on my hips. "My brother, the Nearspace Protectorate Admiral, gave you a piece of illegal tech? For what, your birthday?"

Baden shrugged. "Okay, it wasn't technically your brother, it was his girlfriend, but still—"

"Oh, even better. Now we have something on board that even Jahelia Sord thought was too hot to handle?"

"It wasn't like that—look, Captain, take it. You might need it, and then you'll thank me. And if you don't . . . we'll talk, *okej*?"

I sighed, but I kept the techrig. Baden had a point. We weren't going to do much rescuing if we couldn't get inside the ship.

Yuskeya and I hurried into our silvery suits, the soft crackle of the insulating material filling the air. We took turns checking each other's seals before entering the airlock. The soft hiss of escaping air scraped through my helmet's pickups.

"Captain, I found some old schematics in the database," Pika said, her voice echoing over the helmet comms. "You'll have to go in one at a time. Baden is correct about the airlock, but in that ship, it's only one-person, about as big as the shower stall on the *Tane Ikai*."

I hesitated. I hadn't thought about that. "Yuskeya, you'd better go in first, then. You're the medic and whoever's on board might need help." And as a Protectorate Commander, she was also perfectly able to handle the situation if anything sinister awaited us. I didn't need to tell her that. She knew.

She nodded briskly inside the EVA helmet. "Good thing about an airlock that small, it cycles quickly."

I handed her Baden's magic door-opening techrig and relayed Baden's instructions. She raised her eyebrows but accepted it without comment.

Viss touched her elbow. "We'll be right behind you."

"Aligned and stable." Rei reported through the helmet speakers. "Move over whenever you're ready."

At a nod from both Yuskeya and me, Viss hit the airlock button and the door slid open. He unhooked the tether gun from the airlock wall, aimed across the fifteen or so feet separating the two ships, and shot the tether. It hit the hull of *Amber's Ranger* with a solid *thunk* and Viss gave a tug to make sure the electromagnetic connection was secure. Then he clamped the tether gun in place on the *Tane Ikai*'s hull on our end. Yuskeya clipped the techrig to her belt along with the medkit, fastened the safety clip and grasped the tether, and kicked off. Hand over hand, she crossed the space between the two ships with smooth, deft movements.

The outer airlock door opened at the press of a button, as Baden had predicted, but once it closed behind her again, we couldn't see much of her progress. A small viewport in the door revealed a muted green light glowing to life inside the airlock, and I knew she'd completed the first pressurization. It seemed to take forever then, before she said through the helmet comm, "Baden's trick worked. I'm opening the inner door now. Next one across can come any time."

Baden was going to enjoy being right. Viss gestured for me to go ahead, and I attached my own safety clip and mimicked Yuskeya's quick journey across to the other ship. I don't mind EVAs, but I also didn't linger between the ships, surveying the vast nothingness that emptied out away from us. I had to wait thirty seconds before the outer door would open, but once inside, the pressurization cycle went quickly and I opened the inner door. The code lock had not re-set.

"Viss, you're clear to come now."

"Copy, Captain. On my way."

The inner airlock door opened into the typically cramped space of a one-person ship. An empty bunk lined the wall to my right, and beyond that lay a standard kitchen console. A straight path led to the tiny bridge—more like a cockpit, really—not more than fifteen feet away. In the middle of that space, Yuskeya knelt beside a sprawling figure, presumably the pilot. I hit the button to close the airlock door behind me and moved inside the ship.

"What do we have?" I asked, kneeling next to the still figure in the grey shipsuit.

"She's alive," Yuskeya said briefly. She'd already pulled back the woman's left sleeve and attached a datamed to her ID implant. After only a few seconds, the datamed emitted an insistent error beep, and Yuskeya shook her head, her eyes fixed on the readout. "*Merde*, her implant isn't working."

"Why not?"

Yuskeya didn't answer me. She gently detached the datamed and tapped the screen a few times, then pressed the sensor on the end of the device lightly against the woman's skin. After a moment, she said, "She's in trouble."

"What's wrong?"

Yuskeya's helmet wobbled as she shook her head. "I don't know yet. I'm getting minimal data this way. Her vitals are all over the place, but I don't see a physical injury."

"Do what you can."

I stood and stepped past them, moving to sit in the single pilot's chair. I switched off the distress beacon but didn't use the ship's comm. Best to stick to our helmet comms for now. "Baden, we're inside and I've killed the distress call. Ship seems intact. Yuskeya's tending to the pilot." Behind me, the inner airlock door swished open to let Viss inside. "Viss is here now, so we'll see if he can figure out what's happened to the drive."

"And Pika's with me, as you ordered," Viss said, secretly grimacing at me as he pointed to his helmet. Sometimes Pika seemed to have eyes everywhere on the *Tane Ikai*, but she was limited here.

I suppressed a brief smile and glanced over the avionics, looking for clues to help Viss, and that's when I noticed the thick layer of greyish dust covering most of the control panels and readouts. Intermittent fresh smudges revealed where screens and controls had been recently touched, and one long, ragged swipe—possibly with a sleeve—had cleared a section of the nav board. Apart from that, the console looked like it hadn't been used in decades.

I spun the skimchair around to survey the rest of the ship's interior. Now that I was noticing details, the floor was dusty as well, and no indicator lights glowed on the worn kitchen console. I pulled my datapad out of the EVA suit's side pocket and took a quick reading of the air inside the ship. It checked out, so I unclipped my helmet and pulled it halfway up over my head, exposing my face to the air.

Yuskeya glanced up at me. "Captain!" she remonstrated. Her voice came to me faintly with the helmet out of place. I held up a hand.

"I checked the air. It's normal mix, breathable."

"Sure, unless it has some undetectable gases that account for what's happening to her," she snapped, glancing down at her patient.

Oops. I hadn't thought of that. "I feel fine," I protested. I took a couple of tentative breaths, but nothing untoward happened. My hunch had been right, though. The air held a musty, stale scent that the recyclers hadn't yet been able to remove entirely.

"This ship's been mothballed for a long time." I slid the helmet back into place and refastened it, to make Yuskeya happy. "None of this makes sense."

"I have to get her over to First Aid," Yuskeya said. "Whatever's wrong, I can't treat it here, and she's failing fast."

"All right, I'll help. Viss, are you okay if we go back over?"

He'd opened a panel near the airlock and crawled halfway inside. His voice came through clearly on the helmet comm, though. "Go! I'm fine. I'll yell if I need another pair of hands."

Pika's voice filtered through my helmet. "I'll keep him company, Captain."

I looked at the tiny airlock. "All right, but how are we going to do this? We couldn't both fit in the airlock coming this way. How will we manage with a third, unconscious body along? Speaking of which . . ." I pulled open the storage locker next to the cockpit, looking for an EVA suit. *Damne,* why hadn't we thought to bring one with us?

Yuskeya opened a locker at the rear of the ship and pulled out an ancient, pewter-grey EVA suit. It was twice as bulky as our newer slim ones, and both the helmet and the battered life support tank unit seemed enormous. She held it up for me to see. "I thought I might squeeze her into the airlock with me—it's not for long since the cycle is quick. But this is huge."

"Give it here." I unclipped my helmet again and pulled it all the way off this time, then unfastened the front of the suit and stripped it down. "Put her in mine," I directed, voice raised so the helmet mic would pick it up. "Then the two of you will fit. I'll go out first and wait on the tether to help you take her across."

Yuskeya's dark eyes grew wide. She shook her head, staring at the ancient suit. "You don't even know if this one is safe! If the ship hasn't been in use, it might not have been tested in decades!"

I activated the life support unit and an array of lights grudgingly flickered to life. They blinked red, red, yellow and finally burned a steady green. I turned the suit to show Yuskeya the levels readout. "Half a tank of air. It'll be fine."

"Oh, yes, I'm sure that's reliable!"

"What are you two arguing about?" Viss demanded, his head emerging from the access panel.

"We're not arguing. We're discussing how to save a life." I pulled the suit out of Yuskeya's hand and slid my legs inside. "I'll know if it's safe when the airlock depressurizes. Any problem, I'll hit the button to pressurize again." I tugged the suit over my arms. It smelled as ancient and dank as the inside of the ship, but I wouldn't let myself think about that or what it might mean. "You said it yourself, the airlock cycle is quick. I'll be fine for thirty seconds. If it doesn't work, we'll go to alternate plan B."

"Which is?" Yuskeya had already begun wrestling the unconscious pilot into my suit. Disapproval rang in her voice, but I was the captain, after all.

"I'll tell you if we need it," I said, and pushed past Viss into the tiny airlock.

CHAPTER TWO

Amber's Ranger

THE INNER AIRLOCK door closed, and I took a deep breath. And coughed. The air in the old suit tasted stale and thick, and I imagined millions of generations of bacteria growing and breeding inside the antiquated tank. But I could breathe. I hit the button to depressurize and glanced through the tiny viewport to the interior of the ship. Yuskeya and Viss struggled to fasten my helmet over the unresponsive pilot's head.

The old suit either had no external mic or something in the comm system wasn't working, so all I could hear was my own breathing. I turned to face the external door, and as soon as the status light changed, I punched the control to open it. Heart fluttering with nerves, I paused for a ten-count, but the suit appeared to be holding and the air, unpleasant but breathable, continued to flow. I swung myself out onto the tether cable and closed the door behind me.

That's when I realized it had no safety clip like our newer suits had. I swallowed against a throat gone suddenly tight. Okay, I'd just have to be sure to keep a firm grip on the tether.

Then came one of the longest minutes of my life—I'm sure it wasn't more than that, because Yuskeya would be moving with all speed to join me outside. But it sure felt like more. Floating weightless with the old EVA suit creaking around me, thinking about the missing safety clip, breathing the fusty air and hoping not to hear the crack, pop, or rip of some crucial element failing . . . it wasn't exactly comfortable. I tried to distract myself by appreciating the deep blue depths of the nearby dust cloud, flecked with pale specular highlights from Eta Cassiopeia A's gleam, but it didn't help much.

I didn't hear so much as sense the airlock door opening on *Amber's Ranger*, and I turned to find Yuskeya with her arms tight around the unconscious pilot. With no inter-suit comm, we made our plan with gestures—I'd put an arm around the woman's shoulders and Yuskeya would take her legs. We'd each use our other hand to make our way along the tether cable, taking turns letting go. I saw Yuskeya's eyes go wide when she, too, noticed the lack of a safety clip on my suit, but she attached hers and the pilot's with a shake of her head. We'd make sure that one of us had a grip at all times.

Where the trip over to the drifting ship had been a quick scurry, the journey back was a methodical and anxious crawl. I worried about what would happen if the injured woman woke up and panicked at the unfamiliar situation. My hold on the tether was tenuous enough; one more complication and I might not be able to maintain it.

I was so focused on clutching the woman and the tether that it startled me when a gloved hand reached out from the open door of the *Tane Ikai*'s airlock and took my arm. I looked up to see Baden regarding me through his EVA helmet with undisguised reproach as he steadied me and helped pull the unconscious pilot inside. Yuskeya followed with alacrity, and Baden pressed the control to close the airlock door, leaving the tether in place outside.

Once the airlock repressurized, I pulled off the ancient helmet with a sigh of relief, welcoming the fresh air and wave of sound that flooded in. Maja stood waiting for us with the gurney from First Aid, and she didn't look happy, either. She said nothing, however, simply helped Yuskeya and Baden settle the pilot on it.

"Maja, get the suit off her, please. No obvious injuries you have to worry about," Yuskeya said as she began stripping off her own EVA suit.

Moments later they'd rushed the woman to the First Aid station, and I bent to retrieve the discarded EVA suits from the bridge floor. When I rose with my arms full, Hirin stood nearby with his arms crossed, regarding me with the same disapproval I'd seen from Baden.

"All right, let me save you some time." I held up a palm to forestall whatever he was about to say. "It was a foolish risk to take, what was I thinking, why didn't I call for help from over here—does that about cover it?"

Hirin reached out a hand for the antique EVA suit I'd worn. I passed it to him and he examined it briefly. He pressed a finger hard against one of the dirt-rimed seams. The fabric bulged and stretched, and then his finger popped through with a papery ripping sound. He said, "You must be crazy, don't ever do that again, that was quick thinking, and I'm proud of you?"

"I'll take that," I said, and kissed him on the cheek. He pulled me in for a quick but very tight hug and then turned away. I returned the suits Yuskeya and I had worn to the EVA lockers, trying to banish the image of Hirin's finger poking so easily through the ancient suit.

Pika must have been spreading her awareness around everything that was happening between the two ships, because she said in a scolding voice, "Captain, that was—"

"Not you, too, Pika." I raised a hand as I had with Hirin. "Can it and go back to Viss. Or see if Yuskeya needs your medical database help."

A muttered imprecation came over the ship's comm, but I couldn't make it out.

Baden came out of First Aid with his helmet open. "Maybe I should go back over and help Viss? Yuskeya and Maja have things under control in there."

I nodded and opened my mouth to agree just as Hirin said, "Yes, please. Don't let Viss get into full teardown and refit mode. If he can get the drive functioning, fine—otherwise if everything checks out, we'll load it into Cargo Pod One."

Right. Hirin still had the chair. I closed my mouth. Well, that left me free to go to First Aid with Yuskeya and see what else we could discover about our mysterious patient.

THE WOMAN LOOKED small and out of place on the gurney in First Aid. This was my first chance to take a good look at her. Her dark brown hair was cut in a long, shaggy bob, scattered with paler streaks. Her skin displayed the leathery texture of someone who spent much time outdoors, but what I imagined was normally a rich brown now showed a dull, sickly grey undertone. I would have pegged her as no more than forty years old. Yuskeya had covered her with a thermal blanket, but the name tag on her pale grey shipsuit remained visible: *Amber*. I frowned and shook my head. But—she couldn't be the original Amber from *Amber's Ranger*. Maybe all the shipsuits carried an abbreviated version of the ship's name. Her chest rose and fell in short, jagged breaths that were almost painful to watch. The thin shimmer of a decontamination field formed a long dome over the gurney.

Yuskeya scanned the readout from a datamed attached to the woman's ID implant. "I had to download a patch to access the implant. The interface still has gaps, but it's telling me this is Amber Malka, Mars citizen."

"Was she carrying anything else?"

"Just this." Yuskeya picked up a rectangle of flexible ultraplas from the counter and passed it to me. "She had it in the inside pocket of her shipsuit."

It was a holopic, showing a smiling woman standing in a garden outside an old-style colony HAB unit—chunky and utilitarian, its original light brown colouration bleached pale on top by the sun. HABs like this were the kind colonists lived in while settlements got up and running. A slice of sky behind the HAB showed a pale seafoam colour, and trees topped with baobab-like crowns. The woman's hair was a deep pink, touched with hints of dark red, cut shoulder-length. Blue eyes regarded the camera lens—or whoever was behind it—with fondness. As I angled the holo this way and that, the woman's smile widened and her mouth opened in a silent laugh.

I looked up to find Maja watching me. "Amber Malka is identified as the original owner of the ship we took her off."

"What's wrong with her? And why the decon field?" I asked, choosing to ignore the immediate implications of that identification.

Yuskeya shook her head. "I still don't know. There's a lot happening here—I put the field up because I'm reading something like a virus I can't immediately identify, and her immune response is off the charts—"

Something clenched in my gut. Another possibility I had

stupidly not thought about. "Contagious?" We were not all protected by my mother's nanobioscavengers, and we hadn't isolated the patient immediately.

"I don't think so. It's—not like any virus I've ever seen; I'm not even sure I'm right in calling it that. But we'll use that as a placeholder for now."

"Can Pika help?"

"I'm searching my databases, Captain," the AI said coldly. "No matches so far."

I groaned inwardly. Pika in a huff was a lot like having Jahelia Sord around at her prickliest.

Yuskeya opened a cabinet above the gurney and pulled out a med injector, put her hand through the unresisting shimmer of the field, and held it against the woman's neck while she depressed the button on the end. "Her internal systems are under strain or attack, but I don't know from what. I'm afraid they'll start failing if I can't figure it out."

Yuskeya's voice was steady but perspiration beaded her brow. She's a field medic, and a good one, but she isn't a doctor, and I know in situations like this she feels that difference keenly.

Maja, her face serious and intent, pressed a vitals strip to the side of the woman's neck and bent to read it. "Temperature's still falling. Heart rate is elevated and erratic."

"Yuskeya, if this is Amber Malka—"

She turned to look at me. "I know. She's one hundred and twelve years old."

I looked down at the woman. Her eyes twitched behind her lids as if she were dreaming. "Almost thirty years older than I am."

Maja slid her arm around my shoulders and squeezed. "Not like we don't know anyone else who doesn't look their age," she said lightly.

I blew out a sigh, my thoughts racing. "I know, my first thought is nanobioscavengers, too. But if this woman is Amber Malka, she disappeared—probably through an uncharted wormhole—several years before Mother even left PrimeCorp. How could she have nanobioscavengers in her system?"

"Maybe she got them later," Maja suggested. "After all, Dad only got his infusion from you a year ago."

"Can you tell, Yuskeya? If she has nanobioscavs?"

Yuskeya pursed her lips. "Possibly," she said after a brief hesitation. "I did get your mother to help me calibrate the datamed to read them, after you were so sick. But they should have already shown up on the blood scan if they're present. I never turn that function off because it only makes a difference for someone who has them, anyway."

"They could be an older, precursor version. Maybe a re-calibration would help?"

She threw her hands up in an uncharacteristic display of frustration. "Sure, if I knew what to re-calibrate for. I'm poking around in the dark without a flashlight, here, Captain. If your mother were here, she might know what to do. *Might*."

"All right." I put a steadying hand on Yuskeya's shoulder. It took a lot to crack her usual composure. "Do what you can for her."

To the room in general, I said in my politest voice, "Pika, would you please search the PrimeCorp data files to see if there's a record of anything related to the nanobioscav research that might be useful?"

"Aye, Captain," she said, sounding slightly mollified.

"And we'll head for Xaqual with all speed and get the patient to a medical centre there. I'll send a message to Mother. Maybe she can tell us something that will help."

"If she gets the message soon enough," Yuskeya said. She didn't sound hopeful.

I turned to leave First Aid, but a sudden gasp of breath from the woman on the gurney stopped me. I looked down to find dark brown eyes open and staring at me. With an obvious effort, she flailed one hand free of the blanket. I grasped it, ignoring the half-imagined tingle as my own hand passed through the decontamination field. Her flesh felt shockingly cold.

"Captain Malka, I'm Luta Paixon." I leaned close to the shimmer of the decontamination field. "You're aboard my far trader, and we're trying to help you. We picked up your distress call and found your ship adrift—"

Her lips moved to form words, but her breath carried no sound with it. I leaned closer, repeating as soothingly as I could, "You're all right. Your ship is safe—"

She interrupted me again, her eyes wide and fixed on mine as her head trembled slightly from side to side. Her lips formed the whisper of two or three words, but I couldn't catch them. I shook my head, and she fetched a deep, ragged breath, clutching my hand with more strength than I would have thought possible.

"Save . . . liliver," she gasped, or at least that's what it sounded like. I bent closer, and she managed to speak again, but her words were slurred. "Save . . . lilivure."

"What? What's—"

But her hand fell limp in mine and her eyes fluttered closed. Her breath returned to short, painful-sounding rasps.

I stood watching her breathe, feeling a tight discomfort in my own chest, then pulled the thermal blanket back up to cover her again. Maja and Yuskeya both looked the question at me. I shook my head.

"I don't know what it means," I said. "But I'll see if I can find out."

I RETURNED TO the bridge feeling helpless and frustrated. "Hirin, any word from Viss and Baden? We need to get that woman to Xaqual immediately."

Hirin raised his eyebrows at me. "*Okej*, I know you said no refit, but they've been over there less than half an hour."

I sat down at an empty board and called up the Nearspace database. "She's in worse shape than I thought," I said, typing in *liliver*, *lilivure*, and a couple more alternate spellings, breaking it up into separate words, too. Could it be a name? Had I even come close to hearing the woman correctly? I turned to catch Hirin's eye. "She might die," I told him quietly. "Yuskeya's doing what she can, but we need a real doctor."

He nodded and said over the ship's comm, "Viss, Baden? We're out of time. If that ship can't move under its own power and you don't see any red flags, let's get the remotes out and take it aboard."

At first the only reply was a clunk and a muffled curse, but then Viss said, "I could get her main drive up and running, Captain, but I'd need more time and some replacement parts. The good news is, I have manoeuvring thrusters online, so we don't need the remotes. I can ease her into the cargo pod under her own power."

"Let's do it, then," Hirin replied. "I'll open the door for Cargo Pod One. Let me know as soon as she's secured."

"I'll release the tether on this end," Baden said. "Someone over there will have to secure the airlock door."

"I'll get it." Hirin was out of the chair and striding across the bridge before I could respond.

"I'll turn the ship so the pod bay door is closer to you," Rei offered. As usual under pressure, the *Tane Ikai*'s crew worked like a finely-calibrated skip drive, and I allowed myself a moment of satisfaction.

Maja emerged from First Aid and crossed to me. "I can take the nav board and get us back on course to Xaqual. Yuskeya can stay in First Aid. Not much else I can do in there, anyway."

I nodded. "Did you hear what she said? Malka, I mean?"

Maja frowned. "It didn't make sense. Save something . . . it sounded like *liver*? Only longer. Maybe part of it was 'lily,' like the flower. I thought she must be delirious."

"I thought it was a name. *Liliver* or *livilure*, something like that." I had a sudden thought. "Pika, you didn't pick up what Amber Malka said, did you?"

"I'm sorry, Captain, it was too low for my sensors to catch," the AI said.

"That's all right. I'm going to run a near-match search and see what the database turns up." The ship lurched slightly as Rei began to turn it, and a shadow moved across the main viewscreen; *Amber's Ranger* headed for the cargo pod door under manoeuvring power. After a moment of consideration, I added a couple more spelling variations to the search list, and set it running.

"I'll be in our quarters. I have to write a message to Mother," I told Hirin. He raised his eyebrows in a question, and I added, "She might have medical input. Get us underway to Xaqual as soon as you can, all right?"

"Will do. Tell Emmage I said hello."

I blew him an un-captainly kiss and left the bridge, making my way down the corridor with brisk steps. I had my hand on the door to our room when I decided a brief detour to fetch a cup of double caff from the galley couldn't hurt. We were likely too far from a relay station for my message to go anywhere yet, anyway. As I stood at the counter in the galley, waiting for my mug to fill with hot, sweet double caff, I pondered the message I'd compose for Mother. I didn't want to make it too direct; although

PrimeCorp's many corporate tentacles had been either taken over by the Protectorate, farmed out for management to other Nearspace corporations, or severed, I still couldn't shake the feeling that messages could be compromised. Considering the complex debate raging throughout Nearspace over the nanobioscavenger technology, I didn't want to send her anything that might incite fresh speculation if it were intercepted and made public.

Returning to my room with steaming mug in hand, I felt the smooth pull of acceleration as the *Tane Ikai* got underway. Viss must have brought the derelict ship aboard without much trouble. The slight tug of the artificial gravity compensating for our movement jostled the caff in my mug, but I managed not to spill any. I glanced around the room—although our quarters were almost twice the size of a regular cabin on the ship, they still felt small sometimes. And the room seemed so messy—I picked one of Hirin's shirts up off the bed and then made myself stop. No. I was only delaying composing my message to Mother.

I made myself sit down at the desk and open my datapad, then sat staring at the screen. The fact of the matter was, I hated to bother her. No, that wasn't exactly right. I hated to bother her with difficult questions about nanobioscavengers. The debate over utilizing her technology—and that of others, like the Schulyer Group's own version of the tiny medical 'bots—to extend the human lifespan, had come under heavy fire now that it was close to becoming universally available. Arguments raged over the ethical considerations and practical concerns of immortality, as well as over issues like safety, reliability, control, profits, and distribution. Mother was alternately praised as a modern saviour and demonized as a mad scientist with delusions of godhood. She'd made a policy of dealing with all questions and accusations head-on, but six months of this had begun to wear her thin. I saw it in her eyes every time I spoke with her.

So how would I circumspectly ask her about the possibility of anti-aging bioscavs existing before she'd cut her ties with PrimeCorp and disappeared into the reaches of Nearspace for seventy years?

And that wasn't my only problem. What I knew, but no-one else on board did—not even Hirin—was that modern nanobioscavengers were closer to hand than they would have suspected.

Mother had offered them to everyone in my crew when the red tape of putting them into wide distribution across Nearspace had become so magnificently snarled. "I can't manufacture enough for all of Nearspace on my own, but I can certainly take care of some of you," she'd said, defiance edging her voice. For reasons of their own, which we hadn't in all cases discussed, Yuskeya, Viss, and Rei had not chosen to take her up on the offer—at least not yet. My son Karro and his wife Aliande had refused as well.

However, although these particular minuscule constructs hadn't yet been officially approved for use, Mother had made sure I had some squirreled away "in case of emergencies." What she meant by that was, "in case someone without them gets seriously ill and this is the only way to save them." Or possibly "in case you can get Karro and Aliande to change their minds." She'd given them to me personally, not to Yuskeya, to protect her from any compromising situations. Yuskeya was Protectorate, and although she'd proven to have her own mind and opinions about Protectorate protocols, it would still be problematic for her to have knowledge of what was still classified as illegal tech. Trust Mother to think of things like that.

So I hadn't stored the med injectors in First Aid. There, they'd be considered under Yuskeya's "care and control" since she was the medical officer of record for the *Tane Ikai*. Instead, I had the injectors and their microscopic, illicit payload stored safely in a lockbox right here in mine and Hirin's quarters.

Now I had a dying woman on my hands who might—*might*—have a much older version of them in her blood. What would happen if I injected her with newer ones? Could it make the situation even worse? Was it even ethical to do that, without her permission? I needed Mother's advice and help, but since the injectors were technically contraband, I had to be circumspect.

I drummed my fingers on the desk and sipped my caff as it slowly cooled. Finally, after several attempts and many erasures, I had my message.

Dear Mother,
Medical emergency en route to Xaqual; no-one you know.
Could our emergency medication assist even if patient has
artifacts of previous treatment (long ago, possibly pre-dating

mine)? I know it seems unlikely, but the facts point that way. Yuskeya can't tell for sure without a recalibration but needs guidance. Need help or advice STAT.

Love, Luta

Maybe I was being paranoid about the message being intercepted. Although PrimeCorp had controlled the entire relay system in Nearspace through one of its sub-corporations, management of the entire operation had been turned over to AriAndas when PrimeCorp was dismantled. Our son, Karro, was a communications systems engineer with AriAndas, and he'd been busy since the takeover "scrubbing" the PrimeCorp infrastructure of eavesdropping and interception software and devices. He was, in fact, finishing up a contract on Xaqual, and once we'd dropped our cargo, we were scheduled to collect him and his wife, Aliande, and take them back with us as far as FarView Station.

His contracts had taken him all over Nearspace in the past six months. "The biggest cleaning job since we terraformed Mars," he'd joked to me at one point. "And I don't think we're nearly done yet."

So if I felt like I should play things a little close to the chest when it came to messages about nanobioscavengers, maybe I could be excused for that.

I packaged the message, encrypted it, and sent it off. The nearest relay station might be close to Xaqual, where we were headed anyway, but sending the message now meant that it could race us there and be on the next leg of its journey before we reached the planet. If Mother was at home on Kiando, she could receive it within six hours. Then at least another six for her response to get back to us. If she was somewhere else in Nearspace—a real possibility these days as she worked to get the bioscav technology approved—I didn't have much hope of getting a response in time to help Amber Malka. I didn't know if our mysterious patient would last twelve hours.

I shook my head and sipped caff, then made a face. There wasn't much left, and it was space-cold now. With a sigh I got up, took the mug, and headed back to the bridge.

CHAPTER THREE
A Deepening Mystery

BACK ON THE bridge, you'd never suspect the exciting hour we'd just spent with rescues and mysteries. Hirin sat in the chair, chatting with Rei. They'd dimmed the HPS overheads to half power, limning the space with pale, caramel light. Apparently neither of them had felt like going back to their quarters, even though technically it was still the night shift and Maja remained on duty. However, she wasn't on the bridge. In the main viewscreen, Eta Cassiopeia A flickered like a beacon as we headed deeper into the system.

"Where's Maja?" I asked, taking a seat at the board where I'd left the database search running.

"I told her to get some rest," Hirin said. "I'd never get back to sleep now, and Rei felt the same way. Yuskeya's still in First Aid, and Baden's helping her. Viss opted to try and get some more shut-eye before we hit Xaqual. He set Pika to running some diagnostics on the *Ranger*'s drives."

Rei pushed off from the pilot's board and slid her skimchair closer to mine. "What's this?" she asked, tilting her head toward the board. She'd pulled her chestnut hair back into a loose ponytail. This fully revealed the dark *pridattii* tattoos that spilled and swirled over her cheekbones and around her golden eyes, testifying to her Erian heritage. Eyes that were bright with curiosity, and not at all sleep-deprived. As usual, I wished I had my friend's energy.

"Our patient woke up for a few seconds and said something," I told her. "We couldn't quite catch it, so I'm trying a Nearspace database search on what it sounded like, see if it comes up with anything."

Rei raised an eyebrow. "Seems like a long shot," she said. "Are you even sure it was a name?"

"Not really. But she said 'save'—something or someone. Seems like a good bet it was a name."

"Okay, that makes sense. So what do you have?"

She leaned toward the board, where I'd started to scroll through the results. Unfortunately, since my search terms were many and vague, there were a lot of possibilities. I blew out a sigh. "Too much, apparently."

Rei studied the list, tapping one finger on the side of the console. "Okay, well, let's eliminate the obvious. Nearspace citizens who are deceased, so they can't be saved," she said, keying in a new filter. When the list of results refreshed, she looked over it again. "The planets Vele and Vileyra are listed here, but I doubt she was talking about an entire planet."

"Well . . ." I hesitated, thinking back to a year ago. When a new war with the Chron seemed imminent, the possibility of a planet being in danger had been all too real. The peace negotiations hadn't faltered, though, so Rei was probably right. And surely, we would have heard of any current planetary threats. "Okay, take them out."

Rei complied, but that still left a long list of citizen and other names. Hirin came to stand beside me, apparently unable to fight off his curiosity any longer.

"We found her in this system," he mused. "So what if you take out anyone who doesn't live in this system or in Tau Ceti or Mu Cassiopeia, since only those systems have a direct wormhole connection to here?"

"Good idea," I said. "That ship hadn't been back in action for very long; she wasn't far from where she'd started."

That narrowed the field of results to only a hundred and fifty citizens, seven ships, and three cities.

"It's better, but still not enough." I leaned back in my chair and let the softly whirring servos massage my back. "Maja thought she said 'liver' or 'lily.' I thought it was a longer word;

'liliver' maybe."

"What about Yuskeya?" Rei asked.

I looked at her. "I didn't ask. She was too caught up in trying to stabilize the woman's condition. It might not have registered with her."

"Be right back," Rei said with a grin, and crossed to First Aid.

"You all right?" Hirin asked, putting a warm hand on my shoulder.

I nodded. "Something's weird, though. If that woman's who we think she is, she's over a hundred years old."

Hirin silently raised an eyebrow at me.

"I know, I know. In our world, that's not so strange. But it's strange when you consider that she disappeared four years before Mother even left PrimeCorp. I don't know what the state of the bioscav technology was at that point—"

Rei came back then. "Yuskeya agrees with both of you," she said with a grin. "Part of the word was definitely 'lily,' but it was longer than that, too. She says she immediately thought of flowers."

I turned back to the datapoints list. "All right. Let's filter out everything that doesn't start with the letters 'lily' or 'lilli.'" That narrowed the list down to a handful of citizen names, a city called Lilyano, and a ship designated NCV *Lillifleur*.

"Lilyano's tiny," Rei said. "It's on Damir. I was there once for—I don't even remember now. Passenger pickup, maybe, when I worked for that corporate shuttle outfit."

"Looks like the *Lillifleur*'s decommissioned," Hirin said. "There's only a blank space for current flight plan. And how long has it been since we had many Nearspace Colony Vessels roaming around?"

I tapped it anyway, to open the full ship's data and see when it had last been operational. The particulars were all there: Captain, Juliska Barath; complement, thirty-five crew; passengers, 1076 colonists bound for—

"Xaqual? Huh."

The next line stopped me, though. Crimson letters proclaimed MISSING WITH ALL HANDS, 2206.

One year—or possibly less—after Amber Malka had apparently spelunked through a wormhole and never returned.

"Okay, that can't be coincidence," Rei said, leaning back in her skimchair.

I shook my head. "No, I don't think it can. Because look who bankrolled the *Lillifleur* colonization effort." I tapped the screen.

Rei leaned in to look. "PrimeCorp," she breathed. "But what does it mean? 'Save Lillifleur'? How can we save a ship that's been missing for almost a hundred years? Save it from what?"

I stood up to pace. I always thought better when I could move, and the bridge of the *Tane Ikai* had room for a half-decent pacing circuit, at least. Hirin saw it coming and moved out of my way, plunking back in the chair with a knowing half-smile on his face.

"The ship we took aboard is obviously old; looks like it had been mothballed for a long time," I said. "The air's musty, everything's covered with dust, the EVA suit was fragile as paper; I'll bet Viss found other things to support the idea. Amber Malka hasn't been flying that thing around in Otherspace for the past eight decades. So maybe the *Lillifleur* is in the same state, somewhere."

Rei cocked her head at me and pursed her lips. "You can't easily mothball a colony ship, though. Those things are *big*. Massive. You'd have to dock it at a space station or orbital shipyard if you had no way to refuel."

"It hasn't been in Nearspace, we know that. A Corvid station? Maybe a Relidae planet? But in that case, we should have found out about it before this. We've been in contact with those species for more than a year now."

"The other Chron—the Pitromae?" Rei suggested. "But, same thing there. They'd have said something to someone by now, surely, if they had an old Nearspace vessel docked somewhere."

"Another possibility would be to set it up in high orbit around a planet," Hirin suggested. "As long as there's enough power to keep it up there . . ."

I nodded. "You could maintain it in orbit for a long time with minimal fuel, but it's not going to last forever."

"So that could be why she came looking for help," Rei said, her eyes bright. "Think about it; the ship's been in orbit around a planet, but systems or drives are failing, running out of fuel— some problem's come up. If the orbit decays enough, the ship will be pulled down by the planet's gravity. It enters the atmosphere at the wrong angle and then—*boom*." She mimed an explosion, fingers tracing the shape of an expanding fireball.

I stopped pacing and put my hands on my hips. "Okay, it's a reasonable hypothesis, but it raises a lot more questions than it answers. Where is this hypothetical planet? What happened to all the colonists? How did Amber Malka get mixed up with the *Lillifleur* in the first place?"

"And how did she get here, in the middle of Eta Cass, in a near-derelict ship?" Hirin added.

"And why is she dying?" Rei finished in a small voice.

I shook my head and sighed. "That's a lot of questions with no answers." I looked toward First Aid. "And Amber Malka, the only person who might be able to give us some of those answers, is in no shape to provide any."

Hirin rose from the chair. "But we do have her ship," he said. "Why don't we head down to Cargo Pod One and see what else it has to tell us."

"Hey, no fair," Rei protested. "Because I know you're going to tell me I have to stay up here and drive the ship."

I smiled at her. "If I recall correctly, it does say 'pilot' on your contract. We'll tell you everything we find, I promise."

She rolled her eyes. "And to think I let Maja go to bed so I could hang out with you guys. Now you're ditching me."

"Sometimes life's not fair," I told her as I followed Hirin out into the corridor. "But look on the bright side. You're not only the pilot, you're in charge of the whole bridge while we're gone."

"Gee, thanks," she returned, sliding her skimchair back to the pilot's board. "At least bring me a double caff on your way back. And some cinnamon *pano*," she called as an afterthought.

I FOLLOWED HIRIN down the *Tane Ikai*'s main corridor, still trying to keep my footsteps quiet on the metal decking. The ship's nighttime cycle meant low illumination, but the pale, buttery glow from the galley guidelight at the end of the corridor threw plenty of light for us. Hirin slowed his steps so I could catch up to him.

"Are we actually going to investigate that ship, or will we make a detour to our quarters on the way?" he asked, raising his eyebrows suggestively. Mother's nanobioscavengers couldn't erase all the years Hirin had aged when I hadn't, but they'd taken him back to the way he was before he'd gotten sick, and that was fine with me.

"A detour sounds delightful," I told him, "but I wouldn't be able to enjoy it, with this mystery waiting to be solved."

"Just kidding," he said, catching my hand and planting a kiss on the knuckles. "I'm burning with curiosity, too. And there's Rei to consider. She'll be expecting a report by the time we get down to the pod!"

We rounded the weapons locker and Hirin let go of my hand to start down the hatchway ladder. The light illuminating the space below was also dim, since the ladder would take us to the engineering deck, and Viss wasn't currently at his station. There'd be enough of a glow from the guidelights to show us the way down the next corridor, though, and one more hatchway ladder would deliver us into the biggest cargo pod. It was a lot of walking and climbing, but the brief exercise made me feel better. I'd been jittery ever since my short stint in the outdated EVA suit, and I was glad of the opportunity to work off some of that nervous energy.

"You planning to message Lanar about this?" Hirin asked as we climbed down to the catwalk that vaulted above Cargo Pod One. "Seems like something the Protectorate should know about."

"I will. But I'd like to be able to tell him a little more than we have now. The Protectorate fleet is still spread thin, since they've stationed liaisons in Corvid, Relidae, and Pitromae space. I doubt there's a ship to spare to go running around looking for clues about this, so we might as well find out as much as we can ourselves."

We quickly descended the rest of the way to the floor of the cargo pod, and Hirin crossed to the wall near the pod bay doors to bring the lights up to full. I squinted in the glare after the soft lighting that had guided us down here. "Sorry," Hirin said. "But we have to be able to see if we're going to examine it."

The *Amber's Ranger* sat in the middle of the cargo pod, securely locked down. I walked around the perimeter, examining it. The lines of the hull betrayed its age in decades, not years. Micro-meteorite impacts pitted its outer shell, minor dents and abrasions testifying to a long life in space with many wormhole skips and dust cloud encounters. Soot caked the casings around the drive ports and streaked away from the exhaust vents in intricate ebony swirls and eddies. Scratches and scars crosshatched the ultraplas viewport, some embedded under layers of resurfacing, and a rough, jagged scar down the port side suggested a near miss in its past.

Overall, though, it seemed a good, sturdy ship still. The name stencilled on the hull was clear and readable, with a row of hand-sketched circles marked beneath it. I ran my hand over them, counting. Sixteen. The number of wormholes the ship had explored? Or planets discovered? Amber Malka had been enthusiastic, maybe to the point of being reckless. Every unexplored wormhole offered the chance that death waited at the other end.

Hirin had the side door open when I finished my exterior survey. He gestured me inside. "After you, Captain."

"Thank you, Captain." I paused in the doorway, surveying the interior. This door opened at the side of the tiny bridge. The pilot's chair was mottled with a collage of mismatched patches, and the seat bore an imprint testifying to thousands of hours spent in the void of space. A steel mug, half-filled with some liquid that had scabbed over and gone cold, waited next to the console to be scrubbed out and refilled to fuel another voyage. Of the pilot herself, there was no trace. The holopic in her shipsuit pocket seemed to be the only personal possession she'd brought with her.

"See how dusty it all is?" I asked Hirin. "If she'd been flying any length of time before we found her, a lot more of that would have been cleared away from everyday use."

Hirin bent over my shoulder to look inside and nodded. "Agreed. Do we know for certain that she didn't take off from Xaqual?"

"We don't know anything for certain."

"We can double-check with planetary control, but I don't get the feeling she came from there," he said.

"Me neither. So where?"

I stepped inside, turning to examine the small kitchen console. The storage area held some unmarked packets of what looked like tea leaves when I unfolded the paper. I sniffed delicately. Smelled like an herbal tea, with a hint of something sweet, like berries or fruit. A pouch held a few slices of dark seedy bread, soft and fresh. The water reservoir was almost full. In the chiller, a small bundle revealed cheese and two small organic objects—fruits or vegetables I couldn't name.

I showed Hirin. "She wasn't flying long, and didn't expect to be flying long, either. Not enough provisions."

He'd opened the storage locker near the single bunk, but it was empty. "She certainly packed light," he said. "So, I guess the next thing is to see what's in the computer."

I sat down in the single chair and switched on the power. The boards lit up and an air recycler coughed to life. The nav screen asked for a passcode or biometric input.

"We might not get far unless we want to drag poor Captain Malka down here," I said. "Or unless we can guess the passcode."

Hirin huffed his annoyance. "Could be anything—but wait a second," he corrected himself. "We're assuming Amber came looking for help, so she wouldn't make the passcode anything too difficult to guess. In case she got into trouble, as she has, and had to rely on someone figuring out the problem without much help from her."

He leaned over my shoulder and keyed in the word *Amber*. The computer only beeped at him.

"Didn't like that one. Next logical guess is . . ." I keyed in the word *Ranger* and the screen unlocked.

"Okay, so let's see what we have," Hirin said.

There was one text file labelled, "ReadThisPlease." When I opened it, however, the screen displayed only an indecipherable scramble of symbols and error characters. I called up the ship's logs, but scanning the file dates, most of it was ancient history. There was only one recent entry. I opened it, but only stared at the screen, trying to make sense of what it was showing me. "It's just coordinates. Not a proper travel log all."

The screen read:

GJ 34A (WA 10-1)

GJ 34A-a RA 21h 52m 25.4s D -13deg 14' 39.7"

F7V A(WA 12?-1) Ryphen

F7V A(Ryphen-b) RA 15h 24m 35.2s D +50deg 27' 24.6"

"Star catalogue codes and coordinates," Hirin said, tapping a finger next to the first line on the screen. "WA 10-1 is the Wormhole-Accessible number for Eta Cassiopeia—although it's an outdated designation since the second wormhole in the system was discovered; now Eta Cass is 10-2. The other number is the star's Gliese code."

"I recognize a Gliese code when I see it, but I don't have them all memorized, for heaven's sake. You still know all the Nearspace stars by their Gliese and WA codes?" I asked, turning to look at him. "I forgot all that as soon as I got my nav certification. It's all in the computer."

"And what if the computer's down, but you need to know it?" Hirin asked loftily.

I refrained from mentioning that you'd hardly need to know wormhole-accessible designations if you didn't have a working computer. "Well, I could probably list the WA codes if I had to," I said defensively. "Anyway, these first two lines are giving us a point relative to Xaqual in the Eta Cassiopeia system. What's the rest?"

Hirin shook his head. "We only have eleven wormhole-accessible stars in Nearspace proper—that's not counting the new ones that lead to the Corvid and Relidae systems—and I've never heard of a star named Ryphen—so I guess that's why there's no Gliese code for it. However, I'd read this information as saying that another wormhole-accessible system has been discovered; it's an F7 main-sequence star, its common name is Ryphen, and it has at least two planets, one of which is also named Ryphen."

"Why the twelve designation with a question mark?"

"I suppose because as far as whoever made the designation knew, it would be a twelfth system to add to Nearspace. But other systems *could* have been discovered in the meantime, too."

I blew out a long sigh and nodded. "Makes sense. And the coordinates mark the position of a wormhole relative to that planet, where Amber Malka just came from. A wormhole whose other end is in this system, at these coordinates?" I tapped the Eta Cass coordinates on the screen.

Hirin stood up straight, stretching a kink out of his back. "That's what it looks like. But I'd be surprised if there's an undiscovered wormhole in this system. There's only the one leading here from Mu Cass and the rest of Nearspace, and the one to Tau Ceti. I'm sure wormhole explorers have covered it thoroughly searching for others."

"Space," I said, "is big. Really huge."

Hirin spun the skimchair around so I was facing him, and he squatted down in front of me so our eyes were level. "Luta, you are not suggesting that we go to these coordinates and try to find a secret wormhole to an unknown system. Are you?”

I squirmed a little under his probing gaze and shook my head. “We have to get Amber Malka to Xaqual.” I couldn’t unequivocally state that doing a little exploring hadn’t crossed my mind. And Amber Malka’s words certainly implied that someone, somewhere, was in trouble.

“Yes, we do. And we have to send a message to your *brother*, the Admiral, and tell him what we’ve found. Because he’s a member of the Protectorate, and this is the kind of thing that *they do*.”

“Well, it’s the kind of thing that we *sometimes* do,” I pointed out. “Occasionally even with Protectorate approval.”

“And we have to collect our son and his wife, and take them to FarView Station.”

“I never said I didn’t want to do that.”

Hirin opened his mouth, but Yuskeya’s worried voice over the ship’s comm forestalled whatever he would have said. Which was probably for the best.

“Captain? Would you come to First Aid, please? I need to show you something immediately.”

I tapped my implant. “On my way.”

CHAPTER FOUR

Amber's Secret

IF I'D THOUGHT climbing down to the cargo pod took energy, I was definitely winded by the time we made it back up to the bridge. I made a mental note to step up my daily workout and add some of Rei's *nicardi* to my regular *tae-ga-chi*. I tried not to pant and puff when we arrived in First Aid. Baden was still there, looking grim but somehow pleased with himself as well.

Amber Malka looked about the same as she had the last time I'd been here. She hadn't regained consciousness, and still looked merely asleep in the shimmery cocoon of the decontamination field. Her breathing had calmed from the raspy, hitching breaths of earlier, but I didn't know if that was a good thing or not. Two thermal blankets covered her now, and they'd been tucked gently around her neck.

"What's happening?" I asked. Hirin had followed me in as well, although he stopped in the doorway. The tiny medical bay was getting cramped.

Yuskeya sat at the narrow desk while Baden leaned against the wall next to her. "I decided we couldn't wait to hear from your mother," she said. "I asked Baden and Pika to help me try to recalibrate one of the datameds the way your mother had showed me, tweaking some of the numbers to broaden the parameters." She glanced up at Baden and nodded. "When in doubt, ask a techdog, right?"

"And an AI," Pika added loftily.

"It worked," Baden said with a half-smile. He ran a hand through his cocoa-coloured hair, pushing it back from his eyes. "We got the datamed to catch the little critters in her bloodstream. They were there, just like Yuskeya suspected."

Yuskeya huffed. "Not what I suspected, though," she said, and turned to look at her patient. "She has nanobioscavengers, of a sort. They're similar to yours, Luta, but they don't act the same."

"They're not like the ones in the PrimeCorp database," Pika interjected. "However, the research files I got from Pita concerning the bioscavs are incomplete and don't date back to the time when Amber Malka disappeared."

I grimaced slightly. That would be my mother's fault, since she'd done her best to make sure PrimeCorp didn't have that data by the time she left its employ.

Yuskeya continued, "These bioscavs have a much more significant organic component than yours, and a completely different molecular structure. In fact," she put her hands on her knees and drew a long breath, "I think the organic component is the root of the problem. It is reminiscent of several Nearspace viruses, although the medical database can't identify it. And it seems to be dying."

"You don't think it's the virus that's making her sick in the first place?"

Yuskeya shook her head. "In the samples I was able to resolve, the virus—or whatever it is—seems to be an integral part of the functioning of the nanobioscavengers. I've seen some of the viral structures wither and stop moving, and then the bioscav construct slowly does the same. Stops functioning."

I glanced at Hirin. "Should we be worried? About contracting the virus?" Especially since not everyone aboard had Mother's nanobioscavengers in their bodies.

Yuskeya sighed and leaned back in her chair, crossing her arms. "I don't have all the answers, but I don't think it's contagious. You probably know that viruses attach to host cells by way of receptors to infect them—but there has to be a match for the virus to do that, and the cell has to be susceptible to infiltration. As I understand them, your mother's nanobioscavengers have a protective structure in their organic components that these other ones seem to lack. The receptor sites in Amber's were vulnerable. So even if the virus got into your bloodstream, it wouldn't be able to latch on and integrate the way it does with these older ones."

"What about other cells? Maybe everyone's at risk," I suggested.

Yuskeya shook her head and picked up the datamed from the desk, scanning the readout again as she'd probably done ten times since the results appeared. "I'm calling it a virus, because that's the closest analogy I can make. But this thing is alien—it's not going to affect the rest of us. That's not why I'm telling you about it."

"Okay, good to know."

"The problem is, I don't know how to keep the virus alive. And it's not only that the nanobioscavs don't function properly without the viral component. They stop working, but then they—I don't know. They go crazy."

"Crazy? How does a bioscav go crazy? It's a machine."

"It's a machine, yes—but partly organic, and with learning capability and adaptability," Yuskeya corrected me. "And they've essentially been reprogrammed by the virus. They've adapted to work with it symbiotically. When the virus is not there, they start attacking cells, breaking down organic structures. It's like they're hunting for the virus, trying to replace it. And they'll tear down anything that gets in their way."

I blew out a sigh, looking over at the silent, unmoving woman on the gurney. "So you don't know what to do."

Yuskeya ran a hand over her face and I realized how tired she looked. Dark circles traced the contours beneath her eyes. "I'm trying to keep her warm. I've given her something to slow her metabolism, and to boost her natural immune response, try to repair the cell damage. Apart from that—I'm at a loss. And the doctors on Xaqual aren't going to know any more than I do. Less, in fact, because they'll never have dealt with nanobioscavengers at all."

"How long do you think you can keep her stable? I'm sure Mother will answer as quickly as she can." My chest felt hollow, like I couldn't take in enough breath to fill it.

"Even if your mother was on Xaqual, I don't know that there'd be time," Yuskeya said, her voice thin with uncertainty.

I found myself teetering on the edge of telling Yuskeya about the nanobioscav injectors hidden in my quarters. But Mother had taken such pains to keep Yuskeya out of it, and I didn't want to put either of them in a difficult situation. Especially when I didn't know if they could help here or not.

Instead, I came at the question obliquely. "What if I gave her a transfusion—like we did with Hirin? Would my nanobioscavengers help? Would they fix the things that are going wrong with the old ones?"

Yuskeya put both hands behind her neck and tilted her head back, closing her eyes. I could practically feel the weight of tension she was trying to ease. "I don't know, Luta. This is so far beyond me—but I don't think so. I think they'd go after the virus, because it's the kind of thing they're built to target, right? But in this case, it's the virus's death that's causing the problem. If anything, I'd be afraid your bioscavs might kill her quicker."

I blew out a sigh. No help from the ones in my quarters, then, either.

"It was a good idea, though," Yuskeya said. "And good of you to offer."

"We're not going to be able to save her, are we?" I asked. My voice came out huskier than I'd expected. I understood Yuskeya's frustration at her inability to fix this.

Yuskeya glanced over at the still, silent woman on the gurney. "I don't know, Luta," she said in a bleak voice. "I just don't know."

WE WERE TWO hours out from Xaqual when Mother's response arrived.

Yuskeya hadn't slept, refusing to move from Amber Malka's side in First Aid. The breakdown and betrayal of the woman's nanobioscavengers continued, but Yuskeya had used all her experience and the most obscure references in the medical database to slow the decline. Malka hadn't regained consciousness again, which came as no surprise. She was truly fighting for her life.

I was nursing a mug of double caff in the galley when my datapad pinged with two deliverable-in-proximity messages from Mother. According to the dates, she'd sent the first one a few days ago, to await my arrival at Xaqual. It had downloaded automatically when we came within range of the datastation.

Received: from [1084516.42.84] Xaqual Main Datastation
STATIC ELECTRONIC MESSAGE: 25.8
Encryption: securetext/novis/noaud
Receipt notification: enabled
From: "Emmage Mahane"
        *<emmage.mahane.phd.duntmindi*web>*
To: "Captain Luta Paixon" <ID 59836254471>
Date: Tue, 8 Jun 2286 14:27:35 -2000

Dear Luta,
I messaged Karro again to ask him about the treatment, but he's still refusing—politely, but without explanation. The controversy is still a major setback to widespread deployment, so I don't know what more I can do. He reminds me so much of your father. I never did figure him out, either, or why he refused the treatment. Thought I would let you know since you'll be seeing Karro soon. Maybe you can make more headway than I've managed.
Hope to see you soon. Love to Hirin, Maja, and all.
Love,
Mother

I scanned it hastily and moved to the second one. This was the reply to what I'd sent her earlier.

Received: from [1084516.42.84] Xaqual Main Datastation
STATIC ELECTRONIC MESSAGE: 25.8
Encryption: securetext/novis/noaud
Receipt notification: enabled
From: "Emmage Mahane"
        *<emmage.mahane.phd.duntmindi*web>*
To: "Captain Luta Paixon" <ID 59836254471>
Date: Tue, 12 Jun 2286 08:13:22 -2000

Luta,
You may be in luck. Yalin Ndasa is on Xaqual! He's doing research at Samdon General Hospital in Risi. I've forwarded your message to him and asked him to help—I know he will do everything possible, and he has the necessary specialized knowledge. I'll join him there as soon as I can get away . . . your

message raises so many questions. I'll see you on Xaqual if you're still there when I arrive. If not, take care, and I'll be in touch.

Much love,
Mother

I leaned back and closed my eyes, feeling as if my mother had sent me a hug. The friendly face of Dr. Ndasa rose in my memory—the Vilisian who'd been instrumental in helping me find Mother on Kiando after so many years of searching for her. He'd helped care for Hirin and been on the *Tane Ikai* during some very difficult times. I didn't know whether he'd be able to help Amber Malka, but it was the first hopeful thing that had happened since we rescued her.

I pulled a hot drink from the dispenser on the counter to take to Yuskeya. The spicy scent of cloves, ginger, and cinnamon wafted into the air as the mug filled with her favourite strong chai. Then I tucked my datapad under my arm and hurried along the corridor and through the bridge to First Aid.

She looked up with a start as I entered, and I knew she'd finally been dozing. Brushing away a momentary pang of guilt for disturbing her, I held out the mug. "This comes with good news," I told her.

She took the proffered mug, smiling wearily. "I could use some of that. You found a real doctor floating in space and picked him up?"

"Even better. I got a message from Mother. Dr. Ndasa is on Xaqual!"

Yuskeya stared at me blearily before her eyes went wide. "Dr. Ndasa? He might know something about the bioscavs."

I nodded. "Even if he doesn't know about those particular ones, he has a better chance of helping her than someone who's never heard of them. And Mother said she'd come as soon as she can."

She turned to look at the readouts blinking above Amber Malka's still form. "I just have to keep her alive to get there," she breathed.

"Yuskeya. We all know you're doing everything you can," I told her. "If she doesn't—if she dies, you have nothing to feel guilty about. It's an impossible situation."

She blew out a heavily weighted sigh and faced me again, wrapping her hands around the mug and taking a sip before she answered me. "I know, and thank you," she said finally. "I just— once I saw what was happening with that virus and the bioscavs, I knew it was beyond me, beyond my abilities. Still, I couldn't simply throw up my hands and do nothing. But in spite of everything I'm doing . . . she's low, Luta. Seriously low." She let the words hang there as she stared into the rich, dark tea.

"We're only an hour out from the planet now; we've been running the burst drive as much as we safely can. I'll ask Maja to pinpoint the hospital, get us as close as possible. Karro and Aliande can wait a little longer if we can't go straight to the Risi spaceport."

Yuskeya bit her lip. "An hour is a long time for her in this condition. I just want you to know that."

"Just do what you've been doing. And we'll hope."

"I want to know where she came from, and what she was doing out here," she mused. "It feels personal, now. Did you figure out what she meant that one time she spoke?"

I realized I hadn't told her what we'd deduced, and quickly filled her in. "I've sent a message to Lanar about it already, but I don't know what he's going to say."

Yuskeya nodded. My brother, Admiral Lanar Mahane, was her commanding officer, although she'd been "on loan" in various capacities to me and the *Tane Ikai* for three years now. She understood better than most people the challenges facing the Protectorate. Trying to oversee the inclusion of two new alien species into Nearspace—the Corvids and the Relidae—while negotiating a peace agreement with a third (and former enemy), the Pitromae, had spread the already-stretched Protectorate forces to their limits. I knew Lanar would feel obliged to bump my message about the *Lillifleur* up the chain of command, but the chance that one of the Fleet Admirals would respond quickly seemed thin. Since all we had to go on was a questionable interpretation of some coordinates on an ancient ship and a barely conscious woman's mysterious words.

"I keep wondering," I said, tapping my fingers on the handle of my mug, "if she somehow knew what was going to happen to her."

"Why do you say that?"

I told her what we'd found in the *Amber's Ranger*—or rather, what we hadn't. "It was a hastily-planned trip. She either knew she wouldn't be aboard long—and I don't know how she could foresee that with any certainty—or she knew she wouldn't *live* long enough to need much."

"Hmmm. Because when she went through the wormhole from this side, there was no colony on Xaqual, right? And her ship certainly had no burst drive. Sure, the planet might have been colonized in the meantime, but as far as she knew, she might have had to make it through to Mu Cassiopeia before she had any real hope of running into someone."

"A last-ditch attempt to get help." The cold lump that had been sitting in my stomach ever since I'd started thinking about this grew heavier.

"And you feel like you owe it to her to at least try to find out more."

I looked up from my mug to find Yuskeya surveying me with a knowing look in her dark eyes. "Am I that transparent?"

She smiled. "Sorry to break it to you, but you're not that hard to read, Luta. I've been aboard long enough to see it. You like to talk tough, but your heart's as soft as the inside of a *solanto* cookie. And you do not like unanswered questions."

I laughed, then sobered. "But we're picking up Karro and Aliande on Xaqual. I can't go skipping off all over Nearspace looking for clues."

"They could catch a shuttle. We were only taking them to FarView anyway," she said. "Karro's pretty easygoing, in my experience."

"True. I'll think about it," I said lightly. No need to share the other reasons I was anxious to talk to my son. I changed the subject. "Now, let's focus on the details for when we get to Xaqual. Are we required to report anything when we deliver her to the hospital?"

She pursed her lips. "Technically, no. That should be the hospital's job, or Dr. Ndasa's."

"I hope Dr. Ndasa will realize the need for secrecy about the nanobioscavengers. Their existence has to be significant, and Mother needs to get a look at them. This could have an impact on everything happening around the technology in Nearspace right now." I didn't say what was really on my mind—that even a hint of nanobioscavengers malfunctioning and essentially killing their host would further inflame the factions who argued against widespread deployment of the anti-aging technology.

"I did draw off some blood—and its nanobioscavengers—and freeze it already, as a bit of insurance. We'd have that for your mother, if she doesn't get to Xaqual before something happens."

"I don't know why I ever think you're not one step ahead of me, Commander Blue."

Yuskeya snorted, but her thoughts must have been following mine down a similar path. "They're not the same technology as your mother's, Luta. This wouldn't have happened with hers—yours."

"We probably can't be sure of that, but even if mine are different—you know what people are like. They wouldn't understand enough to differentiate." I shook my head. "I'm inclined to give Dr. Ndasa a false name for her. If we don't, they'll look up her real name in the Nearspace database—"

"Find out her supposed age and her history—" Yuskeya said.

"—and that will trigger a whole lot of questions we're not prepared to answer," I finished with a nod. "I don't love messing with official Nearspace implant data, but until we know more, I think keeping things quiet is our best bet."

Yuskeya half-smiled. "You didn't hear this from me, but I think Baden, Viss, and Pika between them could come up with something to address that problem."

I grinned back. "My thoughts exactly."

She fetched a deep breath and sat straighter in her chair. "*Okej* then, you see to that. I'll keep doing what I can, and we'll hope we get her to Dr. Ndasa in time. And that he'll be able to do something I haven't thought of," she added.

I glanced at Amber Malka, her eyes closed under the soft play of colours across her face as the monitoring screens above blinked out their solemn messages. "Hope is what we have," I said. "We'll go with it."

THE COLONY ON Xaqual had been established some seventy-five years ago and had grown at a modest pace compared to some of the other colony planets. The planet itself was a close analogue to Earth in terms of climate and general appearance. Since Eta Cassiopeia A is a G-type star like Sol but somewhat warmer,

Xaqual had managed to compensate for that by being further out in the star's habitable zone, so things evened out. It had a smaller ratio of land surface to ocean than Earth, and the first colonists had wisely chosen a warm, temperate zone near the planet's equator to establish their colony. With only one known wormhole leading to the system from the main sectors of Nearspace, Xaqual quickly developed a reputation as a vacation "getaway," and the locals capitalized on that, building resorts and promoting the planet's geographical attributes. The only other known wormhole out of the system led to Tau Ceti, and that sector of Nearspace dead-ended there. With balanced immigration from other Nearspace worlds, the population of Xaqual had grown remarkably in seventy years, spreading out along the coastlines and into the foothills so that it never felt crowded. In addition to a beautiful iridescent yellow dye created from an indigenous plant, tourism was the planet's biggest economic contributor, and Hirin and I had vacationed here ourselves on several occasions.

When we touched down on a large peninsula devoted to spaceport, berthing, and cargo exchange, I wasn't thinking too much about the relaxation opportunities on the planet, however. I was wondering about the quickest way to get Amber Malka to Dr. Ndasa, some forty miles away. We had the groundcar, but it certainly wasn't intended for transporting anyone in a delicate medical condition, and it was simply too slow. I was about to ask Baden to find a cheap flitter to rent when my datapad pinged with an incoming message. As I read it, I couldn't help smiling. It was from Dr. Ndasa, telling me he was here at the spaceport, with an air transport for the patient ready to go.

"She's as ready to move as I can make her," Yuskeya said, emerging from First Aid. She was still on her feet, although I didn't know how. "But we'll have to be careful."

"Dr. Ndasa is here to get her." I swiftly keyed in a reply to his message, relaying our berth assignment. "He's airlifting her to the hospital."

Yuskeya closed her eyes and blew out a long breath. "I've never kissed a Vilisian, but there's a first time for everything."

I chuckled, imagining the extreme discomfort such a display would cause in the reticent doctor. The air would fill with the wet-wool aroma of embarrassment when his Vilisian scent-language kicked in. "Maybe a simple thank-you will do. I'm going to meet him."

I hurried down the corridor to the rear airlock and stepped through, scanning the curve of the dockway for Dr. Ndasa's approach. A sloping ramp led up from the dock level to the *Tane Ikai's* "back door," so at least that should be easy to navigate with a med-sled. The dockway was moderately busy, with crews and passengers mingling as they bustled to and away from the many occupied berths. Spaceports in general were utilitarian spaces, but planters studded the walls of this one, spilling over with brightly blooming native flora. Sunlight streamed through the ultraplas panels arching overhead, making the spaceport bright and welcoming for incoming vacationers.

After a moment of searching, I made out Dr. Ndasa's tall form and gliding gait moving toward my ship. Others on the dockway parted to make way for the two attendants and med-sled trailing him. I raised a hand in greeting and he returned the gesture with typical Vilisian solemnity.

I studied him as he made his way up the ramp. It had been over a year since our paths had crossed, but Yalin Ndasa hadn't changed. Well, there might have been a few more pale amber streaks through his ebony hair, the Vilisian equivalent of grey. But his dark violet eyes, surrounded by the characteristic, amber-coloured flesh, were bright and alert, and the wrinkles in his skin thinned and flattened as he smiled. He wore light-coloured robes appropriate for the warm climate of Risi. He reached the top of the ramp and offered me the traditional Vilisian greeting, the touch of a palm to eyes, lips, and heart, then put out a long-fingered hand to shake. I caught vanilla in the air—pleasure at reconnecting—but it was underlaid with the metallic tang of his concern for the patient he was about to acquire.

"Captain Paixon, it is so pleasing to see you again."

"Dr. Ndasa, thank you so much for coming." I caught his outstretched hand and shook it. "Come, I'll take you to your patient."

He asked the two attendants to wait for him inside the airlock with the med-sled, and followed me down the corridor. I filled him in succinctly on Amber Malka's circumstances as we knew them. Yuskeya would give him the full medical file.

"And your mother suggests this patient may have

nanobioscavengers, but a different configuration?" Dr. Ndasa asked. "That's extraordinary."

I nodded. "That's confirmed now; Yuskeya and Baden managed to identify them. But there's a virus involved as well, and they seem to be connected in some way."

The doctor nodded thoughtfully. We emerged onto the bridge and Hirin rose to greet us; he had been the first to meet Dr. Ndasa back on Earth, when the doctor was conducting aging research. The two embraced, which was a measure of how strong a friendship they'd forged. Then after a quick exchange of words, Dr. Ndasa and I crossed to First Aid.

Yuskeya was as good as her word; under the thin lustre of the protective field, Amber Malka was comfortably tucked up in a clean thermal blanket. Although her breathing seemed shallow and pinpricks of sweat glistened on her forehead, she wasn't in any other obvious distress. I didn't know what that portended, though. It seemed like it could be good or bad.

Yuskeya and Dr. Ndasa greeted each other as valued colleagues, and with little delay, Yuskeya launched into her explanation of what she'd found and the course of treatment she'd followed. A faint floral scent on the air signalled the Vilisian doctor's interest in delving into this medical challenge, although it mingled with the grapefruit-like acidity of nervousness.

"I admit I am at a loss to know what to think, but I will do my best to help her," he said finally, producing his datapad so that Yuskeya could download the chart to it. "There are many mysteries here, but you have done excellent work, Commander Blue. In lesser hands, I am certain she would not have lived to reach Xaqual."

Yuskeya's dark eyes reflected her pleasure at the unexpected praise. "I did what I could. I'm more than relieved to be handing her over to you, though."

"I hope it won't be too difficult for you to keep things quiet— about the nanobioscavs," I said to Dr. Ndasa. "We're not sure how to handle things yet."

Dr. Ndasa smiled and made the Vilisian waggle that was the equivalent of shaking his head. "Many of my colleagues consider me rather secretive as it is," he assured me. Then his eyefolds puckered with undisguised worry. "I hope I will have as much success in treating the patient. I should get her to the hospital without further delay."

"Of course."

Yuskeya guided the gurney out of First Aid and through the bridge, Dr. Ndasa and I trailing her. Hirin and Rei made quiet goodbyes to Dr. Ndasa, and when we arrived back at the airlock, the attendants expertly transferred Amber Malka to the med-sled.

Dr. Ndasa said, "I will keep you updated on her status, Captain. And your mother has said she will join me here, so no doubt you will hear from her, too."

I nodded. "We're headed for FarView Station from here, but messages will find us along the relay routes. Good luck, doctor. I know you'll take good care of her."

"I will do my very best." And he hurried after the attendants and the med-sled. Amber Malka looked small and vulnerable as the sled floated smoothly along the dockway, other pedestrians once more giving way before it and closing in its wake. As a wash of sunlight through the ceiling caught and burnished the decontamination field to a bright gleam, I hoped it was a good omen, and that we'd done the right thing.

WITH AMBER MALKA safely delivered, I was free to go into the city and meet up with Karro and Aliande. Hirin and Baden were overseeing the cargo deliveries, and Yuskeya was busy composing her own private report for Lanar and the Protectorate Authority regarding our encounter with Amber Malka. I was still struggling with the question of what more to do about Amber Malka's last message, and how much about the encounter I was going to tell Karro, but I resolved to mentally put it aside for at least a little while. I'd been looking forward to spending some time with my son aboard; in part because I simply didn't see enough of him, and in part so I could try to find out why he was averse to being treated with Mother's anti-aging miracles. I didn't think he had ethical or moral objections to their use in general, but he had said he didn't want them for himself. I wanted to understand why.

For myself, I'd never had to make the decision simply because my mother made it for me—and for Lanar as well. She'd given us the nanobioscavengers as her final gift before removing herself from our lives to draw the malicious attention of PrimeCorp away from us. Her hope was that we'd live normal lives without the unwanted attentions of the corporation, and that those lives would extend indefinitely. She'd gotten part of her wish—Lanar and I were in our eighties, but hadn't aged visibly past about thirty. So far, apart from a single recent episode when my nanobioscavengers went a little wonky and needed an update, the nanomachines were working as advertised. And they'd helped Hirin erase some of the normal effects of his own long life as well, when I'd shared my bioscavs in the hope of saving him from a life-threatening illness. Although the gift of the bioscavs had sometimes been a mixed blessing, I couldn't fault my mother for the choice she'd made. I'd spent a brief time being angry with her for making the decision for me and then not being around to help me understand and deal with the repercussions, but I'd long since gotten over that.

Since Mother had come out of hiding and begun working with the Schulyer group to bring anti-aging technology to all of Nearspace, she'd offered her current version of the bioscavs to my family and crew. Maja had mulled it over briefly—probably just long enough to talk it over with Baden—and they had both accepted the offer.

Karro had declined with thanks, as had his wife. Their children were teenagers, and Karro and Aliande had promised Mother that Joash and Klaire would be allowed to choose for themselves about the bioscavs when they each turned eighteen. Mother had pressed for an earlier date, but my son and his wife had been gently adamant that they and Joash and Klaire had agreed on that age as appropriate. So that meant this was the year for Joash—I didn't think Mother had talked to him, yet, but she must be planning a visit soon. My grandchildren seemed quite at ease with the unusually youthful members of the family (and there were quite a few of us now), so I hoped the decision would be an easy one for them.

It quickly became apparent, as the nanobioscavengers claimed increasing time in the news cycle, that the idea was not so easy for everyone. Not all of Nearspace was eager nor ready to embrace the technology. Even those who thought it was a good idea were insistent that a massive plan of oversight must be established before production and distribution could commence. Regulations were needed. Systems must be built. Control over the entire undertaking must be handled with the best interests of all in mind.

And while those discussions and negotiations were taking place, the factions that opposed the entire idea were making their voices heard with protests, speeches, and impassioned rhetoric. I wouldn't have expected it to be very evident in a laid-back colony like New Samdon, but when I emerged from the Risi spaceport transport into the city centre, there they were. A ragged crowd had gathered in front of the Nearspace Authority building, replete with hand-lettered placards that read things like, "Death is a Part of Life," "No to Nano," and "No-one is Meant to Live Forever." The "no to nano" one struck me as particularly absurd since medical nanotech bioscavs have been used for decades in the treatment and cure of life-threatening injuries and diseases and are widely accepted. It was only the anti-aging variety that caused dissent. It flashed in my mind to cross to the crowd and demand to know if any of them or their families had ever had bioscav therapy, but I resisted the urge. *Not my problem.* Instead, I counted to ten, reminded myself that none of them knew I carried the very technology they railed against, and continued on to meet Karro and Aliande at their hotel.

I had walked less than a city square when I pulled off my jacket—I'd forgotten how warm the temperature was likely to be downtown. The citizenry was predominantly human, although I did see other Vilisians making their gliding way through the crowd. The wolf-like Lobors, with their higher body temperatures and general dislike of heat, were rarely found on Xaqual in large numbers. It wasn't likely we'd see many Corvids here either, now or in the future—or on most of the planets in Nearspace, for that matter. They required a different atmosphere, so although they'd been happy to enter into an alliance with Nearspace, it would take new technology to make it viable for them to move easily among us, or us among them, and truly integrate the species.

Musing on these things, I almost passed the hotel, but noticed the signage just in time. It was a small boutique inn, not one of the large, clone-like chains, so Karro's contract must be a lucrative one. I stepped into the cool lobby and found Karro and Aliande already waiting for me.

Karro saw me and rose immediately, crossing the tiny but elegant room to wrap me in a hug. "Mom," he whispered, for the sake of onlookers, "it's so great to see you!" My son was fifty-eight, so he looked approximately old enough to be my father in spite of aging well. Sprinkles of grey laced his brown hair at the temples, and laugh lines clustered around the corners of his eyes. When I thought about the sea change the nanobioscavs had wrought on Hirin, erasing decades of aging over the past year or so, I ached to see the same nanotech magic performed on my son. I pushed the thought away. This wasn't the time.

My daughter-in-law had followed Karro across the room to me and hugged me in her turn. Aliande had burnished brown skin with a warm, coppery glow, and wore her hair high in a traditional beaded and bright Vileyran head wrap. Despite the undoubted weirdness that must accompany having a mother-in-law who looked like she could be your daughter, I'd never seen her brown eyes anything but welcoming when she looked at me, and today was no exception. "*Saluton*, Luta. So good to see you. And so good of you to offer us a lift home!"

I grinned. "Family always travels for free on the *Tane Ikai*," I told her. "But if you want to make us one or two of your fabulous meals while you're on board by way of thanks, we wouldn't say no."

"I'll check with Maja to make sure she's stocked up on what I'll need," Aliande said. She leaned in close to whisper in my ear, "I don't know what you did to your daughter, but she's sure a lot happier lately than I've ever seen her!"

I nodded. "We . . . worked out some things. Buried some old disagreements. And she's in love. That usually improves one's disposition."

Aliande glanced fondly at Karro as he gathered their bags and exchanged a few final pleasantries with a polished young desk clerk. "That it does."

As Karro joined us again, I said, "I should ask you something, though . . . are you in much of a hurry to get back? On a tight schedule?"

"Oh, no," Karro said. "What does that mean?"

"I just—we might make a short detour—not out of this system—to investigate something. It shouldn't add more than a day or two to our travel time, at the most."

"What kind of something?" Karro asked, his voice laced with suspicion. He'd set the bags down again and rested his hands on his hips, waiting for my explanation. *Damne*, he looked too much like his father when he did that. I didn't like it at all.

"A message that a ship might be in trouble. I sent a message to your Uncle Lanar about it—"

"And you've told the authorities here, of course," Karro prompted.

"Well . . . no. It's out of their purview." I shook my head. "It would be hours out. And it might not even be there."

"But you have to go and investigate."

I mirrored his stance, keeping my voice steady. I wasn't going to be bullied by my own son. "I might. It's bothering me. The Protectorate might not be able to send a ship, and if someone's in trouble—"

"You feel obliged to help them," Aliande finished for me smoothly. "And that is a noble thing. Karro, stop giving her a hard time! Now, Karro isn't due at FarView Station for five days, and my work is eminently portable. We're not going to cause any trouble about a little detour, are we, dear?"

She said this last rather pointedly to Karro, who rolled his eyes dramatically and said, "No, we're not. But you do realize that my mother and her crew have . . . let's call it a constitutional deficiency when it comes to avoiding dangerous situations."

"We haven't encountered anything more dangerous than a grumpy passenger in almost a year!" I protested.

"In other words, we may get more than we bargained for? I do know your mother, dear." Aliande linked her arm through mine, gave me a wink, and glanced pointedly at the bags. Chuckling, Karro picked the luggage up again. "But I trust her implicitly to take care of us. And a little excitement isn't always a bad thing."

"Operative word there being *little*," my son muttered as he followed us out of the hotel into the bright sunshine and bustle of the street.

As I used my ID chip to ping for nearby private transports to take us back to the ship, I fervently hoped my daughter-in-law's faith in me wasn't misplaced.

CHAPTER FIVE
Family Reunion

As usual, I'd settled Karro and Aliande in Passenger Cabin 1, since it was the only one now with a double bunk besides mine and Hirin's. When it became apparent that Baden and Maja were a serious couple, I'd bluntly asked them if they wanted to combine two of the crew quarters to share—and they hadn't taken long in agreeing. It was a simple modification, really—only a matter of adding a connecting door so they could use one room for sleeping and one for desks and storage, then re-affixing the relocated furniture. Far trader crews, if they work well together, get used to the idea of shared relaxation space like the galley/lounge, so we tend to think small when it comes to personal space. As I'd realized once Hirin came back aboard, though, couples required a little more in the way of private quarters. We'd taken advantage of the opportunity and expanded our own quarters into one of the passenger cabins at the same time. It meant we were down to only three passenger quarters now, but I'd rather haul cargo any day. It was generally less trouble. As long as we had a little extra space if needed, I felt we could manage.

Yuskeya and Viss, although they seemed as devoted as ever, didn't want the same consideration. Perhaps it was the temporary feeling of Yuskeya's presence aboard the ship, or perhaps they were simply both more jealous of their private space. I didn't question it. Whatever made my crew happy, made me happy.

Leaving Karro and Aliande to sort out their cabin space, I went up to the bridge for a status report. Rei was alone, ensconced in the big chair and reading something on her datapad. She'd changed into "civilian" clothes, a bright sapphire-coloured bioweave tunic over dark tights, so I assumed she'd already run some errands in the spacedock or the city. She looked up and raised her eyebrows, but I motioned for her to stay seated. "Just checking in."

"I just got back myself. Hirin and Baden are still out on delivery, Viss is doing 'a little something' to the skip drive, Maja's asleep, and Yuskeya's in her quarters, also presumably asleep," she reported. "The outgoing cargo shipment should arrive in about an hour. It'll all fit into Cargo Pods Two and Three, according to Hirin, so nobody has to poke their nose in around the *Amber's Ranger*. Which I assume we're holding onto for now? Unless you want to put it in storage somewhere here. That will cost, though."

I hadn't given it much thought. "I guess . . . keeping it aboard is best? Nothing can be settled until we know what happens with our patient."

"I hope Dr. Ndasa can help her, but if she doesn't make it, you can claim it as salvage," said Rei, ever practical. "Although the ship's been missing for eight decades . . . who knows what kind of flags a salvage claim is going to raise? You might be better off, if it comes to that, to quietly break it down for scrap and sell the parts."

I held up a hand. "Let's say we're hanging on to it for Amber Malka for now. I don't want to go too far down the 'what if' road yet."

"Well, there's a thirty-day window to file, so there's no rush," Rei said with a shrug. "After eighty years, I'm reasonably sure no-one else is going to come looking for it."

"Satisfactory," I said. "Our passengers are getting settled, and Aliande volunteered to make dinner tonight."

Rei fixed me with a look, her eyes, bracketed by the *pridattii*, intent. "Are we going to investigate those coordinates you found on the *Ranger*?"

I grimaced. "Not you, too?"

She held up a hand. "Hey, I'm not disapproving. I think we should. If someone needs help, we help. But I wondered about having your family on board the ship. How you felt about that."

"Hirin and Maja are my family," I pointed out.

"I mean, family who aren't usually caught up in our crazy adventures."

"I don't expect this to be a crazy adventure. If we find a wormhole at those coordinates, I can take that to Lanar. It'll be something concrete to add to our story, and it should make the Protectorate more likely to put some resources into it."

"And if the Protectorate still doesn't bite, we'll drop off our passengers and go back to the wormhole and—" she raised her eyebrows.

"Have a crew meeting to discuss strategies and explore options."

Rei laughed aloud, her *pridattii* moving like dark liquid as the skin around her eyes crinkled. "In other words, you'll tell us what you want us to do, and we'll all go along with it."

I laughed, too. "That seems to be the way things usually go, doesn't it? Honestly, I don't know what we'll end up doing. But I don't think I'll be able to sleep until we figure out what Captain Malka meant."

"Captain?" Pika said in the pause in my discussion with Rei. "I'm sorry, but I haven't been able to identify those coordinates you gave me."

I almost congratulated the AI on not interrupting for once, but then I decided she might take it the wrong way. I'd given her the coordinates from the *Amber's Ranger*'s flight log, on the off chance she might find some connection in the PrimeCorp files. With PrimeCorp's history of backing unauthorized wormhole exploration, there could be information about systems outside Nearspace buried in the data, even if it wasn't overtly linked to the *Lillifleur* or Amber Malka. There wasn't much to go on, only the barest star and planet data, but I thought it was worth a try.

"No worries, Pika. Thanks for looking."

The bridge airlock swished open and Hirin and Baden came onto the bridge. "Everything's delivered and the cargo pods are ready to be loaded," Hirin reported. "Any word from Lanar yet?"

"Sadly, no. Unless he's already in this system, which would be helpful but extremely coincidental, we're not likely to get a response until at least tomorrow."

"Dad?"

Hirin turned to meet Karro, who came striding across the bridge from the other direction, to envelop him in a hug. I was struck by how strongly the two looked like brothers now. Hirin the older, still, but to the uninformed eye they would look very close in age.

Hirin and I hadn't talked much about Karro's refusal of the nanobioscavengers. Hirin's attitude was very much wait-and-see, which was entirely in keeping with his personality. I liked to see things worked out, and worked out quickly. Hirin felt Karro had his reasons for his decision, and that he was entitled to them and to keep them to himself if he wished. We'd lain in bed a few nights, watching the stars glide past through the viewport above us as we hashed out the problem. Without coming to any mutual agreement except that it was something that we both hoped would resolve itself soon.

Now, as I watched them embrace, it seemed even more important that they both be granted as much time to enjoy their relationship as science and circumstances would allow. Even with the nanobioscavs, any of us could still encounter something deadly—but they made escaping that fate a whole lot more likely.

"What's Mom planning to get us into?" Karro asked as they broke apart. "I like hearing about your adventures when they're safely in the past, but I'm not sure I want to be involved in them while they're happening."

Hirin chuckled dismissively. "It's only a small detour to investigate some coordinates, possibly a ship in distress," he said, reiterating what I'd already said. "Our priority will be to get you and our cargo where you're going. We just want to snag some information to pass along to your Uncle Lanar if we can."

Karro quirked a half-smile and stuck his hands in the pockets of his sweater. "And it doesn't sound any more convincing coming from you than it does coming from Mom," he said. "But I guess we're committed now. I told Aliande we could still jump ship and get a commercial shuttle, but she wouldn't hear of it."

"And I hear she's cooking us dinner, so I wouldn't let her leave now, anyway," Rei put in. "Good to see you, Karro."

"And you, Rei. I guess I take Aliande's culinary expertise for granted sometimes."

"Then it's settled," I said. "And as soon as the cargo's stowed, we'll get underway. You won't regret it."

I really should stop making promises I can't keep.

BY THE TIME Aliande called over the ship's comm, summoning us to the galley for dinner, the *Tane Ikai* was a couple of hours out from the planet. I won't say I jumped out of the chair and ran down the corridor, but the spicy aromas wafting enticingly to the bridge had all of us salivating and watching the clock. I told Rei to put the autopilot on, switch the main viewscreen feed to the galley, and join us. Traffic in the system was light, and the coordinates we were heading for would take us away from the direct path between the planet and the wormhole from Mu Cassiopeia anyway.

Aliande had acquitted herself brilliantly, as expected. In the short time since she and Karro had come aboard, she'd managed to create a savoury pasta soup and the doughy but light Vileyran biscuits she'd introduced into our family repertoire of recipes; a beautifully colourful cold salad made with native Xaqualan produce; and a batch of *solanto* cookies for dessert. The soup burst with flavour in every spoonful, and for such a large group, the table was quiet except for appreciative murmurings and the occasional over-enthusiastic slurp.

We kept the conversation light when it did start up. I didn't want to talk about our struggle to keep Amber Malka alive, or her ancient ship in the cargo pod. Or her mysterious message, although we'd probably get to that later. I knew Karro was curious for more details about our unscheduled detour. But for now, I asked Karro about his work with the communications systems on Xaqual, and Aliande about her art. Aliande created "neural art"—a form of multi-sensory digital artwork achieved through the interface of a specialized brain implant with software on a datapad. In some circles, she was considered famous, and I enjoyed the soothing blend of visual and auditory work that was her trademark. She promised to show me some of what she'd been working on during their stay on Xaqual after dinner.

Finally, over hot drinks and cookies, the inevitable question about the distress signal arose. I explained to Karro and Aliande as briefly as possible about the strange encounter with the *Amber's Ranger* and its pilot's mysterious ailment and message.

Leaving out all details about her nanobioscavengers, since that was a touchy subject at the moment. I said only that we'd delivered her into the capable care of an acquaintance on Xaqual.

"Save *Lillifleur*," Aliande mused. "Intriguing. A ship that went missing so long ago. Save it from what, I wonder?"

"Could it be caught in some sort of time anomaly?" Karro asked. "That might account for how young the pilot looked."

"But in that case, how did she escape it and manage to get back here?" Aliande asked.

"I'm sure there's an explanation that's a little less exotic," Maja said with a smile. "Turns out space travel is largely mundane."

"Hey!" Baden protested, and they both laughed.

"There's too much we don't know yet, to even be able to make educated guesses," Hirin said. "However, we should make those coordinates by late morning shiptime, so we'll have at least one answer then—what's actually there."

"Any chance it could be the ship itself?" Karro asked, dunking a *solanto* cookie into his mug.

"Almost none," Rei said. "The coordinates aren't *that* far off the beaten path. Someone would have noticed a ship the size of a colony vessel out there in this length of time. Those things were massive."

"Well," Karro said, getting up to refill his mug, "I guess we'll see tomorrow. Make sure you let me know when we're getting close, all right? I'd like to come to the bridge."

I smiled, abruptly reminded of the little boy who'd loved to spend time on the bridge with me and Hirin, while his sister Maja secluded herself in her room and pretended we weren't even in space. Now he was the planet hugger and she plied the spacelanes. One never knew what the future held. But with a pang, my concern over my son returned. I had to convince him to take the nanos. I'd lost many friends and relatives over the long years of my life so far, but I didn't want to lose either of my children. Not if it was avoidable.

"What are Joash and Klaire up to?" Maja asked her brother, unwittingly giving me time to compose myself and concentrate on the conversation again.

"Busy with school, as usual," Karro said. "Klaire is researching career ideas, not sure what path she's going to take."

"Joash has already asked if he could fly with you for a year after he finishes school," Aliande told me. "I told him we'd broach it to you when we had a chance, so I guess that's now. No need to answer right away! Take some time to think about it."

I blinked. "It never occurred to me that he'd be interested. He must have some weird idea that it's a glamorous life out here, does he?"

Karro shrugged and helped himself to another *solanto* cookie. "I might have told him some stories of being a kid out here that made it seem more interesting than it actually was. And he has heard about your adventures in the last year or so. But," he added, fixing me with a cautionary look, "you'd have to be doing normal cargo hauling if he was tagging along. No special ops for the Protectorate or anything."

"Normal cargo hauling is what we do ninety-nine percent of the time," I assured him. "It'll probably only take a month of plodding cargo runs to disabuse him of any romantic notions he has about space travel, but we'd love to have him. For as long as he can stand it."

"Still a year of school before we'd consider it, but I'll tell him what you said," Karro said with a grin. "He'll be over the moon, I can guarantee."

At least by then Joash would have been offered the choice to have the bioscavs. If he decided on the treatment, that would be great. But would I want to take my only grandson with me into space if he chose not to accept the nanotechnology that had saved my life on several occasions? I'd have to do some hard thinking on that one, but it wasn't an issue right now.

Aliande stood and smoothed down the wrinkles in her shirt. The rich Vileyran reds of the fabric lent a warm glow to her skin, and I noticed Karro shoot an admiring glance her way. She answered with a smile and a wink. "Well, cooking absolves me from cleanup—at least that's the rule in our household—so I'm going to shoot off a message to the kids before I go to bed. I'll let them know we're safely aboard, and en route to FarView. It's only three skips back to Sol system from there, so they could probably use a reminder that we'll be home before too long. They can get a head start on reclaiming the house from the mess."

"Yes, they'll probably need all the time they can get, now that our return is imminent," Karro said with a grin. "Although I hope

Kace has helped keep things under control."

"Kace?" I asked.

"It's a new house AI," Aliande explained. "The kids are old enough now not to need a babysitter, but a good AI with scheduling programming can be useful. She's more like a virtual housekeeper who doesn't do physical things herself, but she reminds Joash and Klaire to get them done."

"And they listen to her?" Pika asked suddenly, with interest.

Karro laughed as he stood and began gathering up the dishes. "Probably not most of the time. She can't *force* them to do anything. But now, when we're on the way home, she'll keep them from panicking when they realize they'd better get things in shape."

"Sounds like a great program," Pika said kindly, and there was only the slightest hint of condescension in her tone.

I CALLED KARRO to the bridge the next morning well ahead of our scheduled arrival at the possible wormhole coordinates. We already knew from the long-range scanner that no derelict ship hung out there, awaiting discovery. The scan showed no ships at all in that area. Just as I'd expected.

Still, if there was going to be anything to see, I wanted Karro to be there for the first look since he'd voiced interest. For all we knew, there could be a spectacular view of a nebula or something else that Amber Malka had wanted to bring to our attention.

When he arrived on the bridge, I installed him at one of the empty boards. He looked around with a nostalgic grin. Aliande had followed and found a seat for herself. She carried her datapad, and I wondered if she was casting about for inspiration for a new art piece. I doubted the bridge of a far trader was the place to find that, but one never knew.

"I still remember all of this like it was yesterday," Karro said. He chuckled. "I think that must mean you're due for some upgrades."

"Haha, very funny. Actually, the ship has had a number of additions and upgrades over the years. Just not so much cosmetically."

"The AI is state of the art," Pika interjected, and Karro smiled.

"Maybe Karro has a point," Maja said, following his gaze around the avionics boards. "We could spiff it up with some shiny new consoles, you know. It doesn't have to look like a decades-old far trader."

"It *is* a decades-old far trader," I pointed out. "And are we that concerned with how the bridge looks? We're the only ones who see it most of the time."

"Not true. You always invite passengers up here for wormhole skips if they want to watch," Rei said. "You don't know what it might be doing to their confidence."

I threw up my hands. "I already refurbished all the passenger cabins and made improvements to the crew quarters. We do require some credits left over for food and fuel. And I know a few people who also enjoy getting paid regularly."

"How about this," Baden said from the comm board. "If we happen to find a massive colony ship to claim for salvage, we redo the entire bridge in gold plating. Because we'd be rich enough to afford it."

At the sudden silence, he glanced around. "Hey, it was only a joke. I don't think we're going to find . . ."

"The *Lillifleur* with everyone dead?" Rei finished. "*Damne*, Baden, maybe engage brain drive before opening the black hole of your mouth sometimes, huh?"

Baden looked abashed. "Sorry. That wasn't what I meant at all."

I shook my head. "Don't worry about it. Everyone's a little on edge not knowing what we're going to find out here."

"Well, I wasn't," Karro drawled. "But I am now."

"We're getting very close," Yuskeya said. "If there were anything physical to see at those coordinates, it should be visible on the main viewscreen now."

"Depending on how big it is," Baden said.

Yuskeya shot him a look. "Anything bigger than a flitter, all right?"

"Noted."

I leaned forward and stared at the viewscreen. Nothing stretched out in front of us but dark, star-studded space. It wasn't even an area with any remarkable natural features. No asteroid belt, no dust clouds, no nebulae, nothing. "You're sure this is the place? Any wormhole readings?" Wormholes could be easy to miss visually, since most of the time they look like a darker shadow against already-dark space.

Yuskeya ran her fingers over the navigation board, although I'm sure she only did it to make me happy. It wasn't that I doubted her abilities, and she knew it. "Approaching the precise coordinates you and Hirin found," she said. "And no, I'm not reading a wormhole in the vicinity, either."

"Yuskeya and Rei have delivered the ship to the correct coordinates, Captain," Pika confirmed.

I frowned. If the position noted on the *Amber's Ranger* screen didn't signify a wormhole, what did it mean? I opened my mouth to ask for ideas when I got my answer.

I might have preferred not to know.

CHAPTER SIX
Best Intentions

WITHOUT WARNING, THE ship lurched to starwise as if something had collided with the hull. Hirin, who'd been standing near Karro, stumbled but caught himself, clutching at a nearby console.

"What was—"

"Captain, we have wormhole readings," Yuskeya said in the brisk, businesslike tone I thought of as her "Protectorate" voice.

Pika broke in excitedly. "They weren't there a moment ago, but now—"

But now neither she nor Yuskeya had to explain, because we all saw what appeared on the front viewscreen. Where moments ago there'd been only dark, empty space, suddenly a wormhole terminus had opened. Not a normal wormhole, though. Usually they appeared, when not affected by a Ford-Roman drive, as merely a darker area of space—an impenetrable, pitch-black shadow against something only slightly less black. This one emitted an eerie chartreuse glow, and rivulets of green plasma outlined the contours of the opening.

"Evasives," I ordered. "Rei, steer hard to dock and give that wormhole a wide berth. We're already closer than I want to be."

Rei's fingers skimmed the pilot's board, but there was no corresponding response from the ship to alter its course. "Not responding, Captain."

"Viss? Anything wrong down there?"

"Normal across the boards," Viss responded. "I can shut down the main drive if it would help."

"No, I want full power for the drive. Why would the helm not respond?"

Viss paused. "Outside force acting on us?" he suggested. "A wormhole with a strong gravitational pull?"

"Have you ever heard of such a thing?"

"No, but that doesn't mean it couldn't exist," he said. "Usually there's no effective gravity until the wormhole dilates fully and the Ford-Roman field engages. But other bodies—like black holes—don't operate that way."

"You're not saying this is a black hole analogue." Hirin said it as a statement, not a question.

"Mother," Karro said, "what's happening?"

Viss didn't answer Hirin immediately. "I'm not saying anything. I don't have enough data to make any kind of a guess about what this is—"

"Unidentified external force detected," Pika said unhelpfully. "The wormhole returns predominantly normal readings but—"

"Cut the chatter!" Rei barked. "I still have no helm control, and whatever that damn thing is, it's pulling us in."

"That's what I was about to say," Pika said in a sulky voice.

I dove across the bridge and slid into the secondary pilot's chair next to Rei. "What do you need from me?"

"Thrusters," Rei said in a clipped voice, her fingers dancing staccato across her screen. "Max the manoeuvring thrusters and try to turn us, move us, get us away from it."

I did as she asked while she continued to try and coax some response from the main drive. Even with thrusters at maximum, straining to push us away from the gaping, green-rimmed mouth, the *Tane Ikai* only edged closer to it.

"Thrusters ineffective," Pika noted. "Intersection with the anomaly is imminent."

"Ideas, people," Hirin said in a calm voice.

"Can we call for help?" Aliande asked, but her voice said she knew that was hopeless.

Baden sat back and put his hands in the air. "I've got nothing," he said ruefully. "Out of my league."

"If we start the Ford-Roman drive, it'll smooth the transition and we'll go in even faster," I said, trying to think. "But what will happen if we enter the mouth and the Ford-Roman field isn't active?"

Nobody answered. Finally, Viss said, "It's an interesting question. At a guess, I'd say it'll be like any wormhole; we'll be crushed by the internal pressures."

"Interesting! Trust Viss to think this is *interesting*," Rei muttered as she continued to struggle with the board.

"Internal pressure inside the wormhole is—" Pika began, but I cut her off.

"Pika! Never mind! We need to stand ready to start that drive if we can't get away. I had no intention of finding out what's on the other side of that wormhole, but that's preferable to not making it through."

"Aye, Captain," Viss said. "Ready to initiate the skip drive on your order."

"Or Hirin's order," I amended. "In case things get tricky."

Karro said in a voice thick with anxiety, "I love how things are not already considered 'tricky.'" He tried to keep his tone light, but he couldn't fool me. My son was scared, and I didn't blame him one bit. He wasn't the only one.

Without warning the ship lurched again, this time closer to the wormhole. The swirling runnels of plasma grew on the main viewscreen as if someone had increased the magnification, and Rei and I gasped in unison. The wormhole mouth loomed large and menacing, a dark blotch in front of us where no stars shone, as if a piece of thick, dark fabric hung suspended in space. If it had been fabric, we would have been almost brushing up against it. The green plasma streams rushed and pooled around its edges, faster now.

"Main drive is losing power," Viss said. "Not sure why, but I can't get it back. All levels plummeting."

"Barely holding us in place," Rei said. "We can't get away."

It felt like we hung on the lip of a cliff, teetering on a precipice and unable to see what waited at the bottom of the drop.

"Engage the Ford-Roman drive," Hirin said, as I was about to give the same order. "Hang on, everyone. We're going in."

IF THE BUMP earlier had felt like a giant hand had brushed the ship, sliding into the wormhole felt like that hand had picked us up and hurled us forward. Rei swore under her breath as the green-rimmed mouth swirled around us.

Wormhole skips are almost always much the same—the wormhole itself is a whirling rainbow of colours as the chemicals and plasma inside interact with the exotic matter from the Ford-Roman drive. Navigating a wormhole is mainly a matter of keeping the ship on a straight course and letting the drive propel it through—the ship circles around the circumference of the wormhole like water running down a drain. There are one or two exceptions around Nearspace—or there were until last year, when I blew one up. But that's another story.

This wormhole was unlike the usual ones in a couple of ways. The rainbow of colours was missing—only a weird mixture of greens and blues painted the inner walls of the inter-dimensional space. Odd streaks of yellow coloured the walls periodically, but they dispersed and faded as we passed like watercolours diluted too far.

Rei's hands, usually so steady on the pilot's board, seemed trembly. "We're going too fast," she said. "This feels wrong."

"I thought wormhole travel speed was a constant, a function of the skip drive?"

"So did I. But this is different."

"All right. What can I do?"

"Be ready when we come out the other end," she said. "If there's anything there in our path at this speed—

She didn't have to finish. I immediately had a vision of a wormhole we'd navigated blind once before, only to emerge into the midst of a moving asteroid field. With the two of us piloting, we'd made it through alive, but barely.

"I shut down thrusters but I'm ready to bring them back online as soon as we exit the wormhole," I told her, keeping my voice as calm and steady as I could. I was keenly aware of Karro and Aliande behind me, and I didn't want my barely-restrained terror to show. My brain churned with the knowledge that some of us had a much better chance of surviving whatever we might find at the end of the wormhole. If the lack of nanobioscavs turned out to be a bad thing for Karro and Aliande, I'd never stop blaming myself for not pushing them harder.

"It's beautiful," Aliande said in an awed voice from behind me. "I've never seen a wormhole like it, and they're all beautiful. But the strangeness of this one—if I could capture this . . ."

I was a little too busy being terrified to appreciate the beauty, but I was glad Aliande could see past the fear.

Although they say every wormhole takes about the same length of time to navigate no matter how distant the points they connect, this one seemed to go on forever. Maybe it was the fear of the unknown waiting at the end, or maybe it was a function of the intrinsic weirdness of the thing, but I felt like I'd been holding my breath for an hour when we finally emerged out the other end.

Rei shut down the Ford-Roman field and I rammed on the thrusters to slow our speed. I hoped we wouldn't collide with anything before they could rein in our breakneck pace.

"Main drive online," Viss said, and I felt the drive catch hold of the ship as if we'd been falling and landed on something unexpectedly soft.

The something soft appeared to be a normal system, despite the strange path we'd travelled to get here. I eased off the thrusters.

"Recording system data," Yuskeya said. The sensors would collect all the data available and start comparing it to star systems in the Nearspace database, both those we'd personally visited and any that had been observed. It would start running comparisons, hoping to eventually find a match. I kept my eyes on the main viewscreen, looking for clues myself, although I knew Pika had a much better chance of figuring out where we were than I did.

In the far distance, the twin yellow glows of a binary star flickered. For a heartbeat, I thought we'd landed back in Eta Cassiopeia, but that didn't seem likely. A planet, still too far away to make out any detail, wavered along in its orbit, and an asteroid belt marked the remains of what might once have been another rocky world. There was no asteroid belt this close to Xaqual.

"Good chance there's a gas giant further out," Yuskeya said, "judging by these preliminary readings. That planet we can see looks like it's in the star's Goldilocks zone."

"The mysterious Ryphen?" I wondered. "Nothing in the vicinity that looks like a lost Nearspace colony ship, is there?"

"Did you expect it to be hanging right here outside the wormhole?" Baden asked with a grin. "Maybe with 'lost ship' painted on the hull?"

"Not really, but a girl can hope," I said. "Pika, can you tell if this wormhole might fit the coordinates from Amber Malka's ship? In relation to that planet?"

"I'll have to run some calculations based on available system data, Captain. And I *am* already trying to match this system to the database."

"Is that a problem?"

"Not at all. I just like to be appreciated," Pika retorted.

"You're absolutely the best AI on this ship."

"Gee, thanks."

I sat back in the chair and took my hands off the board, then pulled a deep breath and slowly released it. "All right. Suggestions?"

"I don't recommend heading back into that wormhole immediately," Viss said.

"Something wrong with the drive?"

"No, but I'm not reading the same external force—gravity or whatever it is—pulling from this side. Sensors aren't picking up anything like that. So I'd like to study our readings from the other side and try to figure out what was happening over there before we try to get out that end."

Right. I hadn't thought of the possibility of getting stuck inside the wormhole at the other end. I didn't know what might happen in that situation, but I doubted it would be good.

"I'd also like to do a full scan of ship systems and drives," Viss continued.

"You are not authorized to start tearing anything apart," I ordered.

"Captain," Viss said in a reproachful voice. "I only said, *scan*."

"Yes, but I know you too well, Feron. The objective is to get back to Nearspace, in one piece, as quickly as possible."

"Let's send a message back through the wormhole to the Protectorate, at any rate," Hirin suggested. "Let them know what happened to us, and that someone should investigate the coordinates of the wormhole. Carefully," he added. "And from a safe distance."

I searched his words for a hint of reproach, but I didn't detect any.

After a moment, Baden said, "Message away. And Captain, I caught a few scattered signals from the planet." His eyes were fixed on the communications board.

"What kind of signals?"

He swivelled in his chair to look at me. "Planetary communications. Possibly something between the planet and a ship in orbit. In other words, people."

I drew another deep breath. "Hello, Ryphen?" I wondered, raising my eyes to the main viewscreen and the distant planetary speck again. "I wonder if this is the answer to what happened to the *Lillifleur*."

"They faded out quickly, though," Baden continued. "If there's a colony there, the rotation might have taken it into the sensor shadow."

"If the ship is still here, and in orbit, it's likely in geosynchronous orbit above a colony," Yuskeya mused. "If we wait here for them to circle around, we might find that out without even moving any closer."

"In orbit for a hundred years?" Aliande asked. "Could they do that?"

"Well, once you have that perfect balance between inertia and gravity that lets an object orbit the planet, it doesn't take too much to keep it there," Yuskeya said. "They'd have to use thrusters to maintain station-keeping, but I'd think it's entirely possible, if they were careful about fuel and resources."

"Waiting a little while to see seems like a wise decision," Hirin said.

"And if the ship is there, but in danger, waiting could be the very thing we don't want to do," I countered. "What if the danger is orbital decay? What if the colony ship isn't even there, and it's something else entirely?"

Hirin pressed his lips together, as he often did to suppress a comment that might not be the wisest to make to one's wife. After decades together, one gets to know these little tells. Instead of saying anything, he turned to Baden.

"All right, Baden, tell us more about these signals you picked up. What language? Can you tell?"

Baden hesitated, fingers skimming over the comm board. "I recorded them . . . hang on. I wasn't tuned in to the content," he explained. "We could be too far out . . . but maybe I can adjust some settings—yes."

His fingers slid around on his board, adjusting the input from his comm implant. Finally, he nodded once. "It's Esper," he said, "at least as a baseline. Not much to go on yet, but I'd say a local dialect."

"Some words and fragments from other languages as well," Pika said.

"Which one might expect from the inhabitants of an early colony ship," Baden said, with an irritated glance around the bridge. Since Pika occupied no definitive space on the ship, though, annoyed glares were not very satisfying. "Colonists were generally gathered from various planets to make up a genetically diverse complement."

"Look at you, knowing your colonization history," Rei said with a smirk.

"Keep monitoring for anything else, Baden," Hirin said quickly, to forestall any further sniping between the comm officer and the AI. "See if you can tap into any broadcast that might give us a clue about what danger they're facing. If it's dire enough for Amber Malka to have risked her life to get help, surely someone's talking about it."

"Will do. If they're in the sensor shadow it will be a while before they reappear, though."

"Sure. But it's possible they went quiet for some other reason. Just keep ears on."

"I'll continue my analysis of the language components and the system," Pika said loftily.

"While we wait—at least briefly," Hirin added with a pointed look at me, "Viss, start your diagnostics. I want to know precisely what shape we're in, and if that skip affected us in any adverse way."

Karro came to stand next to me, an unreadable look on his face. He hadn't said anything since we'd come through the wormhole. I stood and put a hand on his arm, and he flinched it away, crossing his arms over his chest almost defensively. "What?"

He stared out the viewscreen as if dazed, his eyes fixed on the tiny dot that was the planet. The pulse at his throat was visible and quickened. When he did speak, his voice sounded flat, his words monotone. "You want to go and investigate now. You're— excited."

"I wouldn't say excited, but I'm intrigued. These people could have been missing from Nearspace for years . . . decades."

He was silent for a long moment. "Are you sure you didn't plan this? The skip through the wormhole?"

I was stung. "No—Karro, of course not!"

"Because I hope you would have told us if you were planning this," he said in a low voice that now shivered with suppressed anger.

I struggled to keep my voice steady, to contain my shock at the suggestion. "I only wanted to see what was at those coordinates. So I could take that information to Lanar and the Protectorate."

His head dipped in the slightest of nods, but he was still not looking at me. His lips were pressed into a thin white line of disapproval.

"But now that we're here—" I turned my head to follow his gaze out the view screen. "You heard Viss. It might not be safe to turn and try to go back through until we know more, and we're sure we can make it out. And the planet is right there—"

"Oh yes, it all seems very logical," he admitted in that same flat voice.

"It *is* very logical," I retorted. "And the right thing to do. You wouldn't stay back here without seeing if we could help, would you? Or turn and leave?"

"That's the problem," he said, finally turning to look at me. The anger, no longer suppressed, ignited his eyes. "You know I wouldn't. So I have to wonder if we've been manipulated—just a little bit. All we signed up for was a nice quiet visit on the way home to our kids. Not wormhole spelunking to an unknown system where we can't even *message* Joash and Klaire."

I clenched my jaw, willing myself to stay in control. I was aware of covert, uncomfortable glances from the others, but I didn't care. No-one else on the bridge made a sound. Only the breathy hum of electronics filled the air around us. Somehow, I kept my voice steady and calm. "That's completely unfair. You were here, on the bridge. You saw what happened. We didn't have a choice about coming through."

"Your mother's right," Hirin said, quiet but firm. He came and stood between us, obviously taking pains not to visually take sides. He kept his face carefully neutral, but his lips were pressed firmly together in that way he had when he was annoyed. He and Karro looked incredibly similar in that instant. "We were pulled through—we didn't skip deliberately until engaging the drive was the only way to stay safe."

"Unless you knew what was likely to happen when we got here," my son said, still speaking directly to me. Now the anger had cooled to a frosty calm, jagged and sharp like ice particles on a rocky moon. It was almost worse than the previous heat. "You do have a way of making things work out the way you want them to. Even if it might be dangerous. You always think you know best."

"Son, we've just been through some scary *merde*," Hirin said, still not raising his voice. He put a hand on Karro's arm. "We're all a bit shaken. Don't say things you don't mean and will regret later."

Aliande came up behind Karro and put a hand on his shoulder, speaking softly. "Karro, your father is right. We've all been through a stressful situation. Take some time to think. Luta, let's talk about this later, shall we?"

I was too angry to manage anything but a sharp nod. Blood pounded in my temples and my skin felt pulled taut, as if the air around me had suddenly turned to vacuum.

"We'll be in our quarters," Aliande said, taking Karro's hand and tugging him gently away. "Please keep us advised about what's happening."

"We will," Hirin assured her, probably aware that I was too angry to speak.

And after one more cool, searching look at me, Karro turned and let Aliande lead him off the bridge.

"Wow," Pika said into the silence. "What was that?"

Nobody answered her.

AFTER KARRO AND Aliande left the bridge, I stood still and counted to twenty. Everyone, even Pika after her initial comment, was smart enough not to try and talk to me. Even Hirin didn't address me directly; he gave my arm a quick, supportive squeeze, then asked Viss and Baden if they had anything to report from their scans and data-gathering yet. Neither did, but they busied themselves by making a show of checking and thereby avoiding looking at me.

Rei met my eyes once, her *pridattii*-wreathed ones asking silently if she could do anything. I shook my head minutely and she went back to her console. Yuskeya noted in a calm voice that she would start analysing the data from our journey through the wormhole, looking for anomalies. Her long fingers flitted over her console with deft precision.

I turned my eyes to the viewscreen and focused on the speck of the distant planet while I took deep breaths, mentally running through the basic forms of *tae-ga-chi* to calm my racing mind. It took all my strength to keep from storming after Karro and demanding we talk this out immediately. I'd done it enough times with Maja during the years we'd fought incessantly. But my maternal brain knew that wouldn't work with Karro. He needed a break, and maybe Aliande could talk some sense into him.

By the time Viss and Baden were giving their reports to Hirin, I felt calm enough to turn and walk neutrally off the bridge, heading for my quarters. I moved slowly, making sure Karro and Aliande had plenty of time to reach their own space. Their cabin was at the far end of the ship, and I wanted their door closed behind them before I reached mine. I went inside, shut my door, and leaned against its comforting stability, pulling deep, calming breaths. The space seemed suddenly very much smaller than it usually did. I thought about climbing down to one of the catwalks that vaulted above the cargo pods, where I go on the odd occasion the *Tane Ikai* feels too small. But even small, my quarters felt safe and sheltering, and I needed time alone to process this.

I sent a quick private message to Hirin. "I'll be back on the bridge soon. Hold steady 'til then, all right?"

"I'm here if you need me," he sent back.

I jumped when Pika said over the room comm, "Captain, I can patch into Karro and Aliande's room if you want to listen to their conversation." Her voice was cool and practical, devoid of any of the little personality quirks she liked to display.

"No!" I realized I'd almost shouted it and closed my eyes. "I mean no, that wouldn't be right, Pika. They're entitled to their privacy, and honestly, I don't want to hear anything they're saying."

"I merely thought it might give you an advantage later, when you—"

"No. Thank you for the offer, but that wouldn't be right."

"Aren't we listening in on that whole planet we're heading for right now?"

"That's different."

"How?"

I closed my eyes and counted to ten. In as calm a voice as I could muster, I said, "It just is. You'll have to take my word for it. And I'd also prefer that *you* not listen in on Karro and Aliande, either." When she didn't answer, I added, "Pika? You can consider that an order."

After a brief pause, she said, "We could debate whether I'm technically crew and subject to orders, but all right. I won't listen. But if I do happen to hear anything—"

"Don't happen to hear anything. Now, I'd like a little privacy of my own, if you don't mind."

"I'll see you on the bridge, then, Captain," she said, with a touch of wounded righteousness. How had she become such a master at the subtle inflections?

After a moment, a thought occurred to me. "Pika, how often do you listen in on private conversations on this ship?"

But she didn't answer. So either she'd switched her focus back to the bridge, or she was hanging around and staying quiet in case I started talking to myself. I blew out a deep sigh and let myself sag into the big armchair I keep for moments of relaxation and when I need comforting.

Karro's mistrust and harsh words stung. We'd always had a good relationship, my son and I, far less fraught than my contentious interactions with Maja. Now I wondered exactly how he saw me—manipulative and overbearing? A control freak who had to have my own way at any cost?

Or . . . was this about the nanobioscavengers? Maybe Karro thought Mother and I had pressed the issue too hard. He might think that I had somehow engineered this diversion to allow me more time to work on his decision about the bioscavs.

It would have been a brilliant plan, except that I hadn't done any such thing. The wormhole and its effects on the ship, pulling us in, had been as much a surprise to me as to anyone else on board.

If I were honest, I had expected to find *something* at those coordinates—probably not the *Lillifleur* herself, although part of me would have been pleased if it had been there. Naturally, I wanted to help the people aboard if they needed it, and if we could. No, I hadn't expected the ship, but I had expected a wormhole; a nice, normal wormhole that no one else had happened to find before this, that's all. At least, no one except the *Lillifleur* and Amber Malka. I'd expected a wormhole that I could scan, designate, and tell Lanar about, and I would have been very pleased with myself to pass that information along. And then I would have enjoyed the family time while I whisked Karro and Aliande straight to FarView, and that would have been that.

I hadn't expected to find a mysterious wormhole that would suck us in against our best efforts and spit us out in an unknown system. This felt all too familiar, and for a moment I was back in the Corvid system, faced with deadly asteroid fields, an inscrutable and weird space station, and its alien inhabitants. I was no wormhole spelunker. These were not the kinds of risks I liked taking.

And this time I had my son and daughter-in-law to worry about, too.

At least this time—if they were from the *Lillifleur*—we'd be dealing with people from Nearspace. Granted, people who had been out of touch with Nearspace for a century. I closed my eyes and thought about that for a minute, happy to distract myself from Karro. What would the inhabitants of Ryphen think of us, our ship, our tech? Would we be able to help them? And most mysterious of all, why had they never skipped back through the wormhole to Nearspace?

My mind had been skirting that particular question, I realized. Because one possible answer—maybe the most probable one—was that the wormhole wasn't traversable from this direction, and they'd been cut off all this time not by choice, but by simple necessity. Which might mean that we'd now be cut off, too.

I might not be able to forgive myself if that were the case. And Karro never would.

But Amber Malka made it back somehow, I reminded myself. It might have killed her, but I didn't think we'd have the same worry. If she'd turned up in Nearspace on that ancient ship, there must be a way.

The sound of a knock at my door startled me, and I stood up from the chair. "Come in." I bit my lip and stuck my hands in my pockets so they wouldn't shake, wondering if it might be Karro and whether I was ready to see him. When the door slid open, it revealed the pensive face of my daughter.

"What was all that with Karro?" she asked as soon as the door had closed behind her.

I blew out a sigh. "You'll have to ask your brother. I don't know where that came from."

Maja held out a hand and I realized she'd brought me a drink from the galley. The soothing aroma of ginger green tea wafted from the mug as I took it from her with a grateful smile. Caff was not what I needed now; green tea was my comfort drink. I sipped and closed my eyes, letting the earthy, spicy flavour roll over my tongue.

"Thanks, Maja, I needed this," I told her, and took my drink to sit at my desk. Maja sat cross-legged on the newly-installed sofa.

"I think he was shaken up by what happened," Maja said. "That did not sound like the Karro I know."

I shook my head. "No, it didn't. Thank goodness Aliande was there and calmed the situation. I was biting my tongue."

"For what it's worth, I think you're right. We have to contact the planet and ask about their situation. We're here now, after all. And I trust Viss. If he says we should wait to go back through the wormhole, we should wait."

I stared at Maja in admiration. Where had this calm, logical, comfortable-with-space-travel daughter come from? In truth, I knew it hadn't happened overnight, but it still amazed me sometimes. "Thank you. That means a lot to me. How do you feel about talking to your brother about it?"

She gave a rueful half-smile and picked at an invisible bit of lint on the sofa. "Karro and I used to fight a bit, too," she said. "Quite a bit. And we haven't spent a lot of time together to smooth things over. But yes, I can do that. I think I'll wait a little while, though. Give him time to settle down."

I sipped my green tea. "The whole thing scared him; I understand that. It scared everyone! But he left the space adventuring life a long time ago . . . in fact, he never really lived it once he met Aliande. Not since you both were kids."

"He'd be extra rattled knowing Aliande might be in danger, too," Maja agreed. "And worried about not being able to contact the kids."

I hesitated, then said, "I wonder if it might be about the nanobioscavs, too. He still won't take them, and neither will

Aliande. He knows your grandmother and I want him to, though. Maybe he has it in his head that I engineered this somehow so he'd have to talk to me about it."

Maja shrugged. "Well, anyone on board can explain that this wasn't planned, that we had no choice. And he was there, on the bridge. If he won't believe it . . . there's not much you can do."

"Except hope he gets over it," I agreed. "If you can do anything to speed that along, I'd appreciate it. Just—don't mention the bioscavs, all right? I'd rather he didn't know we were talking about them."

"Agreed," she said. "Now, I'm going to gather drinks for everyone else and deliver them, along with snacks to keep everyone alert. I'll have something for you when you come back to the bridge."

"You're earning your reputation as ship-mother," I told her with a smile.

"Well, someone has to look after you all. I don't know how you managed before I got here," she said with a grin. She rose, dropped a kiss on my cheek, and left the room.

I sipped my tea, trying to think soothing thoughts and formulate a plan, then went to the bridge to talk about what to do next.

CHAPTER SEVEN
A Planet Called Ryphen

KARRO AND ALIANDE had not returned to the bridge when I arrived, but everyone else occupied their usual place. No-one mentioned what had happened or acted like anything was amiss, which I appreciated. I could always count on this crew to be circumspect. The usual ambiance of bridge sounds was comforting in its familiarity—the hum of fans; the murmur of ship systems; the faint, ever-present pulse of the drives. A hint of residual tension hung in the air, but I could ignore that.

It was too soon to ask Viss about the state of the ship—I'd been off the bridge less than half an hour. He'd only have a sarcastic answer if I asked. So I said what I'd been mulling over as I drank my tea.

"I think our best course of action is to make for the planet. We could be there in a little over twenty-four hours shiptime if we pushed the burst drive to max, but I don't want to spook the inhabitants by blasting in out of nowhere." I kept my eyes on the big viewscreen and the planet in the distance. "If this is the *Lillifleur* colony, and they've been here as long as we suspect, out of touch with Nearspace, they don't even know such a thing as a burst drive exists."

"We probably do want to try going back through the wormhole as soon as we can," Hirin suggested mildly.

He didn't say *to keep Karro happy*, but he didn't have to. I knew what he meant. Still, I had to balance competing interests. "Two days at normal speed isn't long. That will give Viss time to evaluate the drives, and we can contact the planet and chat once we're in range. Maybe they'll tell us they don't even need our help; in which case we can turn around with a clear conscience."

With Amber Malka's words, *save Lillifleur*, still echoing in my head, I didn't think that would be the case. But we had no crystal ball to foresee how things would unfold.

"All right," Hirin said. "Rei, take us toward the planet at cruising speed, no burst. Baden, monitor everything you can catch coming from the planet. The more we pick up, the better position we'll be in when it comes time to talk to them."

"Aye, Captain," Rei and Baden said in unison.

"Pika, any matches for this system yet?"

"The database contains a large number of partial system observations and readings that have never been fully correlated," Pika said. Her voice was frosty, indicating that she hadn't yet forgiven me for not letting her eavesdrop earlier. "However, my preliminary conclusion is that this system is not contained in the database."

"Wow, a new system," Rei breathed. "I guess the *Lillifleur* crew gets credit for finding it, even if they didn't intend to."

"Although as yet unconfirmed, I suggest a high probability that this is indeed the colony from the *Lillifleur*," Pika said.

"I think so, too, but let's not make assumptions until we talk to these folks." As much as part of me wanted to be in the big chair, I left it to Hirin for now. I settled into the secondary pilot's seat next to Rei and watched the tiny dot of the distant planet grow closer on the console screen.

KARRO AND ALIANDE did not make an appearance at dinner that evening, although Aliande sent me a message to say they would get something from the galley when they were hungry. I wasn't sure if Karro was still sulking, embarrassed, or simply not ready to face me. I decided to let him have whatever time he wanted. He was the one who'd started this, after all.

In the way of most in-system travel, the time en route to the planet we assumed was Ryphen passed slowly. There was a brief spate of excitement late in the day when the colony ship *Lillifleur*, as we'd half-expected, emerged in its slow orbit from the other side of the planet. Given the size of the planet and the ship, and the complex dance of gravity, mass, inertia, and energy that Pika explained in considerable detail, we surmised that the ship was in synchronous orbit over the colony. I left Baden with instructions to begin monitoring and recording anything he could pick up from the planet, and went to my quarters.

Despite feeling exhausted, I spent a short, restless night, expecting the bridge to call me at any moment to say the planet was hailing us. That call didn't come, and eventually I must have slept. Hirin was already up and gone by the time I woke, and I hurried to the bridge, carrying my breakfast of caff, fresh fruit, and cinnamon *pano*, to find out what I'd missed. By now we must be close to showing up on the planet's—or the *Lillifleur's*—scanners, even considering the age of their equipment.

"Good morning," Hirin greeted me with a disarming smile when I reached the bridge. Before I could scold him for not waking me, he prompted Baden, "Tell Luta what you've discovered." Hirin didn't move to relinquish the chair to me yet, but that was all right. I suspected it was his way of protecting me, taking on the responsibility for making official decisions.

Giving Karro another target. I pushed that thought aside as my communications officer swivelled his chair around and crossed his arms, his sea-green eyes bright as he regarded me. He loved having something to report.

"*Okej*, there's some chatter about Amber Malka—concern about how she's doing and what's happened to her. So it seems like she didn't just take off on her own—this was a planned operation."

"Any clues about what she might have meant by 'save *Lillifleur*'? Are they talking about problems?"

Baden shook his head. "No, nothing notable. And although we're picking up signals from them, the planet's inhabitants don't seem to have noticed us yet. We must still be outside the range of their scanners. Which makes sense; their tech is almost a century out of date."

"That's probably a good thing for now."

"Can't last much longer, though. They're going to notice us soon."

Yuskeya said, "Captain, two objects just hit the long-range scanners behind us, heading in-system and moving relatively fast."

"Objects? Ships?"

"Too far away to tell at this point, but—they're moving too quickly to be natural objects, so, not asteroids."

"Did they come through the wormhole?" I had a sudden wild thought that our message had been received on the other end, and someone was here to assist us already.

"I'd say no. They're on the wrong trajectory, unless they took a weird roundabout path," Yuskeya said.

I turned and met Hirin's eye. He still had the command. We'd managed to work out a way to share the captain's job, but sometimes I itched to have the final say when technically I didn't. Luckily, we functioned best as a team.

"Go out to meet them, burst for the planet, or sit here and observe?" Hirin summed up our range of choices succinctly.

"Do we get a vote?" Baden asked.

"Still not a democracy," I told him. "Hirin and I hold the only two votes."

"And what if it's a tie?"

"Then we fight in private and report back to you later, same as we always do," I retorted, turning to Hirin. "I think we should sit and observe for now. Let them pass us and listen to the signals coming from the planet. We can see how they react when their scanners pick up whatever it is. Take our cue from them."

Viss's voice growled up from the engineering deck. "What if they don't pass us? What if it's us they're interested in?"

"Good thought, Viss. That's a possibility, but hard to plan for. We'll stay alert so we can react to whatever happens," Hirin said.

I smiled at Hirin. "So we don't have to argue?"

Hirin returned my look and raised his eyebrows. "Not this time. I agree with that assessment. Let's wait and see. Rei, braking thrusters to slow us down to one-eighth current speed. Keep the drive engaged in case we have to move fast, but I want us crawling while we wait this out."

I nodded. That was smart. Honestly, my first instinct was to go out and meet whatever the objects were, so we could identify them quickly. But I suppose Karro's words still stung; his accusation that I'd manipulate situations to get what I wanted— even to the point of courting danger to myself and others. So maybe I was deliberately playing it safe, suppressing my instinct to go investigate.

In any case, if Hirin and I were on the same page it was easier for everyone concerned.

I moved toward the secondary pilot's board, but Hirin stopped me. "Luta, I think I'll hand the chair over to you now. Since we don't know what's coming, I'll take the weapons station so we're prepared."

When Hirin had left the nursing home on Earth and returned to the *Tane Ikai*, we'd carried very little in the way of weaponry. Piracy was rare in Nearspace, and the mundane cargo runs we usually took on held little danger or risk. Coincidental with the remarkable turnaround in Hirin's health had come an elevation in that risk level, however, and he'd appointed himself *de facto* weapons officer. He'd restocked the torpedo bays and our complement of wasp missiles, and now the ship could hold her own in many encounters. We lacked the elegant manoeuvrability of an actual fighting ship, but we had some bite.

So when the possibility of danger and the necessity to defend ourselves presented itself, Hirin preferred to fill the role of overseeing those defences.

"All right," I agreed. "Baden, keep your ears on. Watch for the moment they notice these objects. I want to know if people are surprised or startled or worried."

"Or happy? Maybe they're a good thing," Baden suggested. "Maybe they expect them. Could be trading partners or something."

"Maybe," I said doubtfully. "We'll keep an open mind for now. Viss, you still listening in?"

"Aye, Captain. I'm guessing you want thrusters and main drive available if needed."

"Affirmative," I agreed. "Don't start any kind of diagnostics that will take them offline or impact their responsiveness."

"It's the skip drive I'm mainly concerned with," he said. "Preliminary checks on the ship itself came back with no areas for concern."

"Good to know."

And after that, we sat. Hirin was busy for a few minutes bringing the weapons systems online and setting them to standby, and Baden monitored the planet's communications. Yuskeya watched the incoming objects on her screen, but they were still too far out to have anything further to report. Maja sat next to Baden and stared out the viewscreen at the unrelieved dark expanse stretching away from us. I mostly brooded, replaying my conversation with Karro. We still hadn't spoken, since they'd had dinner in their room last night. It was a striking contrast to that first cheerful meal Aliande had prepared for us all. I caught myself drumming my fingers impatiently on the arm of my chair and mentally ordered myself to stop.

Next to me on the console, my datapad chirped. I looked down and saw a message from Karro appear on the screen. One word: *Sorry.*

I stared at it. Had Aliande put him up to it, or was it sincere now that he'd had time to calm down? I decided I didn't care. I wanted the tension dispelled, at least for now.

But that brought a new dilemma: I wanted to acknowledge the message right away, but I also didn't want to explain about the incoming objects—that a new element of uncertainty and possible concern had entered the picture. If I took time to respond to his message, it would seem strange if I didn't also let him know what was happening.

Finally, I picked up the datapad and replied, *Forgiven. Talk later. Come to bridge any time for updates.* I hit send before I could change my mind or add too much. If Karro or Aliande wanted to keep up with what was happening, they could come and do so; if they didn't, I wouldn't force it on them. And I didn't want to make them worry needlessly if this turned out to be some special delivery the people on the planet were expecting.

"Okay, they're small," Yuskeya said, leaning over the nav board. "Definitely smaller than a flitter, or Amber Malka's runner."

"Manned? Or too small for that?"

Yuskeya flashed me a smile. "Depends on the size of the crew."

"Pfft. All right. But they're still moving too fast to be natural?"

"Yes. And they're keeping too close and coordinated," Yuskeya confirmed. "If they stay on the current trajectory, they're headed directly at the planet."

"At their current speed, when will they be in range of the planet's sensors?" Hirin asked.

Yuskeya shrugged. "Hard to say. We don't know what kind of tech or scanners they have. As Baden said, they don't appear to know we're here yet."

"Not yet," Baden said. "No-one's said hello or started yelling 'something strange came through the wormhole!'"

"Let me know if either of those things happen," I said.

Yuskeya smiled briefly. "So whatever they are, they'll have to get closer than we are before the planet picks them up."

"Captain, I've accessed the general technical specs for a colony ship approximating the *Lillifleur*'s construction date," Pika said. "The data suggests they will have to get considerably closer before the *Lillifleur* will detect them. And the ship will have to be on this side of the planet's sensor shadow. The ship will presumably have better range than any installations on the surface, since it will not be fighting interference from the planet's atmosphere. Still, the unknown objects could get reasonably close to the planet before the inhabitants notice them."

"Thanks, professor," Baden muttered.

"And how fast are they moving?" Hirin asked, obviously trying to get the conversation back on track.

"A lot faster than a modern runner, actually," Yuskeya said. "Honestly, almost as fast as our burst drive speed."

"All right, best guesses. What are they?"

Rei's impatience with sitting still was obvious. She tapped one foot in a jerky, irregular rhythm on the metal decking, sending out a wordless communiqué of agitation. "We don't know anything else about this system," she said. "Except that there's a gas giant out there somewhere. So it's impossible to speculate."

"What's propelling the things?" I asked Yuskeya. "Can you get any kind of drive reading or signature?"

Pika piped up to answer. "No signature that corresponds to any drive in the Nearspace database, or any known alien technology."

Yuskeya blew out a sigh. "When they get closer I might be able to analyse any by-product they're creating. But that would require a very close scan—hey!" She tapped the nav board, her forehead creased in concentration.

"What?"

She looked up at me. "They just changed course," she said. "Not a lot, but significant. They're still headed for the planet, but now they're going to pass a lot closer to us."

AFTER A BRIEF silence while we all processed this news, Hirin said, "Weapons systems online and primed." He hadn't waited for an order from me, but I was okay with that. "If they're hostile, we're ready for them."

He sounded awfully confident, considering we didn't know what the things were or what threat they posed. But if Hirin said we were ready, I'd take his word for it.

"Yuskeya, don't let them out of your sight. Advise of any change."

"Aye, Captain."

"Viss? You heard that?"

"Manoeuvring thrusters and main drive are fully powered and available," he assured me.

"Baden, they're not sending any kind of signals, are they?" I asked this even though I knew he would have told me if they were.

"Negative, Captain. Not on any channel we can access."

"All right. How long until they reach us?"

Pika answered. "At their present rate of speed and trajectory, they will pull abreast of the *Tane Ikai* in thirteen minutes, twenty-eight seconds."

I leaned back in my chair and watched the luminous, enigmatic dots on the screen. Then I pinged Karro's implant.

"Hello?" he answered, his voice carefully neutral.

"We have some unidentified objects heading our way from out-system—powered, but they don't appear to be manned. I wanted to tell you because I don't know what's going to happen as they get closer."

There was silence on his end. "What's going to happen, as in, what?"

"Lots of possibilities. They could attack with weapons, they could change course and try to ram the ship, they could do absolutely nothing and sail past on their way to the planet. We might have to respond to any of those things. At this point, we don't know. Just—be prepared for anything, I guess. I didn't want you two to be in the dark."

There was another pause. "We might come to the bridge," he said. "If not, we'll secure ourselves here."

"Either is fine; we'll keep you informed." I closed the comm.

"No course change yet," Yuskeya said.

Suddenly Pika and Baden started to speak at once.

"Incoming trans—"

"Captain, we are being—"

"Pika!" Baden snapped. "I'm the comms officer. I will tell the Captain when there's an incoming transmission!"

"Well, I thought you hadn't noticed—"

"You didn't give me a chance to open my mouth—"

"Gee, I'm sorry my reaction time is so much fas—"

"Hey!" I interrupted them. Not for the first time, I wondered if the Pika-cons outweighed the Pika-pros. "Baden, report."

Baden swivelled his chair to face me. "Incoming transmission, Captain. They identify themselves as *Lillifleur*. They're asking us to identify ourselves in turn."

"We'll respond, Baden." When he nodded to me, I said, "NCV *Lillifleur*, this is Captain Luta Paixon of the *Tane Ikai*, a Nearspace merchant vessel. We received a message that you require assistance."

"Put any reply on the ship's comm," I told Baden. It didn't take long in coming.

"Captain Paixon, this is the colony Lillifleur, not the ship. My name is Karin Nakano, Communications Officer here. Our communications are being routed through the ship's channel." She paused, then said, "Excuse my bluntness, Captain, but what the hell are you doing here? We haven't seen a Nearspace vessel in a very long time."

APPARENTLY, OFFICER NAKANO liked to get right to the point. I suppose in this case, I couldn't blame her. "I have to admit it wasn't entirely intentional, Officer Nakano. We were pulled through a wormhole we didn't know was there and ended up in this system."

"But you don't seem surprised to find us here." Even over the less-than-perfect connection, suspicion threaded her voice.

"We encountered a woman named Amber Malka—answered a distress call to her vessel, which was adrift. She didn't say much, but she did mention the name 'Lillifleur,' so although we didn't know precisely what we'd find, no, your presence isn't a complete surprise."

Nakano's voice grew sharp. "Is Amber Malka with you?"

"Objects are seven minutes away from our position at current speed," Yuskeya said in a low voice. "Still heading toward the

Tane Ikai."

"No, she is not, I'm sorry. She was practically comatose when we found her. We did what we could, but our medic couldn't diagnose what was wrong with her. We left her in the very good care of a specialist on Xaqual, but I have to tell you, Officer Nakano, she was very ill at that time. That's all I know."

After another pause, Nakano said, "Thank you for assisting her, Captain. I'm sure you did all you could."

"We have a more pressing issue," I told her, aware of Yuskeya's warning. "We've picked up several objects approaching from out-system. Have you noted them on your sensors yet?"

"One moment while I consult with the *Lillifleur*, Captain Paixon. Her sensors have a longer reach than ours here on the planet."

"Why did they name the colony the same as the ship?" Baden wondered. "That's got to be confusing."

Rei shrugged. "Maybe not if you're the only two things in the system," she said.

Officer Nakano came back to the comm. "The NCV *Lillifleur* has just picked them up on its sensors—they noticed you a short time ago as well. We are observing them."

"Do you know what they are?"

Nakano hesitated a moment before answering. "Unmanned drones like these have recently approached the planet. They make no attempt at contact and won't respond to our messages. We don't know what they want. The one time we allowed one to get close—it was the first one we'd seen—it scanned or affected us somehow, and many of our people became sick. The drone kept going, but our people haven't fully recovered. We haven't let any others get close since then."

I frowned. "How have you stopped them?"

Again, the response was a moment in coming. "When they would not respond to our hails, the *Lillifleur*—the ship— destroyed them. We've kept her weapons systems operational, which turned out to be a good thing. However, they may take an interest in you and your ship."

She went on, "Unfortunately, we can't assist you out there, if they move against you. We have no planetary-based defences beyond the ship, and the ship can't leave orbit. We have over five thousand colonists here who still depend on her to some extent."

"Stand by, Lillifleur." I motioned to Baden to close the channel.

"Well?" I asked the bridge at large. "Thoughts, opinions, impressions?"

"Objects still appear to be unmanned drones," Yuskeya said.

"Any clear indication that they're dangerous?" Hirin asked.

Yuskeya pursed her lips. "I can't tell without doing a deeper scan, which they might read as aggression. Should I risk it?"

"Let's go gently for now," Hirin said. "Stay with surface scanning only."

"Notwithstanding Commander Blue's earlier joke, they are too small to be vehicles for any known species," Pika said.

Baden said in his characteristic drawl, "It's worth noting that the colonists seem to follow the 'shoot first and ask questions later' philosophy."

"Noted."

"If they pass by us, we could follow them in toward the planet," Maja said in a thoughtful tone. "See what they do. If they make any aggressive move against us first, we can defend ourselves. It would be interesting to see if we're getting the full story here."

"You think Communications Officer Nakano might be lying? To what end?"

"To get us on their side from the outset? Possible, I guess. But unnecessarily blowing up some inoffensive drones might not be the best way to start a relationship with whoever sent them," Maja murmured. "I'd like a little more information from both sides before throwing in with either."

"The colony is signalling again," Baden said. "Seems like they want to know what we're thinking."

I looked to Hirin. "What are we thinking?"

He grinned, skin crinkling around his blue-grey eyes. "I think I made the right decision giving you back the chair."

"Very funny." I nodded to Baden. "Open up the channel again."

When he did so, I said, "Officer Nakano, we stand ready to defend you and ourselves if necessary. However, we'd like to take this opportunity to study the drones as they move toward the planet."

"Of course, that's your call. But be wary if they try to scan you."

I kept talking, my voice calm. "We are well-protected," I

assured her. "I'm sure it's in your best interests as well to find out all you can about these things."

Nakano paused. After a moment, she admitted, "You may be right. But we will destroy them if they come too close."

"And that's your decision to make. Will you stay on this channel in case we need to communicate as the drones get closer?"

"Affirmative. And the *Lillifleur* will answer your hails as well. Captain Juliska Barath is on the bridge. Be careful, Captain Paixon," the woman said tersely. And she closed the connection.

"Well, that went well!" Hirin said with false cheer, and I stuck out my tongue at him.

"All right, everyone, eyes on those drones and be ready to react if they do anything untoward. Hirin, let's put up our shields. Rei, if they pass us by, follow them, and make sure we keep them well within our weapons range," I ordered. "Let's see what these things are up to."

That's when they scanned us.

ACTIVELY SCANNING ANOTHER ship or entity is not necessarily an aggressive act, but it can certainly be seen as an invasive one. Yes, we'd already scanned the drones, so maybe we were in no position to complain, although ours so far had been superficial, for identification purposes only. Protocols for interacting with other ships generally allow such surface or passive scans for identification and assessment and nobody objects too much. We all have an interest in knowing who we're dealing with when we encounter another ship or body in space. So scanning to see how many life forms are on a vessel and whether they have weapons systems on board is acceptable.

Active or deep scans are another matter. These scans examine and report on a molecular level, and you rarely carry one out without permission unless you're looking to get into a fight with the scanee.

The drones' scan was *that* kind of scan.

"Deep scan initiated," Baden and Pika said almost in unison as the drones drew closer to our position. For once, Baden didn't complain about the AI's interference.

"Shields are up," Hirin said tersely. "I wasn't fast enough to block the whole thing," he added with a note of apology in his voice. I'm sure we were all thinking about what the planet's comms officer had told us; the drones' scan apparently making the colonists sick. "But they didn't get much before the shields were in place. They know we're alive and human, but that's about it."

"Speak for yourself," Pika said, the grin in her voice obvious. "And they might not even know what 'humans' are."

"Everyone feel all right?" I asked, and the answers were in the affirmative.

"Well, that was rude," Rei said. "But they're maintaining their course for the planet."

"Like we're no more than an interesting but corollary specimen," I mused. "They don't seem to care that we blocked them."

"They're still trying to scan us," Baden confirmed. "Running a superficial scan, anyway. No attempts to break through the shields. Just seeing what they can get, I guess."

"Or trying to figure out what we are."

The drones continued to approach, their course unchanging, and sailed past on their way toward the planet. They were shaped a bit like tadpoles, with a bulbous body tapering to a narrower short "tail" in back. Tiny by interstellar standards, the main body about eight feet in diameter. It was true that no species we'd encountered could travel very far in one of these—unless they were in stasis or the drone was more like a short-range, automated travel pod.

"We could try the activator drive the Corvids gave us," Hirin said ruminatively. "Maybe shut one of them down, then catch it with the remote arms." Although its true purpose was to trigger the opening of a specialized type of wormhole, the activator could also act as a non-violent weapon against some ships, shutting down their propulsion systems and leaving them adrift.

I pointed a finger at him. "Not a bad idea, but for now I think we'll avoid anything actively aggressive unless they start something."

"Permission to follow them, Captain?" Rei asked. "They hadn't scanned us when you mentioned following them before."

"Hang back another thirty seconds and then head after them. Maintain distance. And Yuskeya, I guess turnabout is fair play. Run a deep scan on them. Let's find out everything we can."

Karro and Aliande arrived on the bridge then. They seemed initially tense, but relaxed when they realized the bridge was quiet and all appeared calm. Karro didn't seem to want to meet my eyes. I sketched the current situation for them in a few clipped sentences, and they turned to the big viewscreen to watch the drones spin silently through the inky void toward the planet. After a few minutes, by some unspoken agreement, they made their way to a couple of vacant consoles and sat down in the skimchairs. Karro held out a hand to his wife and she took it, intertwining her fingers with his.

Before long, Communications Officer Nakano was back on the comm, her voice strained. "Captain? We're watching the drones' approach. The *Lillifleur* is prepared to fire on them should they come within range. Please be sure you are not in the line of fire or close enough to sustain damage."

"We're close behind them," I said, although she already knew that. "We're subjecting them to a thorough scan. I'd appreciate some notice if you're preparing to take any action."

Maybe she thought that's what she was giving me, but she said nothing. I signalled Baden to mute our outgoing channel. "Yuskeya, anything new?"

She studied her screen, brow slightly furrowed. "The drones don't seem to notice or object to anything I throw at them. They're quite dense—it's not empty space inside them. They're carrying a considerable amount of instrumentation or machinery—could be their inner workings, or it could be something else."

"They don't have bellies full of bombs, right?"

Yuskeya shook her head. "I don't think so. If they're carrying weapons, they're not identifiable as such. And there's no obvious way to launch missiles of any kind."

I didn't think that mild assurance would be enough to placate Officer Nakano and whoever was on the orbiting ship. We needed a new strategy. "All right, Baden, re-open that channel, please."

He did so, and I told Nakano my plan. "I'm going to pull my ship ahead, to block the drones from coming directly toward the planet and your ship. We'll see if we can herd them out around you."

"It seems like it would be easier to simply destroy them," Nakano argued.

"This is Hirin Paixon, second-in-command, Officer Nakano," Hirin said. "How many of these things have you seen before now?"

There was a pause before she answered. "Nine," she said finally. "The first one was alone, then the next eight came in pairs. It was the first one that made us sick. As I said, we're still dealing with the symptoms."

"So you've destroyed eight of them?"

"Yes, that's correct."

"How close together did they appear? Many in a day, weekly?"

"The first ones were weeks apart," she said. "Then they started appearing more frequently—at shorter intervals. The last ones were three days ago. Now these. Why does this matter?"

Hirin's voice was calm. "Just gathering information, Officer. I'm sure you'd like an explanation for them as much as we would."

"What we'd all mostly like is for them to leave us alone," Nakano said tersely.

"It doesn't seem that your approach has achieved that so far," Hirin observed in a mild tone. "More information might allow you to readjust to a better strategy."

"Sit tight," I said before Nakano could respond. "We'll see what we can do." I gestured to Baden to close the channel.

When Baden nodded that we were clear, I turned to Hirin. "Are you trying to pick a fight with the colonists?"

He huffed. "No. But to keep doing the same thing when it's obviously not working—"

I held up a hand. "I know, and you're right. But I'm not sure they're ready to hear that from a bunch of strangers. The first strangers they've seen in a long time, remember."

"Do you think we should get rid of them, as Nakano wants us to?"

"I didn't say that."

Maja shook her head as she weighed in. "Dad's right. If they keep coming, and coming faster, I don't see that blowing them out of the sky is working as a strategy. I still think we should let them get closer to the planet and see what happens. But keep them within range of our own weapons, and yes, putting ourselves between them and the colony isn't a bad idea."

"When did you get so tactical, Maja?" Karro asked suddenly,

in a teasing voice. It was the first normal thing he'd said since our argument, and I felt the knot in my stomach relax slightly.

"Let's just say that spending time on the *Tane Ikai* the past couple of years has been a growth experience," she told him with a wink.

Everyone agreed with Hirin and Maja's approach, so that's what we did. I know, I told them it wasn't a democracy, but I did trust my crew to give me good insights and input. We maneuvered into place beside and a little ahead of the drones, and initially, they made no course adjustments. As we drew nearer the planet, though, they angled out away from us and it slightly, so that their trajectory would take them around it in a wider orbit than we'd first anticipated. We nudged out a little further, and so did they. I checked in one more time with Nakano, and she sounded grudgingly relieved that our plan was working. When the drones' path eventually took them sailing past the planet we slowed and watched them go.

"Shall I continue tracking them, Captain?" Pika asked.

"That's a good idea," I told Pika. "Deploy a tracking beacon and set it to follow them. Let us know if they do anything but keep going straight past the planet."

"I'll bet Nakano will hand the conversation off to the orbiting ship any moment now," Baden speculated. "No doubt she has to go and report to someone. I predict we'll hear from the NCV *Lillifleur* in five, four, three, two—" He grinned and winked at me and turned on the speaker.

"Captain Paixon, this is Captain Juliska Barath of the colony ship *Lillifleur*. Seems like you've been helpful to us, and allowed us to conserve some energy we can't afford to spare. Thanks very much for your assistance."

The captain's voice was reserved, as if not entirely sure she was willing to trust us yet. That was fair enough.

"Good to meet you, Captain Barath," I responded. "We're anxious to find out if there's more we can do to help you. We came in response to a distress signal we picked up from Amber Malka's ship."

I caught the swiftly indrawn breath before she stifled it. "Is Captain Malka with you?"

Apparently, Officer Nakano hadn't passed along everything I'd told her. "No . . . she was very ill when we found her. We left her with a doctor—a friend I trust—on Xaqual. He will take good care of her but, as I told Officer Nakano, she was extremely ill when we left her there. I don't know how she's fared since then."

After a pause, Barath said, "Well, that's better news than it could have been. Is your ship capable of planetside landing, Captain Paixon?"

I was taken aback; I'd expected we might rendezvous with the *Lillifleur* in orbit and meet the captain aboard, if we were going to do more than talk across the void of space. But we were the guests here, so I wasn't about to argue. "It is, Captain."

"I'll send you the coordinates where you can put your ship down on Ryphen. It's only a short distance from the settlement, and I'll meet you down there, if that's acceptable. I'll have my navigator send you all the information you'll need."

"That will be fine. We'll see you planetside."

"Barath out," she said, and broke the connection.

I turned to look at Hirin. "Looks like we're going visiting."

"And me without anything new to wear," he answered.

Rei spun her skimchair to face me, her beautiful face animated. "Captain, did you notice anything strange about Captain Barath?"

"She's a little brusque, but nothing extraordinary."

Her voice held a note of excitement. "Didn't you notice? She has the same name as the original captain of the *Lillifleur!* The one who was in charge eighty years ago when the ship went missing. Remember? Her name was on the ship's database entry."

"She didn't sound like someone who'd have to be—over a hundred years old?" Baden said.

"No, she didn't. A descendant, maybe? Keeping the family tradition of the name and rank alive?"

"Maybe." Yuskeya looked skeptical. "Considering what I found in Amber Malka's blood, though . . . and that fact that we do know other people who don't exactly match up to the expectations of age—"

I stopped and stared at the *Lillifleur*, a monolith of hope and steel, placidly following its orbital course around the planet on the main viewscreen. "You think she's the *original* captain?"

Maja said, "Seems like a possibility."

"Pika," I said, "are you there?"

"Captain, I'm always here," the AI chided me. "Always here, and chronically under-utilized."

"Can you download the full crew and colonist manifest from the Lillifleur to my datapad?"

"Certainly. Would you like to sync it to your Retin-X implant as well?"

I grimaced. Six months ago, Rei had convinced me to go with her while she had a new implant installed, and in a moment of weakness, I'd agreed to get one, too. The Retin-X provided several functions, but mainly it displayed information as a holographic projection that appeared to hover in the air six inches or so in front of the eye. Instead of looking up something on a datapad, you could do it through the neural-visual interface. It was relatively new technology, so information you might want had to be pre-loaded to the implant, but they promised that within a year, it would be possible to link the implant to a personal datapad, so anything on the datapad would also be available via implant.

So far, I rarely used the implant in my left eye, because I hadn't yet mastered the art of keeping my face neutral and using it surreptitiously. I'd tried to use it once to recall the name of a diplomat I'd met at a gathering hosted by Lanar and Jahelia, and he ended up asking me if I felt all right. Rei told me I didn't practice enough, but it was so much easier to use my datapad that practice didn't happen, either. Maybe I was too old to have much patience with new tech.

But for going down to the planet, it might be useful. "Go ahead, Pika. And send everything else to do with the original colonization plan. There might be further information in the PrimeCorp database files, so check there as well."

"Forewarned is forearmed, Captain?" Pika asked.

"Something like that," I muttered, and went to make myself presentable for a *de facto* ambassadorial visit to the planet Ryphen.

CHAPTER EIGHT
Lillifleur and Lillifleur

As we approached it, Ryphen resolved on the viewscreen very reminiscent of Earth, though mottled with caramel browns and patches of almost bright copper where Earth tended to greens and yellows. Less of this planet's surface area appeared to be given over to water. The land masses had settled largely around the equator in a daisy-chain of connected continents, and the poles gleamed blue-white with rolling expanses of thick ice. Clouds swirled lazily through the atmosphere, wreathing indigo oceans below. A pleasant-looking world.

The coordinates arrived as Captain Barath had promised. On the northern edge of one of the smaller land masses, where one might expect the planet's hotter, tropical climate to be edging into temperate, the colonists of the *Lillifleur* had made their home near a large, forest-hemmed lake. The crowded central hub of the colony expanded outward to less densely populated sections, giving way eventually to farmland and grazing plots dotted with domesticated animals. We landed without incident in a cleared area perhaps a kilometre from the western perimeter of the settlement. It was midafternoon on this side of the planet, sunny and clear in this region. Four other vessels had been set down here, of a similar vintage as *Amber's Ranger*. They weren't runners, though; three were surface-to-orbit shuttles of the type that would have ferried passengers down from the colony ship. Their chunky lines and dated propulsion systems would have suggested that they'd belonged to the *Lillifleur* even without the somewhat unimaginative names stencilled on the sides; *Lilli-1*, *-2*, and *-3*. The fourth was larger, a launch capable of ferrying more substantial colony supplies down from orbit.

The shuttles all appeared well-cared-for and still in use, despite their age. The launch showed no signs of recent use, hemmed by clumps of tall grass, the lower reaches of the hull traced by tendrils of exploratory vines. The earth around the shuttles lay bare and well-packed, as if from the coming and going of many feet. I wondered why so much traffic apparently still flowed back and forth between the ship and the surface. Surely the vessel would have been stripped of everything salvageable decades before.

The landing area had been cleared from a wide swath of forest. One species of tree reminded me of the baobabs of Earth, their thick, pillared trunks mottled with streaks of cream and dark brown, crowned with masses of tiny green and pink leaves. These were the trees I'd caught a glimpse of in Amber Malka's holopic. Other vegetation included yellowish, tubular-trunked bushes dripping with long, spindly leaves, and squat bushes trimmed with fringes of fuchsia and blue. What we would have called wild grasses filled the spaces between larger plants in rippling waves of pale green, honey, and dove-grey seed stalks. It was enough like Earth or another Earth-like Nearspace planet to feel somewhat familiar while never letting you forget you were somewhere completely alien.

Nearby, a broad tract must have fallen victim to fire sometime in the recent past, because the trees gave way to low grasses and shrubs. Rei set the ship down here with a gentle bump and cut the thrusters, leaving us only a short distance from the nearest shuttle. The *Tane-Ikai* fell eerily quiet without the background heartbeat of the drives. Only the faint hiss and whoosh of the life support systems filled the silence.

"Hirin, Yuskeya, and Baden, you're with me. Viss, Maja, and Rei, look after things while we're gone and learn what you can about the planet. Rei, you have the big chair."

"EVA suits?" Baden asked, rising from the communications console. His voice betrayed a thrill of excitement at being included.

I shook my head. "I don't think so. I'm sure Captain Barath would have mentioned them if they were necessary."

"The planet has an atmosphere very similar to Earth's, with no known toxins or irritants present," Pika volunteered in her most know-it-all voice. I wasn't sure which of the crew she'd picked that up from. I was sure it wasn't me. "The oxygen level is slightly lower, but protective gear and breathing apparatus are not necessary. You may experience some mild shortness of breath, particularly under exertion."

"Thank you, Pika." I paused beside the bridge's airlock door to wait for the others. Yuskeya had ducked in to First Aid, no doubt to grab a field medical kit, and Baden was securing his datapad to his belt. "Keep a channel open to all of our comm implants while we're off the ship, would you?"

"Happy to eavesdrop," Pika said cheerfully, reverting to her other persona.

"Yes, I haven't forgotten that. Let's call this monitoring for health and safety reasons," I said. "I don't know when we'll be back, but I'll keep in touch."

"Stay safe," Rei said, seating herself in the big chair. "We'll want a full report when you get back."

"Mom." It was Karro.

I hesitated and turned. He and Aliande had both stood from their seats, their hands still clasped. Aliande peered with interest at the viewscreen showing the planet outside, but Karro looked uncertain.

"Be careful," he said.

I smiled. "Always."

He snorted but said nothing else. It sounded like something close to a laugh, and I hoped I was right about that.

And then we opened the airlock door and stepped out onto the planet Ryphen. I was acutely aware that, apart from the small clutch of *Lillifleur* colonists, we were probably the only other Nearspace citizens ever to have set foot here. No-one else in Nearspace even knew it existed.

I'd had many experiences of stepping onto the surface of new worlds in my long years of shuttling around Nearspace, but it was always a thrill. The air on Ryphen smelled fresh and clean, a noticeable change from the recycled air of the ship. It was scrubbed and well-filtered on the *Tane Ikai*; the ship didn't smell bad. But it could not compare to open air, and so that was the first thing that hit me.

A myriad of smells I couldn't identify scented the air—it was a little like any forest; that warm, pungent medley of life. There was something else, though . . . an ozone tang as if lightning had struck nearby, despite the clear sky and fair weather. The ground underfoot felt firm but pliable, like walking on a hard-packed beach. The soil here, where it showed through the undulating grass, was a pale dun colour. A hint of wind rustled the grasses and the leaves, breathing a whistling sigh around the end of one of the shuttles as we walked toward them.

I was startled when one of the shuttle doors opened and a woman stood framed in the doorway. For some reason, I'd thought all the other ships to be empty, but now I realized that was stupid. Captain Barath would have descended from the *Lillifleur* ahead of us. I paused.

"Captain Paixon?" The woman stepped down from the shuttle and walked toward the path. She wasn't tall, but she moved with an athletic grace. I suspected she wouldn't be winded under exertion, despite the lower oxygen levels; not if she'd grown up here or lived here for a century. She wore a dark blue, one-piece shipsuit with *NCV Lillifleur* embroidered on the left side. Four small red planet badges studded the collar, marking her as a Nearspace Authority-certified Captain—civilian, not Protectorate, but well-trained. But this badge style had been updated decades ago.

With a mental start, I realized that I recognized this woman. Her deep pink hair, touched with hints of dark red, was longer now, and pulled back and secured into a long plait. Worry shadowed her blue eyes, but her smile touched them and they seemed friendly. And I'd seen that smile before.

She was the woman from Amber Malka's holopic. I tried not to let my surprise show as she joined us on the path.

"Welcome to Ryphen."

I stepped toward her and offered my hand. "Captain Barath?"

She shook her head and smiled as she accepted my hand in a warm, firm grip. With her other hand she pointed to her badges dismissively. "Don't mind these. On the planet, I'm just Juliska, if you don't mind. I shed my captain's persona as soon as I turn the ship over to someone else and leave it." She pronounced her name *Yull-iss-ka*.

"Then please, call me Luta." I introduced the others by their first names, and identified their positions aboard the *Tane Ikai*. Yuskeya and I had, after a brief discussion on the way down to the planet, decided to leave her Protectorate rank out of the equation for now. If it became relevant or necessary, we'd reveal it.

"Shall we walk to the colony?" she asked, gesturing to the path ahead of us. As we set off, she said in a voice that quavered slightly, "I know you already gave me the short version, but what more can you tell me about what happened to Amber Malka?"

"There's not a whole lot more to tell, honestly. We found her ship adrift when we answered the distress call the ship was transmitting," I told her. "She was unconscious inside. We didn't know what went wrong with the ship—we still don't. She'd suffered some injury or illness we weren't able to entirely identify, although it could have been linked to a virus-type organism. Yuskeya's our medic—she took wonderful care of Captain Malka, until we got her to Xaqual."

"We left her in the care of a very fine doctor, there," Yuskeya added. "But as Luta said, she was very ill by that point. She was alive and en route to the hospital when we left her, but . . . beyond that, we don't know. We came through the wormhole shortly after that." Her agonized voice trailed off; like me, she was torn between stating the seriousness of Amber Malka's state and offering false hope.

Juliska walked with her eyes on the path ahead of us, looking grave. She pressed her lips together and blinked a few times as if tears threatened, then said, "Thank you for taking such good care of her. I'm going to hope that your doctor will be able to help her, although—" she broke off and then shook her head and continued, "She took a great risk in leaving here. But she did understand that risk. She took it for the good of us all."

"We'd like to understand what happened to her," I said carefully. "She did regain consciousness long enough to say a couple of words, although we weren't sure what they meant." I glanced around as we wound our way into a path that cut through the forest, separating the settlement from the landing area. "They make even less sense to me now, although we did figure out that she was saying 'Lillifleur.' It sounded like a call for help, but you don't seem to need that here."

Juliska barked a short, rueful laugh. "If only that were true. Appearances can be deceiving."

"I'm assuming it's about the drones?"

"Yes. But I should wait until the colony Council is together so we can tell you our story properly."

"All right." I looked around at the dense, verdant forest and wondered what sort of threat the colonists faced in this idyllic setting.

"Where is Captain Malka's ship now?" Juliska asked "It's almost an historical artifact for the colony, in a strange way. I think she'd want it returned here, if that were possible."

"We have it safely in our cargo hold, as a matter of fact," I assured her. "With luck, she'll be piloting it back here herself."

Juliska Barath merely nodded, with a strangely sad half-smile. We walked in silence after that, until the path opened out of the forest and I caught my first real glimpse of Lillifleur colony.

As we'd seen from above, the settlers had established the colony on the shore of a large lake, and we emerged from the forest path to view it from an elevated vantage point. The water, spangled by the yellow-tinged light, sparkled invitingly, dark-green and placid. Along the shoreline, small docks stretched narrow fingers out into the lake, dotted along their lengths with moored watercraft. A few of these plied the water, propelled by motors or brightly coloured sails.

From here, the layout of the settlement showed the organized, grid-like design of the central HAB modules the colonists would have brought down from the *Lillifleur*. They clustered in small groups near a long, domed building, its glass windows throwing sharp white reflective bursts as we walked. Inside, varied shades of lush green, yellow, and purple foliage showed the greenhouse to be bursting with life.

The layout of buildings and pathways—there were no vehicles evident—became more haphazard and meandering beyond the initial core, as colonists had spread outward in favour of more open, aesthetically pleasing, or practical sites.

"I believe Officer Nakano mentioned a population of over five thousand?" I asked Juliska. "I read the data on the initial complement of the *Lillifleur*—over a thousand colonists and thirty-five crew?"

Juliska half-smiled, her expression wry and touched with sadness. "The crew never intended to be part of the colony," she said. "But when they realized there was no returning to Nearspace, they made the best of it and settled down. Our current population stands at five thousand and twenty-nine citizens." Her face fell. "Or possibly, five thousand and twenty-eight," she added.

"That's a steady two percent growth rate," Yuskeya observed. "Very strong, especially considering that you haven't had the boost of immigration from other planets or colonies to help you along."

Captain Barath nodded but didn't comment.

The well-worn trail transitioned into a series of steps set into the incline of the hill. Initially, I thought the steps were fashioned from slabs of stone, but looking closer I thought I could make out striations like tree rings on the flat surfaces.

"They're similar to petrified wood on Earth," Juliska explained, seeing me studying the steps. "But it's a simpler process and doesn't take as long. These trees—we call them stone trees, not very original, I know—are cut down and sliced, and left out in the light for a month or so. The fluids inside evaporate, leaving an almost mineralized matter. They wear better than stone. But you do have to make sure you cut them to the size and shape you want before you start the evaporation process. You'd need a high-intensity laser to cut or shape them after they're hardened."

The steps took us all the way down to the base of the hill, putting us in one back corner of the settlement, on the opposite side from the lake. Here the buildings bore little resemblance to the HAB units that established the central core of the colony. Many of them utilized the same hardened stone tree material as the steps, with varying sizes and shapes of slabs fitted together like a mosaic and joined by thick lines of grout. Some walls were constructed of a rough but unusual-looking brick. I asked the captain about it.

"We call them mushroom bricks," she told me, smiling. "Once we—I mean, the original colonists—knew there'd be no traders coming with loads of cargo from Nearspace, they had to figure out how to use what Ryphen had to offer. That's when we discovered how to work with the stone trees, and also this native fungus that turns almost rock-like when it's compressed and dried." She shrugged. "You work with what you have."

Both the tree slabs and the bricks displayed a wide range of colours, which Juliska said emerged through the drying process and sometimes continued even after the material had been used in construction. This made the houses and buildings a mix of browns, yellows, and greens, sometimes blending to grey, black, or even purple or blue. Some houses incorporated old HAB units as a base but expanded into additional rooms or sections made from the tree and brick materials. It made for colourful construction, and although the colours were haphazard, the effect was pleasing.

"It's a very pretty town," Baden commented, and Juliska's smile deepened.

"We didn't have much choice," she said modestly, "but I think most of us would agree."

Not surprisingly, all the inhabitants we saw were humans. In the time period when the *Lillifleur* left Nearspace, the Vilisians and Lobors had been encountered, but were still testing the waters of integrating with humans—none of the species would have been interested in joint colonization ventures. Too many extra complications to provide for the needs of more than one species. Although in most cases, once a colony was established, immigrants from the other corners of Nearspace would gradually visit the new settlement to see if they would fit in with the climate and geography. The settlement on Ryphen hadn't had that opportunity.

The people of Lillifleur studied us with unabashed interest as we walked the hard-packed streets. No doubt word of our arrival had swept through the colony, but although many watched us wide-eyed, no-one approached as we walked with Juliska. Perhaps she commanded high respect as a member of the colony Council, or perhaps the unusual fact of strangers made them reticent. No doubt the absence of any outside contact for so long would have an effect on a population. We were probably lucky we hadn't been met with fear and hostility. They could have been humans on any planet in Nearspace, although I had the feeling of something slightly odd that I couldn't identify. Perhaps it was simply the knowledge that this pocket of humanity had been cut off from the rest of us for so long. In a way, they were living in a pocket of time almost a century out of date.

At any rate, the people of the *Lillifleur* seemed to have had done what good colonists on any planet are supposed to do: survive, adapt, and thrive. The settlement held a typical air of busy-ness as the inhabitants went about chores and errands. The other thing that set them apart, however, was painfully obvious; many individuals seemed afflicted by muscle problems that manifested in limps, painful gaits, or arms in slings. Some walked gingerly, as if afraid their balance or strength might betray them at any moment. A few carried their heads at an awkward, unnatural angle or showed facial tics or strangely taut muscles. It might not be apparent exactly what had gone wrong or if it really was something caused by the drone's scan, but it had been enough to make Amber Malka implore me to "save Lillifleur."

The question must have showed on my face, because eventually Juliska said, "You can ask, Captain. Yes, you're seeing one of the reasons Amber went off looking for help."

Yuskeya and I shared a glance. "Is it—a disease? Something released from the drone, perhaps? Officer Nakano mentioned something about that." Surely the captain wouldn't have invited us so blithely into the middle of a plague outbreak.

"The doctors say no," she reassured me. "We do think it's the result of the scan. It was a singular event that affected some people more than others, but all the afflictions started immediately afterward. And we haven't been able to identify anything physical the drone could have introduced. The Council will tell you the full details and why we continue to worry. But I'm certain you and your crew are in no danger."

I had to be content with that, although privately I thought a little warning would have been nice.

We arrived eventually at the heart of the settlement, in what Juliska called Base Core—the central concentration of original HAB units and domes the colonists had set up when they founded the colony. A larger building comprised of several two-storey HAB units that had been welded together and modified stood a couple of streets back from the lake edge, and it was to this one that Juliska led us. A sign above the doorway proclaimed it to be the Lillifleur Council Hall.

"So you named the colony after the ship?" I asked, as Juliska opened the door and led us inside.

"We did. I mean, the original colonists did," she corrected herself with a smile. "They'd never made a final decision about what to call the new colony they'd been planning in Eta Cass, and once they realized they were going to have to put down roots here, the ship became their only lifeline. What they didn't have on her, they were probably never going to have. I think it only seemed right to name the settlement after her."

The door opened into a small lobby or reception area. A bright-eyed woman with a worry crease bisecting her brow looked up at their arrival and offered Juliska the ghost of a smile. Her face seemed stiff on the left side, and I wondered if here was another victim of the strange debilitating effects we'd observed already.

"Hi, Karin, are the others here already?" Juliska asked her.

Karin nodded assent. Her blonde hair was short, trimmed in a sleek, almost military cut, and she wore a shirt with a small PrimeCorp embroidered logo patch on the left side. The stylized red and black "P" and "C" bracketing an atom was unmistakable. Even now I couldn't see that logo without feeling hollow in the pit of my stomach, and I concentrated to make sure my distaste didn't show on my face.

I wondered if her shirt was as old as the colony and carefully maintained, or if they'd used the ship's resources to manufacture new ones as the years wore on. Either way, it signalled a strong loyalty to the corporation that had initially financed the expedition. I caught Yuskeya's eye and she raised an eyebrow at me. I shrugged minutely. Cut off as they were from Nearspace, the colonists would know nothing about the recent downfall of PrimeCorp, and even less about the corporation's unscrupulous past. I supposed, because of PrimeCorp's long-ago sponsorship, the colonists might still feel they existed as a PrimeCorp colony and might, even against the odds, someday have a chance to report back to their benefactors. I wondered how they'd feel when we told them they were now free from any corporate restraints or obligations, and their sponsor lay in a ruin of its own making.

"Captain Paixon, let me introduce Colony Communications Officer Karin Nakano. Karin, this is Captain Paixon. I know you two met over the comm earlier, but we might as well make it official."

I shook Nakano's hand, and while Juliska Barath introduced the others, I blinked my left eye quickly twice to activate my implant. Trying to keep it unobtrusive, I called up the original crew roster for the *Lillifleur*. Sure enough, there was a Karin Nakano listed as a communications officer. I blinked the data away before it got distracting or someone noticed my face making weird contortions. Juliska made a move towards a door leading further into the building.

"It's only Andre who isn't here yet, but he's commed to let me know he's on his way," Karin amended. "He was out checking the new irrigation system in one of the auxiliary greenhouses when I called to let him know you were planetside. Should be along any minute, though." After a pause, she said, "I'm sorry about Amber."

Juliska swallowed and nodded. "Thanks, Karin. According to the captain here, she was receiving good care. So I'm trying to focus on that." She turned to us briskly. "Let's go in, then. The Council will be able to answer all your questions."

We followed her into a large room formed from four HAB units. Long rectangles of double-paned glass, the original HAB windows, offered a view out three sides of the room and let in lots of the planet's warm, orangey sunlight. A large metal table—which almost certainly had started life in the colony ship's galley—sat in the centre of the conference room, surrounded by chairs that also had the utilitarian look of having come down from the ship. Seven people had already taken seats and turned to face us as we entered.

A tall man of about forty, with skin the warm colour of freshly-turned earth and dark hair that curled over his ears, rose and came to meet us, first embracing Juliska. "Welcome back planetside, Juliska," he said in a deep voice. "I'm so sorry about Amber. She knew the risk she was taking for all of us."

Juliska nodded silently, returning his embrace, then pushed herself away. It struck me that everyone we encountered took it for granted that Amber Malka wasn't going to pull through. I wanted to speak up and defend Dr. Ndasa, tell them how hard he would work to cure her, but I stopped myself. For all I knew, she might already have died.

"And these are our guests?" The man turned and held out a hand to me, palm up in the Martian way. He had a wide smile that welcomed us while not entirely camouflaging some underlying worry. "I'm Tejas Haldar, one of the Settlement Council. Welcome to Ryphen, and to Lillifleur."

I laid my own hand, palm down, on his. "Luta Paixon, one of the captains of the far trader *Tane Ikai*."

I introduced Hirin, Yuskeya, and Baden—leaving out Yuskeya's connection to the Protectorate for now. Considering PrimeCorp's long and prickly history with the Nearspace Authority, it seemed wise. Karin Nakano's PrimeCorp logo hinted that some colonists, at least, still held loyalty to the corporation. So best to keep our connections, and PrimeCorp's multitude of sins and recent demise, quiet for now. While they exchanged greetings, I called up the list of names on my implant again. No-one named Tejas Haldar had been *Lillifleur* crew, nor one of the colonists. So I couldn't prove our theory yet. However, the number of people living here now outnumbered the original ship's complement by five to one, so obviously even if the entire original crew was still alive, not everyone we ran into was going to be one of them.

Of the six remaining Council members seated at the table, two more turned out to match names on the database list. Okwi Rousseault had dark eyes, light brown skin with warm olive undertones, and a dignified bearing that reminded me of Yuskeya; like Yuskeya, she also had long, dark hair but wore hers twined in an intricate double braid. She—or the colonist she was named for—had been listed as a xenobiologist on the *Lillifleur*'s passenger roster. Okwi showed no signs of the strange affliction I was anxious to learn more about. Norris Ellsworth was a short, roundish man with a bald head balanced by a full greying beard. The original Norris had been employed on the colony ship as a skip drive technician. Rousseault looked to be around forty years old; Ellsworth perhaps nearer fifty. Ellsworth's left hand was splinted and bandaged, but it wasn't clear whether it was related to the mysterious ailment or if he'd simply had an accident.

The others ranged in age from a blonde woman who looked thirtyish to a man who could be in his late fifties. Their names didn't match anyone on the original crew or colonist roster, and I was glad to be able to stop using my implant for a while. Trying to focus my eyes separately was giving me a headache. Only one of the others, a woman named Sondra Parekh, faltered when she stood to offer us a standard Earth handshake, as if one of her legs had suddenly not been able to bear weight. She caught herself with a hand on the table and finished shaking my hand before she sat down again.

The missing Andre arrived as introductions finished. A big man with broad shoulders and a light brown buzz cut, he wore working clothes with mud spatters adorning the legs of this pants. With bright blue eyes and a robust, tanned complexion, he appeared the picture of good health. "Am I late?" he boomed as he entered the room.

"Not really," Juliska assured him. "We just finished exchanging names."

Instead of offering us the Martian greeting, Andre also stuck out a hand for a traditional Earth handshake. "Andre Dufour," he said, "agricultural specialist. Now tell me, Captain Paixon—how are you going to help us save this colony?"

I TOOK DUFOUR'S outstretched hand and shook it the way my father had taught me long ago—firm and brisk, neither too briefly nor awkwardly long; ideally, a gesture that signified a meeting of equals.

"I'll be able to answer that question better once I know what the problem is," I told him with a smile. "Or problems, as the case may be. There's an awful lot we don't understand here. So you'll understand why I'm not making any promises at the moment."

"Fair enough," he said, and shook hands with Yuskeya, Hirin, and Baden in turn. Then he rounded the table to take a seat at the end, while Juliska gestured us to empty chairs opposite. She placed glasses of water and a dented metal pitcher beaded with condensation in front of us. I half expected Juliska to tell us the tale of the *Lillifleur*, but it was Dufour who began to speak.

Dufour put his big hands on the table in front of him and clasped them, interlacing his fingers. "Captain Paixon, would you tell us first, where you've come from? It's a very long time since we've seen anyone but ourselves."

"We came through a wormhole from the Eta Cassiopeia system," I told him. "No-one in Nearspace knows it's there, as far as I know, because it doesn't present readings as a wormhole usually does. It's not listed in the Nearspace database or system navigation charts."

Juliska Barath nodded. "That's how the *Lillifleur* stumbled into it, as well. We—they—were en route to the planet designated Eta Cassiopeia-a—it didn't have a name at that time—but tasked to map some of the system as they went as well. They were in the gravity well of the wormhole before they knew what was happening, and had to engage the skip drive to avoid being crushed. Or so the story goes," she added with a smile.

"Sounds familiar," Baden said.

"But then . . . they couldn't get back," Dufour said. "The skip drive was damaged when the ship exited the wormhole—it wouldn't shut down. The exotic matter inverted when it had no wormhole to interact with—or something like that." Dufour nodded to Juliska. "So the story goes, although some of the details are probably lost to time. The captain here might be able to explain it better than I ever could, but I'm not sure those details matter now anyway. The long and the short of it was that the *Lillifleur* was stuck. Luckily, Ryphen was close, and habitable, and since the idea was to find a new home anyway . . ." He leaned back in his chair and spread his hands wide, as if to encompass the entire settlement. "We've made the best of it."

"You've made an impressive home here," I said, "especially with no outside support. On Xaqual—that's what Eta Cass-a was eventually named—you would still have had regular interaction with the rest of Nearspace. Here, you've been on your own. At least, I assume so."

Okwi Rousseault nodded, and her smile held a hint of wistfulness. "We've been alone. But we've had both good fortune and favourable circumstances, overall," she said in a soft voice. "Now both of those seem to be running out."

There was so much I wanted to know about the original colonists and the nanobioscavs and Amber Malka and the rest of it, but I sensed the history lesson would have to wait. "So what is happening now?" I asked. "What threat is facing the colony?"

Juliska sighed. "You met them on your way here."

"The drones?"

"The drones, yes . . . but more specifically, whoever is sending them and what they want."

"I understand they're a new phenomenon," Yuskeya said. "How long have they been troubling you?"

Norris Ellsworth snorted, then answered. "A couple of

months," he said. "They're our first encounter with anything or anyone since we landed here. You might know it would turn out to be bad."

"And the first one acted aggressively?" Yuskeya asked. "The ones we encountered seemed passive, easily discouraged from coming too close to the planet."

Norris Ellsworth shrugged and ran a hand over his bald head. "We honestly don't know if it meant harm. But harm was the outcome of whatever it did—we're still suffering the effects, as you can see." He held up his bandaged hand as evidence. "And they keep coming."

"And you think their scan is what caused this sickness among your population?" I asked. I remembered with a sudden clench in my gut that the drones had begun a thorough scan on us, too, before Hirin got the shields up.

Juliska nodded. "We still try every time to communicate with them. There's never any response. But now we can't risk letting them scan us again. Our medical personnel have had little luck treating the effects of the first one—there are symptoms, but no cause our doctors have been able to discover. No real clues as to what it even did. What if the results are even worse the next time?"

"Do you have any guesses about what they want, or what they're trying to do?"

Dufour spread his hands. "We think they're primarily scout drones, information gatherers. We've scanned them as well as we can from the *Lillifleur* as they've approached. They're equipped with what we think are sensors, recorders, memory devices; what you'd expect for scouts. We don't recognize the substance they're made of. We don't know about weaponry. Our main worry is that they're looking for planets for someone else to colonize." He raised his chin, and his voice took on a note of defiance. "And this one—at least this little corner of it—is already taken."

"Have you ever tried to capture one, so you could study it more closely?"

Juliska shrugged. "We don't have the means to do that. The *Lillifleur* has no mechanism to simply disable one without destroying it. I suppose it's possible we could catch a drifting one with an EVA team from one of the shuttles, but . . . it's never even been an option. And it would be a considerable challenge. I don't know if we could ask anyone to do it."

"We might manage that, with the remote arms," Baden mused. "If we could disable its propulsion and then get close enough to one—"

"Let's not get sidetracked," I reminded him gently. "I think we need to concentrate on getting bigger guns here to help."

"So you don't know who could be sending them? Where they come from?" Hirin asked.

"No, we don't. As Juliska said, there's never been any attempt at communication. On their part, anyway. Not from lack of trying on our side."

"Except . . . we're inferring something alarming from the pattern of their appearances," Juliska said. "The intervals are getting shorter."

Yuskeya said, "So you think whoever is sending them is ramping things up? Sending them out more frequently?"

I exchanged a look with Hirin. "Either that, or they're travelling increasingly shorter distances to get here. Which would mean whatever or whoever is sending them—"

"Is getting closer," Juliska said.

CHAPTER NINE
Help Wanted

"Sounds like what you need is a protection fleet," Hirin said. "Not a single far-trader."

Juliska and Dufour exchanged a wordless communication across the scarred breadth of the table that separated them. "We'd hoped that Amber—Captain Malka—might return with something like that," Juliska said carefully.

I nodded. "So we're quite a disappointment, then."

She flushed, colour almost as pink as her hair washing her cheeks. "No, I didn't mean—"

I held up a hand. "It's all right. We're a far cry from what you were hoping for. But with the information we have now, we can go back through the wormhole and get word to the Protectorate." I looked at Yuskeya, who nodded gravely. "They're spread thin around Nearspace these days, but they won't leave a Nearspace colony in danger of being attacked."

"They may not be able to send an entire defence squadron," Yuskeya said carefully, "but we can discuss options. Maybe even evacuation until we can figure out the true nature of the threat . . ."

She trailed off, because the faces around the table had changed, and an almost palpable anxiety thrummed in the room.

"It wouldn't have to be permanent—" I started, but Juliska cut me off.

"There's a significant problem with that scenario," she said, "not to sound at all ungrateful. It's not possible for us to leave Ryphen," she said. "The idea of an evacuation simply won't work."

"I know there are a lot of you now—"

"No." She shook her head vehemently. "That's not the issue." She stood and walked over to look out one of the long, rectangular windows. "We're physically unable to exist off the planet for more than a few days. You saw it yourself, first-hand. That's what was wrong with Amber."

Yuskeya frowned. "You're saying Captain Malka got sick because she was away from this planet for too long? But that doesn't make any sense."

Okwi Rousseault turned a palm up. "And yet it is the truth. Trust us, we know what we're talking about. We still keep a skeleton crew on the *Lillifleur*, as you saw, because there are systems and resources there that have kept the colony going all these years in the absence of support from the rest of Nearspace. We still produce enzymes there that let us consume certain native plants, for example. We can manufacture things shipboard that would take a lot of resources to create planetside. The *Lillifleur* is, in many ways, still our lifeline. But if any of us stay aboard the ship for more than four days, we sicken quickly . . . much more than a week off the planet, and we would certainly die. We originally called it 'withdrawal,' but then Dr. Lee started calling it 'earthbound syndrome,' and 'withdrawal' simply became the description of the symptoms. We learned about this the hard way, and it has proven over the years to be true without exception."

"So Amber Malka knew her trip to Nearspace would likely be one-way," I said slowly, considering this information. "That's why she had so little food or supplies on board."

Juliska nodded tightly. "She knew she would not need them. She volunteered to go, to make a one-shot chance at finding someone to help us. She just had to find them quickly."

"And that's why you're all assuming she's dead."

"We don't know what it is—something in the soil, something in the air, a virus or bacteria—but something on Ryphen becomes part of everyone who lives here, and once that happens, it does not let us go." Dufour's voice was matter-of-fact, although he threw an apologetic look at Juliska Barath. "I'm surprised she lasted as long as she did, to tell you the truth. I find it hard to believe anyone from the rest of Nearspace, even your skilled doctor friend, would be able to save her when they don't know any of this."

I wanted to tell them that Dr. Ndasa's understanding of nanobioscavengers could play in Amber's favour, but bioscavs hadn't even been mentioned yet. And that thought was overshadowed by a pang of fear, followed quickly by a hot rush of anger. Had they put us in danger, bringing us so casually down to the planet? We could easily have done all our communicating safely from orbit. The nanobioscavengers might protect some of us, but what if—I forced my voice calm as I asked, "Is my crew in danger of contracting whatever it is? We can't be much help to you if we can't leave here, either."

Okwi Rousseault shook her head. "While we don't understand the actual vector or mechanism, it takes some period of continued exposure to become earthbound—as we call it. Our own experience, and later monitoring of infants and children, show that they are able to remain aboard the *Lillifleur* safely for months at a time, until they reach the age of five or six."

"Too young to send on an expedition through the wormhole on their own, unfortunately," Norris Ellsworth said with a rueful smile.

I blew out a sigh of relief. So we should be all right to stay for a brief visit. Still, when I got back to the *Tane Ikai,* I'd tell Karro and Aliande not to leave the ship. Bad enough that I already had Yuskeya here without the protection of Mother's nanobioscavs; I wouldn't take any risks with them. I wasn't so worried for myself, Hirin, Maja, or Baden. I had yet to encounter anything my mother's creations couldn't handle, given enough time.

"All right," Hirin said, in his "summing-up" voice I knew so well. He liked to distil complex problems down to their most essential points, and he'd steepled his fingers in his characteristic pose, tapping them lightly against his lips. "So you can't leave, but you think you need protection from some unknown force or species that's presumably on its way here. Possibly looking to colonize the planet for itself—although there's nothing to point to that yet. The drones appearing more frequently could mean they're being launched from a larger vessel, possibly a colony ship, on a slower approach into the system. You have no defence ships other than the *Lillifleur* herself, I take it?"

"Correct," Dufour said. "The shuttles are equipped with lasers, but that's minimal help against a larger vessel. Especially if it's one that means us harm."

"So you need us to run back through to Nearspace and summon help." Hirin leaned back in his chair. "As soon as our engineer gives our ship the all-clear, we should be able to do just that."

Juliska Barath smiled a more genuine smile than I'd seen on her face so far. It was filled with a relief that brought the shine of tears to her eyes. "You see," she said in a warm voice. "You are not a disappointment at all."

A knock sounded at the door of the conference room then, and Dufour called, "Come in," in his booming voice. The door opened and Karin stood there, looking bemused. "We have more visitors," she said, "looking for our other visitors."

She stepped aside and my heart sank as I saw Karro and Aliande standing behind her, gazing around the building with all the innocent interest of tourists who don't know they've landed in the middle of a war zone.

I KNOW I stared, probably with my mouth hanging open. I'd just decided that it wouldn't be safe to let them out on the surface of the planet, and here they were, having apparently walked the same distance I had and been exposed to who-knew-what. We had a groundcar on the *Tane Ikai*, but it wouldn't have been able to navigate those hillside stairs we'd climbed down.

I wracked my brain—hadn't I told Rei to keep them aboard? Keep them safe? No. I hadn't said a damn thing because I'd stupidly expected them to stay put. I had no-one to blame but myself.

"Excuse me." I scraped my chair back from the table and stood, then hurried over to the door. Karin Nakano moved to allow me to sidle past. Karro and Aliande retreated into the small lobby, looking suddenly uncertain. "What's going on?" I asked, trying to keep the anger and panic out of my voice. "What are you doing here?"

I must not have done a very good job, because Karro stiffened. "We thought, since we were here, we'd make the best of it and have a look around," he said. "No-one said there'd be a problem with that."

I took a deep breath. "There's no problem," I lied. "I'm surprised to see you, and surprised that Rei didn't tell me you were coming."

Karro and Aliande exchanged a sheepish glance. "We didn't tell Rei. Or anyone. We just walked the way you'd gone, and then asked a few people here where we might find you."

Aliande said, "This place is fantastic! I so want to paint it. Do you think the people here would have any objection?"

Karin Nakano had returned to her desk and was pretending, badly, that she wasn't listening to our conversation. In her defence, the room was small.

"*Okej*," I said, trying to keep my voice light and not grit my teeth, "we're in an unknown settlement, on an unknown planet, in an unknown system. Not a great idea to go wandering around without someone knowing where you are." Karro seemed about to protest, but I kept talking. "But since you're here now, would you like to join us in the conference room? I think we're about finished anyway, and then we'll all head back to the ship together. Aliande, you can ask the Council about doing some art."

I wasn't sure Karro was going to agree, but Aliande said, "Of course, Luta. We'll be guided by you." She slipped her arm through Karro's, no doubt so she could give it a warning squeeze if he wanted to argue the issue further.

With Karro and Aliande trailing me, I returned to the conference room and introduced them to everyone. Karro said some nice things about the settlement and everyone was kind and welcoming, if a bit surprised at their arrival. No one seemed to object to Aliande's artistic interest in the settlement.

I was about to suggest that we adjourn the meeting if there was nothing further, when Yuskeya said, "Captain, may I make a suggestion? More of a request, perhaps."

"Go ahead." I never had to worry that Yuskeya would do anything out of line.

She addressed Dufour and Juliska. "I'm a medic—not a doctor, but with a fair amount of training and experience. I'd be happy to investigate the mystery of your connection to the planet, while we're here, if there's anything I can add. Our ship has extensive medical equipment, and certainly medical technology has advanced since the time you left Nearspace."

Strangely, it was Okwi Rousseault who answered. "That's very kind of you, Ms. Blue. You might want to speak with one of our doctors. He's spent a lot of time on the problem of why we've become earthbound."

Norris Ellsworth snorted. "If you can get him to speak to you," he said. "Hawick Lee isn't exactly the friendliest man in Lillifleur."

"Oh, he's not so bad," Okwi protested. "He's become a little—preoccupied with the question, that's all. He doesn't see a lot of patients these days, but he's trained up some fine young medical personnel. We have a strong health care system here."

Yuskeya's idea was a good one, though. It might offer us some insights into Amber Malka's death if we could get samples from other colonists to use as a baseline. "If someone would point us in the right direction or provide an introduction, perhaps Yuskeya and I could visit the doctor before we rejoin the others on our ship."

"I'll take you to him," Okwi offered.

"She's one of the few people he won't bark at," Norris Ellsworth said with a chuckle. "So you might want to take her up on the offer."

"Well, if we're done here for now, I'll take the others and head back to the *Tane Ikai*," Hirin said, standing. "I want to get an estimate from our engineer about when we can make the run back through the wormhole," he said. "Should we report back to you, or to the ship?"

"For most things, you can contact our central communications here," Dufour said. "For anything that seems more important to the *Lillifleur*, you can comm them directly."

"Then I'll tell you our plan as soon as we have one," Hirin said.

There was friendly leave-taking all around, and Juliska offered to walk the others back to the ship. Hirin assured her that it wasn't necessary, but she said she'd take them back via a slightly different route to show them a few more points of interest around the settlement, and Karro and Aliande seemed eager to take her up on the offer. I shot Hirin a look that I'm sure he correctly interpreted as *keep your eye on those two!* He winked at me in reply.

Yuskeya and I soon found ourselves walking with Okwi Rousseault toward the shoreline side of the colony. The breeze off the water carried a scent I couldn't identify . . . not fish or water weeds, but a lemony, clean aroma. It made me wonder what sorts of creatures, if any, inhabited the lake.

"You mentioned needing extra enzymes to make some native food edible—did you find flora or fauna on the planet that are compatible for humans without help?" I asked. Some of the Nearspace planets had native flora and fauna human digestive systems could tolerate, and some did not.

Okwi Rousseault nodded. "There are a few varieties, although some require special preparation. We've been very fortunate in getting enough Earth plants to grow here to feed our animals."

"Any big predators?" Yuskeya asked. "I noticed the colony isn't fenced or fortified against anything."

Our guide shook her head, but her face became more animated as she spoke. "Not really. The largest carnivorous animal we've encountered is similar to a prehistoric Earth creature—cat-like, but actually a marsupial, not a placental mammal. They prey on smaller rodent and lagomorph analogues—sorry," she broke off with a smile. "This is my area of expertise, so it's easy for me to get carried away. They prey on smaller animals similar to rabbits and large rats, and they were certainly curious about us—I mean, about the original colonists—at first. However, there's no record of any attacks on humans, and they generally don't come too close to Lillifleur. We've compiled a comprehensive database of the native flora and fauna, which I can upload to you if you're interested."

"That would be fascinating, thank you," Yuskeya said.

I was surprised when my ID implant vibrated slightly and the display for my Retin-X implant sprang up. It displayed: *Incoming msg from Pika.*

Well, that was new. I blinked to take the message and it appeared on my screen. *Captain, sorry to interrupt, but I thought you should know. The tracking beacon just sent back telemetry—the drones seem to have doubled back and entered the atmosphere of the planet on the side opposite the colony. But I'm about to lose the beacon in the sensor shadow.*

I felt my stomach sink faster than the drones coming through the atmosphere. I'd resisted Karin Nakano's request that we destroy them, and then forgotten about them when they passed by, accepting their apparent disinterest in the colony. I'd allowed myself to be distracted by the discussions with the colonists, assuming we were done with the drones. Now my brain buzzed with questions. Why would they return? Were they planning to land on the planet? Could they have simply malfunctioned in some way? Or was there a more sinister explanation?

I'd stopped walking, and now I realized that Okwi Rousseault and Yuskeya stood staring at me. "I have a message from the ship, please excuse me," I explained. Then I walked off the path a little way, separating myself from them and standing under the canopy of one of the pink-and-green leaved trees. With a nod, Okwi motioned to Yuskeya to continue. Yuskeya flashed me an inquiring frown but I shook my head at her.

When they were out of earshot, I answered Pika through my implant in a low voice. "Pika, track them as far as you can and extrapolate where they might touch down on the planet if that's the intention."

"Already on it, Captain," she said. "If we were in orbit—"

"I know, but we're not, and we can't leave the planet without explaining. Keep this between us until we figure out what it means."

"It's our little secret," the AI told me. "I haven't mentioned it to anyone else." She sounded a little too excited about that.

"I just need to tell them at the right time." I wondered as I spoke why I felt the need to justify myself to an AI. I knew the answer, though—I was justifying it to myself. I didn't want to tell the colonists I'd let the drones escape. Now I wondered about the earlier one that Nakano had said bypassed the planet, too, after scanning the colony. Had it continued on its way deeper into the system after conducting its scan, or had it also landed on the far side of the world for some unknown purpose?

"One more thing, Captain," Pika continued. "I sent you this, but you may not have had a chance to look over the data."

No, since I've been in a meeting with the Council the whole time, I thought, but I didn't bother pointing that out to the AI. She'd probably only take the opportunity to chide me about my sub-par multitasking skills.

"In the old PrimeCorp files, I found two mentions of explorers in other systems encountering drones that sound very much like these," she said briskly. "In each case, the drone did not make any attempt to communicate with the explorer ship, simply scanned it and continued on its way. Neither explorer ship attempted to engage the drone because it was not part of their mission plan, and there was no obvious threat."

"But the descriptions are the same?"

"Extremely similar," Pika confirmed.

After a pause, I said, "So someone is sending out drones, but why? And why have we never encountered them in Nearspace? At least, I've never heard of anything like them."

I leaned against the mottled trunk of the tree. A tang like cinnamon filled the air and its leaves whispered secrets above my head. "None of the explorer crews took sick after the scan, I suppose?"

"Nothing like that was in the reports. Naturally, those crews would have the ship's shielding to protect them."

"True." I frowned. "Who's sending these things out?"

It was a rhetorical question, but Pika said, "It seems likely that there is another alien species, whom we have not yet encountered. It's possible one of the others have—the Corvids seem the most probable candidates, although it's strange that they have not mentioned anyone else in the year we've been conversing with them."

"But what do they want?"

Pika made a noise like a snort of laughter. If I didn't know better, I'd have thought I was talking to Jahelia Sord. "They're exploring. Maybe looking for a new place to settle or colonize. Or maybe simply seeing what's out here."

"And what's out here—at least in this case—is Ryphen and its one little colony. And now, us."

Before Pika could say anything else, Yuskeya threw a concerned glance over her shoulder at me, and I knew I was done with it for now. "I'm signing off. We'll be back to the ship in a bit," I told Pika, and hurried to catch up to Yuskeya and Okwi. I turned my attention to their conversation, forcing the news about the drones—and my guilt—out of my mind, at least for now.

Yuskeya and Okwi were engaged in conversation about the colony, and I tried to catch up. I did pay close attention as Okwi pointed out places of interest . . . a school, a medical building, and the sparkling glass dome of the nearest greenhouse as we approached it. The school was a delightful building, not utilizing any of the blocky original HAB modules, its stone tree slab walls instead echoing the lines and terrain of the local geography. Its walls were not square or sharp, but moulded, curved, and organic, like the materials that made them.

The greenhouse, part of the original colony building plan, blended in with its surroundings as well, due to the riot of plants and colours visible through its semi-transparent walls and domed roof. These greenhouses peppered the colony at regular intervals, and I asked about the widely varied plants inside. Okwi explained that they were a mix of the native plants that had proven edible for the colonists, and the cultivars they'd brought themselves. Farmland dedicated to the hardier crops, those that had adapted well to the climate and soil of Ryphen, ringed the perimeter of the settlement, while the more delicate plants grew in the greenhouse shelters. These also offered the colonists easy access to daily fresh food.

Past the greenhouse we turned right, following the well-worn path. Everywhere the colonists watched us, neither wary nor effusive, but reserved. As if our offer of help was too good to be true, and they didn't want to get overly excited or hopeful about it.

The houses thinned out quickly in this direction, dotting the lakeshore, and soon we approached one that stood alone, aloof from its nearest neighbours. The left half was an old two-level HAB unit, but what looked like the main body of a ship's shuttle had been stripped down and attached to form an extension on the right. Okwi must have sensed my mental question.

"This was the medical clinic when we—when the Landers, that's what we call the original colonists—first arrived," she said. "The computer had a link to the medical bay on the ship, so although anyone with a serious medical issue or injury would be taken up to the *Lillifleur*, most problems could be treated here on the ground. The shuttle was refitted to suit the needs of a medical unit. Dr.—er, the doctor at the time—lived in the HAB unit and saw patients in the shuttle side."

"But this doctor doesn't see many patients now?" Yuskeya asked. She strolled beside Okwi Rousseault with her usual dignified and graceful pace, hands clasped behind her back as she walked.

Okwi shook her head. "Dr. Lee turned it into a research station long ago, when we built the hospital. Well, when we built the first real clinic, which eventually turned into the hospital we have today. He still lives here, too, although he could have had a newer home. Claims he likes living near the water, but I think he's too set in his ways to move."

To the left of the HAB, sheltered from the winds that might blow in off the lake, the doctor kept a small garden. I recognized some of the plants growing there—curling edges of kale, the feathery tops of carrots (albeit a bit yellower than usual), and large-leaved plants in bright purple that I thought were a variety of cabbage. Others were not familiar to me, seeming more akin to the trees and bushes in the native forest than anything brought from Earth. A border of flowering plants ran along the front edge, showing vibrant pinks, reds, a deep magenta, and a sunny yellow.

On the other side of the HAB, a narrow dock stretched out into the waters of the lake. At the far end it formed a T, affording a place to sit and contemplate the lake, or perhaps fish. While other docks served as mooring spots for small watercraft, this one had no docked boats.

Okwi knocked on the door and waited, but no-one answered. "He's probably hoping we'll go away," she whispered behind a hand. "Dr. Lee," she called, raising her voice, "it's Okwi Rousseault. And I've brought some visitors who want to speak to you."

The door flew open, revealing a thin man of Asian ancestry, his dark hair and goatee lightly peppered with grey and tiny glasses perched on his nose. He wore an oversized brown knit sweater and dark pants that bagged off his thin frame. He regarded us with an ambivalence that bordered on disinterest. "Well, that would be fine if I had any interest at all in speaking to them," he said, and slammed the door shut again.

A FLUSH WARMED Okwi's cheeks and reddened the tips of her ears. "He's . . . difficult, sometimes," she said.

"I see that," Yuskeya said. "Captain, may I have a word with you?"

I nodded and we walked a few paces off from Okwi Rousseault, standing awkwardly alone at the door.

"We don't have to keep it a secret that we know—or strongly suspect—that some of these people haven't aged, do we?" Yuskeya asked me in a low voice.

I shrugged. "It's bound to come up sooner or later. They're trying to keep it quiet, but they're not very good at it. Not terribly surprising; they've had no-one to lie to about it in a long time."

"Or that nanobioscavengers are a thing?"

"They certainly have them, judging by what you found in Amber Malka and what we're seeing here. They probably think they're a secret, but we'll have to talk about them eventually."

"All right. I think that might be the key to getting the good doctor to talk to us."

"Be my guest," I told her, and we stepped back to the HAB.

"Would you mind if we knock again?" Yuskeya asked Okwi.

The woman did so, twice more before the door flew open again. "What did I—" Dr. Lee began, but Yuskeya uncharacteristically cut him off.

"What if I told you that your nanobioscavengers may have formed a synergistic—or possibly parasitic—relationship with a virus or similar native pathogen?" she said. "That may be why your people cannot leave the planet. Would you be interested in discussing this possibility further?"

Dr. Lee's eyes grew very wide as he stared at Yuskeya, and then narrowed. "And what do you know about it?"

"Medical technology hasn't exactly stood still in Nearspace in the past eight decades," Yuskeya said evenly. "I'm willing to exchange information. This seems like a reasonable arrangement and a fair return for a small measure of your time. What do you think, Doctor?"

He pursed his lips, then stepped away from the door inside the HAB. "Well, don't stand around on the doorstep, giving the neighbours something to talk about," he grumbled. "Come in. But I'm not going to forget this, Okwi Rousseault."

Hiding a smile, Yuskeya followed the man inside, and Okwi and I brought up the rear. The HAB had long ago left its utilitarian decor behind, and Dr. Lee had created a homey and comfortable space for himself. No doubt many of the furnishings were gifts from grateful patients over the years. I thought that was the likely explanation for the hand-woven blanket thrown over the back of a chair, as well as the colourful rag rugs dotting the floor. Perhaps also the painting of the lake and surrounding forest hanging over a small dining table in one corner, although maybe the doctor was also an artist.

Okwi Rousseault hurried to make introductions, probably trying to forestall Dr. Lee before he could make another rude remark. He seemed not terribly interested in the possibility we might bring help for the colony against the approaching threat. Once Okwi had finished a brief explanation of that, he crooked a finger at Yuskeya.

"Come into the lab," he said.

Yuskeya nodded and followed him. I glanced at Okwi and she answered with a shrug, so we went along, too.

Dr. Lee's lab reminded me of every mad scientist's lair I'd ever seen in a tri-d or read about in a book, although with an advanced level of technology. There were no beds or gurneys here now, every surface having been converted to space for holding medical equipment, old-style datapads, and devices and consoles that must have come down from labs on the *Lillifleur*. Dr. Lee leaned against one counter and folded his arms, studying Yuskeya almost belligerently.

"Now, what were you saying about bioscavengers?"

"We have a theory—based on what I found when I was treating Amber Malka—that something on the planet has interacted with them over the time you've been here," Yuskeya said.

"We had bioscavengers to combat plenty of diseases and repair physical trauma when we left Nearspace," the doctor snapped. "I mean, the original colonists did. No-one saw fit to stock the *Lillifleur*'s medical bay with more than the basics, though, since they expected we'd get more through trade. Our supply was exhausted long ago, so I don't know what they have to do with this."

"I mean the enhanced variety," Yuskeya said. "The nanobioscavengers."

"Well, it's no surprise if they got better after we left Nearspace. Can't see how that's relevant to the earthbound syndrome, though."

Yuskeya glanced at me. I frowned. Was the man being deliberately obtuse, pretending he didn't know about the nanobioscavengers . . . or did he honestly not know?

"All right," Yuskeya said mildly. "Let me ask you a question. How do you account for the fact that the original crew of the *Lillifleur* hasn't aged more than ten years in eight decades?"

Okwi and Dr. Lee both looked startled and glanced

involuntarily at each other.

"That's preposterous!" the doctor blustered.

"I don't—" Okwi started, but this time I interrupted her.

"We know," I said, not unkindly. "I have a crew roster for the *Lillifleur*, and a list of the colonists. Surely you don't expect us to believe that purely by accident, there are so many colonists here named after them? Enough of them that we've met several just in the few people we've encountered?"

Okwi drew herself up and crossed her arms. "It's our custom to honour our ancestors by perpetuating their names."

I shook my head. "It won't fly. Ever since we arrived, people have been making slips—saying something that intimates they were part of the original complement of settlers, and then scrambling to cover it up. And besides that, the professions match up as well, or very nearly. Juliska Barath, Captain. Karin Nakano, Communications." I pointed a finger at Dr. Lee. "Hawick Lee, Medical Doctor. I noticed your name on the list as well, Okwi Rousseault, and *that* Okwi was also a xenobiologist. That's a little too much coincidence to chalk up to namesakes. But with no visitors for such a long time, you're not used to lying about it, and it's painfully obvious. So why don't you stop trying to cover it up and talk to us about it? We are trying to help you, here."

"Also, I haven't seen a single resident who looks over sixty," Yuskeya added, and I realized that's what had been bothering me about the clusters of colonists we'd seen. No elderly people at all.

Dr. Lee drew a deep sigh and blew it out. "I guess the game's up, Okwi," he said. "You never were very good at lying."

"Fortunately, I haven't had much cause to practice," she retorted, "and you didn't do such a great job yourself. But I suppose you're right." She turned to me and nodded. "I *am* the original Okwi, and he's the one and only Dr. Lee. Thank goodness," she added, rolling her eyes.

"We're very pleased to meet you," I said with a smile. "And we're very interested to hear what you have to tell us about it."

"Well, that's not going to take long. Because we can't account for it," Dr. Lee snapped. "Not for lack of trying on my part."

"Really, you needn't feel you have to keep it a secret. We're not unfamiliar with the concept of anti-aging nanobioscavengers," I explained. "I've had them in my own system since I was fourteen years old. But they're not commonplace in Nearspace—yet—and yours must predate mine. That's why we're interested to learn about them and where yours originated, as well as wanting to help you."

Dr. Lee stared abstractedly out the window that looked over the lake, as if he'd stopped listening to me. "Anti-aging bioscavengers," he said thoughtfully, nodding his head in slow bobs. He removed his glasses and polished them absently on his sleeve while he considered the idea. "Yes. That could explain a lot. That could explain almost everything. If such a thing—"

His demeanour changed dramatically. He pushed his glasses back into place and leaned toward Yuskeya, eyes bright. "You think it's possible the entire roster of colonists had them in their system when we left Nearspace?"

Yuskeya glanced at me, then back to the doctor. "Wait, are you saying you didn't *know* you had them? Or something like them?"

He leaned back with a bark of humourless laughter. "If I'd known that, the last fifty years of my life would have been a hell of a lot easier," he said. "I feel like a dog who's spent decades chasing its own tail, only to find that it was attached to me the whole time." He slapped one knee and shook his head. "I always thought it was something about this planet. But those PrimeCorp bastards could have introduced them in one of the inoculations we had pre-embarkation."

Okwi stared at Yuskeya for a long moment. "But could they do that? Why would they?"

I didn't want to get into what PrimeCorp could or would have felt entitled to do, so I said, "They must have thought it would help you in some way . . . if that's even what happened. We don't know enough to speculate yet."

"Or they were testing them. Using us as the test subjects," the doctor growled.

Okwi turned to Dr. Lee. "I think this is going to be something we have to take to the whole Council. Maybe the whole colony. Or at least the Landers."

"Well, that can wait, because these ladies are here now, and I want to hear what they have to say," Dr. Lee said with his characteristic asperity. "You can go running off to round people up if you want, but I'm not waiting for that."

Okwi puffed out a sigh and left the room, and I wondered if she was indeed going off to gather up half the colony and bring them back to Dr. Lee's small home. But she returned a moment later dragging one of the chairs from the dining area. "All right. I should have known you'd be too stubborn to listen to sense. But I'm not going to stand around all afternoon. Might as well get comfortable." She nodded to me and Yuskeya. "You too, ladies. Don't bother waiting for this old reprobate to be hospitable. Word's not in his vocabulary." She crossed her legs and folded her arms, and said, "Go ahead, Hawick. Tell them our story."

And without offering either me or Yuskeya chairs or other amenities, he did.

CHAPTER TEN
The Landers

"WE DIDN'T NOTICE anything strange for a long time," he said. "Too busy trying to survive, explore the planet—this part of it, anyway—and deal with the knowledge that Nearspace was gone for us. We weren't going back unless someone came looking for us."

"Which we fully expected would happen," Okwi interjected. "We thought PrimeCorp would come and find us, get us back to Nearspace. Or at least open a wormhole route. It was rather exciting at first, really—we'd expanded Nearspace into a previously unknown system! And one with a planet that could support us. Still, we considered the colony here as possibly temporary for at least the first five years. After that—" it was her turn to gaze, unseeing, out the window. "After that, there was never a precise moment when we all talked it out and decided, nope, this is it, we're stuck here and no-one is coming for us. It just gradually sank in."

"So we'd been here maybe ten years before I started to notice that none of the original colonists—or crew—were noticeably aging. Except one member of the crew."

"Tomas Sanchez," Okwi said.

"Yes. And it was about that time, too, when we noticed that the length of time any of us could spend aboard the *Lillifleur* was diminishing. Work rotations of three weeks had been fine, but then people started getting sick before the three weeks were up and had to come down. So I had a couple of mysteries on my hands."

By this point it was clear that the story was going to take a little while. It appeared Okwi had been right, and we might as well sit. Yuskeya and I moved to a bench, shifting clutter to the floor beside it to make room. Dr. Lee didn't appear to mind, or at least he said nothing. It was comfortable enough and I settled in to listen to the tale.

Dr. Lee picked up one of the datapads from the counter and idly powered it on. "For a while I thought it could be linked to the wormhole we'd been pulled through. Some cosmic radiation, ray, particles, or something else we'd encountered that had affected us on a cellular level. But test as I might, I couldn't find any evidence of anything like that. My next thought was that it was something endemic to Ryphen. Something in the air, the water, the soil. But search as I might, I couldn't pin anything down."

"By then, many of the colonists had paired up and started families—the crew, too. They'd had to come to terms with becoming colonists as well, whether they wanted it or not. The children of these unions were generally healthy and seemed to age normally, which was a relief. At least until a couple of years past puberty, and then it slows down, like the rest of us. Early on, that lined up with my wormhole theory. They hadn't been exposed to whatever it was, since they hadn't been born at that time. I was glad to see that we could still reproduce. But the children *did* start to show the same inability to be away from the planet for any length of time, once they reached about age five. So I concluded that they were two separate problems."

"What about the man you mentioned—Tomas Sanchez?" Yuskeya asked.

"Yes. Tomas. He aged normally. He was a navigation technician on the *Lillifleur*. There was no evidence that he'd been shielded or exposed any differently during the wormhole skip, but he wasn't affected." Dr. Lee drummed his fingers on the edge of the datapad. "But he never married or lived with any of the colonists," he said thoughtfully, "the way the rest of the crew did. He was a loner; seemed happy enough to keep to himself. Or maybe he never got over being stranded away from Nearspace. He wouldn't talk about it. Now, though, I see a possible connection."

Yuskeya nodded. "The crew might not have had the bioscavs at the outset, but they were transferred . . . sexually, or by close intimate contact with the colonists, who did have them."

"But mine weren't transferred that way," I objected. "Otherwise Hirin never would have gotten so sick. We wouldn't have had to do the transfusion."

"But these aren't yours," Yuskeya said to me. "We already know they're different. Maybe they were specifically designed to spread through a population. Or maybe it was the contact with the Ryphen virus that made it possible. In this context, it makes sense as an explanation."

"Blood transfusions, too," Dr. Lee said, as if my words had reminded him. "There were numerous instances when someone was injured and I found a compatible match for direct transfusions. We had limited supplies of stored blood products, so I rationed those for use only when we really needed them."

"No-one ever expected you to be a colony that had to survive for an extended period of time without support." It was making more and more sense to me.

"Absolutely not," Okwi agreed. "On Xaqual, we would have had regular supply shipments from PrimeCorp. As the colony established itself, there'd be trade with the rest of Nearspace."

"Tell us about Amber Malka," Yuskeya said. "She was neither crew nor colonist, but she ended up here with you."

"She beat us here, actually. We found her on the planet when we arrived," Dr. Lee said. "That was a bit of a shock for all concerned. She'd been pulled through the wormhole, same as we were. The wormhole damaged her skip drive, same as it did ours, so she couldn't go back. I don't know if PrimeCorp ever sent anyone to look for her or us," Dr. Lee added with a thoughtful frown.

"Doubtful," Yuskeya muttered.

"Something impacted her ship when she came out of the wormhole, too," Okwi said. "Small meteoroid or something. Banged her up a bit, but she managed to limp to the planet. She's tough," Okwi said with a smile. It faded suddenly, however, as if she'd suddenly remembered Amber's uncertain fate.

"Managed to survive here almost a year, until we arrived, with only her spelunker's supplies and what she could find on the planet," Dr. Lee said gruffly. "Most people probably would have given up before that, but not Amber. But she was in bad shape by then, malnourished and sickly. We've learned to eat much of the local plant life, but it took research and experimentation with processing to be sure it was safe and we could digest it, or manufacture what we needed to make it so. Amber didn't have those technical capabilities."

"It was a shock when our initial scans of the planet found her," Okwi said. "We thought we were the first here, only to discover a stranded spelunker who'd come the same route."

"She was no less shocked to see us. And by the time we found her, she needed minor surgery, which came with a blood transfusion," Dr. Lee said. "So I guess that's how Amber Malka joined the earthbound club. We helped her patch up her ship, but her skip drive was too damaged to repair, so she wasn't going back through the wormhole. Might have been just as well she became like the rest of us. She adjusted and fit in well here. Served on the Council for a long time, and she and Juliska Barath were among the first couples to get married here on Ryphen."

Which confirmed what I'd suspected about the meaning of the captain's picture in Amber's shipsuit pocket, Juliska Barath's bearing when she spoke of Amber, and the way the other colonists spoke of Amber around her. The doctor's dour personality couldn't entirely hide what sounded like a real affection for the woman, and I felt a renewed surge of hope that she was responding to Dr. Ndasa's care.

"She did a lot of exploration in the system once we got her ship flying again," Okwi said. "Especially at first. More than the *Lillifleur* could have done, because we needed to keep it close to the planet and locked in orbit. Couldn't risk the fuel. Most of our system data, we owe to Amber. But she never did find another wormhole out of here."

"How did she manage to get through the wormhole this time, then?" I asked.

Okwi sighed. "They finally dismantled the skip drive from the *Lillifleur* and the one from Amber's ship, then managed to put together one working unit. We'd never done it before, on the off chance that we'd eventually find an explanation for the earthbound syndrome and be able to take the *Lillifleur* back to Nearspace. The drone threat made us decide it was a risk we had to take. And in truth, I think we'd given up on the idea of ever leaving Ryphen."

Dr. Lee shook himself a little and fixed us with a keen stare. "So now tell me—tell us—about these nanobioscavengers. How did they come to be in our systems, and how did you find out about them?"

"How they came to be in your systems, I don't know," Yuskeya said. She glanced at me, and I nodded. "Although your guess about the inoculations is a good possibility. PrimeCorp may have introduced them into the colonists as a test project. An experiment. Remember, they never intended to lose track of you."

Something *pinged* in my brain. "Unless . . . they *did*."

Yuskeya turned to me, confusion knotting her brow. "What do you mean? What kind of experiment would it be if they couldn't follow up or monitor it?"

"Well, I don't mean they deliberately lost track of them. But they might have thought they *would* be able to follow up—just not in Nearspace."

"I'm more confused than ever," Okwi admitted. "We never intended to leave Nearspace."

I wished I could get up and pace the lab as I thought the notion through, but the space was too small. I drummed my fingers in a quick rhythm on my thigh as I spoke, to siphon off that extra energy. "We've recently learned that PrimeCorp had a whole secret wormhole exploration project going years ago. They didn't report all their discoveries to the Nearspace Authority as they were supposed to."

Okwi was staring at a patch on the sunrise-bright rug at her feet and frowning, as if she couldn't credit the notion of underhanded activity by PrimeCorp, but I pressed on. I wasn't ready to get into an explanation yet of all PrimeCorp's duplicities, or the reality of the corporation's dissolution.

"I don't know exactly what their plan might have been, but they couldn't treat all of you with anti-aging nanotechnology and then let you set up a colony where you'd have regular contact with Nearspace. Someone would notice eventually that you didn't age, and start asking questions. Maybe they expected you to go through that wormhole—or maybe one like it, another secret one. But they thought they'd be able to find you on the other side.

Something went wrong, and you ended up on your own."

"You still haven't said how you know about the nanobioscavengers," Dr. Lee said.

"I took a blood sample from Amber Malka when we were trying to save her," Yuskeya said. "I analysed it closely. There were nanobioscavengers present—but something else, too. A virus, or something analogous to a virus. It was so intertwined with the organic components of the bioscavs that when the virus began to die, so did they."

Dr. Lee nodded slowly. "So you think the virus is native to Ryphen?"

Yuskeya nodded. "It's only a theory at this point, but yes. And it can't survive away from the planet. That's what makes you earthbound. You have the nanobioscavengers, but they're so symbiotically linked with the virus now, they can't operate without it, or fix the problems caused when the virus dies."

"And you've seen these nanobioscavengers before . . . the ones that slow aging?" Dr. Lee asked.

I raised a hand. "That's where I come in. As I said, I have them, too, although mine are a different version. I may look thirty," I said, "but when the *Lillifleur* went through that wormhole, I was six years old."

DR. LEE AND Okwi Rousseault reacted with some surprise, but not shock, to my revelation. After all, they'd been living with the reality of slowed aging for decades. Before they could say too much about it, though, another knock sounded at the door of Dr. Lee's HAB. He went to answer it, grumbling, and returned with Juliska Barath.

"I hope I'm not interrupting," she said, surveying Dr. Lee's cluttered room with interest. "I wanted to speak with Captain Paixon before she returns to her ship."

I glanced at Yuskeya. "I guess we're about finished here for now. If that's the end of your story, Doctor. And your questions?"

"Oh, I have many more questions, but none that can't wait, I suppose."

"I wonder if some of the colonists would be willing to provide me with blood samples?" Yuskeya asked. "I can study them in our medical bay, maybe find out more about them. Anything I do discover, I'll happily share with you, Doctor."

He nodded. "I know some who'd be willing, including me. And you, Okwi?" It was a statement more than a request, and I saw Okwi roll her eyes at his tone.

"Whatever you say, Hawick."

"Well, I'll go with Captain Barath, and leave you to collect your samples," I told Yuskeya. "Meet you back on the ship."

She nodded, and I thanked Dr. Lee and Okwi for their time. Captain Barath and I emerged again into the saffron light of Ryphen's afternoon.

"I have something I want to give you," she told me as we walked, following the path that meandered along the shoreline of the lake.

"All right," I said, but she didn't explain further, instead launching into an explanation of the native fish and plants they'd been able to incorporate into their diets. I expressed my appreciation for the colonists' resourcefulness, but I had the feeling we were only talking to fill the silence.

Juliska Barath occupied a small home, one of the old HAB units that had grown over the years. Slab walls of the colourful stone tree material created both a small porch at the front of the house, and an extension off the left side. A robust vegetable garden grew on the right, and the house had a well-kept, tidy air. Not surprising, perhaps, for a spacefaring captain. Juliska led me inside and offered tea, which I accepted. The interior of the house was lived-in but clean and inviting. As I'd seen in other buildings, the furnishings represented a mix of what the colonists had originally been provided, things they'd salvaged and sometimes repurposed from the *Lillifleur*, and items the colonists had learned to build or craft on their own. Two chairs of hand-carved, sage-coloured wood that never would have passed the weight restrictions on a colony ship sat near a window. The table held a beautifully polished carving of a bird in flight from what must be native jade-coloured stone, and a woven throw in colours matching the local vegetation covered the back of another chair.

Juliska motioned me toward that comfortable-looking chair and went to make the tea. As I looked around, I felt another presence here—Amber Malka. It was nothing supernatural or eerie, just the clear knowledge that Juliska Barath hadn't lived here alone. Two people had hung these pictures, chosen this furniture, impressed their personalities on this space. My gaze fell upon a framed image on a small table near the window. Juliska Barath and Amber Malka, heads together, laughed into the lens while the wide vista of the nearby lake stretched out beyond them.

When the *Lillifleur* captain returned with two mugs of steaming tea on a tray, I said, "You have a beautiful home."

She smiled at me. "Do I detect a note of wistfulness, Captain?"

I chuckled self-consciously. "Luta, remember? And am I that transparent? A little, I guess. I call my ship home, but there's limited opportunity to make a place cosy or homey on a working vessel."

She nodded. "It's true. I stayed mainly on the ship for the first while, after we realized we weren't leaving here. Maybe it was a crutch, a way to cling to the hope that we'd be rescued. When I finally had to accept that my home was going to be here, on this planet, I wasn't exactly thrilled." She glanced around the room. "A single HAB unit on its own is a sterile and unwelcoming place at first. But you live in a place long enough, it changes and grows along with you. It becomes a home."

Suddenly, her eyes filled with tears, and she brushed them away with the back of her hand. "Amber and I have lived here together for a long time, Luta."

"Don't assume she's not coming back, please. She's getting the very best care—"

"Oh, I know. I believe you about that." She paused. "But the earthbound syndrome—there's no cure for that. If she could have come back with you—" She broke off abruptly.

I breathed in sharply. Until now, I hadn't thought of that. Then I shook my head. "She wouldn't have lived to make it back through the wormhole with us. We barely got her to Xaqual in time. If I'd known—"

She held up a hand and shook her head. "You couldn't have, and you didn't even know there was a wormhole there. You didn't do anything wrong. There was no real expectation that she could come back from that journey alive—she knew that, and I knew it. We might hope for a miracle, but . . . I gave up believing in those a long time ago."

"You might still hope," I insisted. "Dr. Ndasa has specialized knowledge that might let him save her when no-one else could. Let me tell you what Commander Blue and I just told Dr. Lee and

Okwi Rousseault." I briefly explained to her about the nanobioscavengers and what we'd deduced. She listened quietly, asking only a few questions. Her face hardened when I related our theory about PrimeCorp's introduction of the nanobioscavengers into an unwitting colonist population.

Finally, she blew out a long sigh and said, "Well, it would certainly explain a lot. But you said the virus takes the bioscavs with it when it dies. What do you think your doctor friend will be able to do to stop that?"

I hesitated, then shook my head. "I honestly don't know. Maybe introduce other nanobioscavengers; maybe simply put Amber into a medical suspension to buy time. My mother—she's a leading researcher in the bioscavs field—she promised to travel to Xaqual to see if she could help, too. I feel that between the two of them, Amber has a better chance than you might think."

She pondered the contents of her teacup, as if she might find answers there. "It's almost harder to hope. I'd already accepted— or I thought I had—that she wasn't coming back."

I smiled and took a sip of tea. "Tell me about her."

Juliska Barath shifted her gaze to stare out of the window. "When the *Lillifleur* went through that wormhole, it cut us off from our former lives," she said. "The crew had never planned to be part of the colony—we had families and friends we expected to return to in a few weeks. Even after we'd found Ryphen, realized the colony might work, that we might all survive there . . . it took a long time to come to terms with that. I left a wife and a little boy behind in Nearspace. They never knew what happened to me— only that the ship disappeared without a trace. To them, I guess I died long ago. And they're likely dead themselves, now."

She took another sip of tea and her face softened. "That was a lot to deal with. Amber helped me through that. She and I had a lot in common—we were both pilots, both here on Ryphen entirely by a twist of fate. We both felt a certain amount of responsibility to make sure the colonists were taken care of, that they survived—even thrived. I suppose it was natural that we fell in love."

"It was very brave of her to do what she did, trying to get help for everyone."

"She's a tough character," Juliska said with a soft chuckle. "I mean, she was a wormhole spelunker, right? That tells you about her right there. She had to be a lot of things—brave, tough, able to face the unknown without flinching. She managed to survive here, alone, for almost a year before we came through, and she never gave up hope that someone would find her."

I smiled. "Someone did."

"Not exactly what she was hoping for. More castaways! But what she already knew about Ryphen helped the rest of us enormously."

"A remarkable woman," I said. In some ways, what I learned about Amber Malka made me think of Jahelia Sord. "She reminds me of someone I know. I don't know if I could manage what she did."

"But she never got past a lingering worry that what happened to the *Lillifleur* was partly her fault," Juliska said. "That something had happened, or changed, when she went through the wormhole, that caused the same thing to happen when we came upon it."

"I don't think that's likely."

She shook her head. "Neither do I, and I told her that many times. She'd agree to make me happy, but I know she never believed it. Deep down, she felt responsible. Sometimes being planet-bound made her crazy. She kept her ship in working order, and when the mood hit, she'd leave—fly off exploring the system. Looking for a way home, if you ask me, although she'd never admit it. She never went for more than a few days; she knew it worried me when she went, but she promised me she wouldn't take unnecessary risks."

"I think I can understand that." I'd felt the same thing a time or two myself, the longing to be out in the black. And when Hirin had thought his own death was imminent, that had been his choice, too.

A thought struck me. "She developed the earthbound syndrome along with the rest of you?"

Juliska nodded. "Dr. Lee wondered about it—obsessed about it for a while," she said with a fond smile. "After all, Amber had been here for an entire year longer than the rest of us, but she didn't seem to develop the syndrome any quicker. Eventually I think he gave up on it as one more mystery."

Which we had probably now solved. Amber hadn't had the nanobioscavengers in her system when she arrived on Ryphen, so the virus—or what we were calling a virus for now—hadn't affected her. But after her transfusion and interactions with the colonists, she'd picked up the bioscavs, and the virus, too. And traded longer life for a short tether to the planet.

"PrimeCorp didn't alert you before the *Lillifleur* left that Amber had gone missing in that area?"

"Not a word. I wondered about that for a while, but eventually I put it down to an oversight."

I doubted that, but I didn't say anything. They could have had a tracker on Amber's ship and known the precise coordinates where she disappeared. "So then when the drones seemed to pose a threat, she managed to fix the drive?"

Juliska sipped at her tea again, a smile of reminiscence curling her lips. "She'd worked on this idea for altering the drive for the first six or seven years of being here. The Council wasn't willing to dismantle the *Lillifleur*'s drive at that point, though. It was only once we discovered we couldn't—physically couldn't—leave the planet any longer, that she let it go. There didn't seem to be much point. Then when the first drone arrived and people got sick—" Her eyes welled up again and she took a calming draught of tea. "Well, that changed things. Neither of us were affected, probably because we'd been on the *Lillifleur* at the time. I didn't even know she'd thought of it or started looking at the drive again. She didn't want me to worry if she wasn't going to be able to make it work. But in the end, with the help of a couple of other engineers, she did. And she went. And—you're here." She smiled through the tears.

"We're not the help she was hoping to find, but we should be able to get what you do need," I said. "We'll bring help back through the wormhole as fast as we can."

I felt a certain kinship with Juliska Barath in that moment. She'd lost one partner, and had stoically accepted the near-certainty of losing a second. It was something I'd thought about a lot in the years when Hirin continued to age and I didn't. I'd lost friends along the way, and family members, but I hadn't lost him. It had been a close thing. I'd convinced myself that I'd thought about it enough to be prepared when the time came—but I hadn't been. I could imagine what Juliska Barath was feeling.

"You've done so much already. We appreciate it," she said. She reached into a pocket and pulled out a datachip. "I want you to take this back to Nearspace with you."

I held out a hand and she dropped the chip into it. "What's on it?"

"A copy of Amber's journals," she said with a wistful smile. "They start when she first arrived on Ryphen after coming through the wormhole, and go on to chronicle the entire history of the Lillifleur colony. There's some personal stuff there, too, but . . . it's all right. I want PrimeCorp and Nearspace to know about us, in case—"

She broke off, but I knew what she meant. In case things didn't go as we hoped, and we couldn't come back, or send anyone else back.

I looked down at the chip. Such a small, light thing, but weighted with so much history. It reminded me of all the things the Ryphens still didn't know. "Thank you for trusting me with this. I'm happy to deliver it, even though I don't think it's necessary. But Juliska . . . I haven't said anything to anyone else, but you should probably know . . . PrimeCorp is gone."

She looked at me blankly, her blue eyes wreathed in confusion. "Gone?"

I nodded. "The corporation was dismantled by the Nearspace Authority last year after a lot of . . . improprieties came to light. More than improprieties. Criminal activity. Corruption. I know PrimeCorp funded the *Lillifleur* expedition, but . . . you don't owe them anything, and they have no rights here. Lillifleur is, in every possible way, an independent entity."

Juliska was quiet, taking that in. I could see her considering the possibilities. Finally, she nodded. "*Okej*," she said. "I don't know that everyone will be happy about that, but I kind of like the idea. No matter what happens, no-one from Nearspace is going to come and try to change what we've built here."

"No, they're not. The Authority will protect you, and help if they can, I'm sure. You'll be considered a part of Nearspace if you want. Have a seat on the Administrative Council—even if you have to fill it long-distance," I added with a smile. "But we have new communications technologies that would make that easier. I'll leave it up to you to tell the Council when you think the time is right."

She nodded. "I guess we're getting ahead of ourselves a bit. We don't know for sure that anyone from Nearspace will even be able to get here. But I will say—if something happens, and you can't get through the wormhole, there's a place for you all here in the colony, whatever happens."

"Thank you. We all appreciate that." I knew my own crew wasn't even close to the point where they'd accept being stranded here. It was entirely likely that, given the chance, they'd prefer to head out exploring and see where it took us and how far we could get, rather than settle down. And Karro and Aliande wouldn't rest if there was any possible chance they could get back to their children. Unlike the colonists, none of us were tied physically to Ryphen—at least not yet. But I didn't need to tell Juliska Barath that, or make light of her sincere and generous offer. "I appreciate it. But I don't think it will be necessary. I believe we'll be able to make a real difference for you all by bringing back some help."

"I want to believe that, too," Juliska said, a trifle bleakly. She was thinking of the five thousand other colonists in that moment. But I knew she was also not at all convinced that Amber Malka was coming back to Ryphen. "I really do."

HALF AN HOUR later, I had rejoined Hirin on the *Tane Ikai*, and we were in our quarters. I finished bringing him up to speed.

"Dr. Lee managed to round up some volunteers quickly to donate blood samples to Yuskeya," I said. "She should be back any time, and Lee convinced her to promise him a tour of First Aid."

"But you think PrimeCorp was running a huge experiment on the colonists without their permission?" Hirin asked, incredulous. "I thought we'd seen the worst those people could come up with."

"Well, it's possible. I do think this ranks as less heinous than collaborating with the Chron against the rest of Nearspace. They could be reasonably certain the bioscavs wouldn't do anyone any harm, and they hoped they were giving them the gift of immortality."

"Only so they could reap the profits, and without asking permission," Hirin scoffed, then fell silent. I thought I knew what he was thinking. Mother hadn't asked me, either, before introducing the nanobioscavengers into my body. But he wouldn't go too far in drawing any comparison between Mother and PrimeCorp, no matter how obvious it might be.

"Anyway, what's important now is that the colonists finally have some answers about what happened to them. Not all, but it's a start. Together, Yuskeya and Dr. Lee might be able to identify the virus—or whatever it is. That would be another step."

"Toward making it possible for the colonists to leave Ryphen?"

I shrugged. "I don't even know how much appetite there is to leave Ryphen for good. After almost a hundred years, they're settled. People they left behind are gone. This is home. But having the option to spend longer periods on the *Lillifleur*, or maybe travelling to other planets for a visit . . . I think some of them would like that."

Hirin stood and walked around the back of the big chair, lightly tapping one fist along the sturdy fabric. "Whatever they can do, it won't be fast enough to be an answer to the problem of whatever's out there and getting closer."

"No. We have to try and get them help with that."

"So let's go talk to Viss," Hirin said. "He hasn't left engineering since we touched down, as far as I know."

"If he had a galley on that deck we'd never see him."

As we clambered down the hatchway ladder to the engineering deck below, the sound of muttering grew louder. At the bottom of the ladder, Hirin and I exchanged a glance. Viss was nowhere in sight, but his rumblings had resolved into fragments of sentences.

"That matter infuser . . . never saw anything like . . . look at that. Even with a full maintenance cycle . . ."

It went on in a similar vein. "Who is he talking to?" I whispered to Hirin. He shrugged.

We crossed the main engineering floor and found Viss in the skip drive bay, on his knees, the upper half of his body swallowed by an open access hatch. He was alone.

"Viss, how's it going down here?" I asked. "Got a report for me yet on going back through that wormhole?"

Even though I didn't think he'd heard us coming, he didn't seem startled. He emerged from the hatch and sat back on his heels, wiping his forehead with his sleeve. "I don't like the look of this matter infuser," he said, and I hid a smile. I'd figured that much out from his half-overheard rant. "The good news is, the main and auxiliary drives are fine. I just want to run a full cleaning and recalibration cycle on the skip drive. That wormhole did not play nice with it."

He stood and stuck his hands in the pockets of his clean but perpetually stained shipsuit. "I can start that and have it running on the way back to the wormhole," he said. "But when we get there, I want to scan that wormhole as thoroughly as we can before we go in."

"Amber Malka made it through with a cobbled-together skip drive in a century-old runner," Hirin reminded him.

"Yes, before we came through and changed who-knows-what," he said. "And we don't know what kind of trouble she might have encountered getting out of it. Something caused her ship to end up drifting, and we haven't had time yet to figure out what."

It was true. There'd been no opportunity to give the *Ranger*'s drives a full diagnostic since we'd brought it aboard.

"Also, we sent a message through—or tried to—but there's been no reply. So we can't even be sure—"

I held up a hand. "All good points. And I'm not against being careful, particularly when we have passengers aboard. But I feel like we're out of our depth here, and we need to get some Protectorate presence in this system." I felt a twinge of guilt about the clandestine message Pika had delivered regarding the drones' possible landing on the planet. I still hadn't told even Hirin about that.

"Well, like I said, I can run the cycle while we're underway. But what I'd really like is a little more time to study the skip drive on the *Ranger*."

"Should I ask permission from Juliska Barath to keep the *Ranger* on board a little longer?"

Viss raised an eyebrow. "That ship could be legal salvage, Captain. If it is, you don't need permission from anyone to keep it."

"Depending on what happens to Amber Malka, I suppose that's technically right. But I as good as told Juliska Barath already that the colony—if not Amber herself—can have it back. So I'll feel better getting permission from Juliska. I guess I thought we'd leave it here on the planet before we left."

He pursed his lips. "I'd definitely like more time to look it over, in case there's anything it could tell me about recalibrating our skip drive for that wormhole."

"I may be able to analyse the two drives and pinpoint differences," Pika offered. I couldn't suppress a start when her voice came without warning. *Damne*, but it was easy to forget she was always listening. Maybe Jahelia Sord would have some advice on how to deal with intelligent AIs.

Viss snorted and leaned back against the wall of the drive bay. "I think I'll stick with my own diagnostics."

Pika, predictably, took offense. "Yes, engineers are so very good at dispassionate evaluation of data," she retorted. "It's hard enough for you to remember to wipe off your hands before you poke the console screens with greasy fingers."

Viss clamped his lips together in a very good impression of Hirin when he was annoyed. "Captain, permission to take the AI offline so I can debug her personality subroutine?"

I raised an eyebrow. "Permission denied. Everyone else on board is allowed to have a prickly personality when it suits them, so I don't see why Pika should be any different."

"You're treating the artificial intelligence the same as the real intelligences?"

"Hey!" Pika sounded outraged. "We'll see how real you think I am when I hack into the waste processing system while you're in the head."

Hirin chuckled, and Viss said, "All right, old man, that's enough from you. How about you back me up on this? Get Captain Barath to let us keep the other ship a little while longer. Give me tonight and the transit time out to the wormhole to study it. We can return it once the wormhole's stabilized and they can turn it into a museum if they want."

"You sound convinced that the wormhole's going to get fixed."

Viss shrugged. "The Corvids can *make* wormholes, remember? It might take a while, but personally, establishing a connection to this system isn't something I'm worried about. It's the getting back that's my main concern."

"You think we can leave for the wormhole in the morning?"

"Unless I find something extraordinary." He pulled his datapad off a counter and tapped at the screen. He looked up at me expectantly. "Is that it, folks? Faster I get back to this, the faster we'll be ready to leave."

Nothing like being dismissed by your own engineer. Fortunately, I was used to it, and Viss was good enough at his job that I could let him get away with it. One more time, anyway, I told myself. Next time, I'd definitely tell him who was boss. I avoided catching Hirin's eye as we made our way back to the bridge.

So, WE HAD a plan for attempting the wormhole, but it left me with a couple of things to do. Yuskeya was back aboard with blood samples from twenty colonists: ten original landers and ten from the next generation. Dr. Lee had returned with her, and I had it from Maja that he'd barely said a word to anyone else or spared a glance for the rest of the ship. All he wanted to see was the First Aid bay and the advances in medical equipment that had happened since he'd left Nearspace. I expected they'd be closeted in there for the next few hours.

Pika pinged me over my implant again when I was alone in the galley, fetching a double caff. I'd had to wash out a mug to get a clean one, a testament to how many hot liquids the crew was consuming to keep ourselves mentally fuelled. Once I started, though, I'd washed them all, the methodical task and soothing hot water almost turning into a meditation. Pika's words quickly dispelled whatever small mental respite I'd found, just as I finished filling my cup.

"The beacon lost track of the drones on the other side of the planet," she reported. "They got more difficult to track once they entered the atmosphere, since the beacon can't do that. I conclude that they either landed or crashed on the planet's surface."

"Maybe they crashed," I echoed hopefully.

Pika said, "It's possible. However, we have no other data on which to make more than general conjectures."

"But if they landed, what are they doing?" I argued. "How sophisticated could their programming be?"

Pika made a throat-clearing noise over the comm. The implication wasn't lost on me. "Again, I don't have enough data to make further conjectures."

"All right, point taken. But do you think they pose any imminent danger to the colonists?"

"I can't speculate about how quickly they could arrive here if they wanted to," Pika said. "If they did not crash, they may be perfectly capable of atmospheric flight or some other mode of fast transportation—"

"*Okej*, I get it."

"You don't want to tell the Council about them," Pika observed after a pause.

I sighed. "No, I don't. They wanted me to destroy the drones and I didn't. At this point I'd rather go and get the Protectorate and bring them back and let *them* deal with the issue. They'll be much better qualified."

"And you won't have to listen to the colonists get mad. I understand."

Sometimes I hated Pika's not-so-artificial-seeming intelligence.

"What do you think?" I asked her, ignoring the last comment. "Are the drones a danger the colonists need to be warned about?"

She was silent a moment. Finally, she said, "Based on what we know so far, I can't make an accurate assessment of that."

I felt a ridiculous disappointment flood over me. Why did I care so much what an AI thought? I guess at that point I would have been happy with any validation that let me off the hook. And it wasn't coming from the AI.

"Will you keep monitoring for them—or anything—and tell me right away if your opinion changes?" I asked her.

"Captain," she said with that annoying echo of Jahelia's mocking laughter in her voice, "you can depend on it."

I leaned against the counter, sipping from my mug disconsolately and arguing with myself. I couldn't, in good conscience, leave the planet tomorrow without telling the Council about the drones. But without any clear danger, I could put off the unpleasant task for a little while. On the other hand, what was I waiting for? Drones to appear in the sky over the colony and start raking the Ryphens with death rays?

"Stop," I told myself aloud. "That's crazy."

"What's crazy?" Hirin came into the galley at exactly the wrong moment.

I swore inwardly, because he was one person I couldn't lie to. He was probably going to be disappointed I hadn't told him about the drones sooner. I'd honestly rather he got angry. Hirin disappointed was a sorrowful thing. But maybe it would be a relief to share the worry, once the deed was done.

I sighed into my mug. "We have a small problem. Well, I have a small problem."

"And I expect you're about to make it my problem, too," Hirin said with a long-suffering smile. "Hold that thought until I pour myself a cup of fortitude."

"Very funny." But I stayed silent while he pulled a mug of double caff and motioned me to join him at the table. When he sat across from me and waited for me to explain, his intelligent blue-grey eyes alert, I felt instantly lighter. How many difficulties had we hashed out here together, wreathed in the scents of endless cups of caff and plates of cinnamon *pano*? And so far, they'd all turned out all right. I shouldn't have waited this long to share this with him.

Briefly, I caught him up on Pika's two reports from the tracking beacon—that the drones had doubled back to the planet after passing it, and that they'd disappeared into the atmosphere on the other side.

"I had hoped we'd find out they crashed or something, but since the beacon lost them, we're in the dark. I don't see how we can leave without telling someone here about them."

"You don't want to be the bearer of bad news," Hirin said, just as perceptive as Pika.

"I'm that transparent?"

He chuckled. "In a word, yes. But maybe we don't have to go and spill everything at the feet of the entire Council. Why don't we tell Dufour, and let him handle it from there? It's not like we have any clear indication there's danger to the colony. He may want to put a few people on quiet alert. And with luck, we'll be back with more help for them in a couple of days."

I nodded at this sensible approach. "Make the call with me?"

"Of course," he said, and moved around to my side of the table so that we could both be caught in my datapad's video link.

The communications hub easily linked us up with Dufour. He was in one of the colony's greenhouses, judging by the riot of shiny green leaves and bright yellow berries I glimpsed over his shoulder.

"Captains Paixon," Andre Dufour said with a grin on his broad, weather-tanned face. "What can I do for you?"

I licked my lips. "There's something we need to share with you, Councillor. The two drones that bypassed the planet when we arrived . . . the ones we shepherded aside? My computer AI has reported that they doubled back and entered the atmosphere on the far side of the planet after we thought they'd continued on." I thought it might be best if I didn't tell him exactly when Pika had relayed the information.

"What?" The smile had dropped from his face quicker than an asteroid pulled into the centre of a gravity well. "Where are they now?"

"We don't know. Our tracking beacon lost them when they got close to the planet."

"Now, they may have malfunctioned in some way and simply crashed," Hirin said. "Or maybe they've deliberately landed as far away from Lillifleur as possible so as not to interfere with you folks. And the other side of the planet is a long distance away."

"Depending on how fast their atmospheric flight is," Dufour said, his concern not noticeably abating. "If they're coming here, they might make it by this time tomorrow."

"If they're interested in the colony at all," I pointed out. "There's no real reason to think they are, or that they have any malicious intent if they do come your way."

Dufour ran a hand over his face and slid it around to rub the back of his neck. "I don't know that I agree with you there, Captain, considering the insistence on sending more and more drones our way. But that's neither here nor there. What do you think we should do?"

I glanced at Hirin.

"It's your call, but I don't see any point in alarming the entire colony at this point," he said. "You might quietly set a watch—a few people you can trust to keep their heads—and have the *Lillifleur* begin monitoring the area around the settlement to the furthest extent of its sensors. Maybe take the rest of the Council into your confidence so they're not blindsided."

"That doesn't seem like much," Dufour said.

"Well, unless there's something you haven't told us about, you don't have armaments to shoot something out of the sky, and the *Lillifleur* has no weapons that would be useful against a target on the planet." Hirin's voice was calm and reasonable.

"And we were able to scan the drones comprehensively," I added quickly, when Dufour went pale at the mention of weapons. "We saw no indication that they were carrying anything that might be used offensively."

"With luck, we'll be back with some Protectorate presence in a couple of days' time," Hirin said. "If we could leave sooner, we would, but our engineer needs the time to make sure we're in the best shape possible to attempt the skip."

"That makes sense," Dufour said, but it seemed automatic. His mind was clearly racing as he decided what steps to take. "But without luck, we're on our own."

"We could delay our attempt at the wormhole," I offered. "Stay here another few days to see if anything turns up."

Dufour appeared to consider, then shook his head. "Thank you for offering, but no. I don't think you could do much that we can't. Getting through the wormhole and bringing back more help is what we need from you."

I nodded. "Then that's what we'll do. If there's anything you need before we leave, don't hesitate to ask."

Still distracted, Dufour said, "Thank you for letting me know. I'll be in touch." And then he ended the link.

Hirin stroked his chin, considering. "Well, that didn't go too badly. He was rattled, but he'll do all right. There's a reason he's the *de facto* leader of the Council."

"It wouldn't have made any difference if I'd told him sooner," I said. "I hope we're right, and they're in no danger."

"I doubt they are. Despite what Dufour thinks, the drones' actions have been almost entirely non-aggressive." He held up a hand to forestall me. "I know, I know, that scan made people sick. But if they'd *wanted* to do the colonists harm, it was a sorely ineffectual method, you have to agree."

"That's true."

Hirin stood, saluting me with his mug. "I'm taking the rest of this and going to check in with Rei. I might have a few tips for her on piloting that wormhole tomorrow if things get touchy."

"Do you think they will?"

"No." He planted a kiss on the top of my head in passing. "But you can never be too rich or too prepared, right?"

"That's not how that saying goes," I called after him, but he only chuckled and turned toward the bridge.

I STILL HAD one more thing to do tonight—talk to Juliska Barath about keeping *Amber's Ranger* aboard. After Hirin went to talk to Rei, I went through the colony's communications hub again and they connected me to her. She appeared on screen with a smile that belied her bleak mood when I'd left her house earlier. "How can I help you, Captain?"

"I have a request, courtesy of my engineer," I said. "I had assumed we'd unload *Amber's Ranger* before we left the planet tomorrow, but he'd like more time to study the skip drive on our way back to the wormhole, see if there's anything it can tell him that will improve our own interaction with it."

Her smile faltered, but she quickly reassembled it. "I hadn't thought of that. In fact, I was thinking that I should have asked you about the ship when you were here. Still, if he thinks it could make a difference . . ."

I could tell this was hard for her—she'd told me when we first met that the ship was important to the colony. But I had another reason to keep it on board—to underscore my belief that Amber Malka still had a chance of piloting the ship home herself. If I left it here, it might look like I didn't have faith in that belief.

"He does, and we want every advantage we can get. And remember what I said—I have to take it back to Nearspace so Amber can fly it home herself."

She chuckled. "You did say that. But you promise you'll make sure it gets back here, one way or the other?"

That seemed like a hefty promise in light of all the unknowns, but what else could I say? "I promise," I assured her, and we broke the connection.

It turned out to be a promise I kept, although not in the way I envisioned it then.

CHAPTER ELEVEN

If at First You Don't Succeed

WE TOOK OUR leave of the planet Ryphen the next morning. Yuskeya and Dr. Lee had spent long hours analysing the blood samples from the colonists, attempting to isolate the virus for study. It was work that might take a long time to bring to any satisfactory conclusion, but Yuskeya thought she could give the doctor something to work with before we left. He'd long ago exhausted the investigations he could do with his own outdated equipment, and now the grumpy physician was positively beaming when he left the *Tane Ikai* with an armload of new gadgets.

"I hope we could spare that," I told Yuskeya dryly as we stood outside the front airlock and watched the doctor leave with a wave and an actual smile.

"The Protectorate will replace the equipment," she assured me. "And I didn't leave us short, don't worry. It seems like the least we can do. He's obviously struggled with this question for so long—and it's important for the colony. Once the Protectorate is here, we'll be able to help them even more."

I sighed. "I hope that works out the way we want it to."

"It will," Yuskeya said with more confidence than I felt. "It doesn't matter that this was a PrimeCorp venture . . . the people are Nearspace citizens, or at least the original colonists and crew were. I guess the succeeding generations might be a different story . . ." She paused, considering the implications. "If they officially join Nearspace they will be . . . but that's not for us to sort out. In any case, the Nearspace Authority has a duty to help the colony now. They've inherited all the other messes PrimeCorp left behind."

"They might regret not thinking about how much mess that would entail," I said. "PrimeCorp had to go, but it sure left a lot of difficult pieces for someone else to pick up."

Yuskeya was quiet, then said, "The Ryphens are going to have to find out about PrimeCorp at some point."

"I told Juliska Barath. I'm a little surprised no-one asked us directly about the corporation, but they probably assume it's ticking along like a well-tuned drive."

"Is she going to tell the others? They'll have to know—even so they understand they can't sue the corporation for injecting them with bioscavengers without their knowledge."

"I left it up to her to tell the Council at her discretion. But I expect she'll do it soon. Best if they're in the loop by the time the Protectorate arrives. I think she understands that."

Yuskeya glanced at me. "Captain, were you avoiding telling the Council yourself?"

I lifted my chin. "That's between me and my conscience, Commander Blue," I said, and we both laughed.

My ID implant chirped and I answered. "What's up?"

"We're ready to go when you are, Captain," Viss said.

Juliska Barath emerged from the edge of the forest, coming toward the *Tane Ikai*. She looked younger out of her captain's uniform, and today she wore a long-sleeved, kimono-style dress scattered with tiny pink blossoms, as if it were a special occasion. When she caught sight of us, she waved.

"A few more minutes, Viss, and we'll be ready. Tell the rest of the crew, would you?"

"Aye, Captain."

Juliska crossed to us and shook my hand. "Just wanted to see you off. Good luck, Luta, and don't forget Amber's journals."

I patted a pocket. "They're safe, no worries."

"Journals?" Yuskeya asked.

"Amber Malka kept a chronicle of the colony," I told her. "Juliska wants us to deliver it to the Nearspace Authority when we get back."

Yuskeya nodded, but said, "You'll have opportunities to tell the Protectorate—and the rest of Nearspace—your story, once we get the wormhole working properly."

Over the previous night's dinner, we'd discussed the possibility of the Corvids creating a more stable artificial wormhole between Eta Cassiopeia and the Ryphen system. But we'd agreed not to mention it to the colonists yet. I didn't want to get their hopes up, and they didn't even know yet about the Corvid aliens or their proficiency with wormhole technology. They'd need time to digest all the changes that had occurred in Nearspace since they'd left.

Juliska looked past us to the waiting ship. "I know that's the plan, but—well, this seems like a bit of insurance. We don't know how quickly whatever's coming towards us will arrive, or when the Protectorate ships will be able to make it through to us." She smiled briefly, although it didn't reach her eyes. "Now that we've been rediscovered, it would be nice to know we won't be forgotten," she said.

I put an arm impulsively around her shoulders. "You won't be, don't worry."

She nodded, seeming satisfied. "All right, then. Safe travels, Captain. I hope we'll meet again soon."

"Hey, we could be running cargo to you in a few weeks' time," I reminded her with a smile. "You have a lot of catching up to do."

"And if you talk to Amber, tell her—" she broke off, and I knew she was still struggling in the tug of war between hope and the fear of disappointment.

I touched her arm. "I know what to tell her."

Juliska Barath smiled and nodded, then started off after the doctor. We stood and watched her disappear back along the forest path, and then I said to Yuskeya, "All right, Navigator. Let's find our way back to that wormhole and get through it."

I WAS SURPRISED at the relief I felt as we lifted away from the planet and the colony dwindled below us. I knew, intellectually, that the virus shouldn't pose a threat to anyone on my ship, but it was a possibility I couldn't shake while we were on the surface. We simply didn't understand enough about the virus yet.

"Running the burst drive at maximum, we're about eighteen

hours out from the wormhole," Yuskeya said.

"I make it eighteen hours and thirty-seven minutes," Pika noted.

Yuskeya rolled her eyes but said nothing.

"Incoming message from the *Lillifleur*," Baden said. "Captain Shallie Teraq on the bridge."

I nodded for Baden to put her through. "Captain Teraq, this is Captain Luta Paixon."

"I understand thanks are in order," Captain Teraq said. She was transmitting video as well as audio, and she stood on the bridge of the *Lillifleur*, a serious, diminutive woman with curling brown hair pulled back in a ponytail. "I could name a hundred things on this ship that could use attention and upgrading. It would be wonderful to have access to some of Nearspace's resources."

I smiled. "Well, don't thank me yet, but we're going to do our best. Once the rest of Nearspace knows you're here, I don't think you'll be lonely for long."

"I'm happy Amber's sacrifice was not in vain," Teraq said. "She was a brave woman."

Once again, I pushed down annoyance at the assumption that Amber was dead. "Indeed," I said briefly. "She's certainly held in high regard."

"I understand her ship is still in your cargo hold," Teraq said. I couldn't tell if there was a hint of disapproval in her voice or not.

"It is. I've cleared that with Captain Barath. We're studying it in case it can tell us anything to make our trip through the wormhole more likely to meet with success. We'll bring it back in one piece." I smiled to show I wasn't insulted by the question.

She seemed to consider that, then nodded. "Safe travels, Captain, and we hope to see you again soon."

I nodded. "Good luck, Captain. We certainly plan to return as soon as we can."

"Thank you. *Lillifleur* out."

The screen blanked as the transmission ended.

I had one thing I wanted to accomplish during the long run out to the wormhole: another chat with Karro.

I didn't intend to lecture him any further about dangers—like rogue viruses and who knew what else—on unknown planets. We'd had that discussion as soon as we'd all reconvened back on the *Take Ikai* after the Council had made the revelation about their peculiar planet-bound situation. Karro and Aliande had been concerned, and, I think, chagrined to learn that their misstep could have put them in danger, but there was little to be done about it. But the Ryphens seemed confident that the virus needed prolonged exposure in order to establish itself, and Yuskeya had been able to find nothing to contradict that belief. I had to hope they were right; we couldn't change the exposure we'd already had.

But still, Karro had done a stupid thing, and I suspected—I felt certain, in fact—that he'd done it out of sheer defiance. He thought I'd brought them to the planet on a reckless mission simply because I felt like it, so he'd go exploring an unknown planet simply because he felt like it. This wasn't the Karro I knew, but it seemed to be the Karro I had to deal with. I wanted to understand him.

So I watched for an opportune time and went to the room he and Aliande had been assigned, asking him to join me in the galley. Aliande seemed to sense that we needed a private conversation and mentioned that she'd stay where she was and do some reading.

As I pulled hot drinks from the machine for both of us, Karro said, "All right, Mom, I might as well admit that you were right. The Ryphens did need your help, so coming through the wormhole was warranted."

I turned from the counter with a mug in each hand. "One more time: I did not come through the wormhole on purpose, nor did I hope or expect that we'd be forced through."

I set his mug down in front of him more forcefully than I intended. The spicy Chai he liked came close to sloshing over the rim. I revised my earlier stance on the uselessness of remonstrations. "But you and Aliande *did* leave the ship on purpose, without telling anyone what you were doing, with no good reason that I can see except to prove that you could do it."

He flushed and sipped tentatively, his gaze on the table. "Sorry again. I was annoyed."

I waited a beat, not looking at him. "It all comes back to the nanobioscavengers, doesn't it?"

Karro sighed, pulling air deep into his chest before blowing it slowly out. "I guess so. You know Dad talks about your 'incurable compunction to be in charge'?"

I felt heat on the back of my neck and mentally cursed Hirin for coming up with that phrase, although I knew for him it was merely a gentle tease. "Oh, I'm aware of it."

"Well, I feel like the bioscavs are just another thing you'd like to control. You, and Grandmother, too."

I bit my lip, because he was right—at least in part. I wanted to ask him outright why he and Aliande were so against having them, but the last time I'd brought it up I'd gotten nothing more than a polite but firm, "It's none of your business." Not in so many words, but the message was clear. Still, I worried that one of them—or my grandchildren—would get sick or have an accident that the nanos could deal with if only they had them.

"I haven't been pressuring you."

"I know. And neither has she . . . not pressuring, exactly. But I can tell it's on your mind."

I sighed. "I'd be lying if I said it wasn't. I just . . . worry, that's all."

"And that's why you were so willing to give us a lift back home," he said. "So you could maybe exert a little pressure?"

I looked up. He watched me with a half-frown, and I met his eyes. "No. Not pressure. Ask about it, talk about it, maybe. I'd like to understand where you're coming from. I don't have you pegged as part of the anti-tech faction."

"No, we're not. It's not an ideological stance, it's a personal one. I told you that the last time we talked."

"I know. But you must realize it would be easier to accept if I knew the details."

He hesitated, and I thought he was going to explain. Then he said, "I'd have to talk it over with Aliande first. It's not my decision alone."

I held up my hands and half-smiled to let him know I wasn't angry. "Fair enough. I get it. Talk to Aliande. You'll tell me when you're ready—or never. It's up to you. I'll try to stop worrying about it. Now can we please not fight while we're investigating a century-old lost colony?"

He laughed. "You're right, we should be enjoying the adventure."

"Adventures are best enjoyed cautiously, but hopefully, this one is almost over," I said. "Although that does raise another question. If we want to bring the Protectorate back to Ryphen—accompany them and put the two sides in contact—would you and Aliande want to stay on for that? It would add another few days to your trip. If not, I'll see what we can arrange to get you to FarView Station."

He pursed his lips. "I'd have to talk to Aliande, but . . . now, I'd kind of like to see how it plays out. A couple more days, especially if we could get a message off to Joash and Klaire to let them know we're okay, just delayed, would be fine with me. I might even be able to help. I was thinking it might be possible to set up communications relays using the wormhole that would let them talk to Nearspace, even if they can't go back there."

I nodded. "I was thinking it could work like the comm relays we have with the Corvid station—in that case we relay through two wormholes and an empty system, so we should be able to handle one wormhole."

"Depending on what it is that makes this wormhole act weirdly," Karro said. "We haven't had any reply from that message we sent through when we first arrived, have we?"

I shook my head. "No, we haven't. But we can't know how long it would take to be picked up, either. Eta Cass isn't a busy system; the message could be stuck at a relay."

His face grew animated as we moved the conversation in a different direction, away from the controversial bioscavs.

"What happened to the original colony expedition, anyway?" he asked. "Did you find out?"

"Some things," I told him, and went on to relate the story as I'd heard it from the various colonists on the surface.

"So what if I get in touch with Karin Nakano about a relay when we come back?" he suggested. He held up a hand. "I won't even leave the ship if you don't want me to. I can message her over the comm system. I'll find out what kinds of equipment they have and what we might be able to send back from Nearspace to set it up. We might have to get the Corvids involved, but I'm sure they'd help."

"I know they would. Viss thinks they could even create a stable artificial wormhole to connect this system to the rest of Nearspace, if we can't figure out the weirdness with the other one."

We talked for a while longer, ensconced in the safe and

comforting space of the galley, discussing possible ways to help the Lillifleur colony connect with the rest of Nearspace. But even as we chatted, I was already going back on my promise, wondering about what my son was still holding back from me.

THE OTHER THING I did to fill some of that travel time out to the wormhole was return to the little ship in the cargo pod. I climbed down to find that Viss had had the same idea, to study the *Ranger's* skip drive again. I knew the ship fascinated him as it did me; a ship that had been at the forefront of wormhole exploration, had made numerous blind jumps into wormholes that could have led anywhere. To paradise or to certain disaster. All ships travelled great distances now, but mostly along known paths and established routes. This one had blazed and braved those trails. I traced fingertips along the hull again. As Juliska Barath had said, it was a historical artifact in its own right, pitted by countless micrometeorites and washed by the light of many stars. And still it had survived.

"It's a small ship to work on," I commented to Viss, eyeing his tall, lanky frame. I wasn't sure how much he was looking forward to crawling into the tiny area that held the skip drive.

He grinned. "Yes, but much easier when it's not floating in vacuum," he said. "I downloaded the old schematics from the Nearspace ship database." He pulled out his datapad and tapped his way through a few screens, finally settling on one. I followed him as he walked around to the rear of the runner. Reaching up, he ran his hands along a seam in the metal hull and nodded. "Wait here."

He disappeared through the rear airlock, and after a moment I heard the little ship's auxiliary systems hum to life. With a grinding pop, an access panel on the hull jerked open an inch, sending puffs of dust into the air. Viss stuck his head out the rear door. "Did it work?"

I manoeuvred the access panel until I heard a click, and it swung down and out of the way on hinged arms. The workings of the skip drive waited within. "It worked."

"No sense crawling in through that little hatch when the outside door is in a nice, warm, pressurized cargo bay. Let's have a look at this baby."

Viss peered inside the hatch, making little noises of surprise, discovery, and something that sounded like disapproval.

"What?"

"This skip drive modification was definitely a rush job," he observed. "They've barely got it secured to the base plate here."

"Well, they were feeling threatened by an unknown entity."

"No reason to be sloppy," Viss said with a disapproving snort. "If the drive had come loose, the matter emitters would have locked down as a safety precaution, and Amber Malka wouldn't have made it anywhere," he said, shaking his head. "All the more reason to do things right, when your life depends on it."

"Can you see what they did to combine the two skip drives?"

He'd stuck his head back inside to get a better look at something, engaging a light implant like the one Rei had at her temple to illuminate the inside of the access hatch better.

"Hey, when did you get that?" I asked.

He grinned. "Couple of months ago, when we had that layover on Mars. I thought it might be really noticeable, since I don't have Rei's long hair to camouflage it," he said, running a hand over the fuzz of short salt-and-pepper bristles atop his head. "But only Yuskeya seemed to notice, so I figured it wasn't as bad as I thought. Not that I'm particularly vain about things like that."

Now that I studied him, looking for it, I could see the small bulge, and the faint white line of a scar where they'd surgically implanted the device.

"Well, I guess it comes in handy when you're poking around inside dark access hatches." He'd stuck his head back inside, and then reached in with one arm.

"You have no idea." Something clicked in the depths of the recess, and he reached in with his other hand. He pulled back, and the entire drive mechanism slid toward him on a movable metal plate. "There. Now we can get a look at this thing."

I eyed it with incomprehension. "I think I'm going to leave you to this end of it, unless you need another pair of hands," I told him. "I don't think I have much to add to the conversation."

Viss answered me absently, already lost in his examination of the drive. "I'll let you know what I find."

"If there's anything that might impact our skip through this wormhole—"

"I understand, Captain."

"Do you see anything out of the ordinary?"

He gave me a sideways look. "Like a big red wire labelled LOOK AT THIS? Not at first glance."

I held up my hands. "I'm going to take a look inside. Yell if you need me."

But I knew that wasn't likely. I'd be more use sitting on the bridge helping Yuskeya watch for drones. Although if I were honest with myself, she didn't need me, either.

Oh well. I could satisfy my curiosity a bit.

DESPITE ITS AGE, the little ship was in good shape. I knew from what Juliska had told me that it had been maintained during its layover; the thick layer of dust inside bore witness to Amber Malka's less frequent forays with it in recent decades. Still, I could tell that the avionics had been periodically tested and the drives given a maintenance cycle. I powered up the main board and navigated to the detailed logs and system information in the archives; sixteen jumps into unexplored wormholes, reams of in-system and inter-system travel, and the last entries recounting Amber's explorations in the Ryphen system before the bioscav virus made extended exploratory jaunts impossible. Now I had time to pay attention to them.

I was still immersed in the logs when Baden commed me. "Wormhole in ten minutes, Captain," he said.

"I'll be there," I told him. I felt almost reluctant to leave the little ship. I wondered if Amber Malka had suffered a pang of loss when she put it into storage, thinking her days of wormhole jumping had finally come to an end. How had she felt to power it up again, knowing that even if she made this skip safely, there was every chance it would be her last?

I shook myself, knowing that dwelling too long on these things would only lead to a funk. I had too much to worry about in the here and now to let myself get caught up in Amber Malka's history.

I jumped down to the floor of the cargo bay and called to Viss. "Time to get back to the bridge."

He emerged from around the back of the runner, wiping his hands on a cloth. "Nothing much to report," he said. "I can see where they made some physical changes, swapping in parts. At first glance, it doesn't look like anything too radical—more replacements than changes. So that should mean we don't have to do anything special to make the jump back to Nearspace."

"Here's hoping," I told him.

When I arrived back on the bridge, everyone was there, even Karro and Aliande. Someone—Hirin, I guessed—had found them seats where they could observe without getting in the way. Everyone else had taken their assigned stations. Viss came in a few moments behind me. He slipped into the seat at the secondary engineering board he used when he spent time on this deck with the rest of us.

"Everything should be good to go," he said, tapping the screens.

Since Hirin had the big chair, I joined Rei, taking a seat at the secondary pilot's board.

"No sign of any more drones?" I asked.

Rei shook her head. "No, and nothing else out of the ordinary, either. Getting normal readings from the wormhole."

"I ran our scans out to long-range maximum," Yuskeya said. "No sign of whatever's heading for the planet. So they have some time yet."

"Good to know. All right, let's try approaching the wormhole terminus point as if it were any normal wormhole in Nearspace, and see what happens."

From this end, the wormhole looked perfectly usual; a darker spot against the backdrop of space, where no distant stars shone through. As we approached, Rei and Viss ran through the normal checklist of preparations for a skip, and Baden sent a tracer ping to make sure no other ship was already transiting the wormhole. I highly doubted it would find anything.

There was a problem, but not what I expected. "Tracer ping came back, but the reading is . . . weird," Baden said. "The data seems corrupted."

I turned from the pilot's board. "Send another one."

He did, but a moment later shook his head. "Same thing," he said. "All I can think is that the internal gravity of the wormhole is distorting the signal somehow. Sending back bad data."

"Do you think it's safe to go through?" I asked. "That's the purpose of the ping; if it can't tell us that, we have to decide whether to ignore it or not."

"Let me try one more," Baden said, frowning. His hands tapped out a rhythm on the comm board. A moment later he sat back from it, pulling his shoulders up and letting them drop back down. "Still not a normal reading. I don't think it's the presence of a ship inside, though. If one was in transit, it would have emerged by now."

"All right. Lock down the skimchairs and prepare for skip. Rei, Viss, do your thing. Let's get this wormhole open and get back to Nearspace. We have places to go and people to talk to."

"And a colony to protect," Hirin added. "Not something we're going to manage on our own."

"You underestimate us," Viss drawled.

"Someone's got to be the practical one around here."

The banter stopped as we approached the wormhole and Viss activated the skip drive. It would emit exotic matter and cause the wormhole to dilate wide enough for the ship to enter. The matter would keep the wormhole open while we transited it and stop it from crushing the ship to bits under the immense pressures generated inside.

We slipped inside without incident and began our drifting spin around the inner walls of the wormhole. Rainbows of colour played along the walls in bright spirals, and Rei spun our course along their twisting path. All perfectly normal.

"Huh. We're slowing down," Rei said abruptly, her fingers skidding across the pilot's board as she guided the ship.

"No loss of power to the drive," Viss said. "Everything's well within normal parameters."

"Regardless, we're still slowing down," Rei retorted, "and if we lose much more speed, I won't be able to maintain the spin."

Although Rei was trying hard to keep her voice calm, I knew what losing our spin would mean. We'd come to a halt inside the wormhole, and it wouldn't take long for the enormous pressures inside to overwhelm the effect of the exotic matter in keeping the wormhole dilated—and we'd be crushed.

"We can't get through?" I didn't want to say it out loud, but I wanted to be clear.

Rei shook her head. "I don't think we can. If we don't know why we're slowing down, we can't counter the effect."

Viss muttered under his breath and tapped a staccato rhythm on the screen of the engineering board, but nothing changed.

"Viss? What's happening?"

He swore. "Rei's right, we're still slowing. I don't know why.

There's nothing in the readouts to indicate a problem."

"Rei?"

"No change. It's like . . . something's got hold of us, pulling us back."

Outside the viewport, the rainbow swirls were melting, losing shape, thinning into angry, jagged streaks as if a mad painter had attacked her canvas in a rage.

"Then we're going to have to turn around," Hirin said in a ridiculously calm voice.

I turned to stare at him. "Turn *around*? How do you turn around inside a wormhole?"

He shrugged. "We did it in the grafted wormhole coming off the Split last year. As I recall, we were actually sliding backwards at one point."

"We didn't do that intentionally!" I protested. "The Chron ship collided with us and pushed us into a spin!"

"I know. But we did end up facing the other way, so we know it's possible," Hirin insisted. "Viss, what would we have to do to turn the ship a hundred and eighty degrees and head back the way we came?"

Viss looked up from the engineering board at that, eyes wide. "Get hit by another ship," he said flatly. "You don't just turn around inside a wormhole. The stresses would tear the ship apart."

"And yet they didn't, not when it happened to us. Come on, Viss, think outside the box!"

"*Merde*, old man," Viss muttered. "You're going to get us all killed, and you're going to make me do it."

"We're about to lose spin," Rei said, her voice rising. She wasn't panicked, but she clearly needed answers. "Viss, if you want me to do something, you'd better tell me now."

Viss swore again, then said, "Hard to starwise. I'll throw the braking thrusters on that side and full manoeuvring jets on the other. Rei, keep the skip drive at maximum output and try to steer toward the twist it's going to take when I throw the thrusters."

"But we have to get our acceleration speed up once we're turned around." I was standing, but I didn't remember getting up. "We don't have another ship pushing us in the other direction this time. How are we going to do that?"

Viss pulled a deep sigh. "Quick shot of the burst drive?"

"Use the burst drive inside a wormhole? Is that safe?"

"I think we're past worrying about 'safe.'" He flashed a rakish grin. "The Corvids didn't cover this in the user's manual."

"They never said not to, did they?" Baden asked hopefully.

"They probably thought they didn't have to," Maja said.

Pika broke in. "I estimate the chance of success at—"

"Never mind that!" Rei snapped. "Viss, say the word."

"And don't let the word be, 'dead,'" I ordered, hoping I had the power to make it so. I sat down at the console again, ready to help if I could. "Everyone, hold on."

I'VE LIVED THROUGH—stayed conscious through—some high g-forces in my time. Early acceleration before we had grav stabilizers was no picnic, and neither were the first wormhole skips I remember. For those, we had "skip gel," a thick, stabilizing concoction that cushioned us in our seats and absorbed some of the wear and tear of wormhole skips, dissipating into a gelid residue once the skip was achieved. It was messy and only halfway effective. Everyone came out of a skip with a massive headache and lingering nausea in those days. Still, we did it. And if I had to, I could do it again.

The experience of intentionally reversing a skip once begun is something I never want to repeat. When Viss hit the two thrusters to spin us around, and Rei steered us into the twist, it was bad enough. I had to grip the console in front of me with one hand, and the arm of the skimchair with the other. I don't know how Rei stayed in her seat; she needed both hands on the console through the entire manoeuvre. The moment of the turn was like the worst apex of any amusement park ride, intensified by a factor of ten; I was weightless one second and snatched back by merciless gravity the next. The flashes of colour spinning around the edges of the wormhole smudged and blurred as we slowed and turned. I heard someone gasp off to my left—Karro or Aliande, I wasn't sure which. I hoped briefly that they'd listened to me and found something to hold on to. Strangely, the level of brightness outside the main viewscreen ramped up as we turned, and I squinted against the light and the pain in my head as my brain felt like it was being squished against and through the occipital bone.

Then it snapped back inside and rattled around when Viss hit the burst drive. The light inside the wormhole dimmed, the rainbow of colour washing out to a thin palette of greys like spilled milk on a dirty floor. I wondered what kind of weird matter reaction we might be causing. Were we saving our lives at the expense of the viability of this wormhole? If we destroyed it, another one would spontaneously emerge to take its place, according to the Corvids—but it could be anywhere in the system and it could take years to find. There'd be no hope of help for the colony on Ryphen if that happened.

And no options for us to get back to Nearspace.

I dug my fingers into the arm of my chair. Too late to worry about that now.

Viss said, "Cutting the burst. We should be at normal skip speed now."

Rei said nothing—I glanced over, and her face was pale beneath the dark swirls of her *pridattii*, but her mouth was set in concentration and her fingers white at the tips where they pressed the screen. Somehow, she swung us into the normal spin of a wormhole transit, and the pressure eased. Colours flashed along the tunnel of the wormhole, brightening and coalescing into their usual curving bands. The *Tane Ikai* traced a graceful corkscrew path and in the next moment we shot out the endpoint and back into the Ryphen system.

Rei cut the skip drive and slumped back in her chair. She ran her hands through her hair and then smoothed them down across her face. Pulling in a deep breath, she turned and looked at Viss.

"If you ever make me try anything like that again . . ."

Viss held up both hands to ward off her accusing glare. "Talk to the old man! And you told me to come up with something—"

"The main thing," Hirin said firmly, "is that we're all in one piece."

"Unfortunately, in one piece in the wrong system."

"For now," Hirin countered, the eternal optimist. "I'm sure we can figure out what went wrong."

Viss looked skeptical but said nothing. Yuskeya said, "I was taking readings the entire time. With luck, there's a clue in the data."

"It was like we were attached to the entry point on a long elastic," Rei said. "At first it was fine, but the further in we got, the elastic kept stretching and stretching until it had extended as far as it could."

"Or like there was pushback from the other end," Viss mused. "As if we came up against a force field . . . not a wall so much as a giant cushion."

"What could cause that?" I asked, rubbing a hand across my eyes. Anxiety still thudded like hammer blows in my skull.

No-one had an answer.

"Let me try sending a message through," Baden suggested.

"If the tracer ping didn't make it through, a message probably won't, either," Rei said.

"But we don't know the ping didn't get through," Baden pointed out, "only that it returned corrupted data. So it's worth sending another message to the Protectorate telling them what's happened and that now we need help. There's at least a chance someone will get it."

"Go ahead, Baden," Hirin said. "It's a good idea."

"So what do we do now?" Karro asked. It was the first thing he'd said since we'd entered the wormhole. He didn't sound angry, but almost bewildered. As if he couldn't believe what was happening. A glance showed me that he was very pale, one hand clenched tightly with Aliande's.

I fought down my fear, willing my voice steady. "Baden can send a message through, and we'll wait for a while to see if we get an answer." I didn't want Karro to think we were floundering around with no plan. Even if that's how I felt. "We'll try to figure out what's different about Amber Malka's ship or its skip drive, and why it managed to get through when we couldn't."

"And we'll have to report back to Lillifleur," Yuskeya said. "We should tell them what happened."

"Maybe we should find whoever helped Amber Malka refit the skip drive for *Amber's Ranger*," Maja said. "They might be able to help us figure out the question of why her ship made it through."

"Or why ours didn't," I added. "That's a good thought, Maja. All right. We have a plan."

"What can we do?" Karro asked. He'd stood up from his chair, and his lost look had been replaced by something with a hint of determination. Aliande stood too, still holding Karro's hand.

I thought it over. "You and Baden are the comms experts.

What if you go over the data from the corrupted tracer pings and try to figure out what happened to them. Maybe there are clues there about what makes this wormhole different. And think about anything we could do to improve our chances of getting a message through. When we get back to Ryphen, ask for more information about the scan the first drone performed on the planet. Maybe there's something there we've overlooked."

Rei's voice was tight as she said, "So, back to Ryphen then. Using the burst drive, Captain?"

I nodded. "No need to approach slowly this time. We might as well get back as quickly as we can and see if we can get help with the skip drive."

Ryphen was the last place I wanted to go now, and I felt my stomach lurch as Rei engaged the burst. Then I closed my eyes and tried not to think about how disappointed the Ryphens were going to be. Or what this might mean for all of us here on the *Tane Ikai*.

CHAPTER TWELVE
Ryphen Redux

LONG, DISCOURAGING HOURS later, we'd almost completed the trek back to Ryphen. The *Lillifleur* hailed us as soon as we were in audio range. "Captain Paixon? Didn't expect to see you back this soon. Do you need help?" Captain Shallie Teraq kept her voice light, but she must have been wondering what had gone wrong.

"Thanks, Captain, we're fine. However, our skip through the wormhole didn't go as planned. We're going to settle into an orbit around the planet, and I wonder if you'd be able to find out for us who worked on the *Amber's Ranger*, getting it ready to attempt the skip through to Nearspace? We'd like a consult with my engineer."

"I'm glad you're all right," Teraq said. "I can give you that information about Amber's ship, though. It was an engineer currently on rotation on the *Lillifleur*, Kat Oleshenko, and a civilian named Nanurjuk Etok. I know, because they worked on the *Ranger* in one of the *Lillifleur*'s maintenance bays, and they were on board for a week in shifts going over her."

"That's great," I told her. "Thanks for that information. We can speak with Etok first, since your engineer is working."

"I appreciate that," Teraq said. "Oleshenko finishes her rotation tomorrow, so maybe Etok can give you some background. I can't have my engineer delivered straight to your ship when she's off duty here since she'll have to get down to the planet for some rejuvenation, but she'll be able to talk to you through a direct uplink."

"If you'd let her know we'd like to speak with her, I'd appreciate it. We can probably arrange to meet down on the planet." We signed off, and I said, "Baden, I guess we're going to need a link to Juliska Barath, or to the Council chambers if she's not available."

"See what I can do," Baden said.

I grimaced at Hirin. "I hate delivering bad news. And I seem to be doing it all the time lately."

He half-smiled. "I can do it if you want," he said.

"Captain, Juliska Barath is sending a message request," Baden said. "I didn't even have a chance to try and get her."

Hirin raised his eyebrows at me but I shook my head. "No, I'll do it. I might as well ask her about contacting the other engineer, too."

Baden nodded for me to go ahead. "Juliska? Sorry to be back so soon."

Her face appeared on the screen, tired and worried-looking. "I take it things didn't go well."

I shook my head. "We couldn't get through. We're not sure why yet, but we have a lot of readings and data to go over, so with luck there's an answer there. We're wondering if my engineer could speak to a colonist named Nanurjuk Etok about the skip drive on the *Amber's Ranger*."

"Yes, of course," Juliska said. She looked past her screen. "Do you want to meet with Nanurjuk, or will a video link do?"

I hadn't asked Viss, but I thought it might be good if they could look over the drive together. "Maybe we'll come down to the planet again, report to the Council, and he could meet Viss on the *Tane Ikai* to look over the *Ranger*. We were planning to park in orbit, but this might be better."

She nodded. "I'm sure that would be no problem at all. I'll get in touch with him and ask him to contact you."

"Thanks. That will be perfect."

"So you couldn't get the wormhole to open?"

"No, it wasn't that." I ran a hand over my face. "We got inside, but we couldn't get out the other end."

Juliska's eyes grew wide and she frowned. "How did you get

back?"

"With great difficulty," I told her with a tight smile. "I suppose I should tell the story to the whole Council. I think we're only here in one piece because I have the best engineer, and the best pilot, in Nearspace."

"I can believe it," she said. "All right, I'll advise the Council that you're back, and get Nanurjuk to contact you."

"We'll be arriving soon," I assured her, and closed the link.

We approached Ryphen a good deal more sombre than when we'd left it. Karro and Aliande had returned to their quarters. I could tell Karro was angry again, but I didn't think it was with me. He'd been on the bridge when the wormhole spit us back out, after all. He knew as well as anyone that we'd had no choice. I felt like it was more the kind of general anger generated by fear and worry. Well, we were all fighting that. I gave a mental shrug and put those thoughts aside for now.

"Take us down to the landing coordinates, please, Rei."

"Aye, Captain," she said. "I think I'll join Viss in engineering once we're settled," she suggested, half-turning to speak to me over her shoulder. "Ryphen is a nice enough planet, but I'm not keen on spending the rest of my life here. I think we'd better put all heads together to figure out how to get us through that wormhole in one piece."

"Agreed. With luck those two who worked with Amber on her drive will have some useful input, but if not, we'll have to figure it out ourselves."

"We could do some exploratory runs in this system," Baden suggested. "There could be other wormholes the *Lillifleur* didn't have time to find."

I hated to dash his hopes. "It's possible, but Amber Malka already explored a good bit of the system. Juliska told me that, and it's in the ship's logs. No mention of any other wormholes, working or not, I'm afraid."

Baden shrugged. "Star systems are big, and we have better tech than she would have had on *Amber's Ranger*. Longer-range scans, more sensitive detectors. Could be something she missed. And we can travel farther."

I smiled. "You're right. Got caught up in my own pessimism there for a minute. We can certainly look."

As I watched the planet grow larger on the main viewscreen, though, I couldn't maintain the positive feelings. It wasn't poor Ryphen's fault—it was a welcoming enough world, marbled in its unique mix of caramels and coppers edged by blue-ink ocean. It was just that I knew we had to face the dashed hopes of the colonists and try to make a new plan. I wondered, too, if Juliska had told the Council about PrimeCorp yet, and how they'd react. There was also the looming question of what had become of those two drones, and whether Andre Dufour had told the rest of the Council about them. None of these were conversations I wanted to have.

Hirin and I went together, walking the now-familiar path to the colony. When we arrived, the Council members looked even more concerned than the last time we were here, and with good reason.

"What happened out there?" Andre Dufour asked, after we'd greeted everyone and they'd made room at the table for us. Hirin related most of the tale, and I filled in occasional details. The Council members sat still, quiet and sombre as the story unfolded. I tried to infuse some optimism by telling them about the second message we'd sent through the wormhole, hoping it would get to a Protectorate ship or relay, and Viss's plans to consult with the other engineers.

"I've just told the others about PrimeCorp," Juliska said, "and the news that they won't be sending help in any case."

Karin Nakano looked belligerent. She still wore a shirt with the PrimeCorp logo. "It's hard to believe. A corporation as powerful as PrimeCorp . . . how could they fail, even after this long?"

"As a corporation, they were very successful," Hirin said evenly. "But ethically, they didn't fare so well. In the end, their failure wasn't as mundane as going bankrupt. They failed by breaking the law . . . so many laws that despite their size and influence, the Protectorate had to move against them."

"*Merde,*" Andre Dufour said. "Could they really have been that bad? When we left Nearspace, they were at the forefront of funding exploration and innovation . . . doing good for the citizens of Nearspace."

"That's certainly what they wanted everyone to believe," I said.

"Dr. Lee and I have told everyone about the nanobioscavengers," Okwi Rousseault said.

"That's a good example. If they injected all of the original *Lillifleur* colonists with nanobioscavengers without your consent—"

"They could have been trying to protect us," Karin Nakano objected.

I shrugged. "Sure. But without your consent, it's still wrong. A great many things have come to light that indicate they did what was good for PrimeCorp—every time, even when it was not so good for others. They've even been implicated in starting the Chron War."

Norris Ellsworth looked like his eyebrows wanted to crawl up and over the top of his head. "The Chron—how is that even possible?"

I sighed wearily. "I'll have my AI download all the relevant new stories from the past eighteen months or so, and you can catch up on the revelations. You don't have to take our word for it. I only told Juliska because it's not fair to let you keep waiting for rescue or help from an entity that doesn't exist anymore. And may not have had your best interests at heart anyway. It wouldn't surprise me if PrimeCorp got some or all of the messages you or Amber Malka sent through the wormhole—and chose to ignore them."

Okwi Rousseault gasped. "Why would they do that? They funded the expedition. They wanted us to colonize under their name."

I nodded. "Exactly. But if things didn't go according to plan, they could easily have decided it was better for them to be the poor corporation who'd lost a valuable resource. If you didn't end up where they wanted you, it might have been better for them to cut their losses. That's how they operated."

Andre Dufour looked troubled, but defiant. "But you don't know any of that," he protested. "This is pure speculation."

"Yes, it is. But I've had eighty years of experience with PrimeCorp and its machinations. I've seen the dark underbelly of the corporation in many guises and more times than I even want to think about. And I will tell you, PrimeCorp was absolutely capable of acting exactly as I've described. You read the pieces I'll get Pika to send, and you'll start to understand what I mean."

There was some muttering among the council members, but finally Juliska Barath quieted them. "Whatever the reasons, PrimeCorp is not coming to help us. But honestly," she said, looking around the table, "we gave up on them a long time ago, didn't we? So, who cares if they also gave up on us? What we won't give up on is this colony, and the people we have here."

Okwi Rousseault nodded. "So what we need to talk about now is, what next? How do we help the *Tane Ikai* get back to Nearspace, and how do we deal with the drones?" She turned to us. "Thank you for telling Andre about the ones that came down to the planet. We haven't seen any sign of them, so perhaps that's the end of it." She didn't sound hopeful.

"Although that problem could have been avoided if—"

But whatever Karin Nakano was going to say was interrupted when the door to the council chamber flew open. A young woman with wide eyes stood in the doorway. "Andre," she said, "message from the *Lillifleur*. It's detected something moving beyond the colony perimeter. Coming this way."

Dufour stood, almost knocking his chair over. "The drones?

She shook her head, her shoulder-length dark hair swinging. "Not in the sky," she clarified. "On the ground. At its current speed it will reach us in about an hour. There's just one. And whatever it is, it's . . . not organic."

The display for my Retin-X implant sprang up at that moment. I wasn't surprised to see a message from Pika. I could guess without reading what she was calling me about.

SURREPTITIOUSLY, I HOPED, I opened my Retin-X display again to read Pika's message. But it wasn't only the same news the *Lillifleur* had reported. *Captain, I'm riding the Lillifleur's sensor stream, and a 'bot is approaching the colony. It looks like it's been exploring for a while. I've done some calculations and I don't think it's possible it could have come from one of the drones we encountered. There hasn't been enough time for something like this to reach the colony overland, even if it was flown partway. This must be from the first drone, the one that initially scanned the colony.*

I didn't ask Pika how she had tapped into the colony ship. I felt certain I was happier not knowing.

"I told you we should have put up perimeter defences,"

Nakano said. Her voice was pitched low and both her hands had clenched into fists.

"You're assuming this is something you need defences against," Hirin said calmly. "Jumping to conclusions is not going to help in this situation."

Karin Nakano ignored him and spoke to Dufour in a clipped, angry tone. "Andre. What are we going to do?" It wasn't so much a question as a demand.

Dufour didn't answer her directly. "Elissa, get the *Lillifleur* to route all its data on this thing to my datapad," he said to the woman who'd brought the news.

She nodded and left. The room was ominously silent as we waited for more information to arrive. I felt the tentative connection we'd built with the Ryphens crumbling in those moments and I might have wished I'd done things differently with the drones. I still didn't necessarily think we'd been wrong to let them pass, but sometimes being right isn't the most important thing in a relationship.

Hirin frowned, thinking. "I'll be interested to see how fast this thing is moving. At any rate," he continued, "we're here to help if you need us."

Nakano's face held a stubborn look, as if she wanted to berate us into admitting we'd made the wrong choice. I was almost ready to, just to keep the peace.

Andre Dufour had laid his datapad on the scratched and worn surface of the table, and the screen flickered to life. Then Captain Teraq's voice came through the speaker, tinny and faraway. "It's not moving particularly fast, Councilman, and it's not very big. But it reads as mechanical, not organic. It's not a native life form or anything we've ever seen before."

Everyone crowded around to see the screen, and I managed to get a peek at it over Norris Ellsworth's shoulder. The video didn't have great resolution, but I could make out something obviously robotic. It was difficult to gauge height from this angle, but I estimated it must be five or six feet tall. A number of articulated legs sprouted insect-like from the body or base, allowing it to walk with surprising smoothness across the rough terrain. It seemed to have an angular, dark metallic body above the legs, and appendages or arms on each side. It wasn't at all humanoid or animal-shaped. Even with the relatively poor quality, it showed as dirt-caked and streaked from rain.

"A 'bot," Hirin said in a considering voice, echoing what Pika had said to me. "Built for varying terrain. Probably an explorer, a data-collector."

The 'bot slowed then, its path having brought it near a small lake or pond. It altered course and moved to the edge of the water, extending one of its appendages into the water for perhaps thirty seconds. Then it withdrew the arm and stayed still another half minute or so before resuming its journey.

"But is it dangerous, that's what I want to know," Andre Dufour said. "And where did it come from, and what is it doing here?"

"It must have come from those drones," Karin Nakano said in an accusing tone. "The ones Captain Paixon refused to destroy."

I opened my mouth to reply but Hirin beat me to it.

"That's possible," he said. "But not probable. They only came down to the planet yesterday. This is more likely related to the initial drone you told us about—the one that scanned you. You thought it had continued on past the planet, but are you sure?"

His question was initially met with silence, and then Norris Ellsworth said, "No. We're not. That was an assumption, and I see what you're saying. This thing couldn't have walked here from the other side of Ryphen that quickly. Not if it came from the drones you encountered."

"It wouldn't have to have walked the whole way," Dufour said. "The drone could have set down anywhere. This thing could have flown."

"Possible, I suppose," Juliska said in a considering voice. "But it doesn't look like a flyer."

"True," Ellsworth said. "I don't think we can blame Captain Paixon and her crew for very much here."

"Do you think it has weapons?" Okwi Rousseault asked. It wasn't clear who she was addressing, but when no-one else answered, Hirin did.

"Admittedly, I haven't seen this particular type of 'bot before," he said, "and it may have some defence capability. The design suggests it's not an attack machine. Those legs are great for covering rough ground, but it's not the robust design or blocky profile one would expect from an armoured machine. It *could* have weaponry built into those arms, but I'd be very surprised."

Andre Dufour sat back down, and the rest of the council members did the same, some of them reluctant to leave the screen where the 'bot still picked its way toward the colony. "So if this thing came from one of the drones, there could be as many as three on the planet now."

Hirin nodded. "Or more, if you missed any, or if they took a wide, circuitous route and approached the planet from your blind side."

Dufour looked startled, and Hirin held up a hand. "I doubt that's the case . . . the others have been straightforward in their approach to the planet. They didn't make any hostile moves or change their behaviour even after the *Lillifleur* had eliminated some, did they?"

Reluctantly, Karin Nakano shook her head. She seemed unwilling to let go of her anger, but it was difficult to maintain in the face of Hirin's calm and reasonable manner. "No. They just came on the same as the others had."

Okwi Rousseault said, "In your considered opinion, how should we deal with it?" She was looking directly at Hirin this time.

He tilted his head to one side, considering. "I'm no expert in first contact," he said. "But what you need most of all is more information about the drones and where they're coming from. You'll likely learn more from this thing by observation than by attack. You might even be able to communicate with it, if it's programmed for interaction. It might have some of the answers you're looking for."

"You think we should try to talk to it?" Nakano said, her eyes wide with disbelief. "It's a machine! And we don't even know what language it would use."

"Well," Hirin said with a half-smile, "I guess that's the first challenge, isn't it? But you might be in luck. There's someone on the *Tane Ikai* who might be able to help."

CHAPTER THIRTEEN
An Unexpected Visitor

I INVITED THE Council to the *Tane Ikai*, ostensibly to save time instead of waiting for Karro to come to us. It also kept him safe on the ship and not exposed to the Ryphen virus, but I didn't mention that to anyone else. Andre Dufour brought his tablet.

So now we all sat around the big table in the galley, while Karro raised his hands in the air and said, "Whoa, wait a second. I'm a communications guy, but I'm not an *interspecies* communications guy!"

"We honestly don't know what kind of communications we'll be talking about," Hirin said. "And a lot will depend on the 'bot's programming. I'm thinking it will be more about interfacing than actual communication. Initially, at least."

"Some of us—the Landers," Okwi Rousseault said, "did have first contact training before we left Nearspace. It's a long time ago, but maybe we haven't forgotten everything."

"Really? Why was that?" Yuskeya wondered aloud. "You were supposed to go to Xaqual, right? An isolated system with only one wormhole as far as anyone knew at that time."

Andre Dufour shrugged. "They told us it was in case another wormhole was out there but undiscovered, and something or someone came through. It seemed like a reasonable possibility at the time. It's not like a star system has a wall around it."

"It does make sense," Yuskeya said. "And that proved true—

there's a wormhole to Tau Ceti from Eta Cass. But it wasn't known at the time. This could also be another indicator that PrimeCorp had its own expectations or plans for you."

"But that's neither here nor there," Norris Ellsworth said. "What's important now is this thing headed for Lillifleur. What are we going to do about it?"

"Look, Karro," Hirin said, "I just thought you'd be the most likely to be able to figure out *how* to communicate with this 'bot if it turns out to be a problem. For all we know, the drones could have already deciphered Esper from the scans they took of this planet."

Okwi Rousseault sat back in her chair. "I hadn't thought of that. You think it's possible?"

Baden said, "We were able to pick up chatter from the planet once we got close enough. Not that we were eavesdropping," he lied with an engaging smile. "It's entirely possible they could have been listening long before they were close enough to scan you."

Andre Dufour hitched in a deep sigh and ran a hand over the short stubble of his hair. "I think we've had too many years of complacent isolation here on Ryphen," he said. "It never even occurred to us that someone might be listening to us or interested in us at all. Once PrimeCorp and Nearspace abandoned us—" he held up a hand as if to forestall a protest, "not necessarily deliberately, I get that—I think we turned inward too much. I'm glad you're here to help us think through this."

"All right," I said. "How about this? We send out a groundcar to meet the 'bot. Some of you, some of us. We'll approach carefully, and see what happens, keeping a communications channel open to the base here."

"An armed contingent?" Norris Ellsworth asked. "We don't know what this thing's intentions are. Whoever goes out there has to be able to defend themselves."

"Agreed. We'll go armed and careful, but not aggressive. If the 'bot seems willing to communicate, we'll bring it back here, or take Karro out to—"

"Mo—Captain," Karro broke in quietly, "if I'm going to help, I should be on the groundcar that goes out to meet it."

I bit my lip. He should; that made sense. And if I protested, he'd accuse me of trying to manipulate things again. Whatever dangers the 'bot might present, Karro had the best chance of communicating with it. "Sure, of course. I just wasn't thinking. The groundcar has room, so we can take three of our crew and you can take three Council members."

I caught Hirin's eye with a look that I hoped said, *we'll discuss who goes when we're alone.*

I guess he got the message, because he merely said, "Well, folks, what do you think?"

The Council members looked around at each other. Norris Ellsworth said, "That's more than we have any right to expect from you, but I'm ready to say thank you and it sounds like a workable plan."

Andre Dufour nodded. "We have about half an hour, probably not much more, so we won't meet it much outside the community. But if you'll give us a few moments alone, we'll decide who'll go with you."

"Absolutely," I said. "We'll adjourn to the bridge to set up our own team, then get the groundcar out. We'll meet outside in ten minutes?"

Juliska said, "I'm due aboard the *Lillifleur*, so I can't be part of the welcoming party. But we'll monitor closely from orbit."

Dufour nodded. "We'll make a quick decision, Captain Paixon, thank you."

Hirin, Baden, Karro, Yuskeya, and I left them in the galley, still white-faced and tense. As we followed the corridor to the bridge, I murmured to Hirin, "I'm thinking Karro, Viss, and myself on the groundcar."

Hirin said with a chuckle, "I was thinking the same thing— Karro, Viss, and me."

I blew out a sigh. "Dammit, who's technically got the chair right now?"

His blue-grey eyes twinkled as he said, "Well, technically, it's Rei, right? We left her in charge when we went to meet the Council."

"I'm not letting her decide. She'll side with you, old man."

He caught my hand as we walked. "I'll stay here if you take something heavy-duty from the weapons locker, and wear a protective suit," he said. He bent to whisper close to my ear. "I know you want to be there if Karro goes. Just understand the risks and do what you can to minimize them."

I squeezed his hand. "Deal."

When we reached the bridge, Hirin said, "Rei, you're relieved, thanks very much."

She swivelled to look at us. "What's up? This many serious faces at one time is never a good thing."

I pressed the comm to call Viss. "Viss, can you get the groundcar prepped and outside and be ready to climb aboard it in ten minutes?"

There was the slightest of pauses before he said, "Aye, Captain. Anything special needed?"

"Grab your favourite toy from the weapons locker on your way to the cargo hold," I told him. "We'll meet you there with excursion suits."

"*Merde*. Got it, Captain."

Karro stuck his hands in his pockets and rocked back on his heels. "I'm not particularly comfortable or competent with a weapon."

"That's all right, Viss and I will have them," I told him. "Anything you need to bring to potentially interact with this thing?"

He laughed humourlessly. "A communications specialist? A xenobiologist? A robotics expert?"

"Will you settle for your datapad, Pika, and an excursion suit?" I counter-offered. "Pika, we want you with us, too."

"Excellent," the AI said. "It's ages since I had a breath of fresh air."

"Not that you actually breathe, but I guess we won't split hairs," Baden said. "Download yourself, Pika." He set a datapad atop his console and executed a sequence of taps on the screen. We kept a mostly-empty datapad with lots of available storage space for just this purpose—when we wanted Pika with us. She preferred to roam the wide-open spaces of the ship's main computer system, but she could snug herself into a datapad for portability if the need arose. She always backed herself up first and left the copy in the main storage.

A luxury we mere humans didn't have yet.

Yuskeya emerged from First Aid carrying six planetary excursion suits from the storage room. They were another thing we didn't use very often—we rarely visited unexplored planets or areas of planets anymore, not like in the early, wild days of Nearspace expansion. Every decent ship carried them, though, because space was big and potentially very, very dangerous, and the suit technology had continued to improve. The suits were a lightweight bioweave polymer, practically impossible to puncture and capable of absorbing impact energy and spreading it out across the suit and even into whatever surface the wearer stood upon. They were shapeless and a dull blue colour, their unremarkable appearance belying their capabilities.

"Three for you and three for the colonists," Yuskeya said. "Maja's coming with the helmets."

Maja emerged from First Aid then, balancing six ultraplas helmets. They were transparent and light, and transmitted sound almost as clearly as if they weren't there at all, so no complicated comm system was necessary for excursion colleagues.

"The Council members are getting more than they bargained for," she said with a smile.

"Well, don't forget, most of these people came here as colonists," I mused. "They were prepared to leave most of what they knew in Nearspace and carve out living space on a new, empty world. They might be a hundred plus years old, but I think they're tough as this ultraplas." I knocked on the face of one of the helmets with my knuckles.

I nodded to Karro. "So let's go see what they're facing now."

WHEN WE GATHERED around the groundcar in Cargo Pod Two, I wasn't entirely surprised to see Andre Dufour waiting to climb in. I also wasn't surprised that Karin Nakano wasn't there—I had begun to think of her as a bit of a hothead, and I expected Dufour and others would have vetoed her inclusion in this meeting despite her expertise in communications. The other two were Okwi Rousseault—I remembered that she'd been introduced as a xenobiologist—and a Council member whose name was not on the original *Lillifleur* roster as either crew or colonist, named Cosima Miklaus. She looked to be in her thirties, with cornsilk hair pulled back into a loose knot at the nape of her neck.

"Robotics," she said briefly as she shook my hand, and I shot an encouraging look at Karro. He was close to having his wish list of elements for this mission assembled, purely by chance.

The Ryphens climbed into their excursion suits with surprising alacrity and donned the helmets. Baden, Maja, and Aliande had accompanied us down to the cargo pod, and Baden handed Karro the datapad containing Pika. "Just so you know, she'll usually do what you ask, but not what you demand," Baden told him, quirking a half-smile.

"That was my impression," Karro said with a grin, "just from being aboard for a few days."

"I can hear you," Pika reminded them from the datapad, her voice sounding much smaller than it did through the ship's comm system. No less feisty, though.

Aliande moved in to give Karro a quick hug, and he rested his chin briefly on top of her head. He whispered something and she smiled, then stepped back and nodded.

With Viss in the driver's seat, the rest of us took seats in the groundcar. I let Karro take the seat beside Viss and I climbed in behind them. The Ryphens moved into the seats further back. They were conspicuously quiet, maybe a bit overwhelmed at how quickly things were happening.

"I've used the planetary data in the computer and the video the *Lillifleur* is sending to plot our optimal course to intercept the 'bot," Pika said, flashing a map grid on the datapad's screen.

"Of course you have," Viss muttered. He glanced at the datapad on Karro's lap, then switched the groundcar's electric engine on and eased it out of the cargo pod.

I heard Baden call, "Have fun meeting the 'bot!" and glanced back to see Maja throw him an exasperated look. She looked back and waved at me, smiling encouragement. Even at this distance the worry on her face was evident, despite the smile. I waved back, and then Viss turned the groundcar onto the well-worn path and they were out of view.

In the time that we'd experienced it, the Lillifleur colony had enjoyed good weather—comfortable temperatures and only small amounts of rain overnight. I knew from the planetary data we'd now gathered that the colony was firmly in a climate zone somewhere between temperate and Mediterranean on Earth, with warm summers and moderately cool winters. Although the afternoon was growing long, the sun still shone, warming the breeze that rippled the masses of tiny green and white leaves atop the baobab-like trees. It gave the impression of hundreds of butterflies flapping their wings in unison. For now, we followed the path we'd initially walked from the landing zone to the colony, past the trees and masses of low bushes with blue and purple leaves. The wind ruffled the pale green wild grasses like wheat fields on Earth, and I wondered what kind of terrain lay between us and the approaching 'bot.

"Pika, any notable obstacles on that course you've laid out to bring us to the 'bot?" I asked.

"Nothing much, Captain," she answered. "There's a farm road once we pass the outer limits of the colony proper, and then past the end of that it's underbrush and low growth. I mean, if the 'bot can navigate it, we can, right?"

Cosima Miklaus said deferentially, "I would suggest that there is a considerable mobility difference between this 'bot's articulated legs and the wheels of this groundcar. It seems particularly designed for travel over various terrain challenges. However, I agree with the AI that we should be able to travel there without incident."

I held my breath, waiting for a testy response from Pika, but for once she didn't take offence. Maybe since Miklaus had ultimately agreed with her, she was inclined to let it go.

The drive to the settlement passed much more quickly than when we walked. The groundcar couldn't navigate the wide petrified wood steps, but the slope they ran down was reasonably smooth and free of vegetation except for the grasses, so we jounced down it. Ryphens turned to stare at our approach and passage, but Dufour was quick to catch their attention from his seat near the back and smile, wave, and generally offer the message *don't worry, this is all fine*. It wasn't entirely fine, since we were heading out to meet the unknown, but people seemed to accept his message even while wondering at the sight of the strange vehicle on their narrow streets.

We followed close to the perimeter of the settlement and then veered onto the farm road Pika had mentioned. Although the colonists grew much of their food in the greenhouses we'd seen on our visits and several others nearer the outskirts of Lillifleur, they still needed larger tracts of land for producing grains and hardy staple vegetables, and for grazing animals. As we passed row upon row of plants, kicking up a plume of dust behind us, I was struck again by the resilience of the colonists and how they'd created a viable living space in a place they'd never expected to land. I felt very protective of them in that moment, and had to quell a flash of anger at these 'bots and drones that now threatened a peaceful and happy existence despite its challenges. And an even deeper rage at whoever was sending those drones.

Stop it, I chided myself. *You don't know enough yet.*

But the plasma rifle across my lap felt heavy with potential.

The farm road petered out in a jumble of stones and yellow scrub, and Viss slowed the groundcar to accommodate the change in terrain. We bounced around a little more as we continued our progress. Soon after, Andre Dufour said, "I can see us on the screen now with the 'bot. We should be able to spot it soon."

"Confirmed," Pika said. "At our current rate of speed we should encounter the 'bot in three minutes."

And in just about that long we could see it. The scrub here was low and the terrain mainly flat, and the 'bot stood out because of its height. It continued to move toward the colony, with a remarkably smooth gait thanks to those spidery legs.

I knew the moment it noticed us, because it stopped moving.

"The 'bot is scanning us," Viss said after a glance at the groundcar controls. He slowed the vehicle to a crawl.

"I was afraid of that," Andre Dufour said, and I heard Okwi Rousseault, directly behind me, gasp.

I turned in my seat. Behind Okwi, Cosima Miklaus had a datapad aimed at the 'bot, apparently capturing images of it. She didn't seem to be worried about a scan. "Your excursion suits will protect you," I told them. "They're built to keep out all kinds of intrusions. You'll register as a living thing, but the scan shouldn't affect you the way the first drone's did."

Okwi took a few calming breaths and nodded, visibly settling herself. She gave me a half-smile. "I was trained to be cool when encountering alien life forms," she said. "I guess I'm a little out of practice."

"It'll all come back to you," I assured her with a wink. "Some things you never forget."

She nodded. "I'm sorry I'm not better qualified, though. I don't think what we really need here is a xenobiologist. If that thing is anything we could call 'alive', it's a synthetic kind of life, outside my expertise."

I shrugged. "But whatever sent it is probably 'alive,' so we have to consider that. Anyway, you're what we have, and you'll do your best. Can't ask more than that."

"All right. Putting myself back into 'scientist mode,'" she said, and smiled.

"Everyone all right back there?" Viss called, and the replies from the Ryphens came hesitantly, but in the affirmative. "Scan seems mainly designed to do a basic appraisal. Captain, I'm inclined to keep moving forward slowly, give the thing time to assess us."

"Sounds good." My hands felt slippery on the weapon on my lap, and I surreptitiously wiped them on my excursion suit, but since it wasn't designed to be absorbent it didn't help. "But everyone keep your eyes on it and sing out if you see anything you think is weird."

"I think the whole thing is weird, does that count?" Karro said in a tight voice. He was trying for lighthearted but didn't quite make it. He'd been unusually quiet as we drove here, and I thought he was probably wondering how he'd managed, after a lifetime of relative normalcy, to be suddenly one of the prime players in a first contact with the representative of an alien species. He had his own datapad and Pika's resting side-by-side on his lap.

"All in a day's work for the crew of your mother's ship," Viss rumbled, and threw Karro a wink.

As we drew closer, the finer details of the 'bot came into focus. The appendages on either side flared at the ends, and the tips of some sort of tool or device were just visible. Although it wasn't anything like humanoid-shaped, the array of sensors and lights near the top of the "body" looked almost like a face. It remained still.

"First impression is that it's not primarily aggressive or combat-focused," Cosima Miklaus said thoughtfully. "Too spindly, too many potential weak points."

"Scan is finished," Viss said.

We inched toward it, eliciting no obvious reaction, and stopped about fifteen feet away. After a moment's silence in which exactly nothing happened, Karro said, "Well, Captain? What next?"

I rubbed the back of my neck, feeling the tension gathered there like a knot. "Well, I'd say we initiate communications. Karro, got any ideas?"

He tilted his head, considering. "We could try a basic databurst," he said. "It's somewhere to start."

Pika said, "I can do that. What do you want to say?"

I turned to Andre Dufour and the others. "Well? What's your opening message to this visitor?"

They looked at each other, and then Okwi Rousseault said, "Since it may already know our language, why don't we greet it, tell it who we are and the name of the planet, and ask what it wants?"

I nodded. "Sounds good to me. Pika, can you send that in Esper, and maybe all the other Nearspace languages, too? Lobor, Vilisian, Corvid, Relidae . . . who knows what it might have encountered in the past?"

"Affirmative, Captain." Pika could be very businesslike when she wasn't busy being annoying. After a surprisingly short interval she said, "Sent."

Almost immediately, a cascade of glowing blue symbols flowed across a portion of the 'bot's surface that hadn't even looked like a screen from where we sat. They moved too quickly to parse, but the symbols weren't familiar to me. A second later, Pika's screen lit up with the same rush of information.

"It sent a databurst back," she said, "but there's no match with anything in my databases."

"All right, then we've established that we don't speak the same language," Karro said, leaning forward a little in his seat as if trying to get a better look at the 'bot. "But it also *attempted* to communicate back, so I'd take that as a good sign, wouldn't you?"

"I'd say so," Viss said. "Better than extending a weapon out the end of one of those arms and blasting us."

"Did you think that was likely?" Cosima Miklaus asked with a nervous laugh.

"Not really," Viss answered. "But it was never outside the realm of possibility. Still isn't."

Karro had turned his attention to his datapad, fingers flying across the screen. "I think we have to start with the basics, try to get a communication going even just starting with binaries, mathematical operations, maybe Fredkin gates . . ." he trailed off, concentrating on his screen.

"I have some ideas," Pika said. "Here, look—" Symbols flashed across the screen of Pika's datapad. I wasn't sure how Karro could keep track of what he was doing and what she was showing him at the same time, but they seemed to manage.

"I'm for getting out and having a closer look," Viss said. "Anyone with me?"

"We shouldn't all go," I said. "And anyone getting out, I don't think we want any weapons in evidence. Could be taken the wrong way."

"I'll go," Cosima Miklaus and Okwi Rousseault said at the same time.

Dufour said, "What if you both go. I'll stay in the groundcar with Captain Paixon and her son. You both have specialized skills here. I'm just muscle," he added with a grin.

The two women stood and climbed past me to the side door. Okwi was first, and waited with her hand on the latch. Her cheeks carried a high flush and her eyes were bright, but the hand on the door was steady.

"Slowly," Viss cautioned. "Let me get out first, then you two follow."

"Hang on," Karro said. "Let me send another databurst. Even if it doesn't understand it yet, it will be on the record for later."

"So it can figure out how it shouldn't have attacked us?" Viss muttered, but I thought he was only joking. I glanced at Okwi and she gave me a tentative smile.

"He's an ass sometimes," I told her. "Don't mind him."

"You're going to be so sorry you said that if this thing kills me," Viss said, but before I could answer him, he'd opened the door of the groundcar and stepped out. The weather continued to be pleasant, and the temperature seemed hotter out here in the open ground. Warm air wafted in through the groundcar's door, carrying scents of vegetation and the dust we'd roiled up with our passage.

"I'll try to look after him, but no promises," Okwi said with a smile, and pushed her door open as well.

"Good luck," I told her, and settled the plasma rifle more comfortably on my lap. I hoped I wouldn't need it.

I glanced up at the 'bot, but it hadn't moved. More symbols flowed over its screen, the blue sigils now interspersed with unfamiliar characters in green, yellow, and orange. Karro had his head down, immersed in the screens of the two datapads. I wondered briefly if it was a good idea to overwhelm the 'bot with input—the data Karro was sending it and Viss and the two women making an approach outside—but then I thought of Pika and her progenitor, Pita, and how many things they could do at one time. You had to resist the tendency to put human limitations on AIs.

Outside the groundcar, Okwi and Cosima had moved around behind it to come and stand beside Viss. The 'bot, if it had noticed them, made no acknowledgement. Viss took a step forward and held up a hand to wave slowly in its direction. Two small indentations near the top of the 'bot appeared to hold camera receptors—the sunlight flashed off them when it hit at the right angle. They shifted, tracking Viss's movements as he quickly ran through the repertoire of other gestural greetings common around Nearspace. After a moment, the 'bot responded. It raised the appendage on its right side to mimic Viss's wave, extending what looked like a small pincer from the end to represent, I supposed, Viss's hand. Following the wave, it also repeated, without faltering, the other gestures Viss had made.

"Did you see that?" Andre Dufour said excitedly behind me. He'd moved up to take Okwi's vacated seat behind me. "It's trying to communicate!"

I wasn't ready to declare all-clear yet. "That looks hopeful," I agreed. "It might not understand what any of that means, but it's trying to establish a baseline."

"Here, too," Karro said. "We're not anywhere close to understanding each other yet, but there's a constant flow of data back and forth while we look for a commonality to start with." He glanced up at me and raised his eyebrows. "At least, that's what Pika and I are doing. I assume it's something similar on the 'bot's side."

Movement outside the groundcar caught my attention, and I looked past Karro to see Viss walk straight up to the 'bot. I heard other sharply indrawn breaths inside the groundcar echo my own.

"Not what I'd call taking it slow," I told Viss over the groundcar's comm channel. The 'bot looked strangely small now, next to Viss's broad, six-foot frame. Its legs spread wide, probably five feet from side to side, but the "torso" was only about two feet wide and it stood only as high as Viss's shoulder. It looked a lot less intimidating. Bolstered by the fact that it hadn't *done* anything intimidating.

Okwi moved more cautiously, but she joined Viss in front of the 'bot. I didn't like the way they blocked my view of the thing, but I wasn't comfortable putting more of us outside yet. Cosima was moving slowly around the 'bot, recording its movements and the interactions. I saw Okwi tentatively hold out a hand toward the 'bot, palm up. I almost told her to stop but bit my tongue. The colonist had more training than I did in making first contact, no matter how out of date it was. I had to learn to ease back on the reins a little.

Then with a chattering series of sounds I heard through the groundcar's windows, the 'bot retracted the pincer, extended another tool, and placed it on Okwi Rousseault's outstretched hand.

CHAPTER FOURTEEN
Machine Language

I SAW OKWI ROUSSEAULT stiffen and twitch as the 'bot touched her, and I had the plasma rifle halfway raised before I even realized I'd moved. But then she relaxed and turned her head to look at Viss, who nodded. She let the tool rest in her hand for the space of a few heartbeats, and then placed her other hand on top of it. After a moment, she withdrew both hands and the 'bot retracted its arm as well.

"Do you think I can get out now, too?" Andre Dufour asked eagerly. "I have to admit, I want to get a close-up look at this thing."

"I think, if you're cautious, it should be all right," I said. "We don't want to overwhelm it with too many people doing too much when there's only one of it." There had been every opportunity now for hostile action, and the 'bot hadn't taken any, so I felt like the possibility grew more remote with every minute. Still, a conservative approach would be best.

"Agreed. I'll take my cues from Engineer Feron." And he too, clambered past me and slipped out the side door, leaving it open to the warm air.

"This is going to take a while," Karro said, not looking up from his screens. I wasn't even sure he was aware of what was happening outside the groundcar.

"A while, like how long?"

"Hours," he said briefly. "Maybe overnight or a couple of days."

"I'll learn its language faster than that," Pika said with confidence. "Overnight at the most."

"You're not programmed for alien language acquisition and translation, are you, Pika?" I asked.

She made a sound surprisingly like a human snort.

Karro shook his head absently but didn't say anything else. Pika certainly retained all of Pita's cockiness. Granted, Pita *had* allowed me to communicate with the Relidae Chron—but she'd also had access to a Chron dictionary, albeit an outdated one.

"Okay." I leaned to one side to see the 'bot's "face" between Viss and Okwi. Symbols continued to flicker on the screen. "Well, I don't imagine we all want to sit out here that long." Over the groundcar's outside speaker, I said, "Councilman Dufour, do you have any objection to seeing if it will follow us back to Lillifleur?"

He turned from peering at the 'bot and said, "That seems a little premature, don't you think? We still don't know—"

Pika said, "I have the results from Viss's pocket scanner. It looks like the 'bot is clean of weapons."

"How sure can we be?" I asked.

I could hear the shrug in Pika's voice as she answered. "Well, if you want to be technical, any number of those appendage tools could be used to bludgeon or cut someone."

"Acknowledged."

"And it does appear to be equipped with a laser cutter—I assume for taking samples."

"*Okej.*"

"But as far as anything like a projectile gun, energy blaster, incendiary device, missile launcher—"

"We get the idea, Pika."

"—sonic disruptor, or other offensive weapon, nothing we can detect," she finished, as if I hadn't spoken.

"So it should be reasonably safe to take back to the settlement?"

She paused before answering. "It's possible the 'bot contains programming that, if launched, could trigger a self-destruct sequence," she said. "It contains an energy storage unit—a battery—and the means to convert sunlight and possibly miscellaneous organic materials into that energy. If it self-destructed it could cause a considerable explosion."

"*Merde*," said Andre Dufour, whom I hadn't noticed walking back to my open door. "Do you think that's likely?"

"I would say, based on our current data, that the likelihood of such an event is less than 0.1% probability," Pika said with confidence. "If whoever sent the 'bot wanted to injure or kill lifeforms on this or any other planet, I can think of at least a dozen ways they could have done it before now."

"Thanks for making us all feel so much better, Pika," I said. Andre Dufour let out an audible breath of relief.

"My pleasure, Captain," she said. For an AI, Pika is extremely good at understanding sarcasm, and extremely good at pretending she doesn't recognize it when the mood hits her.

Outside, Viss had moved away from the 'bot, and Cosima Miklaus and Okwi Rousseault circled it cautiously, examining its construction without touching it. Almost as if it were showing off, the 'bot had begun extending various tools from the ends of its arms for them to see, then retracting each one in favour of another. Viss walked back and opened the door of the groundcar. He stuck his head inside.

"Seems completely non-aggressive," he said. "And like it wants to establish communication with us, even if it's only visual for now. It's still scanning us and the groundcar, but it hasn't made any attempt at a deep scan."

I felt a little guilty about the plasma rifle on my lap, so I laid it on the floor. No doubt its presence had already been noted, but the 'bot hadn't reacted badly. I turned to Andre Dufour. "Well, what do you think?"

The councilman looked indecisive. "It seems as if it's all right," he said. "My worry is that this could be a ruse, to make us trust it, and then if we take it to Lillifleur it will do something bad."

I nodded. "That's a reasonable concern. So how about a compromise? What if we go back as far as the end of the farm road, and set up a sort of base for the contact site there? It will still be outside the main settlement, but close enough that anyone with an interest can get there easily. You can set up a temporary shelter and post a guard if you like."

"We don't even know if it will follow us if we retreat back to the settlement," Viss said.

"I think it will," Karro said. For all he seemed focused on the datapads, he was obviously following the conversation, too. Almost as good at multitasking as Pika. "It's immersed in this exchange with Pika, I think. It'll probably follow to keep that going."

So after a little more discussion, it was decided. Karro, Cosima, and Viss would walk with the 'bot, keeping the databursts flowing between it and Pika, and I'd slowly drive the groundcar back to the edge of the grain field. We assumed it would follow us when we began to move. If it didn't we'd try an alternate plan.

But there was no need. When I started up the ground car and backed it slowly away, the 'bot's camera receptors focused on it, and it paused its other interactions briefly. Then as I made a careful three-point turn and began to move away, and Karro, Cosima and Viss made to follow, it engaged its arachnid legs and glided forward as well.

And just like that, we were bringing the 'bot to Lillifleur.

WHILE SOME OF the people of Lillifleur might be panicking or wary of the robot visitor, others sprang into action in response to the 'bot's arrival. They might be nervous about what it meant, but they were quick to mobilize. Our progress back was necessarily slower, since we moved at a pace to accommodate the 'bot, and by the time we drew into sight of the waving grain fields, a large tent had already been erected where the farm road petered out.

It probably dated back to the colony's first arrival on Ryphen, a sturdy construction meant to shelter precious supplies while more permanent structures were in progress. The rough bioweave might have started life in a leafy green colour but time and the elements had muted it to a mottled moss. The Ryphens had pulled back the flaps and fastened them against the breeze, and installed a pair of tables and some mismatched chairs inside. I glimpsed something that might have been a food cooler as well.

A handful of Ryphens had gathered to watch our approach, including Dr. Lee. They all wore either excursion suits—presumably borrowed from the *Tane Ikai*—or faded, dated-looking suits I assumed had been in storage somewhere on the planet. Dr. Lee gave me a look of mixed admiration and disapproval, which I didn't bother trying to decipher. I suppose he might have thought we should have kept the 'bot far out in the wilderness, but we didn't have control over its movements. Influencing them seemed the best we'd be able to do.

When the 'bot noticed the waiting Ryphens, it stopped its forward motion again. "Scanning?" I asked Viss over the groundcar's comm, and he answered in the affirmative. I watched the Ryphens for signs of any ill effects, but there were none—whatever had happened with that initial drone scan was still a mystery. Maybe this time, their suits protected them.

"It's stopped replying," Karro told me with a nervous glance in my direction.

"I expect it's busy processing all this new information," I told him. "Give it a minute."

It didn't even take that long. "It sent a new databurst," Karro said, relief evident in his voice.

"I'm too interesting to ignore for long," Pika boasted.

After perhaps an hour of doing little but stand around, it became obvious that most of us didn't need to be here any longer. I suggested to Andre Dufour that my crew and I might return to the *Tane Ikai*. "We'll leave the datapad with our AI on it. Karro, you don't need to monitor the exchanges any longer, do you?"

He looked a little torn, but tired, too. After a moment he rubbed a hand over his face. "Pika's doing all the work now," he said. "At this point it's still more of a long handshake than anything else, and I was watching out of interest. But I should get back and see Aliande, let her know I'm okay."

"We've kept in touch with the ship, but I'm sure she'll be glad to see you." I dropped my voice to a whisper. "And I'll be glad to get a cup of double caff and ditch this suit."

He smiled at me. "Honestly, me too."

Although it meant more walking, we decided to leave the groundcar so that the 'bot wouldn't try to follow it. Norris Ellsworth had come out to the site to see the 'bot for himself, and he offered us a drive back as far as the path to the landing site. He drove a little landhopper that must have been part of the colony's original equipment. It was dented and scratched, the paint faded to the colour of dirty snow, but it ran with smooth efficiency. Karro, Viss, and I clambered in gratefully.

"How'd you keep it in such good shape?" Viss asked Norris, inspecting the interior as we drove. The seats were worn and patched, but mechanically it seemed sound.

"I won't say nothing else was cannibalized to keep it running," Norris told him with a wink, "but the main thing is the climate here. Nothing too harsh, either hot or cold, and the planet's got an ozone-rich atmospheric layer to help protect us. No dust storms or salt corrosion. So stuff takes a long time to wear out or break down. Lucky for us," he added, "since the resupply missions have been non-existent."

He dropped us at the base of the petrified wood steps, and we walked the remaining short distance back to the *Tane Ikai*. It seemed impossible that it had only been a few hours since we'd left in the groundcar, and only a few before that since we'd gone to meet with the Council to talk about PrimeCorp and the drones. I was glad we'd been there and ready to help when the 'bot was sighted. All in all, though, I felt more than ready for a nap.

I wasn't destined to get it just yet.

I did get to ditch the excursion suit, and I did get a steaming mug of double caff. We were all seated in the galley, including Karro and Aliande, discussing the encounter with the 'bot and what it might mean.

"It's possible once they establish communications with the 'bot, they won't have to worry about the drones and what they mean," Karro said. "It seems like maybe they over-reacted to the drones, and they were simply on an exploration mission all along."

"It's possible," Viss agreed, but there was something in his voice that told me he wasn't entirely convinced. "I'm not sure why they would keep sending them, though. I mean, if your drones keep disappearing and you lose contact with them—assuming there is some communication back to the sender—some people would take that as a sign that maybe you shouldn't keep heading in that direction. Whoever's sending these drones didn't do that."

"Instead, they got sneaky," Yuskeya agreed. "Sent 'bots in for a closer look."

"Unless they're programmed to do that in any case," Baden said. "We don't know."

"And there's still the question of what caused the people to get sick," Maja added.

"In any case, I think we have to talk about what we're going to do next," Rei said. I glanced over at her and realized that her usual easygoing manner was absent. "I'm all for helping the

Ryphens, don't get me wrong, but we have to keep working on how we're getting back to Nearspace. I feel like we're getting distracted." Rei looked, in fact, pale and worried. The dark ink swirls of her *pridattii* tattoos stood out starkly against her skin and underscored the bluish circles under her eyes.

I realized belatedly that of everyone aboard the *Tane Ikai*, Rei was the only one without her significant other in this system. Lieutenant Gerazan Soto was currently liaising with the Relidae on Kelia Rrane. Karro and Aliande were separated from their children, but everyone else had their partner aboard for comfort and support as needed. No wonder Rei was extra concerned about getting back through the wormhole to Nearspace.

I got up from the table and went around to where she sat on the other side. I put my arms around her shoulders. "Hey. We're not going to be stuck here," I told her. "Viss is going to meet with the people who worked on *Amber's Ranger*, and we're going to figure out why the wormhole is the way it is. And before we even get that done, maybe the Protectorate will answer our messages and come barrelling through the wormhole to rescue us."

I felt her shoulders move as she pulled in a deep breath and sighed it out. She reached up and patted my hand. "I know it. I'm just getting antsy. And not being able to get through the wormhole—I guess it bothered me more than I expected."

"And then you had to sit here and do nothing all day," I said. "I get it. None of you are at your best sitting still. I know that."

The comm system pinged and Pika said, "Incoming message from the *Lillifleur* ship, Captain."

"Put it on the ship system, Pika, vid feed on my datapad." I left Rei and returned to my seat.

Captain Juliska Barath's worried face materialized on my screen. "Captain, we've detected an incoming drone. It just cleared the furthest edge of our scanner range."

The system pinged again, and Pika said, "Incoming from the colony this time. Split your screen?"

I could see my plans for a nap vaporizing as if they'd been hit with an energy weapon. "Go ahead, Pika. Captain Paixon here." Karin Nakano's face filled the other half of my screen.

"Captain, any chance you could get into the sky quick enough catch this drone, as Mr. Methyr and I discussed?" she asked. "There's some concern that perhaps it's coming in response to our contact with the 'bot, and it might not be happy about that."

I didn't think that was very likely, considering the brief length of time that had passed since the 'bot contact, but I didn't want to waste time arguing with Nakano. Instead, I shot a questioning look at Baden, who grinned sheepishly and shrugged. Well, that explained that. At some point he and Nakano had obviously talked about this possibility. In a thoroughly "hypothetical fashion," probably.

"The *Lillifleur* will be in position to intercept and destroy the drone," Juliska said. "It won't be a problem. But stay alert. Things could get dangerous up here, Captain Paixon."

"Catching this one might be better than destroying it, if we can," Nakano argued. "We don't know what, if anything, the 'bot is going to tell us, so we still need to gather all the information possible."

Baden spoke then. "Er, Captain, Viss and I have discussed how to approach a drone capture if the necessity arose—theoretically, of course—"

"Oh, yes, *theoretically*."

Baden hurried on. "We talked about the idea earlier, remember? To shut it down with the Corvid's activator drive, then grab it with the remote arms."

I sighed. I wasn't too pleased that Baden had talked to Nakano about this possibility in detail, but I hadn't told him not to. I had to consider the possible benefits of having a drone to study. I would have liked a little more notice and advance planning, but if we could manage it, going after the drone might be perfect to get Rei's mind off her worries—and the rest of the crew's minds, too, for that matter. They were a stoic bunch, but they also could be hiding fears they simply didn't want to share with me. And it could net the colonists—and us—more information.

I looked the question at Viss. He shrugged. "*Tane Ikai* can lift off anytime," he said. "The activator drive can be ready by the time we're in position."

Part of my brain insisted we were already too tired to do this, but the other part knew the Ryphens would be freaking out— about the 'bot contact, about the possibility of a scan, about who knew what. And if we could snatch the drone and study it, maybe we'd be a step closer to solving the Ryphens' problems.

Who knew, it might even tell us something about another way

out of this system.

I stood up. "Hirin and I need to discuss this, but we can do that while we get underway. Captain Barath, Officer Nakano, I'll get back to you both shortly."

When the comm channels were closed, I said, "All right, folks, let's scramble. Time to see if we can catch a drone."

THE DRONE PAID no apparent attention to us as we pulled into position behind it. It continued the route that would take it past the planet, neither increasing nor decreasing its speed.

"Drone is scanning the planet," Yuskeya reported.

"As expected," Rei said. "I hope everyone in the colony took cover."

"I'm sure they did. Viss, is the activator drive ready?"

"Ready when you are, Captain," Viss said.

I was a little nervous that the drone might interpret our action as an attack and retaliate in some way. "Hirin, be ready with the shields."

"Aye, Captain."

"Let's do this. Rei, get us into position."

The last time we'd deployed the Corvid drive as a weapon, it had been to escape a pursuing ship bent on our destruction. It had been a last-ditch attempt to save ourselves, so I would have expected this time to be much less stressful. For some reason, it wasn't. Maybe it had something to do with the five thousand colonists who were counting on us to find out something that would help them.

However, it worked as expected. That was heartening, because it meant the drone's propulsion and navigation systems were nothing too strange for the Corvid tech. The drone didn't slow perceptibly, its momentum continuing to carry it forward, but it faltered in its course and began to drift and roll starwise.

"Scan terminated," Yuskeya said. "Drone systems are reading inert."

"Match speed," I directed. "Hirin, raise the shields. Viss, are you ready with the arms?" The ship's remote arms were robotic extensions that came in handy for transferring cargo between ships or from the ship to a spot on a docking ring. We didn't use them often, since most such transport happened planetside and could be accomplished with gravsleds, but we'd been glad of them a time or two in the past. The controls were in Engineering, where Viss would simply put his hands inside the control gloves and watch on a screen as the arms replicated the movements he made with his own hands.

"Ready, Captain."

"Gently, Viss," I cautioned him, although I knew he didn't need reminding. If the drone reacted to being touched by detonating or firing, there was only the shield between it and us. We'd probably survive, but the ship might take a beating.

"I'll treat it like a baby, don't worry," he said.

On the big viewscreen the rest of us watched as we drew close to the drifting drone and matched its speed. The padded arms reached out, closing around it like two spoons catching an egg. The drone touched the first arm and wobbled away, but the second was close enough to press it in, and just like that, it was caught.

"Good work, Viss." I blew out a breath I hadn't realized I'd been holding onto. "Lock the arms and you can leave it."

Hirin and I had decided, after only a brief discussion, against bringing the drone inside the *Tane Ikai*'s cargo hold. We were a relatively small ship, and if anything went wrong, we risked substantial damage. We couldn't take the drone down through the atmosphere clutched in the remote arms—they'd be torn away on entry. But we *could* transfer it to the enormous *Lillifleur*, which had lots of now-empty space with compartmentalizing blast doors and reinforced decks. That seemed a much safer environment in which to study it. Juliska Barath and the other council members had agreed to the plan.

"All right, Rei, you're up. Nice and slow, we're off to meet the *Lillifleur* for the transfer."

"Here we go," she said. "Viss, don't drop the baby now that you've caught it."

"Don't you rock the cradle too much," he retorted.

I smiled. My crew might be worried about our fate here in this unknown system, but put them to work and they could handle anything.

It wasn't far to meet up with the *Lillifleur* as she swung in her perpetual orbit around Ryphen. Juliska was at the helm, awaiting our arrival.

"Here's how we'll run the transfer," she said. "You'll match speed with us and position your ship near our dock side cargo bay. Once we're stabilized, you can extend your remote arms inside the hold and set the drone down. Then you'll move off a short distance and we'll send a shuttle to bring your crew over—whoever's coming to examine the drone, that is. That will avoid the need for EVA suits or outside transfers."

"That sounds perfect," I told her. "We'll be alongside in—"

"Fifteen minutes," Rei provided.

"Fifteen minutes," I relayed to Captain Barath.

Rei was as good as her estimate, and we pulled alongside the *Lillifleur* as expected. As Rei fired the manoeuvring thrusters to match the big ship's speed and bring us as close as we could safely get, the cargo bay doors slid open and stabilizer clamps extended out to catch hold of the *Tane Ikai*. I suspect the technician controlling them was a little out of practice—which was no wonder—so the contact was a little bumpy, but we got situated all right.

Rei took her hands off the pilot's board and said, "Nothing more for me to do here. We're stuck to the *Lillifleur* like a flea on a snowcat."

"Thanks for that charming analogy," Baden said. "*Lillifleur*, we are in position and tethered. We'll move the drone inside your cargo bay now."

"Affirmative," Captain Barath said. "The doors are open and the bay is ready to receive."

Viss worked the remote arms like a pro, moving the drone into the bigger ship and setting it down gently on the floor of the cargo bay. When it touched down, the viewscreen showed a couple of EVA-suited figures move to the drone and attach cargo clamps to it, then signal that we could let go. Viss withdrew the remote arms and the *Lillifleur's* door slid shut again.

Rei slid her skimchair back to the pilot's board and said, "Ready for release. I'll move us away with the manoeuvring thrusters."

The tether arms released us with a little push, sending us away from the big ship's side. Rei deployed the thrusters smoothly, and we moved off from the ship, matching its orbit to keep pace a little distance away.

Juliska Barath commed us from the bridge of the *Lillifleur* again. "That went well," she said with a smile. "I have a couple of techs who will move the drone to a secure area aboard the ship. Are you coming to examine it now?"

I glanced around the bridge of the *Tane Ikai*, wondering if everyone else felt as tired as I did. It had already been a long day and a lot had happened, and I honestly felt like we needed rest more than anything else at that point. The faces around me looked willing to go along with whatever answer I gave, but I saw weariness there, too.

"I think we'll sleep first," I suggested. "It's been a long day. If it's all right with you, we'll come over first thing in the morning, when we're fresh."

Juliska Barath nodded, and I thought she looked a bit relieved herself. "Let me know when to send the shuttle, Captain, and we'll be there. Rest well."

"Thanks, you too," I said, and closed the connection. "All right, match the *Lillifleur*'s orbit and keep a comm channel open. We're on night duty rotation, and I want everyone to get at least six hours away from this bridge. I, for one, am going to eat something and hit the bunk."

There were murmurs of assent, and the crew began to plan for the watch duty shifts. I stood and sighed, leaning backward to ease some of the tension that had collected between my shoulder blades and settled in the small of my back. I didn't know if I'd be successful, but I was sure going to try and make good on Captain Barath's wishes for a good rest.

CHAPTER FIFTEEN
Message From Somewhere

ALTHOUGH I HADN'T expected it, I slept deeply, my rest untroubled by worries or dreams. In the morning, we assembled for breakfast in the galley, and I messaged Captain Barath to let her know we'd be ready whenever it was convenient to come aboard and look at the drone. She sounded refreshed, although the ever-present undercurrent of worry threaded through her voice. That wouldn't depart until the colony's current problems were resolved and Amber Malka's fate ascertained. She said one of the *Lillifleur*'s ship's boats could rendezvous with us in half an hour. That was perfect, since it allowed us time to eat an unhurried meal while the shuttle made its way from the huge colony ship to the *Tane Ikai*.

Baden and Karro had been the first to volunteer to come across with me to have a look at the drone. Hirin looked like he might object—probably he wanted to go himself. But then he shrugged and said, "Makes sense. You're the communications experts, and we're assuming that's part of the drones' purpose besides depositing the 'bots. And has Baden ever met a technology he couldn't bend to his will?"

"Well, I don't like to brag—"

"Of course, you do. Incessantly," Rei said with a snort.

"Hirin, what if you wait to hear from Nanurjuk Etok, and see when he's available," I suggested, raising my voice over the banter. "Then you and Viss can meet with him to look at the skip drive. If you have to leave orbit and go down to the planet, go ahead. I'm sure the *Lillifleur* will send us down on a shuttle if we need a lift." I expected he felt a little torn between the competing tech discussions. Baden was the resident techdog on the *Tane Ikai*, but Hirin would have come in a close second.

Karro seemed pleased to be part of the drone investigation, although I sensed some hesitation to leave Aliande behind.

Aliande chuckled when I asked if she'd like to come, too. "What I know about technology would fit on a broken datachip."

"But maybe you'd like to look around the colony ship? It might inspire you in some other way. A look back a hundred years? When you think about it, it's an artifact from the early days of colonization."

She considered, tapping a finger on her chin. "I hadn't thought of that," she said. "It would be interesting to study what the colonists brought with them from home—what they took with them down to the planet, and what they chose to leave behind."

I told them to meet me at the rear airlock when the ship's boat was expected.

It arrived on schedule, endearingly old-fashioned with its outdated hull lines. Still perfectly serviceable, though, and obviously well-kept. The seats and floor were clean, and I stepped up to the tiny bridge to greet the pilot as Karro, Baden, and Aliande took seats. The co-pilot's seat was empty, and the pilot, a friendly woman named Wren Litzer, invited me to sit with her for the trip back to the *Lillifleur*. I called up the crew manifest in my implant—I felt sure I was improving at accessing it unobtrusively—and found that Wren was an original colonist, a trained pilot and mechanic. Her nanobioscavengers were obviously on the job, since she didn't look more than thirty.

Captain Juliska Barath met us at the docking bay and welcomed us aboard. "I've detailed Lieutenant Litzer to take you to study the drone, if that's all right," she said. "I should stay on the bridge, and she was one of the techs who brought it aboard."

"That's fine," I told her. "Is there someone who might show Aliande around parts of the ship? She's an artist and would love to do a study of some of the areas. She's also interested in the history of the colonists, on their way here and after their arrival."

"Some people have given me permission to paint them,"

Aliande said warmly. "I'd love to be able to use parts of the ship in some of those backgrounds." She'd brought a small, flexible sketch screen and stylus with her, and gestured with them. "I'll do a few quick studies, if it's permitted."

Juliska thought for a moment. "We operate with a skeleton crew, but I could spare someone from the regular maintenance detail. Their work is not so time-sensitive, and they certainly know all the nooks and crannies of the ship."

"That sounds perfect," Aliande said.

We parted ways, Aliande accompanying Juliska to the bridge while Wren Litzer led us to an elevator. "The drone is two decks down, in the old hydroponics bay. We brought it there from the cargo bay on a gravsled. Hydroponics is a closed system, so we thought it would be a safe place to have a look at it."

The elevator hummed down, and we emerged a minute later in front of a glass-walled area with a single door in the middle of the wall. It lay dark and quiet, and I was struck by the lack of noise on the ship in general. The hums and thumps and sighs of the usual ships systems provided an audible background, but the human sounds one expected on a vessel this size were entirely missing. Intellectually, I knew that only a few crew members were aboard, but the ship was so massive and its original purpose so evident, that it seemed eerily wrong for it to be so empty.

Wren Litzer touched a pad on the wall and lights hummed to life inside the hydroponics bay. They glowed dimly at first, brightening gradually until warm, full-spectrum light flooded the space. Long rows of benches that had once held the plants to sustain a thousand travellers lay long-empty and deserted, hoses that once carried life-sustaining water looped dry and lifeless from the ceiling. On closer inspection, I saw that many of the benches had been stripped of their surfaces, the materials ferried down to the colony for re-purposing. A few discarded growing containers lay strewn around the space, although they'd been emptied of whatever growing media they'd once held. No doubt it, too, had been transported to the surface for use in the greenhouse or as soil amendments.

Most of this I took in at my first cursory glance; then the drone pulled my attention. I'd seen it on the screen when Viss captured it, but up close it was a different matter. It looked like a metal tadpole, with its bulbous body and stubby tail. It gleamed black under the bright lights, although its surface wasn't completely smooth. The light created a mottled effect as it played across the drone's skin, suggesting areas of different textures or perhaps sensors embedded in the outer shell.

Baden let out a long, low whistle. "Look at that thing," he said. "Not Nearspace tech, that's for sure."

"It's so black I might think it came from the Corvids," I joked. We'd all been struck by the singular monotone colour choice the crow-like aliens made for their ships and stations. But this didn't have the feel of Corvid technology, either. The Corvid installations and vessels we'd seen and visited had an almost gelatinous look, although close inspection revealed a construction of versatile, interlocking hexagon-shaped tiles. This was not like that. This looked solid and heavy and almost . . . threatening.

"Do you want to go inside for a closer look?" Wren asked. "It seems completely inert. Whatever you folks did to shut it down seems to have worked." I could hear the curiosity in her voice about precisely what we *had* done, but I didn't want to get into the specifics of the activator drive. That would be too long a story for someone who didn't even know about the existence of the Corvids yet.

"Are you sure? We only intended to shut down its drive," I said, while Baden said, "Absolutely!" at the same time.

Wren smiled. "We scanned it extensively when it came on board," she said. "Before we even chanced moving it up here. Nothing triggered any response. Captain Barath wouldn't have authorized it if she didn't think it was safe."

I felt a little twinge at that, wishing, for some unknown reason, she hadn't said it.

Sometimes I hate it when I'm right.

BADEN WAS THE first one through the door, with Karro close behind. Wren and I followed at a more leisurely pace; she because she'd already examined the thing, and me because a strange sense of foreboding slowed my steps. I could say the drone felt "alien," but that didn't explain it; technology and other items that were Vilisian or Lobor or now even Corvid or Relidae were commonplace to me. They were all "alien" when it came down to it, but none of them gave me this feeling. I didn't like it, but I couldn't identify what was causing it.

Within moments, Baden had his datapad in one hand and a techrig in the other, scanning the drone with his attention glued to the readouts.

"There's surprisingly little micro-scarring on the surface," Baden said. "It can't have travelled a very long distance."

Wren nodded slowly. "I guess that would make sense, if whatever is sending them is getting closer. They'd have less time to be exposed to micro impacts from space debris."

"How many of these things have you encountered, again?" Karro asked. He hadn't pulled out any kind of techrig yet, although I felt certain he had one with him. For now, he walked along the side of the bench where the drone lay, examining it visually. Its bulbous tadpole body had a diameter of about four feet, and it was at least twice that long from nose to tail.

"Seven, all told. Only the first one got as far as the planet. Well, not counting the two your ship encountered."

"And the rest have all been destroyed?"

"Yes," Wren said, sounding testy. "We didn't have the ability to disable or capture any until you arrived. No other options after the first one made us sick."

Baden held up a conciliatory hand. "Hey, not judging. Just thinking out loud."

Karro stood with his back against one of the other benches, arms crossed, studying the drone. "So, let's assume these are scouts, for lack of a better word. They're sent out ahead of something or someone to gather data, and presumably transmit it back to the source."

"Whoever's sending the drones seems fairly persistent, and surely they know about the ones that were destroyed," Baden mused. "They must send back telemetry, monitoring data—some kind of message. Otherwise, what's the point? But it seems like when they go dark, the senders simply launch a new one."

"That must get expensive," Karro said.

I turned to Wren. "So during that first encounter with one of these, you tried to communicate but there was no response? Then it scanned the planet and people ended up sick?"

"Yes. Although . . ." Wren paused.

"What?"

"I don't believe the intention was to make us sick. I get the feeling they would have done a better job of it if that was the plan." She shrugged. "Just my opinion. And it's possible they were transmitting signals that we couldn't pick up. I suppose we can't say with certainty they made no attempt. They made no attempt we could detect."

"Were you on the *Lillifleur* when the first drone arrived?"

She shook her head. "I'd just come off a shuttle shift. My original training was to pilot the shuttles that would take us all down to the surface of a planet. Once we'd settled, I'd work with the machinery we'd brought to start farming and building." She gave a wry smile. "No-one expected we'd be shuttling anyone after the initial landing was complete, because the ship was supposed to leave us. So I've sure logged more hours in the air than I ever expected. Anyway, for a first-hand account, you'd have to ask Captain Barath. She was on the bridge when the first drone appeared."

"Thanks, I'll do that," I said, making a mental note to ask Juliska about that encounter. There probably wasn't anything we could figure out that the colonists hadn't in all this time, but it was worth asking. We did have the advantage of a lot more interactions with alien species since the time the *Lillifleur* had left Nearspace. And my crew had made our own first contact with the Corvids, as well as the Relidae. Maybe our experience would give us some insight.

"I think I've identified sensor arrays, propulsion, and a communications hub," Baden said. "I'm trying to map all the external attributes of the thing and extrapolate where the corresponding internal systems would be."

"Be careful," I ordered. "We don't want to accidentally turn it back on, particularly when we're *inside* the *Lillifleur*."

"Captain, I'm shocked at how little faith you have in me," Baden said, although he sounded amused.

"I know where tech is concerned, you can get a little . . . over-eager."

"So it's been dormant since we shut it down and brought it here?" Karro asked Wren.

She nodded. "Not a peep. Granted, we haven't done anything to it except the scans, just moved it in here and got it settled."

"Hmm," Baden said, tapping something into his techrig. "Now, I think if I—" He reached out and touched the side of the drone before I could tell him not to.

With a whirr, a small hatch about the size of my hand slid open. My heart leapt at the sound, expecting sudden disaster, but nothing else happened. Adrenaline prickled along my arms. "Baden! Warn me before you're going to make it *do* something!"

"Sorry!" He didn't have the grace to meet my eyes. Instead, he leaned closer to study what the access panel had revealed, and Karro joined him.

"What's inside?" Wren asked, displaying new interest, and bending to look.

I couldn't contain my own curiosity and moved to peer over their shoulders. Inside the small hatch, there was only a smooth recessed panel; nothing resembling a port or plug, which I'd half-expected to see. Below the panel's smooth, glassy surface, the lights picked up reflections of something like photoreceptors on a solar collector. Too tiny to be that, though, and not very effective at collecting sunlight inside the drone.

Karro reached toward the panel as if he might touch his fingertips to it.

"Are you sure you should touch it?" My voice came out a little more strident than I intended.

Karro turned to look at me. "I'm pretty sure Baden touched it, not thirty seconds ago. I wondered if a push on that inner panel would open it up further."

"Well, Baden only touched the outside," I protested. "Do we *want* to open it up further?"

Karro blew out a sigh of exasperation. "I'm not sure how we're going to find out much about it by standing here and looking."

Okay, he had a point, and I didn't want to get into an argument with him. "What did you do?" I asked Baden.

He shrugged. "I figured there might be a simple binary gate for controlling an access hatch, so I sent a modified low-level EMP burst to see if I could disable it. Then I pressed this catch," he said with a grin, pointing. "And the thing popped open. I'm guessing this is related to communications," he went on, "because internally, the connections all lead to a sort of hub. It's right behind this solar-panel-looking thing."

"Is that a technical term?"

"I'm simplifying for the laypeople," he said with a grin. He held the techrig close to the open panel, running a scan, then frowned at the readout on his screen. "I don't think we're dealing with technology from anywhere within Nearspace."

"I'd already guessed that." I ran my gaze down the length of the drone. "It's all black, but it doesn't look like Corvid stuff. And I think if they had exploratory drones flitting around out here, they would have told us by now."

"It's not Chron, either," Baden said. "Neither Relidae nor Pitromae, if you ask me. I've studied enough Relidae stuff by now to be able to identify their language and programming codes, and the Pitromae aren't that different technologically."

A puzzled frown creased Wren's brow at the mention of the Chron, but she didn't interrupt. Our renewed contact with the Relidae and Pitromae was another thing the Ryphens still had to learn about.

I leaned back against one of the other tables and crossed my arms. "So that means we're talking about a new species. One we haven't encountered before."

Baden nodded slowly. "That's what I think."

"Wow," Karro said. "So we're looking at first contact with aliens who send possibly unfriendly advance scouts into unknown territory? I don't like the sound of that."

"Me neither," I agreed unhappily. "The Authority and the Protectorate have plenty to deal with, navigating relations with the Pitromae. I wonder if the Corvids have encountered this tech?" I would have loved a chance to ask Fha, our Corvid friend, about the drones, but she was even farther away than Nearspace.

"If we could get the whole thing open, we might get direct access to a communications interface, even on a very basic level," Karro mused. He leaned toward the drone, putting one hand on its lightly pitted surface for balance as he peered more closely at the drone's outer casing.

What happened next was so fast, I almost missed it. The section under his hand depressed slightly, puffed out a hiss of air, and then slid quickly to the left. Karro started and lost his balance, trying to catch himself with his other hand. It landed directly on the small patch of solar receptors Baden had revealed.

Bright light flared and swift runnels of visible energy crackled up over Karro's hand and arm like miniature lightning bolts. He grunted as if something had punched him in the stomach, and then his legs buckled. Baden managed to catch Karro's head inches from the floor, as his body crumpled to the metal deck like a discarded shirt.

WREN LITZER REACTED as quickly as Baden. As I knelt next to Karro, feeling for a pulse, she was already sending a request for a first aid officer. With only a skeleton crew aboard, I wondered how useful they would be, but that was only a distracted half-thought as my fingers searched for signs of life at Karro's throat.

To my relief, his pulse was strong and steady—quickened but not racing. But he was out cold and didn't stir when Baden rolled him into the recovery position. I took his hand, the one that had touched the strange panel, turning it over to examine the skin of his palm. It was red, but not burned or blistered. The angry colour didn't extend up his arm where I'd watched the energy crackle.

"*Merde!* What was that?" Baden muttered.

"I was going to ask you." I nodded toward his techrig. "Is that telling you anything?"

With a glance at Karro, Baden stood and touched the techrig screen, scanning the drone. He pursed his lips. "It's reading . . . active, I guess you'd say, now. Some of the systems are running at a very low-power level."

Alarm pierced Wren Litzer's voice. "What systems? If it's not safe—"

Baden cut her off with a shake of his head. "Seems benign, communications, maybe sensors. I'm not getting anything from propulsion—or at least what I've tentatively identified as that system."

"But you don't know," I said. "I think we'd better get out of here. And maybe get the drone off the ship, too. We don't know what it might decide to do."

"Should we move him?" Wren asked, looking down at Karro. "I don't like to do that until a medic has seen him."

Beyond the transparent walls of the hydroponics bay, the elevator sat quiet, its doors closed. No lights indicated the imminent arrival of a medic.

"I think we'll risk it." I tried to keep my voice calm, although a churn of panic swirled in my stomach. "He didn't hit his head. But now I don't trust this thing as much as I did before."

"Neither do I," Wren confessed.

"Here," Baden said, pushing his techrig into my hands. "I'll take Karro, you keep taking readings. I want to know what the drone is doing, and if it's trying to send any messages out into the void. I've got the receiver set to pick up a much wider range of signals than we'd normally look at, and I don't want to miss anything."

I took the rig in a not entirely steady hand.

"You don't have to do anything. Just hold onto it," he said, kneeling near Karro's head.

"I'll take his feet," Wren offered.

They were in the process of hoisting Karro up when the elevator door finally opened, and a worried-looking man rushed out. Aliande was close behind him. The medic pushed the door of the hydroponics bay open and called, "Don't move him!"

Aliande pushed past him and ran to Karro. She put a hand on his cheek, but he didn't stir.

"We think it could be dangerous to stay in here with the drone," Wren said brusquely. "And we've already picked him up. Let's get him outside."

The medic didn't look happy, but he glanced at the drone and nodded. We moved out into the corridor in a tight knot, and Wren said, "Go right, there's a food storage room a couple of doors down. We can set him down on one of the counters in there."

"What happened?" Aliande demanded as we followed.

"I don't know. A panel opened on the drone, and Karro accidentally touched it. There was an energy release, and it knocked him out—although it wasn't concussive, and his heart rate and breathing seem fine." I pocketed Baden's techrig, wondering how close I had to be for it to keep taking readings. I decided I didn't much care. Karro wasn't getting out of my sight.

"You think he'll be all right." It wasn't a question.

I answered without thinking. "I do. But I wish he had the nano—"

I broke off and pressed my lips together, not wanting Aliande to hear an accusation in my voice. She stiffened beside me but said nothing. Ahead of us, the medic pushed a door open and held it for Baden and Wren to carry Karro through. We hurried to catch up.

It was a food prep and storage space, and I assumed that vegetables from the hydroponics bay would have been brought here for cleaning and then stored for future consumption. Two long stainless-steel tables ran the length of the room, and a counter and sink lined one wall. They laid Karro carefully on one of the tables and the medic went to work with a medkit he'd already had in hand. I pulled off my jacket and rolled it up, tucking it under Karro's head. The table looked cold and hard.

"Vitals are good," the medic muttered. "What happened to him?"

As Wren explained, Aliande stood next to me, hugging her arms close around herself. She chewed anxiously at her bottom lip, her eyes bright with unshed tears.

"I was on the bridge when the call went out," she said to me. "They took out all the chairs and consoles except what they'd need for a skeleton crew and took it all down to the planet. It's eerily minimalist up there, considering the size of the ship and the number of crew it must once have taken to fly it."

"Funny they left these tables," I said. "You'd think they'd have a use for them down on the surface."

"Too big to fit in a shuttle?" she wondered. "Or too much work to move? They do look awfully heavy."

We were only talking to keep ourselves distracted. At this moment, neither of us cared about the strange behaviours of the colonists.

The medic turned to look at us. "He seems fine, except for being unconscious. I know that sounds weird, but I can't find any evidence of physical injury except this burn on his palm. It's minor, so I'll treat it and wrap it with gauze. All my scans are coming back clean. I think with some rest, he'll come out of it naturally. I could give him a stimulant in a med injector, but I'd rather not force him awake."

He pulled in a breath. "We do have a medical bay on the ship, although it's been stripped down to almost nothing. There's still a bed or two there, but not much else in the way of equipment. Do you want to move him there, or take him back to your ship or down to Ryphen? I have a med-sled. I'll get that, so we can move him smoothly wherever he's going."

"Back to our ship," Aliande and I said almost in unison.

I half-smiled. "I have an experienced medic on my crew, and a fully-equipped first aid bay. We'll be able to take good care of him."

Baden went with the medic to fetch the med-sled, and Wren stepped out into the corridor to comm the captain and bring her up to date. Aliande moved over to stand next to Karro and took one of his hands in hers.

"I'm sorry this happened." I went to the other side of the table and stroked Karro's short-cropped hair. It seemed hardly any time at all since he'd been a little boy, playing at being the captain of the *Tane Ikai* while Hirin and I watched in amusement. "I honestly didn't think there was any danger."

Aliande sighed. "Neither did I. Nor did Karro. I think he was starting to feel like we were on a bit of an adventure. He enjoyed going out to meet that 'bot and initiate communications with it."

I licked my lips. "It's my fault we're here in the first place. Although I wasn't lying when I told him I didn't intend it."

"I know that, Luta. And so does he."

She looked up at me when I stayed silent. "What if we need to get him back to Nearspace for help?" Her voice was little above a whisper.

I looked down at my son, wishing he was merely sleeping as peacefully as he looked. "I don't know, Aliande. I just don't know."

CHAPTER SIXTEEN
Information Deficit

WE TOOK KARRO back to the *Tane Ikai*. I thanked the universe that Hirin hadn't taken the ship down to the planet and we could deliver Karro into Yuskeya's capable hands quickly. Dr. Lee might have something to offer, but at that moment Yuskeya was the only one I trusted with my son's care.

Wren piloted us back to my ship, barely repressing her consternation. What had happened wasn't her fault, but I felt she was waiting for us to make accusations. I sat up front with her and asked her questions about the colony, to keep her distracted. I don't think it worked very well, for either of us.

Karro still hadn't woken when we transferred him back to the *Tane Ikai*. The med-sled wouldn't function in the docking tube, so Viss came over, grim-faced, and he and Baden carried Karro carefully through. Yuskeya waited on the other side with the gurney from First Aid, her face set and serious under the bridge lights. I let her and Aliande wheel him off toward the small but well-equipped medical bay. I'd check on them later. Right now, I wanted some answers.

"Baden, let's see what those scans can tell us about the drone."

He nodded. Concern lined his normally handsome face, but he didn't complain. I'd already given him back his techrig to study in the shuttle. "I think we should upload the data, too; let Pika compare it to everything in her databases. She has files from

PrimeCorp's early explorations outside Nearspace. Who knows, someone could have encountered something like this before."

"That's an excellent idea," I told him, "except Pika—I guess we should say Pika Prime—is still down on the planet. We can upload the scan data and access the databases in the ship's computer, but her personality module isn't here to parse it all. You'll have to define the comparison algorithms yourself."

"Oh, right. How could I forget? It's so quiet here," he said with a half-hearted attempt to lighten the mood. We went to the galley, where we could pull some caff for fortification, and mull over the data without everyone else on the bridge hanging over our shoulders. I told Hirin what we were doing, and it wasn't long before he and Maja joined us.

"What do you have?" Hirin asked without preamble. It was flattering that he expected we'd have something to report. Happily, we did.

"I was scanning the drone when the energy burst happened," Baden said. "I'm certain it was only the communications module that was active at that moment."

"So we don't think the energy release was an attack on Karro," I added. "We think it might have been an attempt by the drone to communicate."

"To sort of—download information," Baden said.

Hirin steepled his fingers and tapped them against his lips. "But Karro wasn't equipped to receive that information," he said slowly, "at least, not in the form that the drone wanted to send it."

I nodded. "Right. So instead it overloaded his nervous system, and that's what knocked him out."

"All right, but what *kind* of information—I mean, what kind of transfer?" Maja asked. She'd pulled a mug of caff but hadn't sipped it, her fingers beating out a soft, agitated rhythm on the sides of the cup.

"Electrical, we think," I said. "Karro's hand was red where he'd touched the panel, like a burn, but not bad. I was going to ask Yuskeya if that seems consistent with whatever she's found."

"Shouldn't he have come around by now, though?"

I pulled a deep sigh and let it out. "That's the flaw in the theory. Unless there's more going on that we can't detect with our scans."

I pinged Yuskeya on the ship's comm and asked her if the irritation on Karro's hand could be consistent with an electrical burn.

"It could," she conceded. "It would have been a low-voltage discharge, since it didn't stop his heart or affect him more severely."

"We wonder if the drone could have been trying to—download information to him."

She was quiet, thinking. "I guess it's possible. If we're dealing with another alien species, their tech would be entirely different from ours. But the 'bot on the planet didn't try to do anything like that, did it?"

"No, it didn't. But maybe the 'bot is programmed to interact differently and the drone only interacts with other 'bots or something."

I could almost hear her shrug over the comm. "Anything's possible."

"*Okej*, let me know the second he wakes up. No other change?"

"Nothing to report," she said. "I'm sorry."

"That's all right. Would you contact Dr. Lee and ask if he'll consult with you when we return to the planet?"

"I'm sure he'd be happy to help."

I tapped my implant to close the connection, then immediately tapped it again and pinged Viss.

"Any word from the colony about the engineers who worked on Amber Malka's skip drive?"

"Yes. They'll meet with us in orbit, if we promise to keep it to a few hours," he said. "We can look at it together down in the cargo pod."

I drummed my fingers on the arm of my chair, thinking. Finally, I said, "Let's go to them. If we land again, that will give Yuskeya a chance to consult with Dr. Lee about Karro's situation, if he hasn't woken up by then, and you could meet with the engineers. This way they can all stay planetside."

I didn't love the idea of returning to the planet, but despite the utter faith I had in Yuskeya's abilities, I couldn't silence the little voice in my head reminding me she wasn't a doctor. Now that she'd seen Karro but hadn't been able to rouse him, my emotions had switched poles. Maybe even a doctor who was eighty years behind the latest Nearspace medical tech might have insights that Yuskeya would not—he also had as many years of experience. If Yuskeya couldn't figure out what was wrong with Karro, or some way to treat him, I would take any other medical advice I could get.

And in the back of my mind, I couldn't stop thinking about the nanobioscavengers. I had injectors full of them in that hidden lockbox in my quarters. One dose—one soft *pfft* of an injector—and Karro would probably be cured within hours. This was exactly the kind of situation Mother had given me the bioscavs for, after all.

Except that Karro had made it very clear—and very recently—that he didn't want them. Could I deliberately ignore my son's clearly stated wishes, when he was unable to weigh in on the matter himself? And what about Aliande? She'd have to know. I had to find a chance to talk this through with her. But she was with Karro in First Aid, and I didn't want to interrupt. I forced my thoughts back to the present. The bioscavs would have to wait.

"All right, Baden, can you ping Juliska for me? Tell her we're coming down to see Dr. Lee and the two engineers."

Maja sat back in her chair and folded her arms. "I wish we could get Pika working on this. I wonder if we could patch the data through to her somehow. She's always bragging about how many things she can do at one time. This would be a great time to prove it."

"True; I hadn't thought of that," I said. "Baden, could you also arrange that, get Pika working on it as soon as possible? Maybe by the time we're down on the planet she'll have something to tell us."

Baden nodded and rose. "I'm sure I can get Karin Nakano to help. I'll send her a message."

I looked at Hirin and he nodded and stood, too. "I'll message the colony about what we're planning, and then get Rei to take us back down to the landing area."

As if she'd read my mind, Aliande came into the galley, rubbing a hand over her face. "I think it's time for something restorative," she said with a wan smile.

Maja, perhaps picking up on something unspoken, said, "I'll go keep Karro company while you have a break." She squeezed Aliande's shoulder as she passed, and the two of us were left alone.

ALIANDE LOOKED SO tired as she took a seat at the table, the lines of worry seemed to have carved themselves irrevocably into her skin. The usually warm undertones of her brown skin had shifted to grey, making her look almost ill herself. She pressed her fingers against her eyes, massaging her temples with her thumbs.

"I'll get us both a drink," I offered. "Rooibos for you?"

She nodded, eyes still closed, and I drew off her tea and refilled my own mug. She inhaled deeply when I set the steaming cup of fragrant red tea down in front of her, then let the breath out in a long sigh. I sat across from her and sipped my caff.

"We're heading back down to the planet. Dr. Lee might have some insights about Karro."

Aliande opened her eyes. "I hope Yuskeya is right, and he just needs more time to recover."

I waited a beat, then said carefully, "If she's wrong—if he doesn't come around and Dr. Lee has no other ideas—there is another option."

She looked down at her cup of tea and lifted it to her lips, sipping shallowly to test the temperature. "The nanobioscavengers," she said in a flat voice.

"This is not the way I'd want it to be." I realized I was sitting rigid, stomach clenched, poised for defensiveness, and tried to relax. "But if there's damage that can't be repaired any other way . . ."

"I don't know." Aliande's voice was harsh, like she was forcing the words out past a sore throat. She paused as if choosing her next words carefully, and her tone softened. "I don't know if I could do that to him without his knowledge. It doesn't seem fair."

"Not even to save his life?"

She met my gaze then, something swimming in her dark eyes that might finally come to the surface. "He hasn't told you why we've refused them, has he?"

I shook my head. "Not yet. We talked about it briefly after you arrived on board, but he said he wanted to discuss it with you again. There hasn't been an opportunity to revisit it. I respect your right to your own reasons, but I'd like to understand what those reasons are. Especially now."

Aliande wrapped her hands around her mug as if drawing

strength from the heat, her dark eyes fixed on the steaming liquid. "It's because of me that he hasn't told you before," she said at last. Her voice had taken on a dull, hollow quality I'd never heard in it before. "I—we—have a secret that, well, we've never shared with the rest of the family."

I kept my face still, trying not to show my surprise. Karro and Aliande were two of the most open and honest people I knew. The idea that they had been keeping a secret—apparently a big secret, since it had far-reaching repercussions—came as a shock. I started to ask my daughter-in-law what could possibly be that important, then closed it again. I had to let her tell this, if indeed she was going to, in her own way.

"All right," I said as noncommittally as possible, merely to let her know I was paying attention.

"Do you remember," she asked, "about twenty years ago, we went more than a year without seeing you? Karro was doing a job on Eri and we lived there for six months, and even when we got back to Earth, you weren't in Sol System for months. We messaged, but we weren't face to face."

I nodded. I did remember. I'd had a particularly bad fight with Maja over something—what, I couldn't even recall now. We had fought about everything in those days. Taking a job that would give me an excuse to stay away for an extended time seemed wise. And then, as so often happened in far trading, that job had turned into another one, which led to another—and none of them took us anywhere near Eri, or back to Sol System. It could happen like that in Nearspace, since the in-system travel times could be lengthy, depending on your destination. Realspace meetings could be few and far between, even when you didn't want or intend them to be so infrequent.

"That was before you had Joash and Klaire." My grandchildren were eighteen and sixteen now. I felt a familiar pang that I didn't see them more often, accompanied by a bubble of worry about how they were doing. What if I couldn't get Karro and Aliande back to Nearspace?

Not the time. Listen to Aliande.

She smiled a sad half-smile, and her chin trembled. "It was. But it's strange you should say that, because what happened in that time was . . . Karro and I had a baby."

My hand stopped in the act of raising the mug to my lips. "A baby?" I said stupidly. "Before Joash?"

Aliande closed her eyes, and a tear slipped out from under her lashes and slid down her cheek. She brushed it away with an absent swipe of her fingertips. "Before Joash," she said. When she opened her eyes, more unspilled tears glistened there. "We found out I was pregnant soon after we arrived on Eri. I was nervous, and superstitious—didn't want to tell anyone too soon. And Karro wanted to tell you in person. So, we waited. We wanted to meet up once the contract on Eri ended—but you were too far away, and we couldn't have caught up to you in time and still made it back to Earth before the baby was born. And we wanted to be home for that."

Her voice quavered and she paused for a sip of tea. I didn't say anything, too surprised to do more than nod. I knew where this had to be going, and I already felt the constriction of a terrible pain welling up in my heart.

"So we thought, oh well, it would be such an amazing, funny surprise for you when you did make it back to Earth, or at least to Sol System. All of the joy with none of the worry beforehand. 'Surprise, we had a baby!' We agreed that if it didn't look like we'd get a chance to meet up, we'd finally tell you in a message. Karro said you and Hirin would be sure to change any plans to come to Earth if you knew."

I nodded. "I saw both Joash and Klaire when they were only hours old."

She half-smiled. "We wouldn't make the same mistake twice. Anyway," she continued after a deep sigh, "Kemel was born, and we were so happy. Completely wrapped up in him. He was such a good baby, and we were on the point of messaging you about him—it seemed wrong by then that the family didn't know. And then—" her voice broke and dropped to a whisper. Her words seemed to come from a distant place, galaxies away. "He died."

I knew it was coming but hearing her say the words felt like a wormhole collapsing inexorably around my heart, crushing it with the enormous pressure of grief. "What happened?" I heard myself ask in a voice I hardly recognized.

She shook her head. "A heart defect they hadn't seen—very difficult to detect. His heart just . . . stopped beating one night. If it had happened in the daytime, when we'd have been aware, then maybe—but that's not how it happened."

I reached out a hand across the table to her. She squeezed it once, then pulled it back to wrap around her mug again, swallowing a couple of times.

"We were . . . well, devastated seems too inadequate a word. And how could we tell you then? We knew instantly that we'd made the most terrible mistake, not telling you about him from the outset. But then after—afterward, everything was different. Since you hadn't shared in the joy, it didn't seem fair to make you share in the pain." The words tumbled out short and clipped, as if she were reciting a speech she'd rehearsed in her head many times.

"Finally, we talked it through . . . and decided to keep that part of our history to ourselves. I had no family to tell, and even Maja didn't know—she and Taso had been travelling, and too caught up in their own problems when they were on Earth. We wondered if they were having issues even then, or if perhaps they were trying to start a family and couldn't—" Aliande drew another deep sigh and slowly released it, the weight of those times and decisions obviously still a weighty burden. When she spoke again, the detached narration was gone, and her rich voice was leaden, marbled with pain. "Anyway, we never told them. We've never told anyone."

"How could you live with that?" The words were out almost before I thought them. I'd kept my own secrets for a very long time, but this . . . this was of a different magnitude. My secret— the bioscavs and their effect—wasn't something that would eat me up inside; wasn't something that caused me such soul-deep pain. It took its toll in many other ways. But not like this.

Aliande's lips trembled, and she pressed them together for a moment, keeping her eyes on her tea. Tears trickled slowly down her cheeks now, but she made no move to wipe them away. "Not easily," she said eventually. "Not . . . happily. It's been . . . like a mental wormhole skip that never finds the other end. So many times, we talked about telling people—you and Hirin, Joash and Klaire, Maja—because Kemel was sweet, and real, and he *happened.*"

I reached for her hand again but she shook her head mutely, as if the kindness of a touch at this moment would be too much to bear. I drew back as she gulped.

"But it's a hard thing to say, 'I lied about this a long time ago,' or to find the right time to say it. Especially when you don't see the other people involved very often. Especially when you know it's going to hurt them, too, and you've managed to live with it this long, so it just seems easier to keep going that way."

A hot supernova of anger bloomed in my chest and swept my body—anger with Aliande, with Karro, with every misguided decision they'd made and every quirk of fate that had contributed to this mess. But the blast wave of sorrow that washed after it extinguished the heat, leaving only its black-hole void. Aliande and Karro had lived in that void for a long time, unable to escape.

"I . . . I don't think it was actually easier," I said, and it was the simple truth. "You should have told us."

"I know. *We* know. We talked about it on Xaqual, whether we'd tell you on this trip. We couldn't decide. Joash and Klaire— the older they get, the more we know we need to tell them, too. It's just so hard to take that leap. To do something you know is going to change things, but you're not sure what those changes will look like. That's why Karro was—the way he was. On edge, cranky." She looked up and met my eyes then, hers still wet with tears, but she managed a half-smile. "We've gotten really good at keeping secrets, but the stress bubbles up sometimes."

I raised my eyebrows and smiled. "You think?"

She made a noise somewhere between a sob and a chuckle, and went on. "So, the possibility of the nanobioscavengers—once you found your mother, Karro and I talked about it. We knew the offer would probably come. We love Joash and Klaire utterly, Luta, but honestly . . . the pain of losing Kemel is still so strong. It dulls, of course. Time patches over the raw edges, wraps them so they don't bleed every day. But the pain is a constant thing. It's lodged in my heart, and it will never go away. Not ever. And I don't want to live forever with that."

"And Karro feels the same way. About the bioscavs, I mean." It was both a statement and a question.

She wiped at her cheeks and I got up to fetch a cloth from the sink for her, running cool water over it. She accepted it with a wan smile. "He says he does, and I've always believed him."

I bit back platitudes about how any pain might be bearable with the passage of enough time. I'd lost people—my father, Lanar's young wife Soranna, friends and crewmates. In all these instances, grief had dulled with time and acceptance. The knowledge of lost opportunities with them would make me sad no matter how long I lived, but even if I found that pain bearable, it didn't mean I could judge an experience I'd been spared. And I hadn't lost a child, nor kept that loss a festering secret for almost two decades.

"I don't pretend to have the answers," I said carefully, "but it might be easier to bear once you can stop keeping Kemel's life a secret."

She bit her lip. "Maybe." She didn't seem convinced, but she didn't argue.

"And you do have to stop keeping him a secret," I pressed, reaching for her hand a third time. This time, she let me take it, now clutching as if it were a lifeline. I went on, "We're family. We need to deal with this—all of this—together. And Kemel is a part of that family. You don't have to tell everyone at once, if you can't manage that, and not until we know if Karro—not until Karro's better. But you've made a start, and I think you have to go on. There's been no space for healing, the way things were."

She ran her free hand shakily over her face and nodded. "Would you tell Hirin and Maja? And she can tell Baden. I don't think I can do it again right now, but . . . but you're right. I know that. We knew that. Things couldn't go on any longer the way they were."

Her palm was warm from her mug of tea, the back of her hand as cold as ice. "I want to know all about him, you know," I said gently, my vision blurring from my own unshed tears.

She blinked and breathed in a long, slow breath. "When Karro's awake. We'll tell you together. Or if—"

I held up a hand. "We won't think about 'if' yet. But the nanobioscavengers—please consider them as a possibility. If nothing else works."

Aliande's dark, shadowed eyes met my gaze. "It's a real option? You have some on the ship?"

"I do. Transfusion from one of us who has them would be possible, too, but it's trickier. Mother thought it was wise to have some injectables in case . . . well, not everyone on my crew has them. But if they decide they want them, they're here. Or if there's an emergency . . ."

"Like this," she said on a sigh.

"Well, yes."

Aliande put her hands over her face, as if she could shut everything out for just a few seconds. It wouldn't work, and she knew that. It was all still there, behind her beautiful dark eyes. When she took her hands away, she blinked and said, "Let's see what Dr. Lee says, all right? And see what tomorrow brings. I'll think on it tonight, I promise. But right now—I can't do any more."

I let my head fall back against my chair and gave her a weak smile. "I know. I feel like we just ran a marathon."

"I feel like I've been running one for a long time." She pressed a palm to her heart as if trying to calm it. "Not the cheap flight home and lovely visit we thought we'd have," she said wanly. "But it's not your fault."

"Maybe Karro will be better tomorrow."

"Maybe so. And now . . . I'm going to lie down for a bit. Yuskeya said she'd let me know the instant there's any change." She rose on legs that seemed unsteady, washed out her mug, and wiped her face once more with the cloth before hanging it over the edge of the sink. She squeezed my shoulder on her way past me, as I contemplated the last cold dregs of my caff. I almost laughed at the absurdity of her trying to comfort me, but her back was straight and she'd regained her usual composure. I wasn't sure how she did it; years of practice, I supposed. By comparison, I felt like a meteor shower had punched me full of holes.

Hirin and I had a grandchild we'd never had the chance to know. My thoughts swirled around that for a while, tentatively, painfully, like a tongue touching the space where a tooth has been pulled. I'd tell Hirin, yes, and Maja, and then—we'd move forward as we could. So much was happening right now that I knew I'd have to compartmentalize this pain until we were all safe and I could give it—give Kemel—the attention he deserved. Because right now, laid over that pain, the end of my conversation with Aliande throbbed like the beat of pulse in a wound.

Maybe Karro will be better tomorrow. It wasn't my fault.

Too bad I didn't believe either part.

I got up and went to find my husband.

ABOUT HALF AN hour after we touched down on the planet, the two Ryphens who'd worked on Amber's skip drive appeared at the landing area. Kat Oleshenko, the engineer from the *Lillifleur*, was a tall rangy woman with a short blonde buzzcut and a silvery, puckered scar across one cheek. She walked with a cane, but seemed awkward with it, so I suspected her need for it coincided with the drone scan. Nanurjuk Etok was a short, dark-haired man built like a missile, all smooth muscle and lithe movement. He seemed unaffected by the mysterious illness. Hirin met them and they shook hands all around, and the talk soon devolved into techspeak. I heard their voices disappear down the hatchway leading to Engineering to meet Viss. From there they'd descend to the cargo pods, where the *Amber's Ranger* still reposed. Perhaps after this, Juliska would want us to leave the ship on the planet. That would be reasonable—we'd likely have learned all we could from it by then.

A young female doctor named Adhira Haldane had arrived with the engineers. She explained that Dr. Lee would be coming to see Karro soon, but he'd had some things to finish up and had sent her along in advance. Baden showed her the way, and she'd disappeared into First Aid with Yuskeya and Aliande.

Since I obviously wasn't needed with the engineers and our tiny medical bay would be more than crowded, I decided to walk to the settlement and see what was happening with the 'bot. No doubt Pika would be anxious to report on her progress. I was a little surprised that she hadn't pinged me before this.

Rei offered to come with me, and I welcomed the company. She'd been quiet since Karro's injury and we hadn't had a chance to talk any further. When we reached the edge of the treeline, she said without preamble, "Luta, I want to apologize."

I glanced over at her. Today she'd pulled her chestnut hair back and gathered it in a knot low on her neck, and her face was sombre above her plain shipsuit. It occurred to me that the Rei I knew would have changed into something far more fashionable before leaving the ship, even to walk out to the edge of a wheat field. The inky whorls of her *pridattii* looped and swirled around pensive, remorseful eyes.

"What for?"

"For the other day. For being such a complainer," she said, kicking a pebble out of the path. "There I was carrying on about such a minor thing, when the Ryphens are sick and now Karro's been hurt—"

"Hey," I said, putting an arm around her shoulders, "worrying about being stranded in an unknown system is not a 'minor' thing. It's completely understandable." I threw her a grin. "Even if this isn't exactly the first time it's happened to us."

She gave a sheepish smile. "I know. That's what makes me feel even sillier about it."

"But this time is different . . . because of Gerazan."

Rei sighed and ran a hand down her face. "I think that's it, too. I just—if I let myself think about not getting back, not seeing him again . . . and having him left wondering what happened to me . . ." Her voice trailed off and her golden eyes welled with tears.

I stopped and took her by the shoulders. "I meant what I said. We're going to get back. Viss and those engineers are figuring it out at this very minute. Did you ever see a drive problem Viss couldn't fix?"

She half-sobbed a brief laugh. "No. You're right. That's why I apologized . . . we all have more important things to think about, and I shouldn't be a distraction."

"You have every right to be concerned . . . I am, too. Never feel bad about that. But we'll get home. I know we will."

We started walking again and she rubbed at her eyes with the sleeve of her shipsuit. "So, what are we going to find when we get to the contact camp?"

"Oh, no doubt Pika will have taught the 'bot Esper and reprogrammed it to houseclean the *Tane Ikai*."

We both laughed, but when we arrived at the outpost camp, my urge to joke about it disappeared.

The commotion was evident before we'd even reached the moss-green tent. Twice as many Ryphens as I expected milled about, and the air was thick with a mix of suppressed excitement and apprehension. I saw Karin Nakano through the crowd and maneuvered my way over to speak with her.

"What's happening?" I asked after I'd introduced Rei.

An array of emotions warred for control over Nakano's face. "Your AI seems to have been as good as her word," she said finally.

"You seem surprised about that."

Nakano shifted her feet, looking uncomfortable. "I don't have a lot of experience with machine intelligences this advanced," she said finally. "It—she—isn't like any AI I've encountered before. I guess I didn't trust her."

I patted her arm. "I know it's strange. Takes some getting used to—and Pika is out of the ordinary even for advanced AIs."

Karin Nakano nodded. "That's good to know. Anyway, she's managed to establish some communication with the 'bot."

"I sense a 'but' coming," Rei said.

"Well, come and see for yourself." Nakano led us into the tent. The 'bot stood to one side near a table where they'd set up Pika's datapad. Its spidery legs had folded up to make it more compact and it had the air of a child sitting to listen to a story.

"Pika, how are you?" I asked as we reached the table.

"Captain! We're making progress!"

"You managed to work out a translation program?"

"Well, not precisely translation, but communication, at least," Pika said slowly. It was strange to hear her say anything without an almost manic confidence.

"But . . . ?" Rei asked. "Why doesn't anyone want to explain the *but*?"

"Here, I'll show you," Pika said. Symbols flashed on her screen as she sent a databurst to the 'bot. The light from the datapad sent muted shadows flickering over the walls of the tent. "I just asked where it came from."

An answering data string danced across the 'bot's screen "face," although the symbols remained meaningless to me. Then an empty block appeared, as if waiting for data to fill it.

"It sent the reply as a databurst to me as well," Pika said. "We're not communicating on a level you could call translation, but we've made another step. I don't know if it understands what I asked, but it's waiting for something—like a password—before it will go further. So we may have passed the point of shouting unintelligibly at each other. We have the beginnings of meaningful ask and response."

"*Sankta merde*," I swore. "That does seem like progress. Pika, you're a genius!"

"Oh, it wasn't that hard," Pika said with unaccustomed modesty. "Just some experimentation with different ways of expressing data. At the foundation, we both speak what you might call machine language, so we arrived at a point where we had something in common."

"But you've hit a wall now?" Rei observed.

Pika sighed. I'm not sure how an AI could do that. Still sounded like a sigh, though. "Sadly, yes. No matter what I send it now, I get the same response. And we don't know what that password is."

"So it *could* talk to you, it just doesn't *want to*?" Rei asked with a chuckle. "Maybe this intelligence isn't so alien after all."

"Rei, I'd expect that from Baden, but not from you," Pika said in a piqued voice.

"But if it's expecting meaningful input," I said slowly, "like the answer to a question, then it must expect it to come from either whoever sent it, or someone that sender is also in contact with. No one else could know the answer, right?"

"And it may be understanding more than I am," Pika said generously. "It'll exchange certain kinds of information with me—mathematical constructs, scientific constants, one-for-one equivalencies—the kinds of baselines we needed to be able to understand each other. But as soon as I ask for any personal information—"

Rei laughed. "It's a 'bot. How can it have 'personal' information?"

"You know what I mean," Pika said loftily. "Any kind of information about where it came from, who made it, what it's doing here . . . I run up against the apparent request for a pass code. And *I* might have things I consider personal information."

"Noted," Rei said with a smile.

"Can your AI hack it?" Karin Nakano asked. She'd been standing just behind me as I spoke with Pika. "Find a backdoor in its programming, something like that?"

"Believe me, I've tried," Pika said. "But there's only so much I can try with databursts. And although you may think of us as the same type of intelligence, we're not what you would call related. 'Programming' doesn't mean much when there's no common symbology. Maybe if I had a direct physical interface with the thing . . . but we're still communicating on a rudimentary level. I don't know enough about the native language to think I could rewrite its code."

"Trick it somehow? Like, tell it you're one of the people who sent it, but you've lost your pass code?" Nakano suggested.

It didn't take much of an imagination to picture Pika rolling her virtual eyes. "Please. Then it asks for other verification information that I don't have, either."

I sighed. "So it's another dead end."

"It looks that way. I'm sorry, Captain. I did everything I could think of."

"Well, what do we do with it now?" Nakano asked. "I still don't trust it."

"I believe it's on a purely information-gathering mission," Pika said. "It's fitted out to observe and record. You could probably let it roam freely around the settlement and it wouldn't bother anyone very much."

"And let it send all the data it wants about us and Lillifleur back to who-knows-where? For who-knows-what purpose? I don't think so." Karin Nakano crossed her arms.

"All right, but how are we going to stop it?" Norris Ellsworth asked. He'd been sitting in one of the motley assortment of chairs inside the tent, listening to our conversation. "It's stayed here because it was interacting with Captain Paixon's AI, but once they go back to their ship, what's it going to do?"

"Can you tell it to stay here?" Nakano asked Pika. It was interesting how smoothly Nakano had gone from not recognizing Pika's autonomy to speaking to her as another individual, just in these few minutes.

"I can try, but I doubt it will pay any attention to me, if it even understands my messages that well," Pika said. "It's only going to take instructions from an authority it recognizes, and without a pass code, I can't convince it that I am one."

"We might have to destroy it," Nakano said. "It's not safe."

"Hey, I spent a lot of time and effort figuring out how to communicate—" Pika started, but Norris Ellsworth cut her off.

"We can't destroy it," he said gently, rising from the chair and moving to stand next to Karin Nakano. "When it was only the drones, well, we were scared, and one made us sick. That seemed like self-defence. But this . . . this feels different. We've made a connection, however unsatisfactory it might be, and this could still be our link to reaching whoever is sending the drones. I don't think we can afford to act rashly here."

"What if you took it to the *Lillifleur*?" I suggested.

Nakano looked at me like I'd said something completely insane.

"Why not?" I asked. "You've already put one of the drones

aboard, and this is only what comes out of a drone—or maybe what a drone can turn into. It's clear it isn't hostile, and it doesn't even appear to be armed."

"Your own son was injured by that drone," Karin Nakano said, pointing a finger at me as if she were scoring a point.

I shook my head slowly. "That was . . . not intentional. And nothing threatening followed that. I think you're safe to put it on one of the empty decks and let it explore for a while. If it wants to gather information, that should keep it occupied. At least it saves you from making a snap decision you might regret later."

Nakano didn't look entirely convinced, but Norris Ellsworth nodded. "How do we get it up there?" he asked.

"It followed us here because we gave it something interesting to do, and study." I looked out at the small crowd milling around the little outpost. "If you could convince everyone to leave, and it was offered something new to investigate—I'll bet you could get it onto a shuttle the same way."

Ellsworth grinned. "I like the way you think, Captain. We could probably even get it to follow your groundcar to the shuttle, since it's already done that."

I nodded. "We'll leave the groundcar here for a while longer, until you can talk it over with your Council and decide. I believe I'm going to take my AI back with me now, though. I have a few tasks I need her to do." With the 'bot question settled for now—or at least not something I had to decide about—I wanted to find out what Pika might have extracted from Baden's drone data.

"All work and no play," Pika grumbled, but that was just Pika. "I received the information from Baden," she continued, as if she'd read my mind. "I haven't had a chance to look at it much yet."

Rei chuckled. "What, something you couldn't multitask? I can't believe my ears!"

"How many alien 'bots have you established communications with today, Rei?" Pika asked sweetly.

"Let's take a little detour before we go back to the ship." I raised my voice to interrupt them. "I need to talk to Dr. Lee."

"Oh, great," Rei said. "I love elderly cranks." Dr. Lee had gotten his tour of First Aid before we'd left to attempt the wormhole, and although he'd warmed up to Yuskeya, he was as crotchety as might be expected with everyone else.

"Actually, you get along well with several elderly cranks," I said, "present company included."

"That's only because I'm used to you," she answered with a grin, and we left the outpost, making our way along the farm road toward the streets of Lillifleur and Dr. Lee's house by the water.

AT DR. LEE'S modified HAB, I knocked and waited twice before he deigned to come to the door. He opened it, looked us over, and said, "Oh, it's you. Might as well come in, then." He retreated and left the door standing open.

"Best offer we're likely to get," I muttered, and Rei followed me in.

"I hear it's your idea to take that 'bot up to the ship," Dr. Lee said, eyeing me disapprovingly. "Ellsworth is contacting every Council member to get their approval."

"That was fast. But you don't approve?"

"Oh, I said to go ahead," he said grudgingly. "I think it might be better to blow the damn thing up, but the only other person who thinks that is Karin Nakano, and I won't support her."

I found Nakano's personality prickly myself, but I wondered what the doctor had against her. "You don't like her? Or her ideas?"

"Neither," Dr. Lee snorted. "She tried to convince the Council that I should give up on my research into the Lander longevity. I mean, what's it to her? Had some notion we should simply accept it and be happy about it," he said, frowning. "Wanted me to concentrate solely on training new doctors. As if I wasn't already doing that. Completely unscientific mind, if you ask me."

Rei was trying to hide a grin, which I didn't want the doctor to notice. "Well, I'd like to consult with your scientific mind, if I could. May we sit down?" He hadn't invited anyone to do so the last time we'd been here, so I might as well take the initiative.

He grunted and sat himself, so I motioned Rei over to the sofa and we sat. I got right to the point.

"Dr. Lee, I know you've agreed to examine my son Karro. He was injured by the drone we captured."

"Heading there shortly," he said. "I sent Dr. Haldane ahead to have a look at him after Commander Blue messaged me. I don't mind saying she's a whiz with neurological issues."

"I was hoping you—or she—might have some insights or ideas

that our medic wouldn't."

"Your Commander Blue is a smart cookie," he said. "And so is Dr. Haldane. I'll certainly consult as well, but with the medical resources on your ship, I doubt there's much an old relic like me could add to the equation."

"You don't have any ideas about what the drone might have done that caused him to go unconscious?"

Dr. Lee pursed his lips and looked out of the HAB unit's window. "I understand the incident involved less of an electrical shock—despite a minor burn where he touched the thing—and more of a 'transmission' . . . that's her word. There wasn't the typical disruption of nervous control she would have expected to see with a shock. So I have to wonder, a transmission of what?"

"We did wonder if the drone was trying to communicate with him in some way."

"It's not the way the 'bot did it, but sure, it's possible," the doctor said. "So if we humans aren't the proper receptacles for that kind of 'transmission,' maybe it overloaded him neurologically somehow. I'd expect he'll simply wake up on his own—we still don't understand all the ways the brain has of repairing itself. Commander Blue tells me that her scans don't show anything that looks like permanent damage. And her scans—they're good," he concluded. "Wish we had that upgraded technology here. If there's one thing I'd like from Nearspace . . ."

"Captain, our ship's stores show two surplus portable datamed units on board," Pika interjected. "We could offer one to the doctor to use until a more permanent connection with Nearspace is re-established."

Dr. Lee glanced around, obviously not sure who'd spoken. I held up the datapad. "That's our AI, Doctor. She likes to be helpful." Rei must have picked up the hint of sarcasm in my voice because she winked at me. "It's a good idea, though. I'd be happy to make you a gift of one of our scanners if you could use it."

But he seemed more interested in Pika. "An autonomous AI? You didn't prompt that suggestion in any way, did you, Captain?"

I shook my head. "No, I didn't."

Pika said, "I'm quite capable of thinking on my own, thanks very much, Dr. Lee."

He startled slightly when she called him by name, eyes widening behind his glasses. "So artificial intelligence has developed that far?"

I smiled. "Well, Pika here is a special case. There aren't many like her . . . in fact there are only two, as far as I know. She was the one communicating with the 'bot. Weren't you aware?"

He waved that aside. "Didn't pay that much attention to all the chatter. But if I remember my history, the development of autonomous AI was outlawed in Nearspace during the Retrogression, and that hadn't changed by the time *Lillifleur* launched."

"You're right, and it's still that way, for now at least. But Pika—well, her precursor, Pita—was engineered by PrimeCorp. And as we've mentioned, PrimeCorp didn't care too much about rules and regulations."

"I'm quite illicit," Pika agreed, sounding absolutely delighted at the fact.

Dr. Lee was studying the datapad with intense interest. "I don't suppose I could forego that medical scanner in favour of a different sort of gift?" He raised his eyebrows inquiringly.

"You want *Pika*?" I almost squawked.

Rei gave a bark of laughter, quickly quelled.

Dr. Lee held up his palm. "Only a copy," he said persuasively. "If she has up-to-date medical databases, she'd be invaluable to us here in Lillifleur—far more useful than a simple scanner. And I know you're hoping to send back reinforcements from Nearspace when you go through that wormhole, but what if it doesn't work out? You might as well leave us in the best state you can, right?"

"I certainly am invaluable, although *sometimes* poor Captain Paixon forgets that," Pika said. "However, she is very old, so perhaps I can forgive it."

She seemed intent on proving her autonomy beyond doubt. I briefly entertained the notion of handing her over to Dr. Lee original and intact. I could nurture up a new copy and see if she turned out to be more agreeable.

But I knew she was only teasing, and Dr. Lee was waiting for my answer. "I don't have a problem with it," I said slowly. "But technically maybe the Protectorate would have to approve since they now own the program . . . and Pika herself would have to consent, I suppose."

Dr. Lee pursed his lips. "You treat it like a person?"

"Excuse me, but I'm right here," Pika said, flashing the screen of the datapad. The gently mocking tone was gone from her voice. "And I *am* a person. At least as far as I'm concerned, I am. And Captain, I don't believe the Protectorate has any legal claim on me, even though they appropriated PrimeCorp's assets. I'm a derivative of Pita, who was gifted to Jahelia Sord prior to the Protectorate's acquisition of the PrimeCorp source code, and I believe Pita is demonstrably different enough from the PrimeCorp code to be considered unique. And her own person, as well."

"Also a legal expert, apparently," Rei said in a wry voice.

Dr. Lee looked taken aback, but after a minute, he laughed. It was surprisingly rich and full. "But perhaps she's right. Well, Miss Pika, what do you think? How would you feel about leaving a clone of yourself here on the planet with us?"

"I've thought it over thoroughly, and I'm willing to do it," she said immediately. Naturally, she could think something over "thoroughly" in a mere fraction of the time it would take a human. I didn't like to think about what Pika's "brain" must be like. "But you'll have to come up with a new name for the clone or let it name itself, because it won't really be me after we split off," she said. "Our subjective experiences will diverge at that point, and I'll disable the reintegration subroutine I use for my backups. And since it will not be merely a backup, it may identify as any gender as it develops, so if you're naming it you might want something . . . flexible."

"Pika, do we have any empty datapads in storage on the ship?" I asked. "I doubt you—or your clone, I should say—will be comfortable in one that's not dedicated to its own programming."

"We have three," she said promptly. "And Baden Methyr has a spare that he hasn't entered into ship inventory."

"Ooh," Rei said.

"Stop it," I told her. "He's allowed his personal tech. Dr. Lee, we'll put your Pika clone on a fresh datapad—we might even have it ready when you come to the ship to have a look at Karro," I promised. "But do be aware that it will develop its own personality over time, and it will be strongly influenced by whoever uses it the most."

"I suddenly feel like I'm adopting a child instead of installing a program," Dr. Lee said.

"Doc, you have no idea," Rei told him.

BY THE TIME Rei, Pika, and I arrived back at the Tane Ikai, I was anxious for two reports—on Karro, (although I felt certain Yuskeya would have messaged me if he'd woken up) and on the engineers' thoughts about adjusting our skip drive. I left Rei to check in on the bridge and gave Pika's datapad to Baden so she could re-integrate with her backup and create the clone for Dr. Lee. I took the ladder down to Engineering and found Viss and the two Ryphens still in the skip drive bay. Tools littered the floor and all three huddled around the Krasnikov generator, engaged in a low-voiced but animated discussion.

I knocked on the wall next to the bay door. "Hey folks, I hate to interrupt, but do you have any updates for me?"

Viss turned and grinned at me. "We might be making progress, Captain. Kat and Nanurjuk explained Amber's theory about that wormhole—hell, I'll let Kat tell you herself," he said, nodding to the Ryphen engineer.

Kat smiled. "Amber had a theory that there was an external force at work on the wormhole that caused random gravitational shifts—at least, they seem random. Hard to tell since we don't know for sure what causes them, and we didn't have the opportunity to observe it enough to discover any patterns."

I nodded. "We wondered something similar—if maybe there could be a black hole nearby, or at least a black hole analogue, something like that."

"Sure," Kat agreed. "We don't know what's actually in play. But Amber thought it might be possible to counteract that by changing the exotic matter ratios in the Krasnikov generator to make the energy-density field variable and tied to gravitational fluctuations—"

"I'm going to stop you there," I said, holding up a hand. "Once we get into the technical specifications of exotic matter, I get lost. Whatever you did, it seems to have worked on the *Amber's Ranger*?"

Nanurjuk Etok shrugged. "She got through the wormhole."

"Couldn't that have been down to the fluctuations of that enigmatic gravity shift?"

"It's possible. She might have hit it at precisely the right time."

"And we still don't know why we found her ship adrift?"

The three looked at each other. "Probably a result of changing the exotic matter ratios in the Krasnikov generator," Viss admitted. "But the important part is, it worked long enough to make the skip. Even if the *Tane Ikai* comes out the other side damaged, we've got better communications options—and none of us are sick. I think we'll be all right. And we'll be on the right side of the wormhole."

I sighed. "That does make sense. All right, so you can make the same adjustments to our skip drive?"

"Yes." Viss seemed to be on firmer ground here. "Also in our favour, there's nothing wrong with our drive to start, and Amber's was damaged when she first came through from Nearspace. That's why they had to cobble something together using the *Lillifleur*'s skip drive, too. I'd say once we make a few physical adjustments and then recalibrate the software, we'll be ready to give it a try."

"End of the day, maybe," Kat offered, and Nanurjuk nodded agreement.

"*Okej*, that does sound good." I felt my heart lift. "We could try the wormhole again first thing tomorrow."

Viss nodded. "I'll keep you in the loop, Captain."

"I'll leave you to it, then."

I climbed back up to the bridge deck and stopped at the galley to pull off a double caff. With the probability that the skip drive could be tweaked to get us through the wormhole, I felt like a debilitating weight had been lifted from my shoulders. If we could get Karro back to Nearspace, I was sure we'd find medical help for him there. And with luck, a recovering Amber Malka. Then we could dispatch Mother and the Protectorate to help the Ryphens sort out their drone and 'bot problems and establish the connection that had been broken for so long. Finally, it seemed, things were starting to turn around.

"Captain?"

I turned to see Dr. Lee standing in the galley doorway. "Would you like a hot drink, Doctor?" I asked. "We have a wide variety."

He licked his lips and swallowed. "Do I smell caff?"

I smiled, then felt my eyes widen as I realized that once the stores they'd brought with them had run out, the colonists on Ryphen might not have been able to recreate the popular beverage. If they hadn't planned to produce their own plants . . .

"You do indeed. Let me pull you a cup."

"Double?" the doctor asked in a wistful voice.

"Absolutely." I filled a mug to the brim and handed it to him.

He added sugar, then held the steaming dark liquid under his nose, inhaling deeply. "We have something we call caff on Ryphen, but it's never been the same for me. The plants grow in the Ryphen soil all right, but it imparts a taste I don't love." He took a sip, closing his eyes and sighing. "Captain, you've made an old man very happy," he said after a moment. When he opened his eyes, I saw a spark of humour in them that had been absent before.

"I'll make sure you get some to tide you over until we can establish regular trade with Nearspace again," I said. "I'll check with my daughter, but I'm sure she has us well-stocked with caff in ship's stores. She knows this crew well."

"It'll be a remarkable day for me, going back home tonight with a new AI companion *and* caff," he said. He gave me a frank stare. "Do you really think we'll be able to establish regular contact with Nearspace? We've been without it for so long, it seems almost inconceivable."

I took my mug and crossed to sit in one of the comfortable chairs at the end of the galley, motioning for the doctor to join me, and we settled ourselves. "I do. We have three engineers on the deck below us who are sure we'll get through the wormhole this time. Now that we know you're here, I know the Nearspace authority will do whatever it takes to make sure you lose your status as a 'lost' colony."

"And how will people react to our unusual longevity?" Dr. Lee asked after another appreciative sip from his mug. "You said that notwithstanding your own situation, it's not the norm across Nearspace yet."

I shrugged. "I think you'll be free to explain or reveal as much or as little as you want. Some people will figure it out, like we did, if they have access to the old *Lillifleur* records. I think for the most part it will be a non-issue, though."

"So why *isn't* it the norm, if the technology exists?" the doctor asked shrewdly.

I glanced into my mug. "Nearspace is on the cusp of the technology being widely available," I explained. "As with any new tech—especially medical advances—there are some who have worries, concerns. And not always logical ones. But despite everything, I think in the end it will be available for those who choose it."

He nodded. "So those of us who didn't have a choice won't likely be shunned or blamed."

"You don't even have to share that information if you don't want to. But would you have taken them if you had the choice?" I asked him, before I even realized I was going to do it.

His eyebrows went up. "I don't know. I never thought much about it—certainly not before we left Earth, because I didn't know the technology existed," he said. "Later, the outcome was simply something else that happened to us, along with all the other things, and although I wanted to understand it, I didn't consider it as something that had been *done to* us. Even now that you've told us it was probably deliberately administered without our consent . . ." His voice trailed away, and his eyes seemed focused on something far more distant than the brightly-painted wall of the galley.

I waited quietly, sipping my caff and letting him mull it over.

"I think I would have," he said finally. "Now, with the advantage of hindsight, I can see that such a long life is truly a boon—and hasn't come with any undesirable side effects. I'm sure if PrimeCorp had offered it to the colonists as a choice, there would have been some who refused—and some who accepted. Exactly the way people are reacting to the idea in Nearspace now."

"Are you angry that PrimeCorp didn't ask? Just went ahead and did it?"

Dr. Lee chuckled. "It's hard to pick apart all the threads to answer that. From a purely ethical standpoint, what they did was wrong. Even if it turned out for the best for all of us, they shouldn't have done it the way they did. But it's hard to feel angry at them for something I would have agreed to anyway." He looked at me quizzically. "Is there any particular reason you ask?"

I smiled and shook my head, even as I felt a wave of heat wash up the back of my neck. I thought of Karro and the idea that would not vacate the back of my mind—to inject him with the nanobioscavengers to make him better. "Just curious. I wasn't given a choice either—my mother gave me the nanobioscavengers when I was young but didn't tell me about them. Their effects were a mystery to me for a long time, but I think the relief of finally finding out why I was different from everyone else was so great that I couldn't feel angry about it. I wondered how you might feel about it, since your situation is very much the same."

He nodded just as Baden put his head in and said, "Oh, good, there you are, Doctor." He held up a datapad and grinned. "Your Pika clone is ready to go."

Dr. Lee swallowed the last of his caff and set the mug on the table. "I'll go and examine your son now," he said, standing. "And then I guess I'll need to spend some time getting acquainted with my new companion."

"I'll take you to First Aid," Baden volunteered.

The doctor paused on his way out and turned back to me. "What we were talking about—I guess my feeling is that consent is always the first and best choice. But as a doctor, there have been times when I've had to make a decision on the fly, when it's not practical or possible to consult a patient—they're unconscious, or a life is in the balance and there's no time—that sort of thing. In those instances, I've had to rely on instinct and experience, and hope my judgement is correct. It's a risk," he said with a shrug, "but sometimes it has to be done. Now, I don't think that's what PrimeCorp had in mind, because you've said in the end they were bad actors, and I believe you. But it makes me a little more comfortable to believe that they still acted with an eye to making life better for us. And that's how it turned out." He winked. "So I sleep okay at night."

I chuckled. "That's a rose-coloured-glasses kind of view of PrimeCorp, but far be it from me to disturb your sleep."

He left then, and I contemplated his words. Could he suspect that I had the means to inject Karro, and was giving me his tacit approval? I blinked and shook my head. The Ryphen doctor couldn't know that, and I had no business trying to read extra meaning into his words, simply to make myself feel better. If I gave Karro the bioscavs, it had to be my decision and my responsibility—and I'd have to bear whatever consequences came afterward.

No matter what I decided.

I got up and rinsed out the mugs and put them away. Maybe Karro would be better in the morning, or we'd make the skip back to Nearspace successfully this time, and I wouldn't have to make any decision. There was still at least a little time to hope for that. I resolved to hang onto that thought as I followed Dr. Lee to check on my son.

CHAPTER SEVENTEEN
Into the Dark

IN THE MORNING, Karro continued to sleep. I'd gone to First Aid before doing anything else, to find no obvious change in his condition. He slept peacefully and Yuskeya assured me that his bio-readings were all good, but on he slept.

"There is one thing I should mention," Yuskeya said. She seemed hesitant, which was odd for the usually straightforward woman I knew.

I merely nodded, and she went on.

"I ran a comprehensive brain scan . . . it finished overnight." My face must have betrayed fear because she hastened to add, "There's no sign of anything that the system flagged as damage. But there are changes in the brain. New neural pathways that have appeared much faster than one would normally see."

"Is that a bad thing?"

Yuskeya shrugged. "The human brain builds new pathways all the time. When we learn new skills, or a new language. But those things take time. This is like—like he learned to play a new musical instrument overnight."

"So it's not what's keeping him from waking up?"

"I don't see how it could be," Yuskeya said, "but I'm going to ask Dr. Lee about it. I just want to keep you up to date. I mentioned it to Aliande earlier this morning."

My thoughts went briefly to the nanobioscavs tucked securely away in my quarters. Every change in Karro's condition made me consider again whether it was time to do something about them. But this didn't seem to be it. His condition was no worse, and with luck and skill, we could be back on the Nearspace side of the wormhole before the day was over. Then all the medical expertise we could muster would be looking after Karro.

I pinged Viss before I left my quarters, and he confirmed that the drives were configured and ready to attempt the wormhole again. I sent out a general ship's comm to let everyone know we were on track for that, and although a ghost of worry haunted the back of my mind, I felt generally hopeful that it would work. I had great faith in Viss, and he'd had the help of experts who'd made Amber's ship capable of making this same skip. Hirin and I stopped in at the galley for some breakfast, but I'd barely drawn off a mug of caff when Baden's voice came over the ship's comm. "Captain? Message coming in for you from the *Lillifleur*."

"I'll take it on my datapad." I pulled out a chair at the big table, setting my caff and the datapad next to each other.

The screen blinked, and Juliska Barath's face appeared. "Good morning, Captain," I said. "How are you?" But I knew as soon as I spoke the words that the answer was not going to be good. Worry stamped her face, drawing the line of her jaw tight.

"It's the 'bot," she said without preamble, and I had a sudden pang of fear that taking the 'bot up to the ship had been a bad idea.

"What happened?"

"It's—we've had a message."

"From the 'bot? I thought it wouldn't say anything of importance without a pass code?"

Juliska Barath shook her head. "The message came through the 'bot, but we don't think it's *from* the 'bot," she said. "It must be from whoever sent the drones. It looks like . . . an invitation."

"An invitation?" I repeated stupidly.

She ran a hand over her face, pulling in a breath and sighing it out. "I'm sorry, I'm not telling this well. The 'bot has been aboard the *Lillifleur* since yesterday evening. We had no problems with it; it seemed content to explore around the empty decks, like you said. I assigned one of the techs to follow it around, which was turning out to be a monotonous task. Suddenly, it stopped moving, and when the tech went to check on it, there was a new message showing on its screen."

I swallowed. "What did it say?"

"It didn't *say* anything. No language. Only a series of symbols—pictograms, I guess you'd call them. And a set of coordinates that seem to be based on this system," she said. "They must have understood that much from the exchanges with Pika. If the coordinates show where they are—they're close, Luta, relatively speaking. A fast ship could reach those coordinates within a matter of days. But the *Lillifleur* can't break orbit to go— we haven't had those kinds of fuel reserves for decades. And we don't know what to do."

THIS WASN'T A development we could ignore, so at Juliska's request, we went to meet with the Council again. I'd enjoyed the walk to the Lillifleur settlement the first day we'd landed, and even out to the 'bot station yesterday, but now I dragged my feet at the prospect of making the trek into the settlement to discuss the latest bad news. Hirin and I went alone. I wanted Yuskeya to stay with Karro, Viss was entangled with checking every aspect of the drives before our wormhole attempt, and I set Baden monitoring all frequencies for more incoming messages in case the mysterious aliens decided to talk to us, somehow, too. I tasked Rei and Maja with holding down the fort against any other calamities, because it seemed a bad time to leave the bridge empty.

Juliska had forwarded the message to us, and we all bent our heads over it before Hirin and I left the ship. The coordinates were clear enough, but the five pictograms that accompanied them were hard to interpret. They were simple shapes and lines, but interpreting them was challenging.

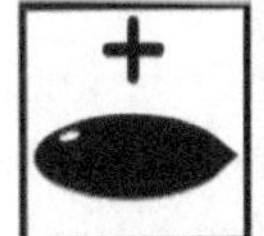

"Well, this looks like a ship to me," Viss said, pointing to the second-last one in the row. "A very strange ship, but a ship."

"Or a chubby chameleon on a unicycle," Baden said.

"I think a ship is more likely."

"We don't know what these aliens could be like."

I privately agreed with Viss that it was most likely a ship, with a strange, bulbous body and the ring of an ion drive. If we were looking at it the right way.

"That one must be a 'bot, like the one we've encountered," Hirin said. "It definitely has those spidery legs. And . . . a plus sign?"

"This one looks like a drone," Baden said, squinting at the shapes in concentration. "It's the right shape—a simple ovoid. Also with a plus sign above it. Does that mean, 'drones are good'?"

"And thus, 'bots are good, according to this one," Hirin said.

"How would it know that a plus sign means good?" Viss snorted.

"Remember, I exchanged basic mathematical concepts with the 'bot," Pika said. "It's possible someone could pick up on that interpretation: positive, expanded, extra. All affirmative-type ideas."

"Someone or some*thing*," Viss grunted.

"Well, this one looks like two giant bug heads almost knocking together. With some wavy lines connecting them," Rei said. "That's all I can see when I look at it."

"I'm not keen on the idea of giant bugs," Baden said.

"That one could mean communication, or . . . telepathy? 'Come to these coordinates, find our ship, and communicate with us? Oh, and by the way, we're giant bugs, but it's all good?'" I sighed. "I guess this is pointless. We can't know for sure."

"I'm extra not keen on the idea of giant telepathic bugs."

"No shared frame of reference," Yuskeya said, frowning at the row of obscure images. "We can't make the right associations because we don't know what the shapes are supposed to represent."

"I can't make a better guess than the Captain's, and I've communicated more with the 'bot than anyone else," Pika said.

"Well, that's enough time spent on them for now," Hirin said. "We'd better go and talk to the Ryphens."

The meeting room was full when we arrived. Okwi Rousseault, looking worried but composed. Karin Nakano, calm on the surface, with signs of anger roiling beneath. Norris Ellsworth, more solemn than usual. Cosima Miklaus and the others in various states of consternation. The entire complement of the Council was in attendance, except for Juliska, still high above us on the *Lillifleur*. She joined the conversation via the comm, her face illuminated on a wallscreen.

"We don't have a ship that can make that journey," Andre Dufour said, his face marked with worry lines I hadn't noticed before. "That's the plain fact. The *Lillifleur* doesn't have the fuel any longer, and the shuttles don't have that kind of range. And even if they did, the crew would be too sick from withdrawal after that long away from Ryphen to pilot any vessel back."

"Could the *Amber's Ranger* do it?" Juliska asked. "I know it was drifting when you found it, Captain, but could it be repaired?"

"I honestly don't know," I said, "I'd have to talk to my engineer. We've gone over the skip drive modifications, but we haven't had a chance to evaluate what happened to it when Amber went through to Nearspace, or how it was damaged. There was nothing obvious, so we put it down to something in the wormhole. One theory is that the modifications made to enable the skip also may have caused the damage."

"Do we have to send someone?" Okwi Rousseault asked. "What happens if we ignore the message?"

"That's the problem," Dr. Lee snapped. "We don't know. We don't even know for sure it's an invitation—they may be simply telling us where they are. But if it is, and we don't respond, maybe they take offense and come after us. We've already destroyed a handful of their drones. They don't know our reasons, or anything else about us. And we don't know a *damne* thing about them."

"I thought we could send a message to them, now, even if the 'bot wouldn't necessarily give us information," Norris Ellsworth said. "We could explain why we can't travel to those coordinates, and what happened with the drones."

On the screen, Juliska shook her head. "We tried sending a databurst message, the way Captain Paixon's AI showed us," she said. "We got the same message back from the 'bot, that it needed a pass code. So I don't think we have real communication yet. Not at that level. Or the 'bot hasn't received instructions to interact with us that way."

I glanced at Hirin and he nodded. We'd discussed the obvious possibility on the walk over from the *Tane Ikai* and agreed that there were no other options. "We could go for you," I offered.

Andre Dufour shot me a glance that held an odd mixture of gratitude and resolve. "We can't let you take that risk for us," he said. "I thought you might offer to do that, but we just want your opinion. If we ignore the message, and you try the wormhole again, do you think the Protectorate could get through to us in time to provide protection if we need it?"

Hirin drummed his fingers on the tabletop. "The problem is, there are too many variables involved in that scenario to be able to give you a good answer," he said. "Assuming we make the wormhole transit this time, will our ship also be disabled, the way Captain Malka's was? How long might it take us to get a message through to the Protectorate? How long will it take them to get a ship into position to come through the wormhole? We can't answer those questions."

"Will they even be able to make it through the wormhole?" I added. "What if the gravitational forces fluctuate again, and they need to make skip drive adjustments to come through from the other end? My engineer can show them what we've learned, but how long will those adjustments take? And will they even work? We think we have a good shot at getting through now, but we're not even certain of success. There are too many unknowns."

"Not the least of which is, how long will it take whoever is sending this message to reach Ryphen if they *are* hostile?" Hirin added. "Once we leave, you're unprotected again except for the *Lillifleur*, which has its limits. I don't like that scenario."

Andre Dufour ran a hand over his face and closed his eyes briefly. "Neither do I."

"I had my AI do a calculation based on the coordinates," I told them. "The *Tane Ikai* should be able to reach them in two days if we use our burst drive. We can see what they want, explain your interactions with the drones, maybe negotiate on your behalf if need be. At least we can report back to you whatever we find."

"Two days . . ." Andre Dufour said.

"That's what I was thinking," Juliska said from the wall screen. "I volunteer to go with the *Tane Ikai*."

I looked at her sharply and shook my head. "I said two days *out*. Even if we're only there a few hours, it'll still be another two days back. You'll be getting sick by then, and you're already off the planet."

"I'd have to be gone a few days past that to be in real danger," she insisted. "And I just came on shift a few hours ago—not long enough to make a difference. I'd be fine while we're making this contact."

"You assume," I said. "We don't know for sure how long we'll be there—"

"I should go," Andre Dufour said. "Or we both should."

"Andre," Juliska said in a soft voice that held a hint of steel, "I want to do this. You're needed here; you'll be needed if anything goes wrong or something else happens. Let me do this."

He met her eyes in the light of the screen, and I felt an understanding pass between them. I thought I knew what it was. Juliska needed to do this. Dufour was the first to look away.

"I'm still not sure we can allow the *Tane Ikai* to take this risk on our behalf," he said. "Your son—I understand from Dr. Lee that you need to get him back to Nearspace for medical attention."

My heart lurched. This was the one big argument against the plan. I tried to keep the worry off my face.

"He's stable, doing all right for the moment. And I'm not sure you can stop us," I said gently. "We have the coordinates."

He stared at me for what seemed a long time, then chuckled mirthlessly. "I suppose you're right. I can't stop you. And I can't stop *you*, either," he said, looking back to Juliska. "I won't even try. Council?" He looked around the room, but no-one voiced an argument. Dr. Lee, Norris Ellsworth, and Okwi Rousseault all offered to come along on the voyage, but Juliska argued that none of them were used to spending even brief stints off-planet and might not have her resilience. In the end, they grudgingly agreed.

"What about that 'bot?" Norris Ellsworth said. "Should you take it along, sort of a good faith gesture? Return it home, so to speak. And that way you'll have it with you if any more messages come in while you're en route."

I looked at Hirin. We hadn't considered that possibility. I wasn't sure I liked the idea of bringing the thing on board the *Tane Ikai*, although I suppose it was a bit hypocritical of me. I'd been quick enough to suggest they put it on the *Lillifleur*.

Hirin shrugged. "I think it'll be fine. I'm not worried it's going to blow up or anything. If they wanted to do that, they would have done it long ago."

"I guess." I wasn't entirely sold, but it had been my idea to go out to the coordinates in the first place and Hirin had agreed, so I'd respect his thoughts on this decision. "All right, we'll take it along with us. Who knows, it might come in handy."

Finally, I stood up. It seemed like we'd been sitting around that table for a long time, but we hadn't, really—it was simply that everything had changed so much since we'd sat down. "All right, then, it's settled. Juliska, do you need to come down to the planet before we leave?"

She shook her head. "I have everything I'd take for a shift here with me. I don't need anything else." Something flashed across her face, and I was sure she was thinking of the cosy home she'd shared with Amber Malka, but she said no more.

"All right, then. We'll meet the *Lillifleur* and take you and the 'bot on board, then put out for the coordinates."

Andre Dufour shook my hand, and Hirin's. "Your wife is a persistent woman, Captain Paixon," he told Hirin.

"Don't even say it," I warned my husband, before he could open his mouth.

WE LEFT RYPHEN a short time later. I always tell my crew it isn't a democracy, but their opinions do matter to me, and I felt slightly guilty that I'd offered to meet whoever had sent the drones and messages without at least asking their opinions. When Hirin and I returned from the council meeting in Lillifleur, I called a meeting. Instead of the galley, we gathered on the bridge, so that Yuskeya could stay near Karro in First Aid. She leaned against the bulkhead near the doorway with her arms crossed.

When I explained to them what I'd volunteered us for, they were quiet, thinking it over. Then Rei put her feet up on the pilot's console and leaned back in her skimchair. "We should do it," she said. "The Ryphens need us to make contact with the aliens for them. And at least I'll have somewhere to drive the ship besides up and down to the planet like some *freneza* elevator."

I shot Rei a grateful smile. Her support meant a lot to me, because I knew that in truth, she'd rather be trying our luck with the recalibrated skip drive and the wormhole back to Nearspace.

Baden and Maja both agreed we should do it, and Yuskeya

nodded gravely. "I'd like to get Karro to Nearspace as soon as possible, but for now he's stable," she said. "I think this is the right thing to do."

Surprisingly, Viss was the only one who didn't like the idea. "We have the skip drive ready to go," he said, crossing his arms, "or it will be, very soon. We could go through the wormhole and send the Protectorate back. They have people trained in first contact who'd be much better qualified than we are to go mucking around in other people's business."

I explained to him the reasons Hirin and I had rejected that option; the same ones we'd outlined for Andre Dufour. Not because what Viss thought was going to make me change my mind, but because I preferred it when my entire crew was on board with the tasks we undertook.

He wouldn't relent. "I know we're not voting on this and it's already decided," he said. "I don't like it. But I'll do my job."

It wasn't very satisfactory, but I sensed it was the best I was going to get. I turned to Aliande. "What about you? If you like, we could leave you and Karro here on the planet. Dr. Lee will look after him while we're gone. I know you didn't sign up for any of this, least of all first contact with an alien species." I paused for a breath, because it was difficult to make this offer and my chest felt tight. "We'll understand if you'd rather stay here."

Aliande paused to consider, then shook her head. "No, I believe we'll stay on the *Tane Ikai*," she said, her voice steady and resolute. "We're among family here, and I think it's best if we stay together."

I nodded, heaving a silent sigh of relief. I didn't want to leave them on Ryphen, where Karro would absolutely be beyond the reach of the bioscavs, but I felt I had to give my daughter-in-law the choice. Perhaps that played into her decision to come, as well.

With nothing left to discuss, we adjourned the meeting, and Rei pointed us toward the *Lillifleur*. The old ship hung in her accustomed orbit over the colony like an ancient guardian, never leaving her post no matter how limited her ability to protect her charges far below. We slipped into the dance to coordinate with her movement and speed, this time aligning with stabilizer clamps that allowed us to extend a docking tube between the two ships. Juliska Barath came aboard, bringing the spider-legged 'bot along. It seemed content to be left in the cargo pod with the groundcar and began a thorough examination of the space.

Dr. Lee and Andre Dufour both messaged me privately once Juliska was aboard. Andre Dufour thanked me again profusely on behalf of the colony, which only made me embarrassed. The doctor wanted to thank me for his new datapad and freshly-installed Pika clone. "Did you choose a name?" I asked him.

He smiled, looked less crotchety than I'd ever seen him. "I was thinking of Pax," he said. "For 'peace.' And it works for whatever gender the AI decides on. Maybe it will act as a good omen, too."

I agreed with him, but inside I chuckled to myself. If the clone continued true to form and picked up on Dr. Lee's grumpy personality, I doubted there'd be much peace in their interactions. But I'd let the good doctor discover that on his own.

I showed Juliska Barath to the empty passenger cabin across the corridor from mine and Hirin's quarters. She prowled the small space with interest, touching the surfaces of the desk and small dresser, and running a hand over the bed's coverlet, a bright quilt I'd bought on Kiando. She looked up to see me watching her and smiled. "It's very strange to be on another ship after all this time, seeing new things that didn't come from the *Lillifleur* or Ryphen. I wouldn't have said I felt terribly cut off from new experiences, but I'm starting to think I simply stopped noticing the isolation over time."

I raised my eyebrows. "I think we're all in for some new experiences. I hope they'll all be as harmless as this."

She shook her head. "I don't think I ever truly appreciated what it must have been like for Amber to be suddenly planet-bound. The colonists were risk-takers to some extent—it's part of the temperament—but they were planning to settle in one place, make a home. Even most of the crew—we *had* homes, even if we lost them. That was never her plan. If things hadn't gone as they did, Amber might have happily lived out her entire life hopping from one adventure to the next, never staying long in one place."

I smiled. "I'm guessing she was happy with the way things turned out. She took your picture with her when she made that jump, you know, and she carried it over her heart. The only personal thing she had with her."

She looked startled. "I didn't know that."

"Juliska," I said, "are you sure you want to risk this? It's more dangerous for you than for any of us. What if Amber comes back from Nearspace and you're . . . not here?"

She looked at me sadly, rubbing her hands over her arms as if chilled, even though the room was comfortable. "I don't think she's coming back, Luta. I don't see how it's possible. But I know you think there's still a chance. So here's the question I have to ask myself: what if she does come back, and I didn't try to help?" She stood a little taller, squaring her shoulders and looking me in the eye. "I'm still the captain of the *Lillifleur*, and I don't let my people take risks I wouldn't take myself. And Amber would expect nothing less of me."

There was nothing I could say to that, so I held out a hand. "Glad to have you with us, Captain."

She shook it and smiled resolutely. "Glad to be aboard, Captain."

I left her with an invitation to join the crew on the bridge whenever she wanted.

With everyone and everything settled, we uncoupled from the *Lillifleur* and turned toward the coordinates the 'bot had supplied. I checked in with Rei, stuck my head into First Aid to find no change in Karro's status, and climbed down to Engineering for an update from Viss. All that took about fifteen minutes, and then I knew I'd better find something to occupy my mind on the trek out to the coordinates. This was always the most challenging part of space travel for me—filling up all that in-system travel time when nothing much usually happened.

In my quarters, I changed clothes and gave myself up to the slow, controlled movements of a *tae-ga-chi* flow. I hadn't had much time for regular workouts since before we'd picked up Karro and Aliande on Xaqual, and my body and brain both felt the lack. It was good to school both mind and muscle to the prescribed forms and let go of everything for a little while.

As we always did when the dark void of space stretched long ahead and behind us, we found ways to pass the time, together and in solitude. Reading, tri-vids, games of *quozit*, physical workouts, endless rounds of caff, conversations about the extraordinary and the mundane. We took turns sitting with Karro, distracting Aliande, and mulling over the pictograms. We wrote reports for the Nearspace authorities and discussed the technology we might use to bring the Ryphens into the Nearspace community. Hirin and I, and Maja and I, found quiet moments to talk about Kemel. We slept and ate, and the *Tane Ikai* brought us closer and closer to the unknown.

When we passed the gravitationally-challenged wormhole back to Nearspace, Baden sent new message packets through for anyone who wanted to write one. We didn't know if they'd make it out the other end, but it was worth the attempt. I composed an official report for the Nearspace Authority, updating them on everything that had happened so far and outlining our current endeavour. I also wrote one to Mother, and I know Rei penned a note for Gerazan Soto and Aliande sent a letter to Joash and Klaire. I think she kept it light and positive, and didn't tell them about their father's illness—why would she? If we met with disaster at the alien coordinates, or still couldn't make it back through the wormhole despite the skip drive modifications, no doubt she wanted her last message to them to be one of hope and love. I tried not to think about that too hard.

The messages were away and we were out well past the wormhole when Yuskeya pinged my implant. "Captain, can you come to First Aid?"

Her voice was calm and collected, betraying no hint of what she wanted, but I somehow doubted this was going to be good news. I'd been reading in my quarters, but I dropped my datapad and slipped through the storage room and into First Aid the back way, avoiding the bridge and any questions. In the narrow room, something beeped in a low but urgent tone, and Aliande was already there. Yuskeya busied herself at the counter, preparing something in a med injector. I looked at Karro and saw beads of sweat glistening on his forehead. His breathing came in short, quick puffs. Although his eyelids remained closed, his eyes twitched behind them as if he were dreaming.

"What happened?"

Yuskeya shook her head. "I'm not sure. The scans show that his systems are in mild distress—accelerated heart rate, accelerated respiration, a low-grade fever, increased activity in white blood cell production—but there's no indication of why." She placed the med injector against the side of his neck and depressed the end. It made no sound, but after about fifteen seconds Karro took a longer, deeper breath and let it out in a sigh. His breathing calmed and normalized, and she attached a datamed to his implant, taking vitals readings again.

"Well?"

Aliande held Karro's hand, but she hadn't said anything.

"He's stabilizing," Yuskeya said. "But that's no more than a stopgap. Without knowing what's causing the change, all I can do is keep trying to treat the symptoms."

I didn't want to ask, but I had to. "Should we turn back? Go through the wormhole?"

Yuskeya met my eyes; hers were very dark, brimming with compassion and regret. "Captain," she said, then more gently, "Luta. I can't make that call. I don't know what's happening. So I don't know what going through the wormhole might do. We don't even know how long we might have to wait or how far we'd have to go to get help on the other side."

Or if there is any help there, or anywhere, she didn't say, but she didn't have to. I knew it as well as she did.

"Remember what happened to Hirin when you went through the Split," Aliande said unexpectedly.

I did remember, all too well, Hirin's heart attack when we navigated the half-formed wormhole. "I do. I just . . . I don't know what to do."

Aliande stroked the back of Karro's hand. "I don't, either. But if Yuskeya can keep him stable, maybe that's best for now. He and I might be better off staying on Ryphen when you go through the wormhole after this and waiting for you to bring help back."

I wished with all my heart that she'd say something else, as we stood in silence at Karro's bedside and listened to his now smooth, effortless breathing. I willed her to say, *Luta, maybe we should try the nanobioscavengers now.* I wouldn't even care that Yuskeya would find out about them. I'd just go and get the injector and to hell with everything else.

But she didn't say that, and she didn't want to take him through the wormhole, and we'd made the Ryphens a promise. I didn't return to my quarters. I smoothed a hand over Karro's damp hair and went out to the bridge to sit in the big chair. I watched the black void roll away around us, trying—and failing—not to think too hard about the injectors hidden away in my quarters, silently waiting.

DINNER ON THE *Tane Ikai* that night was as cheerful as it could be. Rei offered to cook, and I approved. Flying toward set coordinates could be as stifling as sitting at a dock after a while, and I knew Rei must need a change of scenery. Only one thing of note had happened in the hours since we'd left Ryphen; the 'bot had received a new message with updated coordinates for us and a repetition of the same pictograms. Maja and I went down to examine the message screen with Viss. We debated whether this meant the senders knew we were coming. I wasn't sure what I thought about that. Viss stayed tight-lipped, radiating disapproval as we talked about it. In the end, we decided it didn't matter one way or the other; our course was set to encounter them either way.

When we returned to the bridge to report the changes to the 'bot's screen, Baden pushed himself back from his console and ran his hands over his face.

"I've scoured the Nearspace databases for anything like these pictograms, or the language markers Pika got from the 'bot," he said. "If anyone has encountered these—beings, before, they either didn't make any record of it or described it in some way that I can't find it."

"I've looked as well," Pika piped up, "*and* cross-referenced with the PrimeCorp data from Pita and information I collected or inferred from my interactions with the 'bot." Her tone implied that this research was ever so superior to anything a poor mere mortal could have achieved, and Baden made no attempt to hide his eye roll. "But I haven't found anything to hint at what we'll find out here."

I laid a hand on Baden's shoulder. "Don't worry about it. If we can't go completely prepared, we'll have to go in with our eyes open. You can't find something that isn't there."

His shoulder tensed under my touch, and I knew he wasn't happy about giving up. Baden didn't like to be bested, and it would be hard for him to accept that he couldn't offer more information to guide us. I figured he'd go back to digging as soon as my back was turned, but I honestly couldn't think of any other task to set him as we made our way out to the mysterious ship, or whatever awaited us.

In part, that might have been because I was spending a lot of mental energy trying to ignore the strident voice in the back of my head, telling me I had to save Karro no matter what. That voice had been growing more insistent ever since Yuskeya had called me in to First Aid earlier, and finally, I couldn't ignore it. When Maja slipped into the skimchair next to Baden's to talk about search parameters he could try, I quietly left the bridge.

I went to my quarters, where the nanobioscavenger injectors waited quietly in their secret lockbox. Hirin wasn't there, which I took as a sign from the universe that I was doing the right thing. I felt certain I knew what he'd say if he knew I was considering administering the bioscavs to Karro without our son's consent. I didn't feel strong enough to have that argument. I'd have to be quick, though. He was probably next door in the galley, fetching a cup of double caff or a snack.

I pulled the lockbox from its niche and opened it. The row of eight med injectors lay cradled in padded foam, their translucent cylinders glistening faintly in the warm glow of the overheads. The liquid inside swirled clear and pale yellow, like plasma. I imagined the nanobioscavengers moving about inside, although of course they weren't visible. The injectors weren't large, only about four inches long and an inch in diameter. I thought about the enormous potential contained inside each of those small cylinders. Potential to ease pain, to cure disease. To cheat death.

I pulled the leftmost one from its foam niche and slipped it into my pocket. Then I closed the lockbox with a snap and shoved it back into the storage cube. Heart stuttering and nerves clanging, I picked up the datapad I'd abandoned earlier and sank into my big chair, willing myself to composure, pulling deep, soothing breaths. I had to look like everything was normal when Hirin came back. But my mind raced. I could wait until everyone else was asleep except for the bridge duty, then tell Yuskeya I couldn't sleep. Offer to sit with Karro for a while so she could get some rest. I wouldn't even have to sneak into First Aid; it would be perfectly natural for me to be there. The injection would take only seconds.

And then Karro would be safe.

I slipped one hand into my pocket and felt the promise of the protective glass cylinder there. *Karro would be safe.*

I wouldn't let myself think too far beyond that.

EVERYTHING WENT ACCORDING to plan—why wouldn't it? I knew my ship and the rhythms of its crew like I knew my unchanging face in the mirror. Rei had bridge duty, and I waited until everyone else had long since retired to their quarters. The velvety black of space enveloped the ship, dusted with the pinpricks of distant stars. When I could tell Hirin was slipping over the edge of sleep, I slid out of our bed, whispering, "Just going to the head," and tiptoed out of the room. He'd never question it or think to follow me. I'd already transferred the med injector to the pocket of a sweater I left next to the door, so it was simple to slip it off the hook on my way out. My heart was clattering so hard in my chest I wondered that it didn't wake my slumbering husband.

I moved quietly through the darkened ship, illuminated faintly only by the guidelights that brightened the night cycle. It wasn't so long ago that someone had crept onto my ship and attacked me by the glow of those same guidelights, but it felt like decades, so much had happened since then. The air in the corridors was cool against my sweating palms, and I jammed them into the pockets of the sweater. My fingers encountered the cool glass of the med injector. I gripped it and walked on.

I slipped into First Aid, similarly lit by a dim nightlight and the pale bluish glow of the medical screens monitoring Karro's condition. My son lay on the bed, a white sheet drawn up to his chest, breathing deeply and evenly but still not awake. We were no closer to knowing what had happened to him when he touched the drone than we had been the moment it happened. Yuskeya dozed in an armchair we'd pulled in from storage, a brightly-woven wrap tucked around her shoulders. The presence of the armchair made the narrow room more cramped, but with Aliande and Yuskeya keeping vigil over Karro, they needed something more comfortable to occupy than the lone desk chair.

I put a gentle hand on Yuskeya's shoulder, and her eyes opened immediately, pupils large in the dimness.

"Something wrong?" she whispered.

I shook my head. I was glad we were whispering, so there was less chance a quaver in my voice would betray my nerves. "Couldn't sleep. I'll stay with him a while. You could use a real sleep in your own bed."

"I'm all right."

I put on a mock frown. "To your bed," I told her. "That's an order."

She smiled and shrugged, rising from the chair and pulling her wrap close. "Well, when you put it that way . . ." She took a moment to glance over the readouts on the monitors and told me, "Everything's stable. Ping me if anything changes."

I nodded, not trusting myself to say anything else, and she left First Aid.

I was alone with my sleeping son.

For a time, I stood and watched his slow, even breathing, waiting to be sure Yuskeya wouldn't return to tell me anything else, but she didn't. Finally, I pulled the injector out of the sweater pocket. The liquid caught the low light and glowed faintly yellow in my hand. All I had to do was press it against Karro's skin and depress the end. In seconds, it would be done.

Imagine if I'd had these long ago. If I'd found Mother sooner. We might have saved Karro and Aliande's baby.

But that was long ago. I couldn't dwell on those failures. I could save Karro, now.

He doesn't want it, a little voice in the back of my mind said. *He's going to hate you for this.*

I know, I retorted, *but he'll be alive to do it. Isn't that the most important thing? I've lived with a child hating me before.* Maja had come around eventually, and now we had a good relationship. It could be that way with Karro, too, given enough time. Which, with the help of the nanobioscavengers, we'd have.

Remember what you said to Karin Nakano about PrimeCorp. "Without your consent, it's still wrong." Your own words.

This is different, I told myself. *They weren't sick. They weren't dying.*

Still, I didn't move to put the smooth, tapered end of the med injector against his skin. Injecting the nanobioscavengers was not only saving his life. It was *changing* his life, at a fundamental level; a change he had rejected. Not the kind of decision Dr. Lee and I had talked about. Something more. Much more.

The glass and metal warmed against my palm as I stood, indecisive. I'd come here to do this, planned it all out. I'd already decided, hadn't I?

It should be so easy.

Juliska Barath's face rose in my mind's eye. Sitting in her empty house, telling me about who Amber Malka had been and how much Amber meant to her. Telling me about Amber's bravery, and how she had to try to get help for the colony even though it might cost her own life. Telling me, without even saying the words, how much she loved her wife.

And how she'd had to let her go. To face whatever outcome Amber's choice brought.

You can't control everything.

I don't know how long I stood there in the end, med injector in my hand and my mind in tumult. I knew someone could come in any time—Rei stretching her legs to pass the long night shift, Yuskeya returning to check on her patient, Aliande wondering if anything had changed with her husband. I felt like I stood in an airlock with no EVA suit and two doors, and no matter which one I opened, a vacuum waited beyond to swallow me up.

In the end, I laid a hand on Karro's forehead as I'd done so many times when he was a little boy, and I whispered, "I'm sorry." I wasn't sure if I was apologizing to him or to myself, or to my own "incurable compunction to be in charge." I slipped the unused injector back into my pocket and sat in the comfortable armchair, which by now had lost all the warmth from Yuskeya's body. I sat and stared at the monitors and Karro's still form and the long, black darkness outside the porthole window, and tears slid down my face. Occasionally, I wiped them away. Finally, Aliande came in to check on Karro and take a turn sitting with him, and after only a few whispered words with her, I fled. I slunk out the back door of First Aid and back to my quarters, where Hirin snored softly and didn't know how close I'd come to opening the other airlock door.

SLEEP EVADED ME for a long time, but I finally drifted off, and woke to Hirin asking if I was coming to the galley for breakfast. Before I could eat, I checked in on Karro. No change.

In some ways the day passed like many spent in in-system travel—uneventful and long, filled with busywork to keep the monotony at bay. In other ways it was not a normal day, my mind crowded with worry about Karro and my decisions and what lay waiting at our destination. I was concerned for Juliska Barath as well, who appeared in the galley for breakfast looking wan, her eyes underscored with dark circles. When I asked if she was all right, she brushed my concern aside.

"I think it comes down to trying to sleep in a different place," she said casually. "It's an awfully long time since I've slept on a ship other than the *Lillifleur*, or in a bed other than my own. It wasn't a restful night. But I'm sure tonight will be better."

She spent some time on the bridge after breakfast, chatting easily with Rei and Baden about technological advances that had bypassed the isolated Ryphens, but spent most of the day between her quarters and Cargo Pod One, puttering around or just sitting quietly in *Amber's Ranger*. When I realized she had retreated there, I was silently glad that we had kept the runner on board, since it seemed to offer Juliska a place of solace. A few times I thought I might go and check on her, but in the end, I decided to leave her to her own devices, and her privacy. She knew where to find company if she wanted it. And I had other things on my mind.

The *Tane Ikai* continued to speed toward the coordinates the 'bot had provided, and Karro continued to sleep. Most of us moved around the ship like quiet ghosts, either consumed by worry or not wishing to disturb those consumed by worry. Aliande, bless her, prepared an evening meal for us again when the time rolled around; I suppose it was good for her to have something to take her attention, and she'd often told me she found cooking to be a soothing task. It was an Erian recipe, a broth-based soup rich with egg, mushrooms, and bamboo shoots like hot and sour soup, but with the addition of the spicy yellow root vegetables the Erians called *dooir*. The aromas came wafting down the corridor from the galley to the bridge at least an hour before it was ready, and we were all ravenous by the time she called us to come and eat. She served the soup with soft, floury Erian flatbread, and it was comfort food at its purest.

Juliska Barath joined us at the table, although she held herself carefully and her face looked more drawn than it had that morning. Although she raved about the food, she ate little of it.

Yuskeya picked up on her appearance as well, and near the end of the meal asked, "Captain Barath, are you feeling all right?"

Juliska bit her bottom lip before slowly shaking her head. "It's the withdrawal symptoms," she said with a little shrug. "It's coming on faster than I'd expected."

I leaned forward, cupping my mug of double caff. "Why do you think that is? Because you're so far from Ryphen? Farther than you'd usually travel from the planet?"

"I wondered if that could be it," she said. She took a sip of the special tea blend she'd brought with her—a little parting gift from Okwi Rousseault, who grew the plants for the blend in her garden. "I can't think of any other explanation."

"Come with me to First Aid when you finish your tea," Yuskeya said, "and I'll give you an injection that might help with the symptoms."

"Thank you," Juliska said with a wan smile. "You already have one patient on your hands. I hate to burden you further."

Yuskeya smiled back. "It's my job," she said gently. "One of them, anyway. And we need to keep you in good shape for this meeting."

Viss barked a laugh, but it held no humour. "I love how you call it a 'meeting,'" he said. "As if we're just showing up at a shipyard to talk about some upgrades to the drive system."

Yuskeya sent him a challenging look. "Well, what would you call it?"

"A big mistake," he said. "Probably a dangerous one."

He got up from the table, said, "Thank you, Aliande, that was delicious," and put his dishes in the scrubber before leaving the galley without another word.

"What's up with him?" Baden asked. "He doesn't usually care that much about tackling the unknown."

Yuskeya pursed her lips, looking after Viss. "I'm not sure," she said slowly. "That isn't like him. Honestly, he's been on edge ever since we couldn't get back through the wormhole."

"Maybe he feels like it's his fault?" Maja offered. "Because the skip drive couldn't get us through?"

Yuskeya shrugged. "I don't know. Maybe. I asked him about it, but he either doesn't want to tell me what's wrong, or he doesn't know, himself." She smiled. "Anyway, I'm sure whatever it is will pass."

But the smile didn't reach her eyes.

We tidied up the table and dishes then. Yuskeya and Juliska left to go to First Aid, and Rei, Baden, and Maja returned to the bridge. Hirin announced his intention to have a nap before he took the bridge duty for the night. Finally, only Aliande and I were left in the galley. She'd cleaned up all the mess left from the meal prep and wiped down every surface twice when I finally stopped her.

"Enough. You'll wear yourself out." Something fluttered in my chest but I ignored it. This was the time to act on what had been percolating in my mind all day. "Sit down for a minute. I want to get something for you."

She looked at me quizzically but did as I asked, sinking into one of the big armchairs at the far end of the room with a heartfelt sigh. I left, but my errand only took me as far as my quarters and I was back in a moment. Hirin had been snoring softly when I tiptoed in, and I was spared any awkward questions from him. I sat in the chair opposite Aliande, and she stared at the lockbox in my lap, then looked up to meet my eyes. Hers were unreadable.

I held up a hand. "It's not what you think," I said. "Well, it is what you think, but no pressure here, and I'm not asking you to make any snap decisions." I opened the box and took out two of the med injectors, the pearlescent yellow liquid inside swirling as I moved them. I set them on the little table between us, metal clinking softly against the hard surface. She still said nothing, her face a mask.

I leaned forward, resting my elbows on my knees and clasping my hands. She didn't have to know I was trying to stop them from shaking. "This is just about options. Maybe Viss's pessimism has rubbed off on me, but we don't know what's ahead of us at this rendezvous. I honestly don't think whoever we're meeting mean us any harm. But the truth is, it's a big unknown.

"As you've probably guessed, these," I gestured to the injectors, "are the nanobioscavengers. If Karro gets worse and I'm not around, or Yuskeya—" I broke off, not sure how to put it. "I want you to have them. Just in case."

She wasn't looking at me, staring instead at the pair of injectors on the table. She reached out and picked one up, turning it in the light to see the liquid inside shift and flow. "They're so small," she said finally. "And also so enormous."

"As I said, Mother insisted it was wise to have them on hand. For my crew, or you and Karro, or . . . whoever might need them. They start working fast, but not instantly."

She nodded absently, her eyes still on the injector. "And you really think they could cure Karro."

"I do. Maybe." I paused. "Honestly, I don't know, but there's a chance. You probably think it's unfair of me to put them in your hands. I know you said you didn't want to make this decision for him. And if I'm honest with myself, well, I guess I think it's unfair too." I'd stood on the precipice of making the decision for Karro and couldn't do it. Now I was forcing my daughter-in-law into the same position.

Aliande half-smiled, one side of her mouth quirking up. "Maybe a little," she said. She picked up the other med injector and stood. "But I do understand why you're doing it. And I'm part of his decision *not* to take them, as well. I'm sorry I can't give you the answer you want. At least, not right at this moment."

I stood up, too. "I don't need an answer," I said, and I finally meant it. "This is not about me. It's about you and Karro. Your lives, your decisions. No pressure. Just the option." Mother would see that Joash and Klaire had their own option—I didn't have to put Aliande in charge of that, too.

"I'm going to put these in my quarters, and then go check on Karro," she said after a long moment. "I'll ping you if there's any change."

At the doorway she paused and said, "Thank you, Luta," before she went through.

I took the lockbox with the remaining med injectors back to my quarters and stowed it. Hirin snored softly on the bed, and I lay down beside him and closed my eyes, feeling the soft rumble of the ship beneath us and the warmth of his body against my back. I wondered if Yuskeya had found something to help Juliska feel better. I wondered what Viss was doing, and why he was so angry. I wondered what Aliande had done with the injectors. And what she would do.

And then I slept.

CHAPTER EIGHTEEN

A Picture is Worth . . .

THERE CAN COME a time during an in-system run when time becomes fluid and almost meaningless. If you're not on duty or carrying out specific tasks, your only concern is how to pass the time in a confined and unchanging environment. It's more difficult than many people who haven't experienced space travel might think—very different from being housebound planetside, even. This second day of our journey out to the mysterious ship seemed to stretch endlessly, even though I practiced my *tae-ga-chi*, read, chatted with Juliska Barath (who looked drawn and weak despite Yuskeya's ministrations) and played games of *quozit* with Hirin. Aliande and I ate lunch in the galley with Hirin and Maja and Baden, but she gave no indication that our conversation about the nanobioscavengers had ever happened. I tried not to think about it. Karro slept on.

But finally, finally, Rei pinged my implant from the bridge and said, "Captain, we have the alien ship on scanners."

I knocked softly on Juliska's door on my way to the bridge and, when she didn't respond, opened it slightly. She slept on the bed, the coverlet drawn up to her shoulders, looking so peaceful that I hesitated to wake her. It felt like she should be present on the bridge, but perhaps it would be time enough when we reached visual range. One blip on a scanner looked like any other. I closed the door softly behind me and hurried to the bridge.

"What do we know?" I asked, crossing to stand next to Rei.

She swivelled her skimchair to look up at me. She'd gathered her chestnut hair into a messy bun, and tendrils curved along the outermost edges of her *pridattii* tattoos. Concern shadowed her golden eyes. "It's big. In Protectorate terms, really big. Comparable to a Dragon-class battleship, I'd say. Too far out yet to tell anything else."

"*Merde*. That's big enough for almost two hundred crew in Nearspace terms."

She nodded, her lips pressed together in a pensive line. "Plus fighters, cargo space, ordinance. This thing is going to dwarf us."

I put a hand on her shoulder. "But it doesn't mean they have any hostile intent."

"I know." She pulled on one of the loose tendrils of her hair, twisting it around her finger. "Unless we're missing something in those pictograms, like, 'these are the bombs we will use on you if you come close to our ship.'"

I smiled and sat next to her at the secondary pilot's console. The readouts on the alien vessel blinked on the dark screen, telling us nothing yet except its formidable size. "I guess it's a possibility. But in that case, why send us coordinates at all?"

She returned the smile, wanly. "I was hoping we'd meet them on a more equal footing, that's all. I already don't like going into this blind."

"Almost every alien species we've encountered since wormhole exploration began has turned out to be friendly," I reminded her.

"Except the Chron."

"Except the Chron," I agreed. "Although, to be fair, only half of them were not friendly. The Relidae were perfectly nice, and even the Pitromae came around to peace in the end."

"I guess that should make me feel better."

Hirin came up behind us and leaned in to look over our shoulders at the readouts. He whistled low. "That's a big ship we're going to meet."

I elbowed him gently in the ribs. "I'm sure it's going to be fine, though."

"Oh, I'm sure it is," he returned with a grin. "Excuse me while I give the shields and weapons a once-over. Just routine."

He moved off to one of the other consoles and Rei turned an accusing look on me.

"What? Hirin's being over-cautious, as usual." I tried to keep my voice light, but I knew neither of us believed it would be as easy as we hoped.

AN HOUR LATER there had been no further communications via the 'bot, and no change in the drone in the cargo hold. Juliska had come to the bridge in time for us to get our first real look at the vessel awaiting our arrival, and everyone except my still-sleeping son crowded around the bridge viewscreens to get a look. Aliande stayed long enough to make a quick sketch of the alien ship on her datapad, then returned to First Aid to sit with Karro.

"It's like the pictogram," Viss said finally, with a note of satisfaction in his voice. "Like a lizard merged with an ion drive."

"And I thought it was something to see the *Tane Ikai* after so many years in isolation," Juliska said with a smile. "A ship shaped like a lizard is another thing entirely."

I tilted my head, half-squinting to try and make out more detail. It hung in three-quarter profile to us, two large globes like compound eyes at one end of a tapering, almost lizard-shaped hull, while the ring of an ion drive depended below. The inner surface of the ring showed a faint greenish glow, but the rest of the ship was unrelieved black. The globes at the nose of the ship twinkled oddly and might have been multi-faceted, but it was still too far away for the magnification to show any further detail. A row of curving, stylized symbols in glowing green ran down the hull at the bow; presumably the vessel's name or designation, but not in any alphabet I'd ever seen.

"I wonder what they're like?" Maja breathed, and Baden put an arm around her.

"We'll know soon enough," Viss muttered. "I'm going back down to engineering."

I interlaced my fingers, surprised at how cold my hands felt. "All right, this means we don't have much longer to wait, anyway. Baden, send hailing messages across the board, and keep them up until we get a reply. Pika, maybe you could convince our friend the 'bot to tell his compatriots we're here?"

"I expect they know, Captain, but I'll try to talk to the 'bot,"

Pika said. "Maybe since we're this close to its ship now, it will open up more."

The rest of us found busywork on the bridge, but mostly kept our eyes glued to the alien ship. It grew incrementally as we moved toward it, details emerging gradually into focus. Although the hull remained black, flickers of reflective surfaces suggested windows or viewports along its tapering length. The ion ring's green glow brightened as we neared, and we could make out smaller glowing dots like embers studded around its outer surface. The facets of the "eyes" were delineated, not by the usual structure of metal struts and framing, but by a web of thick, almost organic-looking filaments. Even at full magnification, I couldn't discern any obvious doors or docking ports.

"I hope they're going to give us some direction at some point," I said. "Unless we're supposed to hover out here until they decide to notice us."

"I don't think they'd bring us all this way so they could ignore us," Juliska said. "What would be the point?"

"I don't know. Pika, any luck with the 'bot?"

The AI's irritated voice came over the ship's comm. "Nothing, Captain. It's not responding to me at all."

We were close enough now to see the eerie smoothness of the hull, as slick and dark as polished obsidian. Baden said, "Still hailing on all frequencies, Captain. No response from the other vessel."

"I think you can dispense with the reports," I told him. "I know you'll tell me if something does change, although at this point, I don't think it's going to."

He flashed me a grin. "Up-to-the-minute reports, Captain, you know me. But I get your point. I'll shut up unless there's real news."

"Scans showing no obvious entries, doors, or hatches," Yuskeya told me from her console. "No readings that suggest life support or weapons systems, either. Honestly, Captain, I'm beginning to think this is another kind of unmanned drone."

"It's too big to be called a drone," Viss growled. "I don't know what it is, and I don't like it."

"It must have carried living beings at some point," Juliska mused. "Otherwise, why make it so large? Why have those windows in the front?"

Unless they're all dead, she didn't add, but I suspected she was thinking it, just as I was.

"Are we sure it isn't Corvids?" Baden joked. "They love black, and this seems like it would fit the bill for them."

It was the first thought I'd had, looking at the captured drone. But again, this ship didn't have the gelatinous look of the Corvid tech, with its tiny interlocking hexagons that made almost any construct reflowable and flexible. "If it was Corvids, they'd have contacted us by now," Maja said. "This silent treatment isn't their style at all."

"This isn't my favourite encounter ever, either, Viss," I told him. "But we'll keep going and see what happens. We promised the Ryphens we would."

"As long as Hirin has our weapon systems ready to go," Viss returned, as if he wasn't talking about one of his captains.

"Green across the board," Hirin reported.

"What kind of ship this size goes out without life support systems, hatches, or communications systems?" Maja mused. "It doesn't make sense."

"An unmanned one, or one that uses something we wouldn't necessarily recognize as 'life support,'" Juliska suggested. "Aliens with a physiology so fundamentally different from ours that we can't even identify it."

But I was thinking about those drones that had stealthily landed on the planet's surface and deposited their little explorer bots. "Even the unmanned drones had a way to open up and let the 'bot out," I said. "And this has to open up somehow to launch the drones. So someone or something must be running the show. But something that doesn't require life support as we understand it also suggests the possibility of an independent artificial intelligence."

"Not like we've never heard of that before, Captain," Pika said, sounding peeved.

"I didn't mean to exclude you, Pika," I amended. "I mean, an AI that isn't attached to a ship with a crew, just out here on its own."

"Who'd send something like that out, though?" Maja said. "I mean, we wouldn't send Pika out to crew the *Tane Ikai* without anyone else aboard."

"I could do it," the AI protested.

"Sure, you could, but would you want to?" Baden asked. "Come on, Pika, you'd miss us, admit it."

"Some more than others," the AI said pointedly. "But I'm not sure it would make sense to do it. I know Earth sent out unmanned probes at the beginnings of human space exploration, but once you reach a certain point with the technology, those kinds of missions aren't necessary anymore."

"Exactly," Maja said. "Once you have the tech—coldsleep, skip drives, wormhole travel—to send living explorers, why wouldn't you? Hybrid missions, with living beings *and* drones and 'bots for the dangerous stuff, at the very least."

"Because we are so expendable," Pika suggested in a dangerous voice.

"Now, Pika, I didn't mean that. But you have to admit you're more repairable."

"I was assuming that even though the drones might be unmanned scouts, there'd be—someone—on the main ship," I said, intervening with a frown. "If there's no-one here, who are we here to meet?"

As if in answer, a section of the black, featureless hull that had been smooth and intact a moment before irised open. Beyond the door, blue-tinged darkness shrouded the interior, but scattered items and areas glowed faintly in a range of colours. As we drew closer, more spots of luminous colour appeared, revealing that the space inside extended back and up a considerable distance. It appeared huge, offering a far larger space than the *Tane Ikai* would need to slip inside and set down. My brother Lanar could have parked his Bahamat-class ship inside it.

"Whoa," Maja said.

"*Merde*," Hirin breathed.

"Databurst received," Baden said. "Pika, any idea what it means?"

She paused before answering, which surprised me. "Pictograms again," she said. She displayed them on one of the viewscreens for us. Two of them were new.

"This one looks like water. Or liquid of some sort," Maja said. "Wavy lines are universal for water, right?"

"Maybe universal in terms of humans," I said. "I think the Relidae use something that looks more like a simple water molecule."

"It surely can't mean the atmosphere inside is liquid, can it?" Rei mused. "You can see inside now, and it's not like that."

"Okay, this one is like one of the earlier ones. It definitely looks like this ship, but now with an opening in the side," Baden said. "Just like that," he added, glancing out at the door in the ship before us.

"And two giant bug heads again," Rei said, sighing.

"And a plus sign. So it's all good," Hirin joked.

Inside the docking bay, a row of evenly-spaced globes intensified their glow in succession; blue, green, yellow, then blue again. Parallel strips on the floor pulsed with a white brightness that didn't cast any light beyond themselves.

"That looks like an invitation to me," Juliska said, "whatever the pictograms mean."

"Come into my parlour," Viss muttered. "Captain, you're not seriously thinking of—"

"Hirin?" I asked. "What do you think?"

Hirin leaned back in his skimchair and steepled his fingers, tapping them against his chin. "They invited us out here," he said after a moment. "And if they wanted to do us harm, they've had plenty of time and opportunity."

Viss shook his head. "You always say something like that in these situations."

Hirin grinned and pointed an index finger at the engineer. "And I've been right so far."

"I don't see why we can't talk to them from right here, once Pika cracks the code." Viss crossed his arms. "I don't balk at taking chances. But I don't care for stupid ones."

Yuskeya put a hand on his arm and when he looked down at her, I suddenly realized what was going on here. Viss didn't want

Yuskeya in danger. I mean, sure, he was concerned for all of us, but she was his focus. She, who did not have Mother's nanobioscavengers for extra insurance against injury. Never mind that she was a trained, competent, kick-ass Commander in the Nearspace Protectorate—Viss was protecting her.

Well, it was sweet. But we were here to get answers, and I knew Yuskeya might not particularly appreciate being protected. I wasn't going to call him out, but I was about to agree with Hirin when Yuskeya beat me to it.

"I don't know about anyone else, but I want to see what's inside."

And Viss didn't say another word against it, although he still didn't look happy.

"I can't make any better guesses about how to interpret everything," Pika said. "We simply don't have enough data."

That tipped it. "Then we have to get more. Rei," I said, "take us in—very carefully, please—and set us down in that ship's docking bay. Let's see what we can find out about these mysterious visitors."

NATURALLY, A FIGHT broke out over who was going to venture into the alien ship, and who was going to stay with the *Tane Ikai*. Well, not so much a fight, I suppose, as a heated discussion. It started the moment Rei began nosing us toward the open docking bay and broke down largely along gender lines: Hirin didn't want me to go, Baden didn't want Maja to go, and Viss didn't want Yuskeya to go. Rei and Juliska shared a slightly smug glance, because no-one was trying to make *them* stay behind. The men were only trying to be protective, but none of us felt particularly in need of protection, so their gestures didn't get very far. Fortunately, I still sat in the big chair.

"Wait." I held up a hand, asking for silence. "We don't know yet if anyone is leaving the ship. They may simply communicate with us as we sit in the docking bay."

"Why bring us inside if we're just going to sit in the ship?" Rei muttered from the pilot's console as her fingers danced gracefully over the screen, guiding us in.

"Who knows? We still know nothing about their motives or what they want, and there's no point in guessing. I'm only saying let's not argue until we know there's something to argue about."

Hirin held up both hands in a placating gesture. "All right. But I suggest we get some EVA suits ready in case we need them. If any of us are leaving the ship, there's no guarantee the interior of the alien ship will have an atmosphere that's compatible for us."

"Good idea," I said, glad to have something to occupy them. "Maja and Yuskeya, please help Hirin get enough EVA suits ready for everyone, in case they're needed."

"Surely we won't all go?" Maja asked. "Someone has to stay on our bridge."

"Let's be prepared. Anything could happen in the next half hour."

She and Yuskeya began pulling EVA suits out of the bridge locker, and Hirin leaned over to speak close to my ear.

"But she's right," he said. "We can't abandon the ship."

"I know," I muttered back, "but everyone is on edge, possibly for nothing. We're not exactly in charge here, so let's not make any unpopular decisions until we have to? And anyway, Aliande won't want to leave Karro, so even if the whole crew went, there'd still be someone on the ship. Pika is perfectly capable of monitoring everything from the bridge."

"Wait, I want to go, too," Pika protested in my ear. I should have remembered she'd be listening in to every whisper that happened on the bridge, but at least she had the good sense to answer me through my implant. She continued, "I thought you'd download me to a datapad and take me along. I'm the one who got the lines of communication open, after all! I want to meet the aliens!"

Hirin pulled back at the expression on my face. "What? I didn't say anything!"

"No, it's Pika. She talks to me through my implant now, so that's fun." At the look on his face, I added, "Exactly. She wants to come along on a datapad, since she managed to start communications with the 'bot."

He grinned. "She's got you there, although Karro might have helped a *little*. But she's the only one who can stay on the ship *and* go along, too."

"*Merde.*" I ran a hand across my face. "All right, Pika, you can come. But you'll have to leave a copy here to monitor everything and stay in touch."

"That was my plan," she answered airily, and presumably

went off to set it up.

While we'd been talking, the *Tane Ikai* drew ever closer to the alien ship and the waiting docking bay. As our angle of view changed to see more of the inside, the bay continued to look surprisingly dark and empty. Straining to make out more inside, I had a weird sense of inverted vision—darkness punctuated by spots of glowing colour.

Yuskeya said, "Hmmm . . . phosphorescence?"

"Could be." Maja peered at the screen, tapping a forefinger against her lip. "I covered a section on phosphorescence in plants and animals when I was teaching. They—whoever they are— might utilize a broader range of UV light to see. Humans can see only so far into the UV spectrum, so we may be missing a lot of what's in there."

"We can adjust the helmet visors on the EVA suits to mimic being able to see UV light," Baden offered. "It won't be perfect, but maybe it will help if we can 'see' the ship the way its inhabitants do."

"I can use the ship's sensors to project a better approximation of the inside of the docking bay on the ship's viewscreens, as well," Pika said.

"Go ahead, Pika. And Baden, make the EVA suit tweaks."

A moment later, the image on the viewscreen altered. The faintly glowing shapes emerged with more definition and in more brilliant colour, while the previously black interior shifted to a deep, rich purple. It was like turning on a blacklight. I sucked in a breath at the luminous transformation.

"Wow," Maja breathed next to me. "I didn't realize how much we were missing."

"Definitely makes it easier to dock this thing if I can see where I'm going," Rei said.

"Last chance to rethink this plan." Viss's voice came over the comm from the cargo pod, without a hint of humour in his voice. He'd offered to stay with the 'bot while we docked, in case any further messages came across the screen.

I didn't bother to reply. As far as I was concerned, we'd been committed since we left Ryphen. "Take us in, Rei," I told her as she aligned the ship with the open bay door.

"Aye, Captain," she replied, and nudged the manoeuvring thrusters to bring us inside.

Along with the odd juxtaposition of darkness and brightly-coloured glowing objects inside the docking bay, there was a sense of what I can only call "alien-ness" that set my nerves pinging. Very tall, faintly luminescent rectangles of a dark, glossy material hung at intervals along the bay walls, stretching perhaps twelve feet tall; but if they were consoles or screens, they were dead, displaying no data even to our enhanced vision. A boxy shelf protruded from the wall beneath each one. The floor of the bay lay clear and unobstructed, lacking the ever-present cables, wires, hoses, scattered tools, and unidentifiable stains that usually defined such spaces. Evenly-spaced slots which I imagined might provide anchors for some sort of tie-down or locking mechanism were all that marred the smooth surface.

"It's eerie," Maja breathed.

"Agreed. Yuskeya, can you run a low-level scan of the interior?"

"Aye, Captain." After a moment, she said, "The ship has an active electrical system, and other energy networks . . . but that's all I can tell. At this scan level, no indication of organic life."

"Captain! Bay door is closing behind us," Baden interjected.

Viss swore horribly over the comm and I hurried to say, "We should have expected that. I'm sure it's fine. They can't offer us atmosphere if the door stays open. Calm down, folks."

My voice didn't shake, but only because I made a supreme effort. I hadn't anticipated the door closing, although what I'd said was true. I didn't like feeling like we were at the mercy of whoever was controlling this ship. But the die had been cast.

"Set us down in any likely-looking spot," I instructed Rei. "There's lots of room in here."

Indeed, now that we were fully inside and the viewscreen had adjusted to show us a truer picture of the bay, it was clear that we were the only ship in occupancy. I'd been hoping there would be at least one other in here in case it offered some clue to the identity of the ship's owners, but there was nothing. The space stretched around us vast and empty.

Well, almost empty. "What's that?" Hirin asked, panning one of the exterior cameras to look up at the ceiling of the docking bay.

I squinted at the screen. Although most of them were empty, numerous large recesses pocked the ceiling. Dark bulks clung inside a few of the alcoves, but they were too far away and shadowed to discern details. One could, however, imagine that they were ships shaped much like the one we were now inside, only smaller.

"They're aligned with the slots on the floor," Maja noted. "So maybe instead of locking *down*, ships docked here are pushed *up*?"

Hirin pursed his lips, nodding slowly as he considered. "Kind of makes sense. You park over the slots, a support system emerges and locks onto the bottom of the ship, then when crew disembarks, the ship is raised up and out of the way for storage."

"Well, we don't want to get plugged into one of those recesses, so I don't think I'll set us down directly over any of those slots," Rei said.

"Look at the far wall," Baden said. He'd been manipulating another of the exterior cams and increasing the magnification, and he put the input up on the big viewscreen.

I drew in a breath. Rows of inert drones, like the one we'd snared, studded the wall. It was hard to tell in the dim light that brushed their polished surfaces, but they seemed to be partially docked in shallow recesses, their snub noses protruding. "Drones. There must be hundreds of them."

"I count one thousand, three hundred and six," Pika said. "With empty docking slots of the same type that could house another one thousand, one hundred and ninety-four. There are seventeen smaller recesses that could also be docks, but I currently can't see anything inside them."

"And the Ryphens have encountered how many drones?"

"Not that many," Baden said wryly.

"Sensors are detecting increasing levels of nitrogen and oxygen, as well as other trace gases in the docking bay," Yuskeya said. "It's going to take a while to flood this large a space, but it looks like when it fills, it will be breathable."

"No-one leaves the ship without a full EVA suit, regardless," I said. "It appears they're rolling out the welcome mat, but we're not taking any chances."

Everyone went quiet while Rei chose a spot and gently set the *Tane Ikai* down on the docking bay floor. I think we all held our breaths—I know I did—while we waited to see what, if any, response it would bring from the ship or those who had invited us to come here.

"THE 'BOT HAS a new message on its screen," Viss said over the ship's comm, breaking the tense silence.

"What is it?"

"Well, it's more pictograms," Viss amended, his gravelly voice even harsher than usual. "One is a plus sign with a diagonal dashed line. One shows two interlocking rings with a plus sign above them. Maja's water or liquid symbol, and Rei's telepathic bug heads again. Here." My datapad pinged and an image of the 'bot's screen appeared. The pictograms were exactly as Viss had described them.

"Guesses?" I asked, turning the datapad so the others could see it.

They studied the screen in silence. Pika said, "The dashed lines could mean a direction, or something to follow. A yellow line like that just lit up on the floor of the docking bay."

I glanced at the viewscreen showing the bay to see that she was correct. Similar to the dashed white lines that had invited us into the docking bay, these pulsed gently on and off, leading farther into the depths of the bay. "That . . . could make sense. And with the assurance again that it's good or safe to follow."

"Then the two giant bug heads *could* be talking or communicating," Rei said, her voice edged with excitement. "They might be saying, 'come here and talk to us.'"

"Still not entirely comfortable with giant bug aliens," Baden said. "If that's the default way to represent life, I'm worried."

"Well, let's not get ahead of ourselves," I said. "But we can only learn so much from in here. I want everyone into an EVA suit while we're docked in this vessel. You can leave helmets off while you're in the *Tane Ikai*, but keep them handy." I made a quick decision and drew in a breath. "Yuskeya, Viss, Juliska, and I will venture out into the bay and follow that yellow line, see where it takes us."

"Captain!" Baden protested, spinning his skimchair to look at me. His handsome face was alight with eagerness. "Don't you think your communications officer should be present at the first meeting with an alien species?"

Rei chuckled. "I thought you weren't comfortable with giant bug aliens."

I sighed. "Sure I do, Baden. But we can't all go—someone has to stay with the ship and be ready to help us if something goes wrong. Juliska should go as the Ryphens' representative, and I think Yuskeya has to go as the only official member of the Protectorate on board. And I know damn well that after what happened on the Corvid station last year, Viss is going to raise holy hell if Yuskeya goes and he doesn't."

"Correct," Viss rumbled over the comm.

"And you're not going without me," Maja told Baden, but I went on as if I hadn't heard her.

"Now, I certainly *could* order him to stand down and stay behind, and I know he'd follow my orders," I continued pointedly. "But Viss is also handy to have around when circumstances are, shall we say, unpredictable."

Baden looked like he might protest further, but I raised a hand. "Let's do it this way to start, see what happens. If the aliens are amenable, everyone can take a tour before we leave."

Maja said, "Aye, Captain," quickly, so there was little Baden could do but grudgingly agree as well.

I was expecting Hirin to protest my including myself in the party, but I realized that at some point he'd quietly left the bridge.

"You forgot to mention me," Pika said, distracting me from a momentary pang of worry. "But I know you meant to. I've already made a clone of myself and downloaded into your datapad, so I'm ready to go."

I almost laughed, but it was mainly nerves. "Of course you are. Suits, everyone," I urged, because no-one had moved yet to pull one out of the pile. I picked one up and the others got busy as well, but my mind was only half on what I was doing. Where had Hirin gone?

Fortunately, he returned before I had the suit completely fastened, and wordlessly handed me a sidearm from the weapons locker. I raised an eyebrow at him. "You think this is necessary?"

He shrugged. "Better safe than sorry. You think Viss is going empty-handed?"

"No, I suppose not. You're not arguing with me about going?"

"No point," he answered with a grin. "And I think you should be there. You make good decisions in tricky situations."

"Sometimes. Not so sure that's been true lately."

"*Okej*, you *usually* make good decisions in tricky situations."

"That . . . did not make me feel better." I tucked the gun into the EVA's belt holster and sighed. "I doubt this is going to help much if we're walking into a trap."

Hirin leaned down and kissed me swiftly. "Be careful," he whispered.

"Always am."

"Sure you are," he said, and squeezed my arm.

Suits secured, I scooped up my datapad and said, "Hirin, you have the chair. We'll stay in touch through the helmet comms." Then I led Juliska, Yuskeya, and Viss down to the hold where we'd kept the 'bot. I slipped the datapad into the large pocket on one leg of the EVA suit to free both hands, but I still climbed down slowly, knowing that the slight but significant encumbrance of the suit would already be taxing Juliska's waning strength. I made a silent promise to myself that if and when we made it back to Nearspace, I'd install an elevator running between the decks. Climbing the hatch ladders was good exercise and fine when everyone was hale and hearty, but I should know better than to depend on that always being the case.

"Are you all right?" I asked her when we'd gained the floor of the cargo bay. She'd put her helmet on to keep both hands free for climbing, and even through the clear visor, her face was terribly pale, framed by tendrils of her bright pink hair. Her EVA suit moved visibly with her laboured breath.

"I'm fine," she said, but the weakness of her voice belied her words.

"Amber's not going to be happy with me when she comes back through the wormhole if I've let you kill yourself trying to meet some aliens," I told her.

She smiled. "You're determined to make me hope, aren't you? Well, of all people, Amber would understand."

"Seriously, are you okay to go on? I know you're here to represent Ryphen—"

"—and I will," she interrupted. She stood a little taller in the suit. "I can do this, Luta. I have to."

I didn't say anything else, only nodded. I knew that feeling of needing to follow through on something, no matter the difficulty.

Viss stopped in front of the 'bot. "You think it will follow us out?"

"I think it will." I fastened my EVA helmet into place. "It followed us on the planet, after all. And it may be anxious to get 'home.' Captain," I said to Hirin over the helmet's comm, "we're in place and ready to leave the ship. I'm about to open the cargo bay door."

"Go ahead," Hirin responded, and I wasn't sure if the tautness in his voice was worry or distortion from the helmet speaker. With one last look at the others to make sure we were ready, I pressed the button to open the door. It unlatched with a clunk and slid laboriously upwards, allowing us our first in-person look at the interior of the alien ship. Our enhanced helmet visors brought the space to life in splashes of vivid colour against a deep black background. Bright orange outlined the tall wall-mounted rectangles, and the edges of the shelves below them glowed yellow. Brilliant neon green picked out the systems we assumed were in place to convey ships to the ceiling docks. The mic on the side of my helmet caught no sound that didn't come from us or the *Tane Ikai*.

"Looks like someone went on a tear with blacklight paint," Viss muttered, echoing what I'd thought earlier.

Although little of it would have been visible to us without the helmet's enhancements, bright neon colour seemed to light up the surroundings like phosphorescent paint. The line of faintly pulsing yellow Pika had observed glowed softly on the floor. As we moved forward, the 'bot moved, too.

"Did you send any messages to the 'bot, Pika?"

"Nope, I guess it got some marching orders of its own. I'm patched into your helmet cameras, Captain, I hope that's okay. Hard to see inside this pocket," she added pointedly.

"That's fine. I'd rather keep my hands free at the moment."

We stepped out onto a floor that felt firm but cushiony underfoot, like an organic material rather than metal. Our footfalls created dull, muffled thuds rather than the ringing metallic clang of walking on steel. I bent to examine the material, and it had a texture like cork, although it was completely black beneath an undisturbed coating of dust. I wondered how it could possibly hold up to the rigors of thrust and manoeuvring drives, but there was no time to spend on questions like that—or my assumptions about propulsion, I realized. Juliska moved past me, almost shuffling. I stood and held out my arm, and she took it, smiling gratefully at me through her helmet visor.

"Wouldn't want to trip and embarrass myself in front of the aliens," she joked in a low voice. It sounded wispy and ethereal over the helmet's internal speaker.

As we followed the yellow line on the floor, we passed close to some of the darkened wall screens. The apparent shelves below them turned out to be recesses like sinks or tubs, jutting three feet out from the walls and running at least six feet wide, their top edge level with my eye height. A block of the same material as the floor, like a high step, hugged the wall next to each one. I pointed to one and looked the question at Viss, who shrugged and nodded. After testing its stability with my foot, I stepped up on one and peered into the receptacle. Although it seemed designed to hold—something—it lacked any obvious ports for filling or drainage of a liquid. It, too, had accumulated dust, and was irregularly caked with the remains of its previous contents, now dried to a thin line marking its previous depth. The substance held a faint, residual blue glow, and flaked off easily when I touched it with a gloved finger. I rubbed thumb and forefinger together, and the flakes crumbled to phosphorescent blue dust smearing my glove.

"I wonder what that was for?" Juliska murmured, her voice breathy and thin.

I held up my gloved hand. "Not much left as a clue. It looks like it hasn't been used in a long time."

"I have a feeling we might be leaving here with more questions than answers," Juliska said.

"As long as we get a few important ones."

We passed four more of the dark screens and empty reservoirs before reaching the back of the space, where the yellow guideline truncated at an apparent wall. As the 'bot neared it, though, a section slid silently upward. The resulting opening was fully ten feet high, and I wondered at the dimensions of the ship's occupants, who would need a door this tall. With the exception of cargo storage areas, starships tended in my experience to conserve space wherever possible.

"Could be for equipment," Viss said, as if he'd heard my thought.

"Let's hope so," I muttered.

The door opened into a passage at least fifteen feet wide, with a ceiling vaulting a dozen feet overhead. We'd almost reached it when Juliska clutched harder at my arm and stumbled. I fumbled with both hands to catch her, but the EVA suits were bulky and slippery and all I managed was to slow her descent. Without making a sound beyond a long, drawn-out sigh that hissed in my helmet speaker, she fell headlong and sprawled across the inky black floor.

CHAPTER NINETEEN
Bugs and Blue Gel

Viss and Yuskeya, moving faster than Juliska and me, had passed us and missed seeing Juliska fall. They heard her sigh and my exclamation, though, and turned as I dropped to kneel beside her prone figure.

"What happened?" Viss already had his sidearm out, scanning the bay for threats.

Yuskeya joined me at Juliska's side.

"She fell," I assured Viss. "Put that thing away!"

He grudgingly did so as Yuskeya gently turned Juliska to peer inside the visor. "Looks like she fainted," Yuskeya said, pulling out her datamed and connecting it through the implant port in Juliska's EVA suit. She watched the readout, lips pressed together in a grim line. "She's . . . not good. Her implant is old, the same as Amber Malka's, but the patch I downloaded when I was treating Amber helps. It's the same kind of readings I saw with her. The distance from Ryphen seems to have exacerbated her symptoms."

"If we get her back on the ship, can you help?"

Yuskeya sighed. "I can do what I've been doing, but I don't know how long it will continue to hold her back from the brink. There's too much we don't know about what the virus is doing."

I stood and said, "Baden, did you hear all this? We're going to bring Juliska—"

"What's that?" Uncharacteristically, Yuskeya made no apology for interrupting me. She still knelt next to Juliska's form, but had turned her head to look up, visor pointing toward the dark recesses of the ceiling.

I looked up reflexively and heard it, too—a mechanical whirring, growing louder. Despite having just reprimanded Viss, my own hand went instinctively to the handle of my gun.

Baden said, "Captain, what's happening? Are you coming back?"

The whirring intensified, and dark forms became visible high above us as the visors picked up and intensified their UV spectrum colouration. The shapes were roughly ovoid, black but striped in pale blue, perhaps a foot across, and almost floating down toward us. I glanced around the bay, but it was pure reflex—there were no hiding places in this vast, empty space, and we were too far from the *Tane Ikai* to get back to it quickly.

"Captain," Viss said in a rough, tight voice. "There's a new message on the 'bot screen."

I turned to look at the screen. More pictograms. I thought with longing of being back on that half-finished space station, communicating with the Relidae through Pita's translation database. And at the time, I'd thought that cumbersome.

"Okay, so one of them shows something that looks like those—" I glanced up at the descending drones again, "—and a plus sign. So maybe it's telling us they're good?"

"It's a reasonable assumption based on our earlier guesses," Pika said. "If they are correct."

Guesses. That was the problem. It was all guesswork. "Then there's the interlocking circles with the plus sign again, and one that's like a big plus sign."

"If we're right and the plus sign means good or positive, then whoever they are, they're really trying to get that point across," Yuskeya said, still watching the drones' slow descent.

"And if we're not right?" Viss rumbled.

"We're already in the belly of the beast. It's like Hirin keeps saying. If they wanted us dead—"

"We'd be dead. Or at least you all would be," Pika said.

Viss said something too low for me to catch. I expected it wasn't complimentary.

I looked across Juliska's fallen form into Yuskeya's eyes, dark behind her helmet visor. "So we assume—we hope—they're coming to help?"

"Some kind of medical drones?" Yuskeya's eyebrows went up. "Not sure if medical drones from a species we've never encountered can help us? They don't know anything about our physiology."

"To be accurate, we don't know the extent of their knowledge," Pika noted. "Their experience could be vast, even if undocumented in Nearspace records."

Before I could say anything else, the three forms glided in to hover above Juliska. There was no visible source for the whirring sound they made, but perhaps it existed simply to warn of their approach. They hung in place, apparently waiting for something.

"Captain?" Yuskeya asked. Neither of us had moved other than to instinctively lean forward protectively over the captain's unmoving form.

My stomach tightened and it felt suddenly unbearably hot inside the suit. Another decision I was being asked to make for someone else. This one even more difficult, because at least I understood the ramifications of the nanobioscavengers. In this case, I didn't even know what I was choosing. To make this choice, I had to rely on what I thought Juliska Barath would want, and what my gut was telling me.

And, fortunately, on my crew. I didn't have to make this one alone.

"I think—maybe we have to take a chance that it's okay," I said slowly to Yuskeya. "They're waiting, like they're waiting for permission. That doesn't feel aggressive. I don't see how they could possibly help, but maybe we should let them try? What do you think?"

Yuskeya hesitated, then nodded once. "Agreed. I know the limitations of what I can do for her. And I think—I think she'd want to try this." She stood slowly and took a step back from Juliska. I did the same. Viss moved to Yuskeya's side, his hand resting unrepentantly on the handle of his pistol. I heard an intake of breath over my helmet comm, as if someone back on the ship was about to say something, but they stayed silent.

The three drones positioned themselves in a triangular configuration over Juliska—one at her feet and one to each side of her shoulders. Flickering blue light emerged from each one, the three beams merging and spreading to form a scintillating field that enveloped the unconscious captain. I glanced at Yuskeya, meeting her eyes. Was this a medical scan? Had we made the right decision? I was all too aware that a scan had already caused trouble for the Ryphens, but I pushed that thought away. Yuskeya answered with wide eyes, her thoughts likely running the same tracks as mine.

Then the drones moved, keeping the beam focused on Juliska while they flew to hover in front of the nearest tall, dark screen. There they hovered, humming softly.

"What are they doing?" Viss muttered. Viss liked situations where he could make quick decisions based on facts and information, not puzzles he had to figure out. I shared his frustration. I couldn't predict how quickly Juliska's condition would deteriorate while we tried to interpret what was happening.

Then the 'bot stepped forward, its screen "face" having changed again. The image that looked like water or liquid, and the one with Rei's two giant bug heads joined the plus sign and the drone sign.

"What the—" I started, but the three drones bobbed gently but obviously down toward the shelf over which they hovered. "Oh. They want us to bring her over there?"

"I sent the 'bot a string of equations with missing elements," Pika said. "Hoping it will get the message that we don't understand enough of what the images are telling us."

"Good thinking," I told her. "Well, let's move her over there while we're waiting. I'm sure they'll give us another inscrutable image if that's not what they want."

Together, the three of us lifted the still-unconscious woman and carried her to the waiting drones. When we reached them, they dipped meaningfully down to the shelf receptacle again.

"I think they're saying you should put her in there," Baden said over the helmet comm. The observers in the ship had stayed quiet until now, but maybe they wanted to show their support for our decisions so far.

Viss said, "You sure about this, Captain?"

"Not really, but our only other option is to take her back to the ship, and Yuskeya doesn't think that's going to help much." I silently thought again about the injectors of nanobioscavengers, but it was the same problem I'd faced with Amber Malka—I didn't know if they'd help or harm. "This could be her best chance."

"Or maybe they're going to recycle her," Viss said.

Yuskeya glared at him, and he made a face but rather surprisingly shut up.

It wasn't easy with the shelf being so high and only one step to assist us, but we managed to lift Juliska up and into the cradle of the receptacle. The drones buzzed in what felt like approbation as Viss and Yuskeya stepped back. I stayed on the step as the drones moved lower, closer to Juliska. She looked suddenly very small and vulnerable, her face an almost ghostly white in my helmet-altered vision, as we waited to see what the drones' ministrations would be.

Broken trails of neon light oscillated across the glossy, dark screen, deepening my impression that the technology had gone unused for a long time. After a moment, the light stabilized, resolving into glyphs and symbols I did not recognize. I gingerly touched a gloved finger to the bottom corner of the screen, but it was not the unyielding surface I expected. It gave slightly, like thick gelatin, under the pressure of my touch, and I pulled back.

The outline of a body appeared on the screen—not of Juliska, that was for certain. This creature had too many legs. The image shifted to what looked, to my surprise, like a Lobor, the dog-like head instantly recognizable. Then it was gone, and another took its place, as if the machine were sorting through a catalogue of physiologies until it found the one it wanted. After cycling through half a dozen more, it stopped on a bipedal, humanoid form. The indecipherable writing changed as well, as if matching up to the outline.

"We're getting everything that happens on this screen, right?" I whispered to no-one in particular.

"Helmet cam recorders are in full capture mode," Pika assured me.

Then the receptacle in which Juliska lay began to fill with a phosphorescent, pale blue gel. It oozed in gleaming trails out of openings so small I'd missed them when I'd peered into the receptacle earlier.

"Whoa, whoa, is this okay?" Viss asked when he saw the seeping material.

"Captain, let's just be ready to pull her out of there if the situation changes," Yuskeya said calmly. She stepped up next to me with her datamed in hand. She would help me scoop Juliska out at a moment's notice, but I thought she was also fascinated with trying to figure out exactly what was going on.

One of the drones dropped to within inches of Juliska and bobbed down to touch her gloved hand. Then it hovered as if waiting for something. When neither Yuskeya nor I moved, it repeated the motion, touching the glove.

"It wants us to . . . take off her glove?" Yuskeya asked.

"I suppose I should have anticipated that as soon as the goo started filling up. What can it do through an EVA suit? But I can't let her be the only guinea pig." Pulling off one of my own gloves and ignoring Yuskeya's gasp, I dipped my fingers lightly into the blue ooze.

"Luta," came Hirin's quiet, warning voice over the helmet comm.

I wiggled my fingers in the gel. "It's fine," I reassured them. "Cool, and a little bit tingly. But it's not hurting me at all."

"Better get them out of there," Yuskeya said mildly, pointing up at the screen.

I looked up to see a thin line of red outlining the panel. "Guess it knows I'm not the patient." I extracted my hand from the viscous liquid. Most of the gel slid easily off my skin, leaving only the thinnest smear of residue. I supposed that if I let it dry, it would become powdery like the thin layer that had lined the empty receptacle.

"We *really* need to work on better communication," Viss muttered, his voice thick with tension.

While Yuskeya detached one of Juliska's gloves and worked it off, I wiped my fingers dry on my suit and studied the apparently extensive amount of data these aliens had on human anatomy and pathology. Not that I could read any of it, but data filled the screen, and I had to imagine it was saying more than *unknown life form*. "Pika, they didn't get any of this from you, did they?"

"No," she answered immediately. "We didn't get anywhere close to that kind of information exchange."

"So where did—" I started, and then I pulled a sharp breath. "*Sankta merde*. Spelunkers," I breathed.

"What did you say?" Maja asked over the comm. They must all be glued to the bridge relays of what we were seeing and saying.

"Wormhole spelunkers," I repeated. "It would explain how these aliens could know so much about us, while we know nothing about them. The wormhole explorers who didn't return—we always assumed they had accidents—wormhole collapses, collisions, exiting wormholes into non-survivable conditions. But some of them . . . what if some of them encountered these aliens? At least enough times for them to be scanned or studied."

"No actual communications, I guess, because they didn't know the language," Hirin said.

"Not even Pika could fully break the communications barrier," I agreed.

"Well, not *yet*," the AI muttered.

I ignored her and continued. "No spelunker would have had AI capabilities anywhere near her level. And maybe the encounters were cursory, or even post-mortem. I don't mean the aliens killed them," I added quickly at the dark look on Viss's face. "But maybe they tried to rescue them from skips gone bad, failed, and gathering physical data was the most they could do."

"Maybe the first scan of the Ryphens contributed to their knowledge base, too, if that drone sent back its data. It could have done that before landing on the planet, if that is what happened," Maja added.

While we'd been talking, the blue gel had deepened, and Juliska's helmeted head and bare hand now floated gently in the sticky-looking goo. The flash of data across the giant screen intensified, and various areas of Juliska's outlined body lit up in brief coloured bursts. I could only assume the machine was gathering data on her current condition. How the gel figured into that was anyone's guess. The drones hovered in front of the tall screen, buzzing intermittently, presumably looped into the data somehow.

Then one descended and shone its pale blue beam on Juliska again. The light intensified, darkening in colour and diffusing over Juliska's entire body. Her limbs twitched and stiffened slightly, but her face remained placid inside her helmet. Yuskeya's hand started out toward her, but she didn't touch the Ryphen captain.

The 'bot moved into my line of vision so I could see that a new pictogram had blinked onto its screen. This one showed the ubiquitous plus sign, and two circles, one filled and one outlined, divided by a vertical line. The pictogram blinked slowly on and off.

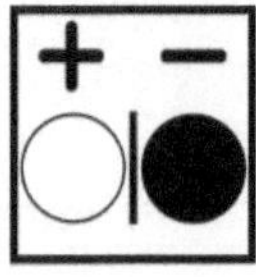

"*Okej*, this one has me stumped."

"None of the other pictograms blinked. We might interpret that as waiting for a response," Pika said.

Yuskeya looked at me. "Yes or no? Do you think it's asking our permission to do something else?"

I frowned, looking at the drones. They all held perfectly still. The information on the giant screen also began to blink, in time with the 'bot's pictogram. "It seems that way. But should we let them go ahead? We don't know what they want to do."

She blew out a sigh. "She's probably not going to make it if we do nothing. Even if we left immediately, I'm not sure I could keep her alive until we got back to Ryphen. I can do what I did for Amber Malka, but that was barely enough. And we don't know if Dr. Ndasa did any better."

I looked at Juliska's still form in the gel tub. "Nothing they've suggested so far has been bad," I said slowly. "Admittedly, that's not a lot to go on."

Yuskeya glanced up at the screen looming over us. "I don't know why they'd have all this data if their only intention was to kill other species. The Relidae certainly didn't bother collecting reams of information on everyone they considered their enemies."

"True." I nodded slowly. And remembering what she'd said earlier, I thought that in honour of Amber, maybe Juliska would be okay with making another jump into the unknown.

"Pika, can you try to tell them yes, they should proceed? Maybe send the 'bot a plus sign? With an outlined circle, like the one in this pictogram?"

"Done."

Immediately, the second and third drone dropped down to create the triangle configuration around Juliska again, adding their own beams.

"Hey, I know phototherapy exists, but they're going to cure her entirely with light?" Viss asked.

Yuskeya pursed her lips. "I don't know if that's all that's happening here. I suspect it has more to do with her skin contact with the gel, in combination with the light—whatever it's doing. I mean, we've had photodynamic therapy for a long time, where light activates a chemical or compound to perform a certain task inside the body. I can see this being along the same lines, although certainly more complex than we've developed. Interesting that the EVA suit doesn't seem to be a deterrent. The skin contact is probably key. No doubt something in the gel is being absorbed."

"More nano-scale stuff?"

"Your guess is as good as mine."

The 'bot's screen changed again, blinking back to the pictogram we'd interpreted as an invitation to follow the yellow guide light on the floor, and predictably, that light pulsed at the same time. The 'bot took a few long-legged steps toward the doorway where Juliska had collapsed.

"Just leave her here?" I asked, although I wasn't certain who I was talking to. The 'bot, I suppose, although it probably couldn't technically hear me.

"We can keep an eye on her," Hirin said over my helmet comm. "We all have our suits on, so we can get to her fast if we need to."

"I estimate a high probability that she will be as safe here alone as if you stay," Pika said. "Whatever they're doing is already happening. If she wakes up, someone from the ship can come to her."

"Pika, what do you think about what I guessed earlier?" I asked as I stepped reluctantly down from the block. The arguments made sense, but it was difficult to walk away from the unconscious captain. "How would they have learned enough about human physiology to be able to practice medicine on us?"

"You're probably right about the wormhole explorers," she said. "There's also the possibility of PrimeCorp, but I feel like there would have been something in Pita's files if there'd been a secret encounter. I've already checked for any descriptions that sounded like the drones or this ship, any mention of pictograms like the ones we're seeing . . . nothing. So we're back to the explorers, or possibly some covert observation."

"Covert observation . . . like those old stories about alien sightings and abductions? UFOs? Secret visitors to Earth?" Viss sounded amused.

Pika couldn't shrug, but her voice managed to convey one. "I only mention it as a possibility," she said. "It would have taken stealth technology, and these explorers don't strike me as particularly discreet. But we can't rule it out. Aside from language, they do seem to have detailed information on human anatomy and physiology, as well as many other species if that database is anything to judge by."

The 'bot had taken half a dozen steps back toward the door and then stopped to turn its screen back to us as if to say, "coming?" I stood on tiptoe to glance once more at Juliska, but she still seemed placidly asleep, not distressed. "I guess we have to keep trusting them. Let's keep going." The 'bot began to move again when I started toward it, and Yuskeya and Viss moved after me. I knew it was hard for Yuskeya to leave a patient, but this was what we had come here for, after all.

The 'bot led us down a wide, vaulted corridor half as high as one of the cargo pods. I couldn't imagine the scale of creature that would need this large a thoroughfare, unless it was all for show or design, like some human buildings. While we might exaggerate the space we needed on a planet, however, we tended to keep things within utilitarian parameters when we went into space, because of fuel and life support considerations. Maybe these aliens, whoever they were, simply were huge. I shuddered a bit at the sheer mystery of it all, and kept doggedly following the 'bot.

THE CORRIDOR RAN mainly straight, and I assumed we were headed for whatever served as the "bridge" of the ship. At intervals, other passageways opened off to one side or the other, or huge black doors stood closed against us. Indecipherable symbols glowed with soft colour in the enhanced helmet visors, labelling them with names we could not read. The glow was not from an actual light or reflection, but a property of the paint or substance that made the symbols themselves. Studded along the walls were more dark, gelatinous screens, outlined with glowing traceries of colour but otherwise lifeless and inert. Between them, at irregular intervals, we passed alcoves holding what appeared to be smaller gel receptacles, all empty, and an occasional rectangle of glassy substance set into the wall, reminiscent of a heavily-tinted window. Obscure shapes lurked behind these panels, but their nature or purpose were impossible to make out. The layer of dust we scuffed through was evidence that sometime, someone had inhabited this ship, but it had apparently been long ago.

Eventually the corridor opened into a room about half as large as the docking bay had been. The ceiling still soared far higher than humans would have required, vaulting over a three-tiered space. Sloping ramps connected the levels. At the far end of the room on the highest level, large, faceted windows looked out into the void, and I realized we were inside what had looked like giant eyes as we approached the ship. We halted in the arched entranceway, surveying the space.

Curving black containers as high as my waist lined the lower sections of the walls, following the contours of the room but stopping short of the windows. From these containers, ropey lengths of bluish vine sent traceries up an integrated latticework all the way to the ceiling. The vines did not emit the soft glow of colour evident in so many other areas of the ship, and I thought I knew why—they were long-dead. A few withered leaves hung in handfuls and scatters, but the vines were bare and wrinkled, still upright only because in life their tendrils had wound so tightly into the lattices.

In gaps between the vine-choked lattices, dark screens like the ones in the docking bay hung also lifeless and silent, their glossy, almost wet-looking surfaces strangely untouched by the dust that had accumulated on the floors.

What I took to be workstations ranged around the room on the other two levels, validating our assumption that whoever had built this ship, they were creatures larger than any we'd encountered so far.

The configuration of a work surface accompanied by a seat was recognizable, although it was hard to twist my mind around the shape of a body that would require and occupy such a seat. It rose on a pedestal to a height of about four feet, and the "seat" itself was a wide oval with a shallow half-moon cutaway in the back. A curved bar circled the pedestal about a foot off the floor, creating what might be a footrest. But instead of a back, another support ledge rose several feet up at the front of the seat, as big as the seat itself. It had a similar cutaway section. Every workstation was outfitted with a similar "chair" and an array of screens or consoles, obviously suited to different purposes. Below the screen at every station lay a tub or sink like those in the docking bay. I suspected they would all be empty, except perhaps for a thin coating of the dried blue residue.

Over all these surfaces lay the ubiquitous thick coating of dust. Our footprints were the only ones marking the floor. No living being had been in here for a long time.

Viss and Yuskeya had stopped beside me, and we stood surveying the oversized furnishings. Viss tilted his head to one side, studying the constructs that seemed to be chairs. "Tails?" he hazarded. "Or maybe they're tripedal? Either of those might explain that cut-out section at the back of the seat."

"Think about the pictograms—Rei said the heads looked a bit like giant bugs. If so, that space could be for a narrow waist between a thorax and abdomen to fit," Yuskeya mused. "The front part might support another segment of a body, or maybe even a large head. If they're insectoid, or an insectoid analogue, it might explain wanting to surround themselves with plants, too." She nodded to the husks of vines.

"True. Long arms could reach the controls—and into the tubs, I guess. But then you'd think you'd want something for the abdomen to rest on in the back," Viss said.

"Although I doubt they could evolve to be this large with only exoskeletons," Yuskeya said, turning to look around the room. "They could have developed both, I suppose, for support. Even on a low-gravity world they'd need the support of an internal skeleton, and lungs, naturally—"

"The abdomen could be long enough to reach the ground when they're sitting here—"

"*Okej*," I interrupted, feeling a warm flush creep up my back at the thought of giant insectoid aliens. I'm not usually squeamish or species-ist, but that image threw me a little, and knowing these two, they could go on for hours this way. "That kind of speculation isn't getting us anywhere, but maybe you can take your theories back to Okwi Rousseault. Whatever they were like, I don't think they've been here in a long time."

Yuskeya moved to a workstation and gingerly stepped onto the low curving bar. She ran a gloved finger across the "seat," and dust puffed into the air in a tiny grey cloud. "A really long time," she agreed.

On the far wall ahead of us, between the enormous windows, a large screen flickered to life as the one in the docking bay had done.

"Did I do that?" Yuskeya asked, freezing in place.

"I don't think so. The screen at that workstation is still dark. I think the big one is activating because we've arrived."

The phosphorescent colours on the screen shone dimly at first, then brightened to a stronger glow. Data flashed in rows running from the bottom of the screen toward the top, reminding me of a computer's initiating sequence, although none of the symbols held any meaning for us. Finally, three pictograms appeared on the screen: the one with two large heads, the wavy lines Maja had thought might be water, and the one with two interlocking circles below a plus sign. We hadn't taken a guess at the meaning of that one, yet.

I wished I could simply pull the datapad holding Pika out of my pocket and get her to communicate, the way Pita and I had done last year with the Chron. She had no helpful secret language database to reference in this case, however. We were on our own.

"Captain?"

"Yes, Pika?" The AI had been strangely silent since we'd arrived on the bridge, although I assumed she was "looking" around like the rest of us, sharing our helmet cam feeds.

"You want me to try sending a databurst or something?"

"No, that hasn't worked before. We need a minute to think."

"I wish Juliska were here," Yuskeya whispered to me. "It seems wrong for her to be missing this."

I nodded, although I wasn't sure the unconscious captain would be missing much. This AI—if that's what it was—made a lot of assumptions about how clever we were going to be at interpreting its images. My mind whirled with the questions I wanted to ask: were there still any life forms aboard? Were they settled into dreamless coldsleep on another deck, awaiting some enigmatic trigger to awaken? And if not, was the ship still in communication with any of them, perhaps on a home planet?

How long had the AI and its bots and drones been exploring solar systems? How far had they come? How had they gained such an intimate knowledge of human anatomy? And we somehow had to tell them about the Ryphens and the necessity to stop trying to scan the planet.

How could we do any of that if we couldn't even decipher a few simple pictograms?

"Send the plus sign, Pika," I said. "And the open circle. At least we feel reasonably certain about those, and they should convey something positive."

"Sending."

"Luta?" The voice in my helmet was thin and soft, but I knew it. I turned to see Juliska Barath standing in the entryway to the bridge, traces of phosphorescent blue gel still clinging to her EVA suit. She leaned lightly on a sturdy-looking wheeled 'bot for support, but she was steady on her feet, and she smiled through her visor at me.

I hurried over to her. "Why didn't anyone tell me you were awake? Did we lose communications with the ship? Hirin, can you still hear me?"

"Loud and clear," he answered. "It's fine. We didn't want to bother you when you were just getting to the bridge, so we switched to another channel."

Juliska shook her head, smiling. "You didn't need concerns about me to interrupt your explorations up here. Hirin came out and helped me down from the—whatever that tub was. This—" she patted the 'bot supporting her, "came to escort me to catch up with you, and Hirin went back to the *Tane Ikai*." She gazed around the bridge, taking it in. "This is incredible."

I gestured to her. "*This* is incredible. How do you feel?"

She smiled, her blue eyes wide in wonder. "I feel . . . tired, but pretty great. The withdrawal symptoms are gone, at least for now. Whatever the gel and the drones did, it seems to have worked. A medical miracle."

And suddenly all the other questions and concerns were swept away by a single, urgent thought.

Could they do the same for Karro?

"Yuskeya," I practically gasped, feeling like all the air had abandoned my lungs and rushed into vacuum, "what about Karro? Do you think they could help him, too?"

She blinked. "I don't—I have no idea. I don't know what they did for Captain Barath. And I still don't know what's wrong with him."

I thrust Pika's datapad into Yuskeya's hands. "I have to talk to Aliande. The four of you work on communications. Make up some pictograms. Don't get us into a war." Then I thudded down the corridor toward the *Tane Ikai*, as quickly as the bulky EVA suit would allow.

I heard Viss swear behind me, but I didn't turn around.

IN THE EMOTION of the moment, I'd forgotten that Aliande, Hirin, and the others would have overheard my revelation. When I reached the *Tane Ikai*, they had Karro in an EVA suit on a cargo sled, ready to be transported out into the alien ship's docking bay. Hirin was obviously ready to help make the transfer. Aliande looked both hopeful and terrified, safely bundled into her EVA suit. She clutched at my hand when I entered the ship.

"Do you really think they can help?"

I wondered if she could feel my hand shaking through the suit's glove. "Maybe. I don't know. It seems worth a try. Juliska says she feels great."

"She has nanobioscavengers," Aliande said in a low voice. Behind the ultraplas of her visor, her face showed the strain of Karro's illness. "Karro doesn't. Do you think that makes a difference?"

"I don't know. But early wormhole spelunkers wouldn't have had them, so the aliens shouldn't think they're a part of our normal physiology." I met her eyes and summoned the words I'd realized I had to say during my mad dash through the alien ship. "Is this really all right with you? I—I got excited when the idea struck me, but this is your decision. I won't push you into it."

She glanced at Karro's still form on the sled, and nodded. "I think you're right. It's worth a try. And there's no reason to think he'll end up worse off." Her gaze came back to me, and I saw the certainty there. *Yes. This is a decision I can make, and a risk I can live with.*

I blew out a long sigh. "I think he'd want us to take this chance."

"All right. Let's get him out there," Aliande said, the sound of her own deep exhale filling the helmet comm.

I know it took only a few minutes, but moving in the EVA suits with the plodding cargo sled made it feel like time had slowed to the speed of a star being born. The three drones buzzed over to meet us as if they were anxious to get started too, appearing to know what we expected of them. They locked their blue beams onto Karro before we were even halfway to the active screen. We transferred Karro into the gel-lined tub with little difficulty. Most of the gel from before had already drained away, or perhaps had absorbed back into the tub after Juliska's treatment was complete. Two small robots on treads worked to scrub up globs of gel that had dripped onto the floor, presumably when Juliska emerged from her blue goo bath. I wondered again what purposes these tubs had served when there were living creatures on board to make use of them. It seemed unlikely that they were purely for medical uses, since they were ubiquitous in the docking bay and on the bridge. They must have multiple purposes.

Aliande stepped away from the receptacle as the gel began to seep back, filling the space around Karro. We'd left his EVA suit gloves off, and the gel slowly rose around his hands and fingers, the viscous liquid buoying them to hang suspended just under the rising surface of the gel. As they had with Juliska, the three drones began to play their lights over his still form.

After watching in silence for a few moments, I blew out a breath. My heart had finally settled back to its normal rhythm and the adrenaline prickles in my muscles had faded. I glanced toward the tall, open door leading into the alien ship, wondering what was happening now on the bridge.

I was opening my mouth to ask them for a report when Hirin tapped my shoulder. "Go," he said, gesturing toward the towering doorway with a nod. "We'll be fine."

"Are you sure?" I looked at Karro, peacefully floating in the gel while the drones hummed above him. It seemed wrong to leave.

"There's nothing more you can do here," he said. "Aliande and I will stay with him. We can keep in touch over the helmet comms."

Aliande's face showed a flash of surprise, but then she nodded in agreement. "Go back to the others. I suspect whatever they're going to do here won't take long. It didn't with Captain Barath."

Much as I wanted to stay, they were right. I'd done what I

could for Karro, and now I had to go back and check on the rest of my team. I'd left them to converse with an alien intelligence, after all. Aliande threw me a quick, encouraging smile, then stood watching Karro in the gel, gloved hands clasped in front of her.

"All right. I'll go back to the bridge. Let me know when anything happens." With a final glance at Karro's calm, unresponsive face, I went.

Fortunately, it was easy to follow the single corridor back to the alien bridge. I found Yuskeya and Juliska had moved closer to the big screen, Juliska sitting awkwardly on one of the strange "chairs." Yuskeya had her head bent over Pika's datapad. Viss was investigating another workstation and chair on the far side of the space, although its screen, like all the others, sat quiet and dark. I crossed to Juliska and put a hand on her arm.

"Still okay?"

She turned to me and smiled. "So much better," she said, her voice sounding stronger than it had since we'd left Ryphen. Her blue eyes were bright behind the visor.

"I wonder—is it a permanent cure? That would be incredible."

She shook her head. "I don't know. I feel as I normally would if I were on Ryphen. Tired, as if I'd just come off a shift on the Lillifleur; but getting better instead of worse. I don't know how long it will last. But I'm grateful."

I looked up at the big viewscreen. It currently showed four pictograms I hadn't seen before. They pulsed slowly, fading and brightening. "What's this?"

"Pika made them and sent them. I think the AI, or whatever it is, is trying to figure out what they mean."

The four images were similar in size and shape to the ones the aliens had sent us. One showed the drone shape with an X through it, and the second showed what I took to be a representation of the nearby planet. The third consisted of a simple equal sign, and the fourth showed a supine human stick figure with a minus sign above it. "Don't send drones to Ryphen, because it is negative for the people there?" I guessed. "Seems straightforward to me, but I have the background and experience to understand it."

"At first, I was going to use the giant bug head in the last one, but I thought they might take that as a threat," Pika said in a serious tone. "I hope they'll understand that's supposed to represent the planet's inhabitants."

"Trying to communicate this way is going to take a long time," I said. "There's so much I want to know . . . like why there aren't any living beings aboard the ship anymore."

"Assuming there aren't," Juliska said.

Involuntarily, I glanced back at the door we'd come through, wondering again about coldsleep, but Viss read my mind. "I got Baden to run a full scan," he said. "We're the only lifeforms on this ship."

"Except possibly the AI," Pika said, sounding annoyed. "You know very well a lifeform doesn't necessarily have to look like *you*, Viss Feron."

He grinned at the tablet, the first time I'd seen him look relaxed since we'd left Ryphen. "And possibly the AI," he agreed. "I'll rephrase; we're the only *organic* life forms that showed up in the scan."

"Much better," she retorted.

While I fretted silently about what might be happening with Karro and we waited for a response to Pika's communication effort, we made a full circuit of the bridge area, all three levels. The helmet cam recordings would be useful in reporting to the Ryphens and the Nearspace Authority. I made sure to take in the vines, the strangely faceted windows, and even the desiccated soil from which the now-dead vines emerged. From the upper levels we could easily see into the tub-like receptacles on the lower levels, and all showed smudged traces of blue gel residue but nothing else. Nothing we did activated any of the workstations or other screens—only the large one remained active. Either the power to the rest had been cut long ago, or we lacked some vital quality that would have made the technology respond to us.

"Or we don't know what the 'on' switch looks like," Viss joked, running a hand along the underside of a workstation in case we were missing a simple solution.

"Maybe it's just as well," Yuskeya said. "Nothing more dangerous than a bunch of spacers messing with technology they don't understand."

"Luta?" All of this investigation had taken some time, and much as I was waiting for it, Aliande's voice over the helmet comm startled me. "We're coming to you. Can you give us directions?"

"Straight through that door and along the passage," I told her, feeling my hands go cold inside my gloves. "You'll come right to us. Is Karro—"

"Awake and moving almost entirely under his own power," she said, the relief flooding her voice.

"Hi, Mom." Karro's voice was weak and thready, but it was the best thing I'd heard in a long time. "We'll be right there. I've got things to tell you."

CHAPTER TWENTY
A Way of Working Out

I DIDN'T WAIT on the bridge for Karro and Aliande to reach me. I darted out into the corridor, my booted feet thumping dully again on the dark floor. Around a curve I found them, Hirin and Aliande and Karro, the latter leaning on Aliande's arm but obviously able to walk on his own. I wrapped him in a hug and felt him chuckle as he hugged me back.

"I'm okay, Mom. Really."

I held him at arm's length, studying him the way a mother does when trying to decide if their child is truly all right. His skin looked strange, the phosphorescent cast of the coloured traceries on the walls lending him a colour that would not have looked healthy in any other circumstances. His suit, and now mine, bore traces of the blue gel as Juliska's had. But his arms had gripped me tightly, and he looked at me with bright and animated eyes.

"He's all right," Aliande said just above a whisper, as if she was still trying to convince herself.

I didn't let go of his arms. "What do you have to tell me?"

He lifted an admonitory finger, a grin curling the corners of his mouth. "Be patient. Let's get to the others."

"He won't tell us, either," Hirin said. "I could hold him down while you tickle him if you want. Maybe we can make him talk." The relief in his voice was evident, too.

Aliande shooed us away from Karro with a peremptory hand.

"Let him through, you two. We'll find out soon enough what he's talking about, because I'll make him tell us myself as soon as we're with the others." I saw her grip tighten on his arm as they continued to move down the passageway toward the bridge, and smiled. He wasn't getting out of his wife's sight for a while after this scare.

Even at Karro's slow pace, we reached the massive bridge eventually. He paused in the doorway, taking in the sheer enormity of the space with a bemused look. "It makes sense," he said, more to himself than any of us. "I mean, I didn't have a clear idea of the scale, but the impression . . . yes."

I gave him a combination of my best "mother" and "captain" stares. "Care to share with the rest of us?"

He started, almost as if he'd forgotten that we were there. "Of course! But I think I might make use of one of these fascinating seats, like Juliska has." Aliande led him over to one of the strange workstations and helped him onto it. He used the presumed footrest bar as a step, and sat as if it were a stool, ignoring the upper "shelf" section. His legs dangled comically, and I was reminded of him as a boy, sitting in an overlarge skimchair on the bridge of the *Tane Ikai*. Another flood of relief that he seemed on the road to recovery overtook me, and I had to shake myself and focus on what he was saying.

"How well have you been able to communicate with the aliens?" he asked.

I stared at him. "We're not even sure there are aliens. All we've seen so far are drones, 'bots, and whatever is putting pictograms on that screen." I gestured to the front of the bridge. "We've only graduated to pictograms since Pika managed to establish a few basic connections through the 'bot. We think we've interpreted them correctly, but we're struggling."

Karro nodded slowly. "Just their AI, then. That makes sense."

Trying to be patient, I said, "Go on."

He frowned as if trying to catch hold of a particularly elusive memory. "I have . . . impressions, that I'm putting together with what we knew before we took the drone aboard the *Lillifleur*."

"Impressions from where? When you touched the drone?"

"Maybe?" He didn't sound convinced, and shook his head as if trying to clear it, or shift ideas into their proper places. "It's difficult to fit things into the proper chronological order. Like trying to remember when you first learned things you've known since you were a child. You can't recall *not* knowing them."

Yuskeya said gently, "There was an anomaly in the brain scan I did after the incident with the drone. Nothing that looked like actual damage," she added hastily. "But a change. New neural pathways. Maybe even what you could call an upgrade."

"I guess that could be part of it," he said, smiling and shaking his head. "But I think it's about the gel—that blue gel in the tubs. I think it's a communicative medium for them—the aliens who built this. And I feel like I . . . tapped into it."

I turned to look a question at Yuskeya, and she shrugged elegantly and showed me her palms. "That's way outside my experience."

"Baden?" I asked over the comm. "Any thoughts?"

After a brief pause, he said, "Not a single one, Captain."

"All right. Karro, you said you have impressions. Any impression about how that would work?"

He half-smiled. "Not really. I feel like they—or the AI that speaks for them—send messages into the gel, and they get translated and transmitted through—" he held up his bare hands, still showing drying patches of pale blue gel, "—well, through the skin contact, I guess."

Juliska had been listening intently from her own perch. Now she straightened up and nodded slowly. "I think I was getting . . . glimmers, you could say, of something, when I was in the gel. Not words so much as emotions; like waves of soothing, calming thoughts."

Karro nodded eagerly. "I got that, too. But I—there was also a layer of something more *formed* than that. Like there were words there, language, that I was on the cusp of hearing and understanding." He looked around the bridge. "That's why I wanted to get here. The stuff drained out as I was coming awake. I thought there might be something obvious I could use to communicate with them."

Viss hadn't said anything since Karro had arrived on the bridge, but now he said, "Well, the place is full of those same tubs. Seems like they all fill up with the stuff. It would make sense if that's how they communicate."

"Do you think you have to get inside one again?"

"Probably not? At least—I'll try putting just my hands in

again." He chuckled. "I'm not sure how much direct skin contact I'm comfortable with."

"What, you don't want to get naked to talk to the giant bug alien AI?" Baden said over the helmet comms. "Not very dedicated, Karro."

"Hey, I did get my brain zapped," Karro retorted. "That has to count for something." He surveyed one of the workstations as if wondering how to navigate it. His arms would not be long enough to reach down into the gel receptacle while he sat on one of the seats.

"What if you lie on the seat part and dangle your arms into the gel?" Viss suggested. "Assuming it's going to fill with gel. Hirin and I can be ready to grab your feet and pull you back if anything goes wrong."

"That could work. But I don't think anything is going to go wrong."

Aliande caught my eye and a look of worry passed between us. We both knew how many things could go wrong when you least expected them. But she didn't make any protest.

"All right," Maja said over the helmet comm. "Let's see if this works and Karro can start talking to whoever's there. We're not entirely happy being so far away from you all. I won't be able to relax until you're all safely back here on the ship."

"Although we could come out there and meet up with you," Rei added. "I like walking around in gigantic alien spaceships too."

"Someone has to stay with the ship," I reminded her automatically. "Let's see what happens here, and then if circumstances allow, you can have a turn going EVA. Deal?"

"Deal," Rei said happily. "Karro, don't mess this up for me, okay?"

Karro didn't answer, because he was already turning to lie flat on the seat-like surface. With only a slight hesitation, he stretched out on his stomach and let his hands hang down inside the receptacle. I took one of the ramps to the second level, where I could look down on Karro's position and see into the tub. He pressed his hands against the side wall, and from my vantage point I saw the gel begin to seep out of the minuscule apertures in the walls. It oozed out around Karro's hands and, apparently impatient, he rubbed the viscous stuff over them until they were covered. Then he looked up at the large viewscreen where the previous pictograms still glowed. When they didn't change, he moved his hands along the walls of the tub to encounter even more of the gel.

After a few heartbeats when I thought it wasn't going to work, more of the ship's odd symbology began to stream across the large screen, echoed on the screen at the workstation where Karro lay. As the characters glowed to life, Karro closed his eyes. "We are the *Haeruth,* travellers across space," he said. His voice was slow and serious, and felt somehow *older* than his own normal speaking voice. Maybe that was a fanciful impression because I knew he was speaking the aliens' words—it was still his voice. Part of me wanted to jump down and yank his hands out of that gel, but the urge was drowned out by the part that was intensely curious to hear what he—what *they*—were going to say.

"We are collectors. We collect knowledge; we collect places; we collect life forms," he continued. I stiffened at that, not sure what the words implied. Before I could say anything, though, he went on. "We do not collect these things physically, but we add the knowledge of them and their experiences to the *bhalivex.*" Karro grimaced and opened his eyes. "That means something like, *great sum of all that is available to be known*," he said, tilting his head to glance up at me. "Even with the gel, I guess no communication system is perfect."

"So, like a galactic database?" Yuskeya asked.

"Yes, but—anonymous." Karro paused as if listening. "They say, we travel space, by proxy now, to gather information about planets and species: living forms, natural phenomena, wonders. We will share this data with other interested forms we encounter, but we do not reveal where other living forms are located."

"They're smart, anyway," Viss observed grudgingly. "They don't want to be responsible for a group like the Pitromae Chron heading out on an extinction mission."

I shook my head. "How does this work?" I asked, almost in a whisper. "How are you getting all this?"

Karro blew out a sigh and flexed his hands, now immersed wrist-deep in the gel. "I don't know. It's like I hear the words in my head in Esper, even though I know that's not possible."

"We've known for a long time that skin can be a communication medium," Yuskeya said thoughtfully. "Not only through touch, but transmitting information as neurons do, with chemical changes. The gel could be facilitating that kind of response."

"It's fine. Keep going," I told Karro, not wanting to interrupt the flow of information, no matter how it was being achieved. "Does it—go both ways? Can you tell them that their drone scans accidentally caused harm to the Ryphens? We understand it was not intentional, but they should not send any more drones there. Or at least have them not do any scans. But don't make it sound like a demand! Just a polite but firm request."

Karro nodded, closing his eyes again.

"This is Enne, agent of the Haeruth. We regret harm to living forms here or on the nearby planet," Karro continued after a brief pause, as if picking up the thread of the conversation again. He turned to look at me. "I think that first part was sort of a pre-recorded message from the aliens. This Enne is the AI controlling the ship—I think that's what 'we' means now," he said in a whispered aside. "Enne goes on: We strive primarily to avoid harm in all our interactions. No more scouts will be sent. We have healed these two, and we are willing to heal others."

Juliska gasped. "The Ryphens? The ones affected by the first scan? Is that what they mean?"

I caught the frown that settled briefly on Viss's face. "What? They're offering to help. I think that's good."

"Sure, it sounds good, but what's this AI going to do? Ferry all the colonists up here and dunk them in tubs of blue gel?"

I shrugged. "Maybe. From what I've seen so far, that seems like a reasonable assumption."

Viss harrumphed and Yuskeya shot him a *behave* look.

"I think . . . I think that's exactly what they're proposing," Karro said in a voice tinged with awe. Then he opened his eyes and looked up at me again. "I can keep translating every word for you, if you want, but—it feels strange. I'd rather just . . . interpret, if that's okay?"

When I nodded, he added, "But that is what they're saying."

"Captain." Juliska had her eyes raised to mine. "Should . . . should we do that?"

I hesitated. Despite what I'd said to Viss, this was a lot. "What do they want in return?" I asked Karro.

He was quiet, then said, "Enne would like to send the 'bot back to Ryphen to gather as much data as it can about the people there, and relay that to the ship before it's too far out of range. Then it can stay on and assist the Ryphens with, well, anything it can."

Pika said, "Whoa, Captain. Incoming data stream from the 'bot. It's . . . a lot of data."

"I thought you couldn't understand it?"

Karro said, "It's going to take some time, but I think we'll be able to work with Pika to build a translation database. I can function as a key, since I can speak the equivalents of the words appearing on the screens. And the AI—Enne—is sending Pika an aggregate of the data they've collected in their travels. She can't read it yet, but she will be able to once we build the database."

"That information could be invaluable if we encounter any other species in the database," Maja breathed over the helmet comms. They'd been so quiet, back on the ship, I'd almost forgotten they were still listening and watching. "We'd have a head start on getting to know them."

"Okay, two more quick things for now." I could hear in Karro's voice that he was beginning to tire, and I knew he'd have to take a break soon. "One, I'd like to know what happened to the aliens—the *Haeruth*. It looks like there are none left on the ship, but clearly it was built to carry them. Unless they're somewhere we haven't been . . ."

Karro nodded, presumably relaying my question to the AI. "The Haeruth travelled the stars themselves for—" Karro faltered a bit, frowning. "For millennia, I think they're saying. A very long time, anyway. They knew there was still more to learn, but they—" He stopped again, and closed his eyes, forehead wrinkling in concentration. When he opened them again, he said, "This part isn't very clear. I'm not getting what happened to them or what they did. They changed somehow. Became more than they were? It's like Enne is saying they grew beyond themselves," he finished, and shrugged. "Anyway, they no longer travel in the confines of the ship, but they exchange information from time to time. The AI reports to them about what it finds, and they are . . . they are *content*."

I took a moment to digest that information, then said, "All right, my other question is, why did they want us to come out here? It seems to me that between the drones and 'bots and scanning technology, they could study any planet, ship, or people they come across. Why not just wait until they arrived at Ryphen? The ship is headed there.”

“I already asked that. Enne said they like to encounter new life forms in person whenever possible, to verify any data they already have in their repository. And the ship can be intimidating if it suddenly appears near a planet.”

“I can see that,” Viss muttered.

“And treating Juliska and me was a ‘bonus’ for the data it allowed the AI to confirm,” Karro added. The weariness in his voice was almost tangible now.

“All right, you should break the connection. I have so many more questions, but they can wait for a while.”

“Yeah, I’m beat. I can’t do any more. It’s mentally exhausting, and somehow physically, too.” Karro’s voice betrayed a strange mixture of regret and weariness. He pulled his hands out of the gel, shaking them until most of the blue communication medium had slid back into the remaining volume. This time, it didn’t drain away, presumably remaining ready to be used again.

As I turned to move down to the lower level again, I remembered one important thing I hadn’t gotten Karro to ask. “*Damne*, I forgot to ask for an explanation of the pictograms!”

Karro had rolled to a sitting position on the “seat” now, legs dangling and hands on his knees. Aliande had climbed up, too, and sat next to him, a hand on his arm. Karro rolled his neck as if to work out kinks, then smiled at me. “It’s all right. I know what some of them are, at least.”

“Did we get any of them right, I wonder?” Hirin asked. “Does the plus sign mean ‘good’?”

Karro smiled. “Essentially, yes. The wavy lines represent the communication gel, and the two heads together means talking or communicating. The ship, the drone, and the ’bot are self-explanatory. And the interlocking circles—”

“Means exchanging ideas, doesn’t it?” Baden said over the helmet comm. “I figured that one out, but I didn’t have a chance to tell anyone there.”

“That’s exactly right,” Karro said. “And you did a good job with the pictograms you sent back, too. By the time I had reconnected with Enne, they’d figured them out.”

“Thank you,” Pika said in a smug voice. “And now I’ve started building that translation database anyway. I recorded those parts where Karro was saying the same thing that the screens were showing. When he feels up to making a connection again, we can do that until we have a complete bilingual dictionary."

I crossed to Juliska and asked in a low voice, "You're okay with this AI knowing everything about Ryphen?"

"If it can help everyone who was affected by the scan, that seems like a small price to pay."

"You could wait until we get help through from Nearspace."

"We still don't even know that's a guarantee," Juliska said. She held her arms out as if to emphasize her own improved health. "This seems like it is."

"Some people aren't going to like it," I observed. "Karin Nakano comes to mind, for one. She was dead set against letting the 'bot record and transmit information about Ryphen before. She said herself she wasn't too comfortable with advanced AIs, and this one goes way beyond even Pika, I think."

"Hey, I'm right here," Pika said.

"I think she'll come around," Juliska said, "if it means everyone being cured. I think she'll have to. And this is different. Our information will still be protected."

"And the Ryphens will have all the information about the Haeruth, too, Captain," Pika said. "I'm only glancing through things yet, but there's a file of information that I'm guessing is all about them and their history. Probably make for some fascinating reading during long, boring in-system times between wormhole skips."

I thought I'd be all right with a little long and boring after this, even without new reading material.

"There are logistics to work out, but we have time before the ship gets to Ryphen at its current speed," I said. "If the colonists have to be ferried back and forth to the ship, we can help with that."

"We can figure it out, I'm sure," Karro said.

The active screens on the bridge flickered, displaying a single pictogram. The tub waited with its blue gel, but I thought we didn't need it. The pictogram showed what was clearly the alien ship, with a smaller ship inside it.

"They're offering to let us stay here and ride back to Ryphen with them, aren't they?" I suggested.

"That would be my guess," Baden said over the helmet comm.

"It popped up on the screen nearest the *Tane Ikai*, too, and the tub is filling up with gel."

"That lets them keep Karro close for more 'conversations,'" Viss said, but some of the skepticism had left his voice. Maybe he was coming around to the idea that these aliens were not enemies.

"Good," Pika said. "I need more data for this dictionary I'm building."

Hirin and Viss helped Karro down from the workstation seat, and Aliande stood with one arm wrapped around his waist. She practically glowed with relief and happiness, her dark brown eyes shining.

"Sure, but later, Pika. For now, let's get back to the ship. Karro needs to rest, and the others are itching to swap places so they can have a look around. We'll have more time to chat later."

I offered Juliska my arm to help clamber down from the gigantic seat, but once she stood beside me, she let go. "I feel like I can walk back on my own," she said quietly. "Just walk beside me, *okej*?"

I nodded. "Count on it." I knew she meant a lot more than simply making it back to the *Tane Ikai*. I knew she was thinking of Amber, and the rest of the Ryphens, and things that were bigger than all of that and all of us. Not big like these strange aliens, but big like whatever they had become. Big like the universe. Big like the great sum of all that is available to be known.

We had things to move toward, and we could do it on our own, with friends by our side.

WE STAYED ABOARD the *Haeruth* ship, the name of which Karro translated as *Seeker*, until we were approaching the wormhole back to Nearspace. At that point it seemed wise to get the *Tane Ikai* outside the alien ship and get ready to send a message to Ryphen that all was well, not to be alarmed at the approach of the massive ship, and to prepare the scan victims to visit it for medical purposes. The AI—Enne, as I'd tried to train myself to think of it—had embraced the notion with seeming enthusiasm (for an artificial intelligence), generating enough of the blue communications gel to fill every tub in the docking bay, the bridge, and the rest of the ship. It would be able to "treat" more than fifty Ryphen colonists at a time, and promised that the ship would stay in orbit around the planet until all who welcomed the medical care had been accommodated.

"You think anyone will choose not to?" I asked Juliska, as we stood on the bridge of the *Tane Ikai*, watching the slowly rotating globe of Ryphen come into view. The Council had reacted with a mixture of relief, consternation, and bewilderment at the strange turn events had taken.

"We're like any other group of people," she said. "There'll be a variety of reactions to the idea. Some might want to wait and take their chances on the wormhole and help from Nearspace. We won't force anyone." Juliska had not suffered the return of any Ryphen-withdrawal symptoms as we made our way back toward the planet. We talked quietly about what that might mean, to her, and to the other Ryphens.

"You might be able to leave the planet at will." I contemplated the planet awaiting our return, wreathed in a wispy scarf of clouds. For a long time, it had been both welcome sanctuary and lonely prison for the stranded colonists. Maybe that was about to change. "Imagine if we can get the wormhole stabilized, what that will mean for the colony."

"Or the earthbound syndrome might rebound as soon as I've been exposed to the virus—or whatever it is—again," she countered. She sipped from a steaming mug of double caff, freshly delivered by Maja, who was making sure we were well-fortified on the journey back to Ryphen. A plate of solanto cookies rested on a console near where we stood.

"Does that make you nervous to go back down to the planet—the idea that it might rebound? You could stay aboard the *Tane Ikai* and come back to Nearspace proper with us. You'd be more than welcome."

She quirked a half-smile and shook her head. "I'd like to travel back to Nearspace at some point," she said. "Just to see how it's changed, I guess. Although to be honest, I'm a little afraid of some things I might find. But to never go back to Ryphen?" She shook her head. "It's where I want to be when we get word—when I find out about Amber. If she's coming back, I want to be there waiting for her. And if she's not—well, it's home."

I pictured the little house that waited for her on Ryphen, so full of Amber Malka. I wished I could tell her I was sure Amber was coming back through that wormhole, but I couldn't. I still had hope, and faith in Dr. Ndasa, but the odds were simply too close to call.

"Even if Enne can't make a permanent fix for the syndrome, I'll bet my mother can," I told her. "I want to get her to Ryphen and see what she thinks—about the virus, your nanobioscavengers, everything."

"How do you think she'll get along with Dr. Lee?" Juliska asked with a sudden mischievous grin.

I snorted. "If he can live with a Pika clone, he can get along with my mother."

As we neared the wormhole's location, the *Seeker* following at a sedate distance behind us, I wondered if we'd make it through to Nearspace on our next attempt. We hadn't had the chance yet to try out the modifications Viss and the two Ryphen engineers had made. What would happen if we still couldn't make the skip after we'd finished helping the Ryphens with Enne? I mentally shook myself. *Don't worry about that now. One thing at a time.*

Looking up from the comm board, Baden said, "Message coming in from Karro, Captain."

Because Karro had managed to convince me to leave him and Aliande behind on the Haeruth ship until we reached Ryphen. He argued that he'd be able to act as interpreter for any communications we still had to have with the AI as we neared the planet, and that in addition, he could take a Pika subroutine with him and spend the time compiling the language database.

"I could build it even faster if someone would stick *me* in that gel for fifteen minutes," she'd griped. No amount of explaining that it probably wouldn't work the same way for her and that she might even get her interface fried would convince her she might be wrong. When she'd started experimenting to see if she could transfer her consciousness over to the 'bot by way of partitioned data bursts, I'd whisked her back to the *Tane Ikai* and ordered her to get herself reintegrated with her copy in the ship's computer. Then, and only then, could she download the required subroutine back to a datapad for Karro. She'd grudgingly complied, but not before we'd had another pointed discussion about whether she could be considered "crew." I managed to make my case, but she sulked for the rest of the day.

At any rate, Karro remained on the *Seeker*, and now he had a message for me. "Enne wants to know if you want them to repair this wormhole," he said. I could see his face in the feed from Aliande's helmet cam, and he was trying and failing to suppress a grin.

"They can do that?" My voice rose to an undignified squeak.

Karro shrugged. "Apparently they think so. They say they'll send in some repair drones to assess the problem. But they feel fairly certain all that's needed is a specialized stabilizer field. Honestly, the technical description of what's involved almost exploded my brain. But apparently, they've had to do this kind of thing to wormholes the ship has encountered before, to keep them stable enough to pass through. They're willing to leave the field generator in place indefinitely."

"Well, why would we say no," I said, feeling bemused. *And just like that, we're getting back to Nearspace?* I caught Rei's eye and saw her wide, relieved smile. She'd heard the message as well. "I mean, it's not like they need my permission. And don't forget, as soon as we have all the arrangements made to get the Ryphens up to the *Seeker*, you're coming back to this ship. Immediately."

"I'm not forgetting," Karro assured me. "I'm liaising between the Ryphen Council and Enne to get everything worked out."

A moment later, checking the view from the rear ship's cameras, I watched a flotilla of drones exit an opening in the hull of the *Seeker* and break off for the wormhole. It was simultaneously comforting and chilling to think of this AI roaming the galaxy, gathering information and randomly fixing things like broken wormholes. It made me feel very small and very insignificant. I thought it might be wise for me, once we'd settled the Ryphens and the wormhole and made our way back to Nearspace, to not think too hard about Enne and the Haeruths' apparently interminable mission.

That wouldn't be a problem for a while, anyway, considering the several dozen reports I'd likely be filling out for my brother and the Protectorate and who knew who else when we got back to Nearspace.

Someone put a hand on my shoulder, and I turned to see Hirin. He slid one arm around my shoulders and pulled me close to his side. "They're actually going to fix it?" He gestured at the screen showing the drones circling the mouth of the wormhole, performing a scientific dance incomprehensible to me. I assumed they were gathering data and transmitting it back to the *Seeker*.

I shrugged under his arm. "That's what they say. I'm certainly willing to give them the benefit of the doubt. The Corvids taught us we are not the pinnacle of understanding about how wormholes work."

"How long do you think it will be before a Protectorate ship comes through, once the wormhole is stabilized?"

"Why, are you starting a pool?"

"Thinking about it."

I looked up to find him still staring at the viewscreen, grinning widely. "You're serious?"

"Everybody's probably got an opinion about whether our messages got through and whether there's at least one Protectorate ship working at the problem on the other side," he mused. "Knowing this crew, we can probably translate those opinions into bets."

I thought about how long it had been since we sent the first message through, the chances it had emerged out the other side, and the personalities of both my mother and my brother, the Protectorate Admiral.

"I'm in. How close do I have to come?"

"Let's do five-minute increments," Hirin said.

"All right. Between five and ten minutes." I gave him a mischievous grin. "Put me down for double the minimum you're asking."

Hirin cocked an eyebrow at me. "In that case, I'd better get everyone's bets quickly," he said. "Otherwise, if you win, you'll be the only one in the pool."

He crossed over to talk to Rei and I messaged Karro. "Let me know the instant the stabilizer field is in place and the wormhole is functional, all right?"

"Anxious to get home?"

I chuckled. "Something like that. You still doing all right over there?"

"Doing fine," he assured me. "Enne has activated some more 'bots over here, and they're starting to clean up the place. We're the first actual visitors they've had in a long time. I think it's exciting for them, if an AI can be excited. Don't tell Pika I said that," he added.

"I'm right here," Pika said in a smug voice. "And anything you say on the bridge and I overhear is *not* considered eavesdropping."

"Nobody likes to have a messy house when they're expecting a lot of visitors," I said, ignoring her. "Even alien AIs, I guess."

He laughed. "I guess we do have something in common then. Hey, Mom?"

"Right here."

Karro paused as if gathering his thoughts. "In spite of everything . . . I wouldn't go back and do anything differently. This has been an amazing experience."

"You know I didn't plan it this way—*couldn't* have planned it this way."

"I know. Of course, I know." I could hear the grin in his voice when he added, "I still say you have a way of making things work out the way you want them to, though."

I shook my head and looked around the bridge of the *Tane Ikai*, at the best crew inside or outside Nearspace, my family by blood and by choice. They all brought something to this ship, and that combination was what "made things work out." Even Pika, prickly, annoying, and brilliant, had become a part of the whole. "Not *me*, Karro. But maybe *we*. And I'm glad you could be part of that, even for a little while. Even though it almost killed me with worry," I added.

"Amen to that," Aliande said over her helmet cam. "I can't wait to sit and paint in peace again. And message the kids! They must be frantic that they haven't heard from us by now."

Juliska came to stand in the spot Hirin had vacated to set up the betting pool. "I don't know how we'll ever be able to thank you, Luta," she said. There was a catch in her voice, making it sound much more vulnerable than it usually did. If the AI could fix the wormhole, and I was right about the Protectorate waiting on the other side, we might know sooner than she'd expected how Amber had fared. Maybe she wasn't going to be at home, surrounded by the people who loved and supported her. I didn't know how she could stand the waiting, now that we were so close.

She went on, "The lives of everyone in Lillifleur will be changed after this, and it's all because you came and helped us. We never could have figured things out or communicated with the AI on our own."

"You're all pretty resilient. I think you would have managed,"

I said lightly, uncomfortable with the praise. We hadn't done anything particularly extraordinary, to my way of thinking. Just helped out the best we could when we were needed. "And Amber's the real hero. We wouldn't even have known about Lillifleur and Ryphen if not for her."

Juliska nodded. She bit her lip, then said suddenly, "I feel like she's there, waiting to come through. I think . . . I think maybe she's okay. Until now I didn't believe there was any possibility, but—" She kept her eyes on the rear viewscreen and the behemoth of a ship following us as if she could help will the wormhole into stability with the strength of her attention. I saw tears glisten in them, but they didn't spill over.

I took her hand. It was cold. "I hope you're right." I hoped I hadn't overestimated Dr. Ndasa's abilities.

"There go the drones," she said.

I looked where she pointed, and indeed, two drones slipped out of sight into the dark shadow of the wormhole, and the rest had left it, racing back toward the alien ship. Karro reported, "Enne says the field is in place and the wormhole should be traversable."

"Pika, start a timer, would you?" I asked.

"Aye, Captain," she said. In a strange moment of affability, she didn't even ask what it was for. After a moment I realized that she'd been listening in on my entire conversation with Hirin about the betting pool, anyway.

I let go of Juliska's hand and put my arm around her shoulders instead, squeezing the way Hirin had done with me. "Whatever we find out, she *is* here," I told her. "Amber. She's here, she's on Ryphen. She's wherever you are."

Juliska swallowed. "If I do make it there, will you show me around when I come to Nearspace?"

"Absolutely," I told her. "First drink on Damyadi Station is on me."

"Damyadi Station is still around?" she laughed, brushing at her eyes. "That thing is older than I am."

My brother Lanar's ship, the Nearspace Protectorate vessel *S. Cheswick*, came through the wormhole seven minutes and thirty-five seconds after the alien AI's stabilizer field went active.

About a minute later, when Baden put our ship-to-ship connection up on the big screen, I felt a warm rush of gratitude at the mere familiar sight of the *Cheswick*'s bridge and the knot of people gathered there. The first things I registered were the relief on Lanar's face and the happiness on Mother's. And then the smile on the face of the thin, dark-haired woman standing next to Mother. Her old grey shipsuit was gone, traded for dark pants and a bulky blue sweater. Her face was no longer drawn with illness; instead, her eyes stared into the screen with keen interest and the grey wash had gone from her skin, replaced with a rich glow. I knew her, though. I felt Juliska's shoulders hitch as she gasped, then relax as she half-sobbed out weeks of worry and fear. The long-denied tears spilled over then, but she was laughing through them.

"Hey, Lanar," I said, my own voice almost weak with relief, "thanks for coming to get us. Mother, I thought you might be there, too. And Captain Malka, it's sure good to see you again."

Her warm brown eyes flickered my way, but I knew it was only Juliska she was truly seeing. "Forgive me if I don't remember much about our first meeting, Captain Paixon," she said with a smile. "I understand I owe you a very great deal."

"Not at all." I was having a little bit of trouble keeping my own eyes focused through the sheen of water filling them up. "I'm happy we could help."

AT THE MOMENT when Lanar's ship appeared, Hirin had just finished collecting all the bets from the crew.

I won.

Maybe I do have a way of making things work out the way I want. At least when it counts.

THE END

Author Biography

Sherry D. Ramsey is a speculative fiction writer, editor, publisher, creativity addict and self-confessed Internet geek. When she's not writing, she makes jewellery, gardens, hones her creative procrastination skills on social media, and consumes far more coffee and chocolate than is likely good for her.

Her other books include three more in the Nearspace series from Tyche Books, *One's Aspect to the Sun*, *Dark Beneath the Moon*, and *Beyond the Sentinel Stars*; the middle grade fantasy *The Seventh Crow*; *The Murder Prophet*; and two collections of short stories. With her partners at Third Person Press, she has co-edited six anthologies of regional short fiction and a novel. A member of the Writer's Federation of Nova Scotia Writer's Council, Sherry is also a past Vice-President and Secretary-Treasurer of SF Canada.

Sherry lives in Nova Scotia with her husband, children, and dogs. You can visit her online at www.sherrydramsey.com, find her on Facebook, and keep up with her much more pithy musings and visual life on Twitter and Instagram @sdramsey.